Home Safe

TRACY BAACK

For those who love someone whose brain was shaped by trauma.
Although your love will never be enough to fix it,
your love is no small thing.

Author's Note

This novel is a closed-door, kisses-only romance. Although it is a contemporary romance novel, there are some weightier themes addressed throughout the book. If you are a sensitive reader, please review these content considerations before proceeding.

This story includes a child who is in process of being adopted out of the foster care system. As such, there are mentions of parental neglect, drug use, death by overdose, and incarceration. These mentions were intentionally kept minimal and vague.

However, a child's trauma responses to triggers are fully fleshed out on page multiple times. If reading those experiences could be personally triggering for you, please seek the opinion of a trusted friend or book buddy about whether reading this story would be beneficial or harmful for where you are in your journey.

CHAPTER ONE

Danae

"This will be your room—what do you think?"

I study Jason's body language, looking for clues as to what he's feeling inside. His nine-year-old face teeters between pensive and awed. The conflict playing out in his expressions mirrors the emotions in my heart.

Excitement. Terror. Tenderness. Anxiety.

I suppose this is our new normal given the life we're beginning today.

"You mean this whole room will be mine? I'll have that whole big bed to myself?" Jason asks, gesturing to the twin bed in the corner.

"Big bed?" I question. "What do you mean?"

"At my dad's place, I slept in the corner of his room. On a little bed." He makes a motion with his hands, indicating the size of a toddler bed. Jason is small for his age but still well beyond the size of a toddler.

I blink back tears.

"Yes! This whole room will be just for you. There's a quilt on the bed for now, but we'll go shopping tomorrow so you can pick out exactly what style of comforter you want," I say. My enthusiasm grows as the smile on his face expands.

"Danae? Could I talk with you in the kitchen for a moment?" Jason's social worker asks. Sandra was waiting in the living room while I showed Jason his room, but I'm sure she has other places to be today.

"Sure. Jason, why don't you unpack the clothes from your duffel bag into the dresser?" I suggest. Jason nods, and I ruffle his orange-red hair before following Sandra down the stairs to the main floor of my townhouse.

We speak in low voices once we reach the kitchen. "How are you feeling?" Sandra asks. It's impossible to succinctly explain the jumble in my heart. I pick at the coat of clear nail polish on my thumb.

"Happy? Sad? Nervous? Like I have zero idea what I'm doing?" I answer honestly. She smiles.

"That's normal," she says. "Take things slowly and try to go at his pace as much as you can. We were able to rush your foster certification since you're considered a kinship placement, but you'll still have a trial period for about six months before the adoption is finalized. So if you ever start to have doubts or think you might change—"

"I won't be changing my mind," I state, cutting off her sentence.

Sandra smiles again. "I'm only saying—*if* you ever have doubts, please reach out and talk to me about it. Sooner rather than later. I'm here to support you in addition to being here for Jason."

"I appreciate it," I tell her. "I'm one hundred percent committed, but I'm grateful for your support. Just to clarify, his father's rights have already been officially terminated, right? There won't be any other legal issues on that front?"

"Correct," Sandra replies. "He signed the papers before he was transferred to the prison. And considering Jason's grandmother personally asked you to adopt him, I can't imagine she would create any legal barriers. There are no other biological family members interested in adopting him. You simply need to get through the adjustment period, and then everything can be finalized next spring. Any other questions?"

I stare at Sandra, trying to steady my racing heart. There are far too many questions running through my mind to ask.

How do I do this? How do you instantly learn to be a mom? Can *I do this? What if I totally mess this up?*

Instead of speaking any of them aloud, I shake my head. "I'll be in touch if I do."

"I'll be here in a week to check in with you," Sandra says. "Oh, and I forgot to tell you one thing—Jason got accepted to go to a special three-day baseball camp put on for kids in foster care. He loves baseball, so I'd entered his name for it before all of this shook out. It's not till after the holidays, though, so I'll get more information to you soon."

"Wait, what? A baseball camp?" I ask, brow furrowed. "Is it possible to cancel?"

Sandra gives me a confused look. "I mean, maybe? I already told him about it, and he was so excited. But I can try to withdraw him, if you want."

I sigh. "No, it's fine. I just hate baseball. But I don't want to disappoint him. Send me the info when you can."

Sandra nods then calls out to Jason. "I'm heading out now, Jason! You know you can call me any time you need anything."

Jason hurries down the stairs to tell Sandra goodbye. "Thanks, Miss Sandra. See you soon."

After I close and lock the door, I turn to Jason. "What do you think? Should we finish unpacking your stuff and then order pizza for dinner?"

Jason shrugs. "I unpacked everything already. There wasn't much." My heart pangs. His eyes light up as he adds, "Pizza would be awesome, though! Can I have plain cheese?"

"You can have any toppings you want. Or lack of toppings," I say with a smile. "I'll even order extra so we can have leftovers tomorrow." Quickly placing an order for medium cheese and medium pepperoni pizzas in the app, I toggle the delivery option on. Usually, I don't pay the extra cost to get delivery, opting for carry-out instead. But for tonight, I think we'll stay put.

"What would you like to do?" I ask Jason. "We could play a board game or watch a movie. What sounds fun to you?" I have no idea what he likes to do at home in the evenings. Then again, I don't know how many options he's been given in the past.

Jason requests a movie, so we find a good option on Netflix while we wait for the pizza. When the pizza arrives, we pause the show to eat at the kitchen table.

"Jason, I thought we should maybe talk about what you want to call me. I know you're used to calling me Miss Collins at school, and that's fine if that still feels most comfortable to you right now. Like we've talked about over the past couple of months, I'm going to be your mom for the rest of your life, okay? Nothing's going to change that. But you don't have to call me 'Mom' if that doesn't seem right to you. You can still call me Miss Collins or Danae—I'll answer to anything for you." I smile warmly so that Jason will sense my sincerity.

He slowly chews his bite of pizza, a contemplative look on his face. I first met Jason when he came to Trailridge Elementary as a first grader. It was my first year as the school librarian instead of teaching one of the third-grade classes. He immediately burrowed his way into my heart with his love for the library and his need for love.

Jason left our school for a few months in second grade during a stint in foster care. I was worried sick about him the entire time he was gone, praying for his well-being every night. Thankfully, he came back when he moved back in with his dad. Trailridge remained a consistent place for him throughout the subsequent cycles in and out of the foster system; sometimes he was with his grandmother and sometimes with other foster families.

"How about I call you Miss Danae?" Jason announces, eyes lighting up with his idea.

I grin to show my approval. "I think that sounds perfect. Do you have any nicknames that you like to be called?"

Jason's face falls, and I wish I could walk back that question. "Not really . . . sometimes my dad used to call me Jase," he says quietly. He fervently adds, "But I don't want you to call me that."

"You got it. I bet we'll think of the perfect nickname for you soon. Although, I love the name Jason, so maybe I won't even need a nickname for you," I say, relieved when his smile returns.

After we're done eating, we return to the couch to finish the movie. I've been around Jason at school for three-and-a-half years, so I'm well-acquainted with his personality—his sweet demeanor as well as his outbursts. I can tell he's making an effort to be on his best behavior tonight. Somehow, I want to communicate to him that this is a safe place to be himself. That this is home, and he's secure here with me.

That I'm not leaving. That *he's* not leaving.

But maybe a long, heartfelt speech isn't quite what he needs on his first night as my son.

At 8:30 p.m., I tuck Jason into bed after he's brushed his teeth. "Would you want me to read a little bit of the next *Harry Potter* book aloud before you go to sleep?" I ask.

His eyes light up, and he sits forward in bed. "Yes, please!"

Despite all of the struggles he's faced in life, Jason's been an avid and advanced reader from the beginning. In fact, maybe it's *because* of the struggles, not in spite of them. I certainly understand the comfort of escaping your life circumstances through a novel. At the end of last school year, I encouraged Jason to try the first book in the *Harry Potter* series. As I suspected, he was instantly hooked. He read the first two novels on his own, and he checked out the third book from the school library this week.

I briefly return to the living room to grab my own well-worn copy of *The Prisoner of Azkaban* from the bookshelf then settle on the bed next to Jason. "How far have you read?" I ask.

"I only had time to read the first two chapters," Jason responds. "I didn't have a lot of time to read this week."

Tears prick my eyes again, and I put my arm around his shoulders to give him a little squeeze. "Totally understandable. We'll read chapter three tonight then."

Inch by inch, Jason leans closer to my side as I read, pulled by the gravity of sleepiness or love, or perhaps both. By the end of the chapter, he's snuggled against my shoulder, and it's all I can do to finish reading rather than wrap both arms protectively around him.

Standing up, I motion across the hallway. "My room is right over there, and I'll leave both of our doors open in case you need anything." My preference would be to keep his door closed for the sake of fire safety, but I know his need to *feel* safe trumps hypothetical fires. "If you wake up scared because you forget where you are, call out for me or come on over to my room, okay?"

Jason nods before scooting down in bed. He looks so small, so vulnerable, tucked under my old quilt, eyes peering up at me.

"I love you, Jason," I murmur, giving him a soft smile. He smiles back and nods again before rolling over toward the wall. I turn off the overhead light, double checking that the night light pushes away enough of the darkness in the room.

After loading the dishwasher and wiping down the counter, I sit at the small dining table and take a deep breath. I run my fingers over the familiar scratches in the wood, courtesy of whoever previously owned my second-hand find. Slowly exhaling, I pull out my phone to text my best friend. Kara teaches music at Trailridge, and she's become a true friend in addition to a colleague.

ME

He's here and settled in.

KARA

How's he doing? How are YOU doing?

ME

I think he's ok. Probably overwhelmed, but he seems happy to be here.

KARA

And you?

ME

Same. Overwhelmed, but happy he's here. I know I've been preparing for this for a couple of months, but I'm not sure anything could have prepared me to flip a switch and suddenly be a mother.

What if I screw this up? What if I wasn't the best choice for Jason?

KARA

Are you having second thoughts about your decision?

ME

Absolutely not. Nothing could change my mind.

KARA

Which in and of itself is a miracle, Miss Pro/Con lists for days, only to second-guess her decision, make more lists, waffle on her choice again, and then repeat.

ME

Ha ha. If you're trying to ease my mind with jokes, I guess you accomplished your mission. Only not really because I'm still freaking out. I'm not afraid I made the wrong decision, I'm just afraid that I can't give him everything he needs. That he won't feel secure with me as a single mom.

KARA

You're going to be an amazing mother, Danae. It's not going to be easy, but I know you can do it. It might be different than me taking Millie home from the hospital, but I guarantee you I didn't know what I was doing either. No parent does.

ME

I know, but I'm still worried that I won't be able to provide everything he needs. A single teacher's salary isn't exactly top-tier financial security.

KARA

You had abundant financial security growing up, and look where that got you with your parents.

ME

Fair point.

KARA

You already love Jason so much. You're going to be there for him in every way you can. That counts the most.

ME

Thanks for the pep talk. I might need a lot of pep talks.

"Miss Danae?" Jason's voice startles me, and I look up to see him standing by the couch.

"What is it?" I ask, jumping up.

"I can't fall asleep," Jason says. "I'm not used to it being so quiet."

"Oh, right," I say. "Would you want me to try downloading a sound machine app on the tablet? Maybe some ambient noise would help."

Once I get the white noise going for Jason, I decide I may as well go to bed early. It's been an exhausting, emotionally-charged day. If we're going to go shopping tomorrow for a bedspread plus Christmas decorations, then I need to get some rest.

As I lie in bed snuggled under the white down comforter, I try to quiet all the "what if" questions pummeling my thoughts.

In the end, I get very little sleep.

CHAPTER TWO

Griffin

"**W**hy can't I bring in reporters to cover Camp Wizard? Think about all the good publicity you're throwing away."

I close my eyes, rubbing my temples with one hand. The cell phone in my other hand is in danger of getting thrown across the room. Although, I shouldn't blame an inanimate object for my agent's refusal to understand my position.

"Joe, we rehash this exact conversation every year. My purpose for this camp is to give kids in foster care a place to come and have fun, learn some baseball skills, and forget their life circumstances for a few days. Kids who deserve some privacy. It's not about positive PR. My entire image already consists of nothing but positive PR. No reporters," I say through gritted teeth.

"Fine, fine. You know I had to try," Joe says, resigned.

"Well, stop trying. If you pester me about it again next year, I'm going to find a new agent," I challenge.

"Sure, sure."

"I'm serious." I am serious.

"Okay, fine, I got it. Have fun with the kids. Just don't let it distract you from your training. You have a lot to prove this season—that you're back and better than ever post-injury. Griffin West, The Wizard of Defense, needs to show the baseball world that he's still the same caliber of shortstop," Joe adds.

I rub harder at my temples. "Thanks for the reminder."

Hanging up without saying goodbye, I transition from rubbing my temples to rubbing my shoulder. It's been over eight months since my injury, and I've completely rehabbed back to playing condition. I served my time down on the lower league farm team that the Kansas City Crowns pulls players from, proving that I could still perform at the same MLB level.

But somehow, Joe's reminder of all that's on the line magically makes my shoulder ache. As if I needed a reminder of how close I came to losing everything I've worked for. Everything I've built.

Who I am.

"What's up, big bro?" Sam chirps, patting my shoulders like drums as she walks past me to the kitchen.

"Just Joe being annoying," I respond.

Sam pulls a face. "So fire him. The whole world loves you, Griff. You could have your pick of agents. Not sure why you keep his irritating face around."

She's never liked Joe all that much, but he's been by my side for my entire professional baseball career, ever since I was recruited out of college. My lingering sense of loyalty has stopped me from getting out of my contract with him.

But that loyalty is *seriously* waning now.

Sam tosses a Gatorade from the fridge to me, and I decide to change the subject.

"Everything good to go for the start of Camp Wizard tomorrow?" I ask.

She takes her time gulping several swigs of her kombucha concoction before answering. "Triple checked everything this morning. We've done it enough times that it's a well-oiled machine at this point."

This is the fourth year that Samantha has been living with me and working as my assistant. What started as a way to give my little sister a soft place to land when she couldn't figure out a direction in life has turned into a mutually beneficial situation that we both enjoy.

There's a nine-year age gap between us, which means I was already off at college when Sam and her biological brother, Ian, were officially adopted into the West family. I was the only one to live at home with them when they arrived as foster placements. My older siblings, Sawyer and Miranda, were out of college when Sam and Ian first came to live with us at the ages of nine and five.

Although we had lots of other kids in the foster system cycle through our home over the years, Sam and Ian were the only two to join us forever. Growing up with other children constantly in and out of our lives had its challenging moments, but it also taught me a level of humility and empathy that I don't think I would have learned otherwise. I certainly wouldn't have learned it from any of the coaches or teammates who constantly treated me like I was a gift to the sport of baseball.

My upbringing is also the reason I hold this camp every January, not to bolster a positive image in the press. It's to give kids with fewer opportunities a chance to feel special. To enjoy a hobby they may not get to play consistently. Even if it's only for a few days.

Giving their foster parents a reprieve at the end of winter break isn't a bad side effect either.

We cap the head count at twenty kids, which always makes me feel guilty about the myriads who don't get selected. But it ensures that I can form some level of personal connection with each individual over the course of three days.

"Have you heard anything from Ian lately?" I ask Sam.

"Yeah, I talked to him a couple of days ago. He goes back for spring semester the third week of January. Sounds pretty eager to get back to it," Sam answers, voice flat. She always served as the protective older sister to Ian, but where she floundered in the college setting, Ian has thrived. Reading her reaction, I don't press further.

"You've been working hard getting everything organized, and the next three days are about to be exhausting. How about we go out for a celebratory dinner?" I offer.

"Aren't celebrations supposed to come *after* a successful event?" Sam replies with a smirk.

"I have so much faith in you that I'm willing to treat you early," I say, flashing her my most charming grin. "How about Capital Gr—"

She cuts me off. "I swear if you finish that suggestion, I'll leave town and let you run this camp solo."

"But—" I try to protest.

"Nope," Sam asserts. "I'm in the mood for sushi."

I groan. "You know that means a high possibility of autographs and photos, right?"

The smirk on Sam's face confirms that she's not only aware, but that it's part of her plan.

"You're lucky you're so indispensable," I huff. But there's no real malice in my statement. I do, however, take a moment to completely tousle Sam's hair, an asymmetrical blonde pixie cut with pink highlights.

Sam shrieks. "Hey! I spent a long time perfecting that today, you jerk. I had it flawlessly cascading over one eye to my chin just so!" She swats at my hand and punches my arm like an indignant little girl, rather than a twenty-four-year-old woman.

"Well, now it's imperfectly swooshing across your face. Right in time for all the photos you're going to subject us to," I tease.

Sam pokes a finger to my chest. "That's it. You're getting me dumplings *and* edamame for appetizers. Move it."

CHAPTER THREE

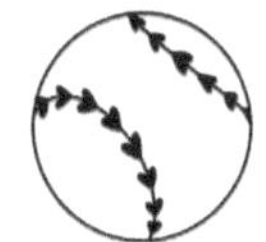

Danae

I rush up the stairs too quickly and stub my toe on the top step. *Ouch!*

I try to ignore the outsized amount of pain caused by the minor injury as I walk into Jason's room. "Jason, we really have to hurry if we're going to make it there on time."

He's sitting in the middle of the floor, arms clutched tightly around his knees. Still in pajamas.

I bite back a comment of frustration, inhaling a deep breath instead. I kneel next to him and ask in a low voice, "What's going on? You've been so excited about this camp. Why aren't you ready to go?"

Jason keeps his head down, but I've memorized everything about his face by now. The piercing green eyes above a splatter of freckles across his cheeks. The fiery red hair that makes my auburn tresses look plain brown in comparison. When he still doesn't meet my gaze, I reach out to rub a hand across his back.

We've settled into a groove over the past month. Or, as much of a groove as possible during the holiday season. We rode the emotional highs and lows of celebrating our first Christmas together. Jason's grandmother joined us for Christmas dinner, and the two days following her visit were filled with emotional land mines. I tried to implement some of the suggestions from the *many* books about adoption that I read leading up to welcoming Jason into my life. But either I executed them wrong, or they're not one hundred percent guaranteed.

Still, I'd wager we're still very much in the "honeymoon phase." We have gotten more and more comfortable around each other, if Jason's willingness to openly snuggle into my side while reading or watching movies is any indication. The increase in emotional outbursts lately might also be evidence of his growing comfort with me.

After another moment of rubbing his back, Jason finally responds with a timid voice. "Is it okay that I'm excited to play baseball? About getting to meet Griffin West in real life?"

"Of course, it's okay for you to be excited! This *is* an exciting thing!" I swallow down the sense of lying through my teeth. The prospect of having anything to do with baseball is the polar opposite of exciting to me. But I know that Jason has been ecstatic about this opportunity.

"Why would you think you shouldn't be excited?" I gently prod.

Jason finally meets my eyes. "It's just . . . it was my dad who always loved baseball. He watched all the games. The Crowns were his team. When he had good days, he'd sometimes take me outside to play catch." Jason pauses, and my heart breaks into tiny pieces at his angst. "Isn't it a little bit unfair for me to get to go to this camp when he's, you know . . ."

As Jason's thought trails off, I don't immediately jump in to pick it up. I've learned to tread carefully the handful of times that Jason has brought up anything about his dad. I never quite know if Jason's going to be defensive of his father's efforts or upset about his failings.

After a beat, I try to toe the line between the two reactions. "You know, I think your dad would probably be happy for you to get to have this chance to meet a real baseball player. And you genuinely love baseball. You're always spouting off stats and facts about the teams. This is *your* passion, not only his."

As much as it pains me to acknowledge. I don't add that final thought.

Jason's eyes glimmer, and he nods solemnly. "It *is* my passion. You're right."

Breathing a sigh of relief that I didn't make things worse, I squeeze his shoulder. "So what do you say we get you changed and ready to go?

We might be a few minutes late, but I'm sure that won't be a big deal." *I sure hope it's not a big deal.*

Thankfully, Jason gets ready in record time. While he brushes his teeth, I check over the details that Sandra forwarded to me. The kids will receive brand-new baseball gear as a part of the camp, which saved me from having to make a trip to the sporting goods store.

The Kansas City Crowns stadium and indoor training facility sits near the Legends Outlets in Kansas City, Kansas. It's only about a fifteen-minute drive from my townhouse in Shawnee, but I lean into my Kansas City driving habits and push the speed limit to get there in ten.

We make good time, but we're still about ten minutes late to the check-in. I hope they're lenient—I don't think Jason could handle the disappointment of missing this camp now.

Rushing through the parking lot, we enter the practice facility through the designated door. The lobby is quiet, but I see a petite young woman with pink highlights streaking her blonde hair still sitting behind a table.

"Excuse me, is this where we check in for the baseball camp?" I ask her.

She looks up with a bright smile. Her eyes dance the line between green and blue, and they light up as she greets us.

"Hey! You must be Jason! My name is Samantha, but you can call me Sam or Sammi if you want. I was hoping you were still coming," she tells him as she comes around to the front of the table. "I don't want you to miss out on anything, so I'll take you back to join the crew and then come out and finish your registration. That sound okay?"

Jason grins at her, then turns to quickly give me a hug. "See you later!" he says before following Samantha down a hallway.

"Have fun!" I call after him. Samantha indicates that she'll be right back. I lean against the table and take a deep breath. I'd been so focused on getting Jason ready for today that I didn't even consider how I would spend my free time. I haven't had even an hour to myself since he moved in. A wave of eagerness washes over me, quickly followed by a wave of guilt that I would be looking forward to time away from Jason.

I'm saved from the pool of guilt by Samantha's voice as she walks back into the lobby.

"I have to tell you—that hair style is *totally* working for you. The blunt bob, the effortless waves, the just-above-the-shoulder length, the full curtain bangs. Fabulous," Samantha declares, making a chef's kiss motion with her fingers.

Laughing, I run a hand through my hair. "Goodness, thank you! What do I need to do to check Jason in?"

"I have some forms for you to sign," Samantha replies. "Are you his case worker or his current foster parent?"

"Oh, I'm his mom. Or, um, I mean, I'm going to be his mom. I was one of his teachers. I mean, I still am. Geez, I need to learn how to answer this question," I stammer. Clearing my throat, I explain, "Jason is with me as a kinship placement for now until our trial period is over and the adoption can be finalized. So, however you want to summarize that on the form."

Samantha smiles. "No problem. You sign here on the liability forms, and I'll make sure it gets notated correctly." She pauses, then asks, "Would Jason potentially be picked up from camp by any other individual? Your husband or boyfriend or anyone?"

My cheeks flush. "Oh, no. I'm single mothering. That sounded weird. It's only me. No one else would be picking him up." Samantha's eyes seem to glimmer, but I'm probably imagining things in the midst of my fluster. "Thank you for letting him come in even though we were late. I swear to you that I am usually very punctual. We had a bit of a rough morning."

Her eyes soften now. "Not a problem at all. We totally understand those rough patches. And I apologize—I didn't catch your name."

"Oh! Right! I'm Danae Collins," I say, reaching my hand out to shake hers. "Do you prefer to be called Samantha?" I ask, indicating toward her name tag.

"Like I told Jason, I answer to any variation of the name—Samantha, Sam, Sammi. No one's ever tried 'Mantha' before, but I'd probably respond nonetheless," she says, and I laugh. "What are you going to do with your free time today, Danae?"

"I was just thinking about that while you were taking Jason back. I haven't had any time to myself for the past month. I can't decide if I should be productive and catch up on all the tasks that I've neglected, or if I should go sit at a coffee shop and read. I suppose I'll have time tomorrow, too, but Friday I have to go back to work for our professional development day."

"Then you should be productive today so that tomorrow you can completely relax, guilt-free," Samantha says with confidence.

"You might be on to something there," I agree. "I promise I won't be late picking Jason up. Three o'clock, right?"

Samantha nods. "You got it. And don't worry! I'll keep an extra eye on him."

"It was nice to meet you, Samantha. Thanks for all your help," I say with true appreciation.

She gives me a half-smile. "Trust me, the pleasure is all mine."

CHAPTER FOUR

Griffin

I watch a ball whiz past me and let out a low whistle.

"Whoa-ho, easy there, Fireball. You've got quite the power on that arm, but we've gotta work on your throwing accuracy," I say to the tiny kid in front of me. His bright red hair adds another dimension to the "Fireball" nickname I'd just bequeathed in response to that wild throw. I motion for him to follow me to one of the throwing practice nets set up on the field.

Half of the kids are working on batting practice with Drew Sheffield, our first baseman and strongest hitter. The other half are working on catching and throwing skills with me. Of course, we have plentiful staff and volunteers milling around helping out as well.

"What did you say your name was again, Fireball?" I ask the kid as he scampers after me.

"Jason!" he says, stars in his eyes. "But you can call me Fireball if you want, Mr. West."

"Only if you call me Griffin," I respond, grinning down at him.

His eyes light up even more but then cloud over. I crouch down to get on his eye level. "Whatcha thinking about there, Jason?"

He shuffles his feet. "I was just thinking that I should apologize to you for being here." He's avoiding eye contact, so I gently poke him in the stomach.

"And why's that?" I ask.

"I shouldn't get to be at this camp," Jason begins. He sniffs hard. "My social worker told me about it a long time ago, and I was so excited. But it's a camp for foster kids, and I'm getting adopted. I moved in with my new mom last month—she's the librarian at my school, and she's really nice. Like, *really* nice. She always asked me how I was doing and listened to me, and she helped me find books that I would like that made me feel better. And now she says she's gonna love me and be my mom forever. So I'm not really a foster kid anymore, and I took the spot of another kid without a mom who could be here instead of me. But I was excited because I love baseball so much that I still came even though that's not fair."

He's spoken so quickly, I don't think he took a single breath. His eyes look like floodgates of tears could burst at any moment, like he's terrified of how I'm going to react to his admission.

The tussle of emotions this kid is experiencing—is expressing—reminds me of all the jumbled emotions that were consistently rotating in and out of our home. My chest hurts looking into Jason's eyes.

I give him a gentle smile. "Hey, little man, I'm so glad for you that you have a new mom who's so nice to you. She sounds amazing. But you have every right to be here at this camp, and I'm happy that you are. I appreciate you telling me that, though. How old are you?"

"I'm nine, but I'll be ten in February," he says, puffing out his chest.

So young to have so much awareness.

"You're awfully thoughtful for your age, you know that, Fireball?" He widens his eyes and nods slowly, like I gave him the world's best compliment.

I nudge his arm with my baseball glove. "You've got a strong arm there, but I want you to work on throwing the ball accurately, not only hard. See how many times you can hit that square in the middle of the net, even if it means you don't throw the ball as hard as you can, okay?"

"Yes, sir!" Jason says with gravitas. He immediately pivots to practice throwing and manages to hit the square on his first try. He quickly looks up at me, eager for positive feedback. I hoot and holler wildly to celebrate his success. The beaming smile on his face is the greatest reward for the simplest "favor" I've ever done.

As much as I'd like to hang here and continue talking with this interesting little guy, I need to spread my attention around to the other kids. I make the rounds to give tips and pointers to each of the kids in my group, but I can't resist the pull to keep returning to Jason. Every encouragement I give him lights up his whole demeanor. The way he soaks up every word I speak makes me want to arrange for him to attend a few games this season. I'm a little sad when his group swaps to batting practice.

At the end of the first day, we make a big deal about presenting each of the kids with their exclusive Camp Wizard gear—baseball gloves, a bat and ball, plus t-shirts and hats, naturally. We give Drew an enthusiastic round of applause for helping with batting practice today, and then we release the kids to the lobby.

Normally, I let the volunteers escort the kids back to their designated guardians on the first two days of camp, saving my face time with the adults for the grand finale of the camp. However, I find myself undeniably drawn to seek out Jason's new adoptive mother, to let her know what a thoughtful, sensitive kid she has on her hands.

Confident that Sam will have her phone on her, I shoot her a text as I duck into one of the offices.

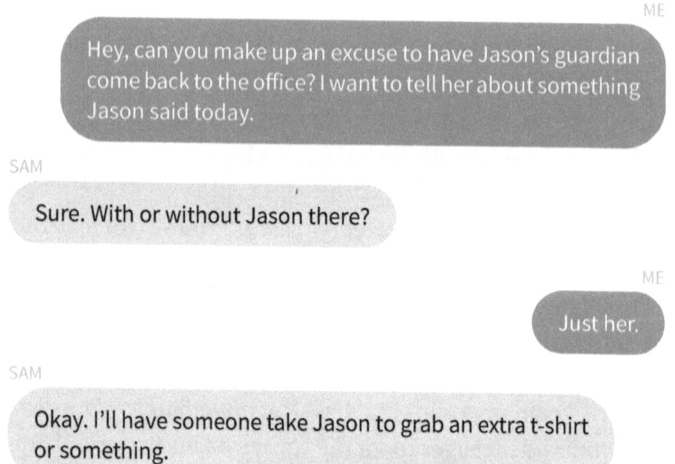

A few minutes later, I hear Sam chatting and laughing with another feminine voice. I step out into the hallway to meet them.

I'm caught off guard by the stunning woman standing beside my sister. Her wavy hair is a deep reddish-brown with copper streaks catching the light. She's taller than Sam by a few inches but probably five inches shorter than my six-foot frame. As she draws closer, I'm taken in by her hazel eyes, golden centers crowded by deep green pools.

The jolt of physical attraction disables my brain long enough to stretch my silence into awkward territory.

Sam shoots me a weird look. "This is Danae Collins, Jason's new mom. You said you wanted to tell her something about Jason?" Sam prompts.

Danae's face visibly falls. "Oh no. Did something bad happen? Did he have a meltdown? This morning was rocky, but I thought we'd talked through everything enough that he was feeling better about coming. I was really hoping he'd have a good day."

"No, absolutely nothing went wrong with Jason at camp," I quickly assure her. "Quite the opposite. He was a bright spot all day. I wanted to tell you about something especially thoughtful he said to me."

I fill Danae in on Jason's conflicted confession. "Not many nine-year-olds have the awareness to even consider whether they're qualified for an event like this, much less to feel guilty about potentially taking someone else's spot. He's a good kid. And he went on and on about how nice you are and how lucky he is to have you as his mom. He talked about you helping him find books that made him feel better when he was younger and how you're going to love him forever now."

Danae blinks back tears. The surprise and gratitude in her eyes only make her look more beautiful as she says, "Oh gosh. Thank you so much for taking the time to tell me that. Hearing that he told you those things . . . I can't explain how much that means." She pauses to collect her emotions, and I'm hit with an urge to comfort her. She shrugs as she continues, "It's only been a month, but I'm constantly questioning myself. I've felt like I'm screwing this whole thing up more times than I could count. To hear that he was so positive today is the encouragement I needed after this morning. I really can't thank you enough for going out of your way to tell me about this."

She wipes a finger under each eye and smiles. "I'm sorry, I didn't even ask your name. Are you one of the volunteers running the camp?" Danae asks.

Sam snorts.

I clear my throat to stop myself from laughing. *Is she serious? She looks completely serious.* Holding a hand out, I say, "I'm Griffin West."

Danae's eyes go wide. "Oh, this is *your* camp? You're one of the players for the Crowns?"

Darting my eyes to Sam, I see the considerable amount of effort it's taking her not to bust out laughing. She'll be teasing me about this for days. Weeks, more likely.

"Yep," I answer. "I play shortstop for the Crowns." I glance down to where my hand is still hanging in midair, which jolts Danae into reciprocating the handshake.

It sounds stupid to say that sparks fly the moment her hand meets mine. That kind of movie nonsense doesn't happen in real life.

Or, maybe it *does* happen, and I had never experienced it before this moment.

Or, maybe I'm wildly intrigued by this striking, compassionate woman who had zero clue who I was. Rather than feeling annoyed by her lack of recognition, it's oddly refreshing. Kansas Citians are *passionate* about their sports teams. So flying under the radar rarely occurs for me.

"I'm so sorry," Danae says, voice higher pitched than it was a moment ago. "I feel so dumb."

"Don't feel dumb," Sam says, mirth in her tone. "It's good for Griff to get a dose of reality every now and then so he doesn't get a big head from all the adoring fans."

Danae looks to Sam with a quizzical expression.

"This joker is my big brother," Sam explains, smile growing wider.

Now, Danae fully covers her face with her hands. "I am beyond embarrassed," she mumbles. She drops her hands, and the pink in her cheeks only makes her more attractive than she already was. "Well, thank you for accepting Jason to this camp. For putting this camp on in the first place—it's an incredible thing that you're doing here. I confess I'm not much of a baseball fan, but this is Jason's dream come true."

The tone in her voice when she confesses to not liking baseball intrigues me even further. I'd like to ask a hundred follow-up questions about where that dislike came from, but I bite my tongue. This is hardly the time or place for a personal interrogation.

I might need to create the appropriate time and place.

"I'd better get Jason back home. He's bound to be exhausted after all the excitement today," Danae says, then turns to Sam. "I promise I'll get him here on time tomorrow."

"And then you'll go sit at a coffee shop with your book all day, right?" Sam insists.

Danae's smile warms, and I'm inexplicably compelled to keep that smile on her face as much as possible.

"Promise," she replies to Sam, then turns back to me. "Thanks again for being so kind to Jason and taking time to tell me about your conversation. And for not making me feel even *more* like an idiot than I already do from not knowing who you were."

I give her my most genuine smile. "I'm glad I got to truly *meet* you."

As she follows Sam back out to the lobby to find Jason, I mull over our interaction. Combing through if I did anything to give off weird vibes. I hope I didn't.

Because I am *extremely* glad I got to meet Danae Collins.

CHAPTER FIVE

Danae

Getting ready for the second day of camp goes much more smoothly. Jason is awake bright and early, dressed and eager to go half an hour before we need to leave. He spends the extra time spouting off every stat about Griffin West that he can remember.

"Did you know that Griffin West's nickname is the 'Wizard of Defense' because his fielding is out of this world? Hey! I bet that's why the camp is called 'Camp Wizard,' don't you think?

"You wanna know when Griffin West got drafted? He was only a junior in college—he didn't even finish college before they wanted him to play! Isn't that cool?!

"Can you believe that Griffin West only played on the farm team for four years before the Crowns called him up to the big leagues?"

I try to sound like I'm listening by adding in, "Oh wow," or "How interesting" each time he takes a breath. But really, I'm tuning out all the baseball talk and thinking about what it was like to meet Griffin West in the flesh yesterday.

And making a total fool out of myself by not knowing who he was.

I'll admit, when Samantha led me down the hallway and I first caught sight of him, I was drawn to the attractive, smiling man standing in front of me. His athletic build—not overly muscular but very fit, with firm-looking biceps and sturdy quads—should have been my first clue that he was, in fact, an athlete. But it's not like he was wearing his jersey. *Are they called jerseys in baseball? Uniform?* He was wearing a blue Camp Wizard shirt and a baseball cap, giving no indication that he was anything more than a regular volunteer.

As we'd walked toward him, his smile widened in a way that can only be described as "charming." In fact, he oozed charm, but not in an artificial way—everything about his smile and interactions seemed genuine. Then, he shared the story about his heartfelt moment with Jason, as though he somehow understood how much I would *need* to hear that information.

I was definitely drawn to him.

And then I opened my mouth and sounded like an ignorant idiot. I wish I could go back and shake my past self. Or cover her mouth with duct tape.

"Did you know that Griffin West had a batting average of .311 when he got injured? He had just come into his power when—poof—it looked like it might be over for good."

Jason's latest fact pulls my attention out of my reverie.

"Wait, what? Griffin West was injured?" I ask.

Jason nods solemnly. "Last spring. Only a month into the season, he hurt his shoulder. Real bad. The replay videos were—" he breaks off speaking and shudders. "I'm glad he's all right and back on the team again this season."

I mull this information over in my mind. *This professional athlete apparently came within sight of his career ending, yet he's still here holding this camp? Surely the upcoming season must be looming over his head. I know that's all I would be able to think about if I was in his position. Fixating on every possible negative outcome. Obsessing over every possible preparation. It's impressive that he wouldn't abandon the camp for a year to focus on getting ready for the season.*

I'm suddenly very curious to know the "why" behind Camp Wizard. What drove Griffin to create this experience for foster kids? But just as suddenly, I shut down my curiosity. I am *not* interested in getting sucked into the world of baseball.

Not even by an attractive, charming, thoughtful man. Not if he's a professional baseball player.

"We've gotta go if we want to get there on time," I tell Jason, shooing him toward the front door.

Twenty minutes later, Jason and several other kids follow a volunteer down the hallway to the practice facility. While I was checking him in, Samantha motioned for me to stick around until she was done.

She turns to me. "So? Do you have your book to go sit and read at a coffee shop all day?"

Laughing, I pull the book out of my bag to show her. "Sure do! I'll actually get to read my book club book this month. Even if I won't be able to *go* to book club to discuss it, at least I'll get to enjoy the story."

"Why won't you be able to go to book club?" Samantha asks, eyebrows furrowed.

"Oh, I don't really have a lot of babysitting options," I say. "I mean, Jason's only been with me for about a month, so I haven't looked into it a lot yet. But most of my closest friends are also teachers at our school, so I'm afraid it might put them in a little bit of an awkward position to watch Jason when they're school authority figures." I sigh. "I'm still figuring things out, I guess."

"Give me your phone," Samantha commands, holding her hand out.

"What? Why?" I ask, eyes narrowed. Yet, I still unlock and hand the phone over to her before she answers.

"I'm putting my phone number in. We all had to pass background checks and take CPR classes to work at the camp this week. I'd love to watch Jason for you whenever you need it, if you'd feel comfortable," Samantha says, tapping away on my phone screen. "He's such a fun kid, and my schedule is really flexible. Perk of working for your brother full time."

"Oh, Samantha, that's really kind of you to offer, but I don't know. Jason's behavior can be a little bit . . . unpredictable sometimes. I still haven't figured out how to handle it, to be entirely honest. I would feel terrible putting you in that position," I slowly explain.

Samantha reaches over to gently touch my arm, eyes full of empathy. "Behavioral outbursts don't scare me. I understand more than you realize because I've been in Jason's position."

My expression must show my shock. Samantha smiles and continues, "My younger brother, Ian, and I were adopted by Griffin's parents after spending a couple of years in the foster system. Ian and I had the same underlying trauma that manifested in different ways outwardly. Not to mention years around other kids in the system. So trust me when I say that Jason's behavior couldn't possibly surprise me."

I'm struggling to process all this new information in order to respond, but Samantha seems to understand that as well. She places her hands on my shoulders, looks me dead in the eyes, and says, "Let me do this for you, Danae. Please. I want you to go to your book club. Or to a coffee shop or out with friends or whatever it is you like to do to keep your cup filled. Jason needs you to be in an emotionally healthy place if you're going to be there for him in all the ways he's going to need you for the long haul."

Tears sting my eyes again, and I clear my throat before nodding. "Okay. That absolutely sounds appealing, but . . . would it be too much to ask if we could maybe get lunch together this weekend first, the three of us? I realize that sounds so demanding when you're trying to do something kind, and I'm sure you have a packed schedule—"

Samantha cuts me off with a wave of her hand. "That's not demanding. That's you being a good mom and vetting the people who might be around your kid. I could do lunch on Saturday if that works for you."

I pause to wipe a tear then huff a small laugh. "Thanks for understanding. Maybe this is the real reason Jason came to this camp—so I could connect with you. Good thing I didn't withdraw him!"

Samantha raises an eyebrow. "Withdraw? Why would you have done that?"

I grimace. "Um, I hope this doesn't make you retract your offer, but I hate baseball. As in, I *loathe* baseball."

She bursts out belly-laughing. "I mean, I did have a little bit of a clue that you weren't a huge fan when you had no idea who Griff was yesterday. I swear I won't hold it against you. Well, I might hold it against you just a little bit that you hate America's favorite pastime but not enough to retract my babysitting services. Why do you hate it so much?"

"Long story," I say, hoping she won't expect me to share said story. Thankfully, Samantha checks her watch.

"I need to get back there to help, but don't think you're avoiding the hot seat forever. I'll be getting that long story out of you someday," she says with a smirk.

Unlikely, I think but don't say. "See you at three," I say with a smile.

Chapter Six

Griffin

"What do we say to Señor Ortiz?" I prompt the kids. They follow with a chorus of enthusiastic "Thank yous," which Adrian receives with exaggerated gratitude. He gives a flourishing bow worthy of the final run of a Broadway show. Even though he'll be back at camp again tomorrow.

Adrian Ortiz is the Crowns' third baseman and my best friend. We hit it off right away when he joined the Crowns five years ago. His playful energy and over-the-top antics have made for somewhat of a media sensation—one I'm frequently included in, since I play right into his mischief more often than not.

He was generous enough to commit to helping out with the camp for two days. We'll also have one of our pitchers here tomorrow working with kids on pitching skills, but Adrian loves this camp almost as much as I do. He may not have any personal experience with the foster care system, but he had his fair share of feeling like somewhat of an outsider when he first came to America from Venezuela. Adrian was a teenager when he got drafted to one of the Crowns' farm teams, where he spent several years developing as a player.

We send the kids out to the lobby and pick up the equipment around the practice field together. When we walk through the hallway to the office, Sam comes through the door from the lobby to meet us.

"I gave an extra autographed poster to the kid who got hit by the fly ball today," Sam announces. "He didn't seem bothered by it, and the liability forms cover everything, but I thought it couldn't hurt to go the extra mile to smooth things over."

"Smart," I tell her, setting a box on the desk. "Aside from that incident, today seemed to go smoothly."

"That little red-headed kid is so cute," Adrian says, grin wide. "He's got a wild throw, but man—kid has enthusiasm."

"Oh, you mean Fireball," I say with a laugh. "His name is Jason, but he was the first to earn a nickname yesterday. He's a sweet kid." I fill Adrian in on my talk with Jason yesterday and the subsequent conversation with Danae.

"*Oooo*, someone's got a crush!" Adrian says, poking me in the sides.

"What? You're ridiculous," I firmly respond, swatting his hands away. "How do you make the leap from me telling a mom about a heartfelt conversation with her kid to '*Oooo*, you have a crush?' You moron."

Adrian waves a hand in front of my face. "It's written all over here. And in your tone of voice."

Sam chooses this moment to fill in the rest of the story about Danae not recognizing me. Adrian nearly falls over laughing.

"Maybe that's why you have a crush—it's all about the challenge of the chase," Adrian says, still chuckling.

"If you stick around after camp is over tomorrow, you can meet her for yourself," Sam says with an impish smile.

"Do not encourage him," I chide her. "Wait, what do you mean after camp tomorrow?"

Sam shrugs. "Danae is a teacher, and they have a professional day tomorrow with a staff meeting that won't end until three-thirty. I told her Jason could hang here with me until she can pick him up."

Adrian rubs his hands together, eyes full of mischievous sparkle. "I'll clear my calendar."

"You're uninvited from participating in camp tomorrow," I deadpan.

"And I reinvite you," Sam adds. The devilish looks shared between them do not bode well for me.

"No way!" Jason's awed voice matches the starstruck expression on his face. "I can't believe you got to meet the GOAT!"

Adrian's face screws into mock offense. "Hold on, hold on—I thought *I* was the greatest third baseman of all time?"

Jason's face pales, accentuating his plentiful freckles. "Oh, I mean, yeah, you're definitely one of the greats, but, you know, he had over fifteen hundred runs scored and even more runs batted in. Not to mention his fielding run value—"

I cut Jason off by ruffling his hair. "He's just messing with you, Fireball."

Adrian holds his fist out to bump Jason's. "That's some impressive stat memorization there."

Jason grins shyly at the compliment. Sam nudges his shoulder. "You keep pulling out those GOAT stats to keep these knuckleheads in their place, my guy." Jason covers his mouth to stifle a laugh.

At that moment, the front door opens, and a flustered Danae steps into the lobby.

"I'm so sorry I'm late!" she says, rushing over to join us. "We were going over some new district safety protocols, and the meeting ran over time. Then there was an accident on the highway, of course, so traffic was at a standstill. I'm so sorry to be a bother!"

Jason races over to practically tackle her. He wraps his arms around her waist with the enthusiasm of a nine-year-old hyped up on adrenaline and sugar (courtesy of Sam's snacks). "I had so much fun, Miss Danae!" he says as he squeezes her tightly.

The emotion that plays out on Danae's face in response to his greeting is truly a thing of beauty to behold. It's the kind of look that reveals the fullness of her heart—that she doesn't take this display of affection for granted. That it hasn't become commonplace to her. That it's something she deeply cherishes.

I almost feel like the three of us are intruding by even being here to witness her tender expression. But I'm not about to walk away from the magic of it.

Sam is quick to dissuade Danae's guilt. "Don't worry about it! Jason was entertaining us with his knowledge of baseball stats and reminding these two that they're not the greatest in the league quite yet."

I reach an arm out to gently shove Sam as Adrian spouts off something in Spanish with an exaggerated sad face. Jason releases Danae to turn back to us, bouncing on the balls of his feet. "I got to hang out with Miss Sammi and Mr. West *and* Mr. Ortiz!"

"Hey Fireball, I thought I told you to call me Griffin," I remind him, smiling. I look up to Danae. "This is our third baseman, Adrian Ortiz."

She holds her hand out and introduces herself. "It's nice to meet you. Thanks so much for hanging with Jason. Or should I call you Fireball now?" she asks Jason, mouth quirked.

"No, you still call me Jason. That's my baseball camp nickname," Jason says, voice serious.

"He earned that on day one with his strong throwing arm," I explain. "The fire-red hair didn't hurt either. He's an impressive little man." Jason's chest puffs up with pride, and he glances up to gauge Danae's reaction to the praise.

After giving Jason an open-mouthed excited response, Danae smiles at me, a look of pure gratitude on her face. Something roars to life in my chest. Because that smile didn't have anything to do with gaining access to who I am as a ball player or any of my athletic skills. That smile was just a mom appreciating someone caring for her son.

I want to see her smile like that again.

Sam clears her throat, and I glance over to see Adrian's Cheshire Cat grin. I turn to grab a large bag from the table.

"We've got a bunch of autographed gear in here for Jason to take home," I say, holding the bag out to Danae.

"Can we hang up the posters in my room?" Jason pleads, and Danae nods.

Sam snaps. "Hold on—I told Jason we'd let him take home a Crowns t-shirt for you too, Danae." She raises her eyebrows at Jason. "You want to come with me to pick one out?"

"Yes!" he exclaims with a leap into the air. He quickly takes Sam's hand, and they exit the lobby to go check out the merch room.

Danae watches them leave with a serene look on her face. She turns to Adrian and me. "Thank you again for putting on this camp and for inviting Jason. This was such a meaningful experience for him—for all of the kids, I'm sure. I really appreciate you taking time to do this. I imagine it's a sacrifice to take time and energy to plan and organize, and that's certainly not part of your job description. It's really amazing that you'd do something so special."

The expression on her face is beautifully sincere, and her praise cuts straight to the deepest part of my heart. "It's a highlight of my year, every year," I respond. "Jason's such a sweet kid. I'm glad he got to participate. It'll be hard to not invite him back again next year," I add with a grin.

Danae huffs a laugh. "He is a sweetheart. Most of the time," she says with a small sigh. The light in her eyes dims, and it's almost painful to observe.

"I don't know Jason's specific story, but I know that whatever has happened in his life that qualified him for this camp isn't an easy history to overcome. For him or for you," I say. "I'm glad he has someone like you to love him as he works through it."

She looks up at me, a fragile hopefulness in her eyes. "Samantha told me that she spent time in foster care before being adopted into your family. She's so upbeat and caring. It gives me hope that Jason and I will get through this. I just wish there was a step-by-step manual to follow. He deserves everything good, and I don't want to let him down." Her shoulders droop as she finishes her statement, and I resist the urge to wrap my arm around them.

"Jason talked about you constantly throughout camp. He knows you love him," Adrian says. I'd almost forgotten he was in the room with us. "That doesn't solve everything, but it gives him a safe place to work through the hard stuff."

Danae nods and gives Adrian a weak smile. I dare to reach out and touch her elbow. "Sam would be the first to tell you that working through childhood trauma is a lifelong journey, not a quick fix. And it becomes a lifelong journey for the people loving you. So make sure you've got people you can lean on for support."

A conflicted look passes over Danae's face, and I want to ask more questions to find out the source. But Jason comes bursting through the door to the lobby, Sam on his heels. "Look at these shirts, Miss Danae! Sammi said I could get matching shirts for you and me. Did I pick the perfect design?"

Danae's face instantly changes to delighted excitement in response to Jason's enthusiasm. He holds up a shirt to her, and she *ooos* and *ahhhs* over it. "How did you know exactly what kind of design I would like?" she asks, and Jason beams.

After tucking the shirts into the bag of signed merchandise, Danae tells Jason it's time to go. "Thank you again for letting him stay a little late today," she says, glancing at Sam, Adrian, and then me. When her eyes catch on mine, I'm overwhelmed by the impulse to invent a reason to see her again.

"I'll see you tomorrow," Sam tells Danae before she gives Jason an exploding fist bump. My head whips in her direction at her statement. Danae and Jason are out the door before I can clarify what she means.

"Why are you going to see them tomorrow?" I ask Sam.

"I offered to babysit so Danae can attend her book club meeting next week, so we're getting lunch tomorrow to get to know each other better. You know I'm amazing, but I have to prove to Danae that I'm amazing so she'll let me babysit that cutie redhead of hers," Sam explains, eyes twinkling. "Lucky for you."

"Now I see why you styled your hair instead of wearing a ball cap today," Adrian comments, eyes holding a similar sparkle.

I run a hand up the buzzed sides of my mid-fade faux hawk, intentionally messing up the longer sandy-brown hair by my forehead. "You're reading too much into things."

Now isn't the time to admit that I did spend a little extra time styling my hair and trimming my beard this morning. I always keep my beard a meticulous full-but-not-long length, but I gave it extra attention today.

Needing to divert the conversation, I place my hands on my hips and face Sam. "Your PA salary isn't enough? You've gotta take up a side gig babysitting now?"

Sam's face softens. "You know that's not why I'm doing it. You *know* how much support Danae needs if she's going to be there for Jason as a single mom. Look at the web of support Mom and Dad needed. And there were two of them."

Feeling properly chagrined, I nod and apologize.

She punches my arm, mischievous grin back on her face. "Besides, now you'll have an excuse to see her again."

"I don't need—"

Sam claps a hand over my mouth. "Stop denying it. I'm your sister, and he's your best friend. We see right through all your fronts. Just admit you're intrigued by Danae."

I narrow my eyes and resist the childish urge to stick out my tongue to punish Sam for covering my mouth. I sigh instead.

"Fine."

Chapter Seven

Danae

I glance down and see Jason enthusiastically waving goodbye to Samantha. We spent nearly two hours together over lunch, and I was surprised by how much I enjoyed her company. This lunch started as an opportunity to scope out whether I'm comfortable letting her babysit Jason, but it became an opportunity to get to know a new friend.

She was open but careful sharing about her past, and I could tell that Jason felt a connection with her through their similar experiences. Samantha even brought me a copy of her background check and CPR certificate, as though the transparent effort would tip the scales of my skepticism.

It might have.

Her genuine interest in me also helped—she didn't treat the lunch like I was interviewing her but more like a mutual conversation. She loved hearing stories about teaching, and we all bonded over a shared appreciation for *Harry Potter* (even if she's only seen the movies—we'll forgive her for that).

Once we're back home, I pull out a notebook and draw a line down the middle for a pro/con list.

The cons of letting Samantha babysit primarily center around the short amount of time that I've known her. *Is it irresponsible to leave*

Jason with her when I don't know her super well yet? What if she's a con artist who's really good at convincing people to trust her?

That cynical spin doesn't sit right, though. After all, she's been helping Griffin with the camp for several years, working with multiple rounds of kids in foster care. She doesn't seem like the con artist type.

The pro side is significantly longer. Those points include Jason having a role model to look up to who understands what he's been through and me enjoying Samantha's company. But the lynch pin of the pro column is that if I am ever going to have time to myself to fill my own cup like Samantha said, then I need someone to babysit Jason. Someone who isn't scared off by challenging behavior. And Samantha seems like that someone, at least right now.

Jason comes over to the table where I'm sitting, holding the tablet out to me. "Could you update this game?" he asks. As I punch in the code, he adds, "Will we hang out with Sammi again soon? She's so cool!"

Handing the tablet back to Jason, I weigh my answer. Glancing at the list in front of me, I look back up to his expectant eyes. "I think we will, bud."

I send Samantha a text confirming Wednesday.

Setting the picture book to the side, I make the quiet sign and wait for the first-grade class to settle down. It takes a moment for them to still their wiggling bodies on the carpet and fall quiet.

Speaking in my soft, soothing library voice, I tell the students, "You can look around to find what book you'd like to take home this week. After you check out with Ms. Pam, please place your book on your table. Then, you may choose a station to play at quietly for the next ten minutes. We'll spend the final ten minutes of library time silently reading the books you picked out."

Light chaos ensues as eighteen first graders mill around the library space, browsing the shelves. I make the rounds to assist students in finding books that interest them, making suggestions to the ones who seem indecisive. The noise level slowly grows as students begin playing in groups of three with blocks, marble towers, and puzzles around the room.

I make rounds through the stations, pausing near groups that are getting a little too rambunctious, encouraging them to use appropriate library voices. The first day back after a long break is always an extra challenge, but I'm grateful to be with our students again. Checking my watch, I announce that it's time to clean up and move to silent reading.

This is my final class of the day, so I'll have a little bit of time to clean up and prepare for tomorrow before it's time to assist with dismissal procedures.

I'm nervous for the day to end, however, because I got a visit from Meghan, our school counselor, during my lunch period. Apparently, Jason had an angry outburst at morning recess. From what she could gather, Jason was sharing about getting to meet Kansas City Crowns players last week, and another student rather rudely pointed out that the only reason he got to meet them is because his mom is dead and his dad is in jail.

At least, *I* think it was rather rude to point out. There's a good chance that Jason was being a little over-the-top in bragging about his experience, but my mama bear instincts have already kicked in to come to his defense.

I know that I need to discuss the issue with Jason—not only what appropriate behaviors at school look like but also how he was *feeling* when the other student brought up those realities.

I just wish I knew how to handle these conversations. How to empathize and validate Jason's very complicated emotions and reactions while also guiding him toward how to better cope with those feelings.

When the students are dismissed, I bundle up in my coat and weave through the hallways to wait with two other staff members for all the students who walk home to the south of our building. The bell rings, and we lead the group down the sidewalk past the car line to the crosswalk. After ensuring that all the students make it across the street safely, we backtrack to the school building.

Kara is one of the other teachers assigned to the south walkers line, along with one of our young paraeducators, Michelle. "So? How was the first day being back with students?" I ask Kara.

"Oh, typical first day back. Felt extra long and extra rowdy, but at least we know to expect that by now," she replies. "You?"

"Same," I say, contemplating whether to bring up Jason's outburst. I sigh. "Jason had a little bit of a rough day back, from the sound of things. I think my long day may be a little longer tonight." I fill them in briefly on what Meghan had told me.

"Poor kiddo," Kara says, and Michelle agrees. "Although, I'm not gonna lie—*I'm* jealous that the two of you got to meet some of the Crowns players! Not that I'm condoning the other student's comments by any means."

I wave a hand. "It wasn't a huge deal. Well, it was a *huge* deal to Jason. I didn't really care about meeting the players," I say. I ignore the temporary increase in my heart rate in response to my minor fib. "But I did get a babysitter out of the deal, so that's exciting!"

Before we go back inside the building, I quickly fill them in on Samantha and her offer.

"Wait, Griffin West's sister is going to be your babysitter?" Michelle asks, eyes wide. "How about I casually drop by your house when she's coming so I can meet her? Griffin West is the hottest player on the team."

Kara's eyes look glazed over. "*Mm-hmm*," she sighs.

I elbow her. "'Scuse me? You're happily married."

She shrugs. "Doesn't mean I don't have eyeballs. Or good taste. You may hate baseball, but even you *had* to have noticed how attractive he is."

Holding my badge over the security sensor, I unlock the door as an escape from this conversation. Jason is waiting for me in the library when I walk back in, feet poking out from the reading tent. Looks like he's enjoying having uncontested access to the most popular reading nook while he waits for my workday to end.

I walk over and nudge his shoe with my toe. "I have a few things to wrap up for tomorrow, and then we can head home, okay?" He doesn't answer but taps his feet together, so I'm counting that as agreement.

Twenty minutes later, we get in the car to drive home. Jason is unusually quiet.

"What sounds good for dinner? I could make chicken tacos, or spaghetti and salad, or maybe some chili?"

In the rearview mirror, I see Jason staring out the window. He shrugs.

"Or does something else sound good? What would you pick?" I ask.

He turns his head to the front. "Could we have some raviolis?"

"Oh, I didn't realize you liked ravioli," I say, darting glances to observe him in the mirror. "We have some spaghetti sauce at home, but we could stop and pick up a bag of ravioli."

"Huh?" Jason sounds completely confused. "What do you mean?"

"You know, like a bag of pasta..." I trail off as understanding breaks through. "Do you mean the ravioli that comes in a can? Not a bag?"

"Yeah, those ones," Jason affirms. "The easy ones that you don't even have to heat up."

I stifle the threat of tears. "Yes, we can have those tonight, absolutely. How about we stop at the store on the way home so you can show me exactly which ones you like?"

He seems to perk up at the suggestion, so moments later, I park in front of the grocery store. I lead Jason to the pasta aisle, and he shows me the generic brand of canned ravioli that he likes. He also leads me to the same brand of boxed macaroni and cheese, citing it as another favorite meal. I put several of each into our cart, and then I lead Jason to the fresh produce section to grab some salad and baby carrots.

"How about we strike a deal? We'll have ravioli for dinner if you have a little bowl of salad and carrots too," I say, holding out my hand to shake on it.

"Deal," Jason says, placing his hand in mine. After solemnly shaking it, I playfully shake his hand back and forth, making him smile.

At home, I ask Jason if he'd like to try the ravioli warm this time, crossing my fingers and praying that he'll agree. Thankfully, he does and eats them with enthusiasm.

I've never had canned ravioli in my life. It's not exactly the type of food my parents deemed acceptable for a refined household. But I'm in this with Jason, so I manage to eat a small serving of ravioli alongside an extra-large bowl of salad.

"Wow, these are even *better* than I thought when they're heated up!" Jason exclaims around a mouthful of ravioli. The bright orange-red sauce on his chin nearly matches the color of his hair, and I can't help but smile at his delight.

Swallowing a bite of salad, I take a deep breath before bringing up the conversation I know needs to happen. "So, I heard that today might have been a little hard for you at school."

Jason's face darkens. "Ms. Benson tattled on me? Since you're both teachers?"

"No, bud, it's not like that," I say. "Any time a student has a hard time like that at school, Ms. Benson calls to let that student's grown-up know about it. Not only because I'm a teacher. It's because she wants to make sure that every student can talk through the emotions at home after a hard day at school."

Jason looks down at his bowl, chasing ravioli with his fork. "Well, Peter was mean. He was bullying me. Screaming was the only way to get him to stop."

I reach over to place my hand on Jason's shoulder and try to re-member the tips Meghan gave me for these kinds of conversations. *Connect to understand. Empathize.* "It sounds like Peter did say some hurtful things to you. What were you feeling inside when he said those things?"

Jason's quiet for a moment, but I see emotion building on his face. "I felt like punching him."

My heart lurches, and I take a deep breath before responding. "Well, I can understand why you might have felt that way. I'm really proud of you for *not* punching him even though you wanted to. Hurting people is wrong, so I'm proud of you for making a better choice." Jason glances up at me, and I take another deep breath. "But what were you feeling inside your heart that made you want to punch Peter?"

For a second, I think that Jason might be about to open up and talk about his deeper emotions. But then his face scrunches up and reddens. He yells, "I don't know! I don't want to talk anymore—talking is dumb. Can I play the tablet instead?"

Adrenaline surges through me as I try to sort out how to react. "I'm not sure that playing the tablet is the best choice right now. We could play a card game or read a book together, or we could build some Legos—"

"No!" Jason's shout cuts off my suggestions. "I don't want to do anything with you! I'm going to my room."

He stomps up the stairs, and I try to follow him. After all, every book I read to prepare me for this unconventional motherhood emphasized connection. Things like "time in" instead of "time out" and being emotionally and physically present for your child when he's struggling.

When I step into Jason's room, he whirls around to face me. "I said I don't want to be around you! Leave me alone!"

I'm a deer in headlights. *Does he actually want me to stay even though he's saying he doesn't? Or does he really need some alone time to calm down? How in the world am I supposed to figure this out?*

"I could sit here with you while you—"

"No!" Jason cuts me off again, stomping his foot for emphasis.

Maybe it's a mistake, but I decide to give Jason what he's asking for this time. "All right—how about we turn on some music and you can chill in here for a little bit while I go clean up the dishes? I'll be in the kitchen if you need me, and I'll come back to check on you when I'm done loading the dishwasher."

Jason shrugs one shoulder. I tell the smart device to start the playlist Jason created over winter break, and I retreat from the room. Putting away the leftover salad, loading the dishes into the dishwasher, and wiping down the table becomes my form of regulation. My own emotions are running on overdrive—mainly anxiety and crippling self-doubt.

When I finish tidying up the kitchen, I slowly walk back up to Jason's room. Peering through the doorway, I see him sitting on his bed with a logic puzzle book in his lap. Blowing out a sigh of relief, I knock gently on the door frame. "Hey there. Just checking in to see how it's going."

"I'm stuck on this part of the puzzle. Can you help me?" Jason asks.

"Sure, I can," I reply, moving to sit next to Jason on the bed. I'm too afraid of restarting the cycle to bring up his emotional response or the day at school again. I help him with the logic puzzle until it's time for him to take a shower and get ready for bed.

We sit together on his bed to read the next chapter of *The Prisoner of Azkaban*. Jason starts yawning halfway through, so I suggest finishing the rest tomorrow. He agrees, and I squeeze him in a hug.

Looking into his piercing green eyes, I say, "You know, Jason, I love you *all* the time. No matter what."

A conflicted look passes over his face. "You do?"

I nod and say, "I do." He still looks conflicted, so I ask, "Do you know what I mean when I say 'I love you' to you?"

When Jason shrugs, I continue. "I don't just mean I like you, or I think you're a really cool kid. Even though I *do* like you and you *are* a really cool kid. It means that you're really, really important to me, and I choose you as my biggest priority." His eyes widen, and I squeeze his shoulders again. "It means I'm with you one hundred percent, forever. I'm yours, and you're mine, no matter what happens. You and me together—that's home. When I say 'I love you,' it means you're stuck with me forever, okay?" I finish with a teasing smile.

Jason vigorously nods his head. "Okay, yeah." He wraps his arms around my waist and hugs tightly. "Thanks for making my favorite dinner tonight."

I know we didn't really address the roots of everything that transpired today—the root of everything that's transpired in his life. But that's going to take longer than one conversation over dinner.

"You're welcome, Jason," I murmur, kissing the top of his head. "I'll see you in the morning."

"G'night," he says before burrowing down under his gray comforter.

Thankfully, after a couple of weeks here, Jason realized he likes sleeping with the bedroom door closed and sound machine on, so I quietly pull the door shut as I exit. Shuffling out to the living room, I collapse on the couch.

Did I do that right? He calmed down, but we never really talked about what he was feeling or how to handle it better next time. Did I chicken out by leaving him alone? Or was that what he needed? What about next time?

I close my eyes and rub my temples. Sitting up, I decide to text Samantha.

ME

Hi, Samantha. I wanted to let you know that Jason had a rough first day back to school today. I really don't want to burden you, so don't worry about coming over on Wednesday. I appreciate your offer so much, though!

SAMANTHA

I swear you're not a burden, Danae! Wait and see how the next two days go. If it doesn't seem like Jason would be ready to be away from you, that's one thing. But if you're only worried about his potential behavior, I already told you that doesn't scare me. So if he seems ok with it on Wed, I'll still come over!

ME

Are you sure?

SAMANTHA

Girl, stop questioning me! I'M SURE. You deserve to go to book club!

ME

Okay, I'll update you on Wednesday.

CHAPTER EIGHT

Griffin

Eyes closed, head leaning against the back of the couch, I try to slow my thoughts. The heating pad on my shoulder is helping my muscles relax after a particularly intense workout today. I just need a heating pad for my brain.

As we creep closer to spring training, the burden of success weighs heavier and heavier on my shoulders. And not only because of the injured one. The Crowns could have a real shot at a World Series run this year, and I certainly don't want to be the weak link that messes that up.

Which leads back to the injured shoulder. I know the baseball world is going to compare my every move this season to my previous success. Watching for any indication that I'm not what I used to be. Ready to over-analyze and dissect any sign of weakness, even though they already had that shot in the month I played for the Crowns' farm team at the end of last season.

I want to be the post-injury success story. I want to be *every* success story. It's what the sports world expects of me and what I expect from myself. I've trained everyone to expect success from me.

Except maybe Danae Collins.

She's kept my thoughts running almost as much as the upcoming season. Sam came home from their lunch raving about how incredible Danae is, how thoughtful she was in getting to know Sam while also being loving and attentive to Jason. Sam's comments only added fuel to the fire—probably intentional on her part.

Sighing, I adjust the heating pad to center lower on my shoulder blade. I drop my head back again, pressing my thumb and forefinger to my closed eyes.

"Oh Griffie, I need you to drive me somewhere!" Sam singsongs.

"Do not call me that. You know this," I rebuke her. She comes waltzing into my line of sight in the spacious living room. "Why do you need me to drive you? Is something wrong with your car? I can call Phil if we need to get it into the shop tomorrow."

"No, no, don't call your repair guy. My car's fine. I just want the pleasure of your company," Sam says.

"Okaaay, that's suspicious," I respond as I switch off the heating pad and stand up from the couch. "Where am I driving you, exactly?"

"You're dropping me off at Danae's house, so I can babysit Jason while she goes to book club," Sam states, like this was obvious information.

I shoot her a look. She smirks.

"What if I have other things to do tonight?" I ask.

"I plan your calendar, dummy. I know you don't have anything going on tonight other than brooding on the couch with your heating pad," she retorts. "Let's go!"

I start to protest. "Sam, don't you think you're being a little—"

"Are you going to stand there and honestly tell me that you're not itching to talk to her again?" Sam cuts in. She sharpens her stare. "Honestly?"

I lose the staring contest. "At least give me a second to change," I say, motioning to my joggers and Crowns t-shirt.

"You have ten minutes."

I utilize all ten of those minutes. After changing into jeans and a long-sleeved Henley shirt, I head to the bathroom to touch up my hair. Giving my reflection a once-over in the mirror, I change my mind and throw on a plain ball cap. The downside of having a very recognizable haircut is that I tend to get, well, recognized. But it's part of my image now, my brand as a player, so I've kept the same hairstyle for the past four years.

Maybe it's time for a change?

I leave the question unanswered in my mind and join Sam in the entryway. "Ready?" I ask.

She scoffs. "Are *you* ready is the real question."

Sam punches the address into my GPS and then proceeds to yammer the entire drive to Danae's house. "I took one for the team and talked to Joe—AKA the world's most annoying agent—this morning to double check your promotional schedule. Tomorrow you're shooting that cereal commercial, and next week you have the photo shoot for the grocery store. A trainer will come over to our house for your sessions on the day of the photo shoot, but otherwise you'll be at the training facility with the other guys."

"And what exactly will you be doing with all your free time while I'm back in training full time? Trips to the spa?" I tease.

"Har har," Sam fake laughs. "Just for that snide remark, maybe I will schedule daily trips to the spa instead of fielding all of your media inquiries, coordinating meals with your chef, and scheduling your appointments like usual. It *would* save me from any further phone calls with Joe."

I reach over to flick her arm.

The GPS instructs me to pull into the parking lot of a large complex of townhomes. I slow the car to a crawl as I peer around looking for the right house number. "Do you see which one is hers?" I ask Sam. She eventually spots it and points me to a visitor parking space. I quickly scope out the area, relieved that the sidewalks are empty at the moment.

"You sure Danae isn't going to think it's totally weird that I came along to drop you off here?" I ask uncertainly as we walk up to the door.

"Oh, she's definitely going to think it's weird," Sam states. I groan. "Just play it off with all your Griff charm," she adds, ambiguously waving her hand in my general direction.

I'm tempted to leave her here, but Sam has already rung the doorbell. And if I'm honest . . . I do want to talk to Danae again. Possibly several agains.

A few seconds later, the door swings open. Danae stands there in black leggings and a pale purple tunic that hugs her curves the perfect amount. She smiles at Sam but startles when she sees me.

"Oh, Griffin, er, Mr. West, I, uh, didn't expect to see you," Danae stammers.

"Definitely just Griffin, or Griff if you'd rather," I say with a warm smile, leaving it up to Sam to explain my presence here.

Danae motions us through the doorway, and we step into the small entry. Sam finally speaks up. "Griff gave me a ride over because my car's been acting up."

Well, then. Didn't expect her to blatantly lie.

Jason chooses just the right moment to come barreling into the entryway to greet Sam. "Sammi!" he yells. When he sees me standing next to her, his grin spreads wider. "And Mr. Griffin! Wow! I didn't know I'd get to see you again too!"

"Hey, Fireball," I say holding out my fist for a fist bump. "I couldn't let Sam here have all the fun. I wanted to say 'hi' too."

"Let me show you my new Lego set!" Jason exclaims, tugging on Sam's hand.

"Hold on a minute, Jason," Danae says, sounding concerned. She looks to Sam. "If you didn't drive yourself here, then you won't have a car to drive Jason in case of an emergency. I got his booster seat out of my car to be ready for you. He's so small for his age that he still doesn't meet the minimum height suggestion to ride without a booster."

"Oh, I didn't even think about that," Sam admits, having the decency to look chagrined. "I mean, I can always call 911, right?"

Danae's face still looks panicked, even though she's trying to hide it.

"How about I drive you over to your book club? That way your car is here in case Sam needs to drive Jason anywhere?" I offer.

It wouldn't take an expert in body language to interpret Danae's hesitance. Sam, for her part, impishly grins at me.

"I guess that would be okay," Danae says. Her voice sounds less than excited. I try not to take it personally. "Let me put the booster seat back in and show you which car is mine," she adds to Sam.

"Great—that gives me time to see this famous Lego set," I say, smiling at Jason.

"Yes!" he yells before grabbing my hand. Danae and Sam go out to the parking lot as Jason leads me to the living room. The space is tidy but homey, with throw pillows and blankets that beg you to settle into the plush couch cushions. The small dining area to the side of the living room leads directly to the kitchen, where a pizza box sits on the otherwise uncluttered counter.

"So, this is a small *Harry Potter* Lego set from when Harry arrives at Hogwarts in the boats. There are all sorts of big sets like the castle, but I don't have those yet," Jason says as he pulls me over to the coffee table. The instructions lay open on the table, the remaining pieces of the half-assembled set organized into piles.

"Super cool!" I say, picking up one of the characters. "Who's this?"

"Well, that's Neville, of course," Jason says. He peers up at me with narrowed eyes. "Haven't you read *Harry Potter*?"

I give a sheepish grimace. "Afraid not. I'm not a huge reader."

"But *Harry Potter* is the best book series ever! You have to read it!" Jason exclaims.

His passion may be contagious, but I tend to avoid reading at all costs. I certainly don't want to discourage *his* love of reading, though, so I reply with a diplomatic, "It must be good if you like it so much!"

Danae and Sam come back inside, and it's obvious that Danae is in the middle of a very detailed rundown of the evening with Jason. As they walk to the kitchen, Danae says, "There's pizza, but if you cook for some reason, there's a fire blanket in the cabinet under the sink. There's also a fire extinguisher in the coat closet and in the linen closet upstairs. Do you know the Heimlich maneuver?"

I hold back a snort of laughter when I see Danae's dead-serious face. Thankfully, Sam maintains her composure as she responds, "Can't say I've ever actually performed it, but I do know the basics from the CPR training."

Danae looks like she wants to say more, but Jason interrupts her. "Can I have pizza with Sammi now?" Danae smiles down at him and holds out her arms for a hug. Jason lunges into her embrace, and you'd need a granite heart to be unaffected by the scene.

"Get out of here and enjoy your book club," Sam says, making a shooing motion with her hands. "Jason and I are going to have a great time."

"Okay," Danae says, releasing Jason from the hug. "Call me if you need anything. I promise I'll be back before Jason needs to go to bed." Her gaze cuts over to me. "Or, I guess, as long as Griffin is able to get me back on time?"

"Of course," I reassure her questioning tone. "Your personal taxi will be available at the drop of a hat."

Jason giggles at that, and I wink at him.

"All right, I suppose we do need to leave if I'm going to get there on time," Danae says. She looks at Jason once more. "Listen to Samantha and have so much fun, okay?"

We walk to the entry, pausing for Danae to put on her coat. Sam and Jason are already talking loudly about their plans for the night, which seem to include fort building and card games. Danae looks back over her shoulder once then looks apprehensively at me.

"Ready?" I ask, giving her what I hope is my most reassuring smile.

The apprehension doesn't leave her eyes as she mumbles, "Okay."

Her apparent reluctance to be in the car with me is so palpable, it's becoming impossible not to take it personally. It's also such an unfamiliar experience that I'm a little baffled as to how to turn the situation around.

As she locks the front door behind us, I stretch my neck from side to side. Winning Danae over just became my top priority.

CHAPTER NINE

Danae

After locking the front door, I turn around to peruse the parking lot. I'm looking for whatever sort of outlandish, expensive sports car I'll have to ride in tonight. My perusal yields no obvious vehicle discovery, and I wonder if Griffin parked a long distance away in order to protect his precious car.

"So, where does your book club meet?" Griffin asks as he begins walking along the sidewalk. I hurry to follow him, which results in me bumping into him when he stops much sooner than I expected. He motions to a large, black Jeep and says, "This is me."

"Oh," I say, flustered after colliding with his rather muscular back. "Sorry, I wasn't expecting a Jeep."

Griffin grins as he holds open the passenger door. "Expecting a cherry red sports car?" he asks before closing the door behind me.

I can't think of a good way to dismiss my assumption in the five seconds it takes for him to walk around the car and climb into the driver's seat. "I mean . . . yeah, I was," I sheepishly admit.

Chuckling, Griffin starts the ignition. "I was obsessed with Jeeps when I was a teenager. Begged my dad for a Jeep to be my first car. Of course, I wanted one of the off-roading versions at the time, which was a hard pass from my parents. I bought my first Jeep when I got called up to the Crowns, and they're all I've driven as an adult."

"But not the off-roading type?" I clarify, gesturing around the vehicle.

He smiles again. "Turns out I'm not much of an adrenaline junkie. I went off-roading once with a friend in college and spent the entire time gripping the panic bar and praying he wouldn't roll the Jeep. I was too afraid of getting injured to enjoy the ride."

I hum, returning his smile.

He looks at me expectantly. When I don't say anything, he asks, "Where are we headed?"

"Oh, right. Sorry," I say, flustered all over again. I was so massively unprepared to see this man standing outside my door tonight. Even though I know Samantha is planning to babysit as often as I need her, I still assumed I'd never cross paths with her brother again.

"The book club is at my favorite local bookstore in Overland Park. Here's the address," I say, showing him my phone screen. He quickly puts the address into the GPS, and I buckle my seatbelt.

I wish there was a proverbial seatbelt to buckle around my nerves. I'm not sure how to handle a conversation alone in a car with Griffin West.

The past few days, Jason has continued showing off his encyclopedic knowledge of Griffin's baseball career, sharing far more statistics than I could ever care to know (or understand). I've resisted the urge to Google Griffin's name because I am *not* curious to know more about him. And I'm certainly *not* interested in analyzing photos to figure out how to classify his gray-blue eye color.

The baseball cap he's wearing tonight makes it hard to study his eye color at all.

Griffin glances over at me with an air of expectation. I must have completely missed him saying something.

"I'm sorry, what did you say?" I ask, sensing my cheeks turning pink.

Even in the dark, his profile lights up with his warm smile. "I asked what book you're talking about with the club tonight."

"Oh, yes," I say. *Stop saying the word "oh," for goodness' sake, Danae.* "We rotate genres each month, and this time it's a historical fiction novel set during World War II. Well, it's a dual timeline, so I suppose only half of it was set during the war."

"Did you like it?" he asks as he glances over his shoulder before changing lanes on the highway.

"Loved it. Everything about the book was incredible. It was so thoroughly researched and well-written. There was a huge twist that made the entire story so much more emotional. It was incredibly moving, and I cried my way through the ending," I reply with growing enthusiasm. I may be mentally struggling with how to interact with this famous athlete, but even he can't smother my passion for talking about literature. "It's one of those books that you know is going to stick with you, that you're going to continue thinking about for a long time. That someday you'll be standing in line at the grocery store and think about a particularly poignant moment from the story and feel the urge to reread the whole thing all over again. I can't wait to discuss it with the book club tonight."

Looking over at Griffin, I see his smile has grown wider. "Big fan of books, huh?" he observes.

I huff a small laugh. "You could say that. I suppose being a fan of books is a prerequisite to becoming a librarian," I say, letting go of some of my apprehension. "Do you like to read?"

Griffin's smile tightens. "Can't say I'm a big reader."

"Oh," I say before pursing my lips. "I suppose you don't have a lot of free time with your baseball schedule. Do you ever listen to audiobooks?"

"Nah, I prefer music or sports podcasts," Griffin replies.

The apprehension starts welling up again. *There goes my one easy topic of conversation.* I turn to stare out the window.

"How long have you been a librarian?" Griffin asks.

"This is my fourth year, but I was a classroom teacher before that for five years. I started taking master's classes immediately during my first year of teaching because I knew my goal was to become a librarian," I say. Griffin is nodding and glancing over at me as often as is safe while focusing on the road. "I was lucky that the librarian at the school where I was teaching retired and they offered the position to me. A lot of librarian hopefuls have to wait a lot longer for positions to open up."

"What made you want to be a librarian instead of a classroom teacher?" he asks.

"Clearly, I love reading. Books have always been my most faithful and trusted companions," I reply quickly, then back away from walking further down that deeply personal explanation path. "I know how much books shaped my childhood, and I've always loved the idea of instilling that same love for reading in young kids. Time spent reading as a child is one of the biggest indicators of success later in life," I say, watching Griffin's reaction. He's focused on the road, but every glance my way is filled with genuine interest, encouraging me to continue. "But library isn't only about loving books—it's about teaching critical thinking skills, even research tools. And it's about providing a safe space for all kids, no matter what they have going on in their lives outside of the school walls."

"That's how you met Jason, at school? At least, he told me you were his teacher before you were his mom," Griffin says. My heart seizes at the thought of Jason saying those words.

"Yes. I wasn't his classroom teacher because his first year at our school was my first year in the library. But we bonded right away when he visited the library almost daily to exchange books. Most first graders only come in on their designated library day, but Jason was there every day that his teacher would let him come. That first year, when the staff began noticing some of his behavior struggles, I started taking him on a weekly walk around the school hallways during one of my planning periods. It was a good way to give him a break from the classroom setting and ask him questions about how he was doing. He always came bounding out of the classroom when I stopped by to pull him out." The corners of my lips turn up at the memory, and when I look over, Griffin quickly turns his eyes back to the road. His lips mirror mine, though.

Ask him a question, Danae! You were brought up with better social skills than this!

"So, um, how long have you played baseball?" I tentatively ask.

Griffin laughs. "I've played almost all thirty-three years of my life," he says, still chuckling. He glances at me, a tease in his expression. "But that's probably not what you were asking. This will be my seventh season starting for the Crowns. I played on their farm team for four years before that."

"Is that a long time to stay with the same team?" I ask.

He shrugs a shoulder. "Yes and no. Some players get traded around a lot more frequently, but it's not unheard of to stay with one team for your whole career. I've loved my experience with the Crowns, so I've always asked my agent to come to an agreement on contract extensions. He hasn't been thrilled about my lack of desire to chase the highest paycheck, but I'd rather have the stability and camaraderie of sticking with the team. Plus, I really like living in Kansas City."

We pull into the shopping center where the bookstore is located, and Griffin finds a parking spot.

"Um, so, I'm not sure what you're planning to do while I'm here, but . . ." I trail off.

Griffin twists in his seat to face me. "I figured I'd come in with you and join the discussion," he says evenly.

My heart leaps in my chest. "Oh, please no," I reply, my voice breathy.

Griffin's face breaks out in a wide grin. "I'm just kidding. How long is the meeting?"

I exhale. "I'm sorry—that was so rude of me. I didn't mentally prepare myself to see you tonight," I say, then blush further at my confession. "We usually talk for about an hour and a half. I can come out and look for you in the parking lot, I guess?"

"I'll find you," he says, eyes locked on mine.

I swallow hard and open the door. My heart is still racing as I mumble, "See you."

Why are you acting like such a bumbling idiot, Danae? Just because the man is famous doesn't mean you should be falling all over yourself. You don't like baseball. You don't care about this man.

My body needs to stop acting like I care about this man.

"The way she wanted to be buried with her husband—it was too much! I couldn't hold back the tears!" Anna says, dabbing her eyes. Our circle of eight book club members nods in solidarity with her. I've had to wipe my own eyes a time or two during our discussion. We sit on an eclectic mix of chairs and the green velvet sofa that Christin has collected over the years for the store. Being surrounded by so many shelves and table displays of books creates the ideal setting for a cozy chat about a novel.

The bell above the door dings, and Christin, the owner of the bookstore, calls out, "Let me know if you need any help! We'll be wrapping up our book club meeting soon." Anna continues on with her train of thought, but I'm distracted when I realize who just walked into the bookstore.

Griffin.

Glancing at my watch, I see that we're nearing the two-hour mark of our discussion. Which means I'm pushing Jason's bedtime and need to leave. *Of course, my first evening away from Jason and I totally lose track of time. Will he ever be comfortable with me leaving again, or will he feel like I broke a promise? Will Samantha even want to babysit again after I didn't come home when I said I would?*

Griffin acts like he's perusing the bookshelves, but he makes casual eye contact with me and gives a subtle wave of his hand that seems to indicate I shouldn't be worried about the time. Then again, I don't really know him all that well. So why do I think I can accurately interpret his body language?

Unfortunately, Griffin's glance in my direction turned his face to us just long enough that one of the book club ladies recognizes him. Mary leans forward and whispers, "Is that Griffin West?" She jerks her head in his direction with zero subtlety. The rest of the group follows Mary's conspicuous behavior by looking very obviously in his direction.

"It is! It's absolutely him!" Anna affirms, voice low but above a whisper.

My eyes can't help but find Griffin, and I see a faint blush of red spreading up his neck.

Well, shoot.

Before I can speak up to turn our attention back to the book, Mary has popped up out of her seat and made her way over to Griffin.

"Excuse me, Mr. West?" she says. I see Griffin square his shoulders a split second before he turns to face Mary, a smile locked firmly in place.

"You caught me," he replies. "I was . . . looking for a gift for my sister."

Mary beams. "You've come to the right place, then! Christin's store is full of great gift ideas in addition to books," she says. She clears her throat. "Would you mind if I take a quick picture with you? My son would absolutely lose his mind."

Griffin smiles. "Of course! You've gotta get some cool mom points."

As Mary rushes to grab her phone from her purse, the rest of the ladies follow suit. They've soon formed a line taking pictures of each other with Griffin, who smiles broadly for every one. He offers autographs, so Christin hurries to find some blank paper behind the checkout desk.

In all the excitement, no one has noticed that I've quietly gathered up my things and slipped to the front door. My heart found its way to my throat the moment Mary made her way over to Griffin. In the midst of the famous-person-induced commotion, the last thing I want to do is call attention to the fact that I know him—that he's my ride home.

I reach the door, and Christin is asking Griffin questions about his sister's interests to help him find a gift. It's not like I can make it home without him, but I'm too panicked to stay in the bookstore with the chaos surrounding him. Before pushing the door open, I glance back and manage to briefly meet his eyes. I give a look that I hope he'll interpret as, "I'll be waiting by the car."

And then I slip outside into the blast of winter air, gulping in the chill. *I should have kept a better eye on the time instead of getting so caught up in the discussion. I should have set an alarm so I knew when I needed to leave. I'm going to be late getting home to Jason because I didn't pay attention. Then Griffin had to come in and get me, and now he's being ambushed by my friends, so we'll be even later getting home.*

I've managed to locate Griffin's Jeep in the parking lot, and I lean against it as casually as possible. *You're messing up, Danae. You need to pull it together and be more responsible if you're going to be a stable person for Jason.*

My thoughts pivot from berating myself to replaying the mayhem inside the bookstore. *Is that what Griffin's life is like all the time?* The way he reacted certainly looked like a well-worn response. Most people probably wouldn't notice the flush of his neck, the mental preparation in the squaring of his shoulders before he faced everyone with that charming smile.

I'm suddenly sad for Griffin. Sad that he has to socially perform in that way everywhere he goes, that he can't just walk into a local bookstore and study the shelves unbothered.

Wait, you don't even know him. Maybe he loves it. Maybe he's not sad at all. Maybe he feeds off of the fame, lets it go to his head until he expects special treatment everywhere he goes.

Even though I don't truly know Griffin all that well, the negative assessment doesn't fit, doesn't sit right in my thoughts. Because he doesn't seem like a fame-hungry, self-absorbed guy in the slightest. He's been thoughtful and disarming in every interaction I've had with him, in spite of his athletic celebrity status.

Which might be even more confusing.

CHAPTER TEN

Griffin

We're on the highway driving back to Danae's townhouse in Shawnee, and she's been deathly quiet. I should have texted her about the time instead of going into the bookstore. We'd exchanged phone numbers after arriving at the bookstore, so it would have been a less intrusive solution.

I couldn't resist the allure of glimpsing Danae in her element at the book club. After she lit up so much when she talked about the book in the car, I wanted to get an additional peek at that passion. But I was overly confident in my ability to be stealthy and remain unnoticed.

The wide-eyed, panicked expression on Danae's face when she slipped out of the bookstore hit like a fast pitch to the ribs. I made the wrong call going inside the store and being seen by her friends. Because I force-fed her a giant helping of the chaos that is my life in public. A chaos I have a feeling she wouldn't be drawn to. Danae strikes me as someone who appreciates the quietness of life in all the best ways.

Of course, I screwed things up right after I spent an hour aimlessly driving and obsessing over how much *I'm* drawn to *her*. Replaying every interaction I've had with her and Jason. Cataloging the times I've seen her smile and the precise causes. Working up the nerve to ask her on a date during the drive back to her house.

I've ruined that chance tonight.

"I'm sorry you got mobbed by a bunch of book ladies," Danae finally says. I chance a glance over at her. Her profile stands out in the dark, accentuating the dip of her nose and the fullness of her lips.

Flashing a smile, I wave her off. "No big deal. Nothing you need to apologize for."

"Still, if I would have kept track of the time, you wouldn't have had to come in there after me," she says. After a pause, she asks, "Is that pretty much the way it always is for you?"

I'm tempted to lie. To downplay the attention. To give the illusion of a calmer life.

"Out in public, yeah, that's fairly typical," I confess. "But there are some places I can go where I'm less likely to be recognized. And if I'm in another city, it's not as frequent. Kansas City locals are zealous about the city's sports teams."

"*Hmmm*, truth," Danae replies with a nod. "Does it . . . bother you?"

I'm caught off guard by her question. Because I handle crowds and attention so naturally, everyone assumes I must love it all. Danae's question is more intuitive than she probably realizes. I blow out a breath before answering. "'Bother' might not be quite the right word. Most of the time, I'm happy to engage with fans, take photos, and sign autographs. Especially when there are kids in the mix. Seeing their faces light up with excitement is worth the hassle. But it does seem like a hassle sometimes."

It's a hassle if it will affect people I care about, I think but don't add.

I'm desperate to dispel the melancholy weighing Danae down, get her back to animatedly talking about her passion for books. Even if I don't particularly like books, I like hearing her talk about them.

"How was the book club discussion? You know, before I came in and made a scene," I joke, hoping to alleviate the tension.

I'm rewarded with a small quirk of her lips. I'll take that quarter-smile.

"It was great. I always enjoy hearing what parts of the story stand out to other people—to give a scene I may have glossed over a second look. Of course, there are the key moments that all of us equally obsessed over. This month's book provided ample discussion," she says.

Glancing over at her, I see a bigger half-smile on her lips as she adds, "Clearly, considering I stayed past curfew."

I reward her teasing with a full laugh. "We'll have to find out from Sam how grounded you are. She can be a bit of a killjoy when she wants to be."

"I have a hard time picturing that," Danae says with a chuckle. "She seems way too upbeat and kind." Her expression tightens. "But Jason may rescind my 'leave the house' privileges after I didn't come home when I said I would."

"Don't get too worked up over the possibility yet. Sam's a pretty fun person to be around. Jason might be totally unbothered," I try to assure her.

"Or he might think I'm just like his father." Danae's voice is resigned.

We're stopped at a red light, and I can't resist the urge to reach over and touch her shoulder. "I don't know anything about Jason's father, but I can confidently say that you're nothing like him. And Jason knows that."

She looks over at me, and the unguarded vulnerability in her eyes has me coming undone. This woman clearly loves that boy more than anything, and she's also clearly terrified that she's not loving him enough.

"Danae." I say her name slowly, savoring the shape of it on my tongue. "You're doing an amazing job at being Jason's mom."

Her chin quivers ever so slightly, and it's all I can do not to move my hand up to cup her jaw. She whispers, "How do you know? We've only been around each other a few times. How could you possibly know that?"

The light has turned green, but there are no cars behind us in the turn lane, so I maintain my eye contact with Danae. "I heard the way Jason talked about you at camp. I see the way he relaxes around you. I know it because you were prepared to miss your book club in order to not leave Jason. And I see it in your panic about how he's going to respond to your being late tonight. You're doing a great job, Danae."

We've missed our chance to turn at this green light, but I don't mind waiting through another red. I don't mind giving Danae an extra minute to process the truth of how amazing she is. A truth I'm only beginning to discover myself.

I don't mind a few extra moments with her quiet presence next to me.

The light turns green. "Thank you," she says quietly as I turn onto her street.

When we park in front of Danae's townhouse, one of her neighbors is locking her front door. Neither of us makes a move to exit the vehicle until the neighbor is safely in her car and the sidewalks are clear.

Danae unlocks her front door, and I follow her inside. I hear Sam's voice theatrically yelling some sort of nonsense word, immediately followed by a similar response from Jason. The look on Danae's face shows familiarity and amusement, so I piece together that this might have something to do with *Harry Potter*.

"I'm back!" Danae calls as we walk toward the living room.

"Miss Danae!" Jason's face lights up when he sees her. He holds up his Lego figurine. "I'm glad you're back, but can Sammi stay a little longer? We're in the middle of an epic duel!"

I hope his response is enough to calm Danae's anxiety about being late.

"I know you're having a good time, but we need to get ready for bed," Danae responds.

Jason groans loudly. "But I don't want to go to bed yet! I'm not even tired!"

Sam jumps in with a nice save. "My guy, I've gotta get Griffin home. He has an early morning. But you know we'll pick up the battle again next time I'm here. I'm going to study up on my spell options because I'm determined to win."

Jason looks slightly disappointed but nods in agreement. Danae tells him, "Jason, why don't you tell Sammi and Mr. Griffin goodbye and then go get some pajamas on."

Jason gives Sam a hug then offers me his fist to bump. "Thanks for bringing Sammi over to hang out with me," he says, voice serious.

"Any time, Fireball," I respond. He grins at my use of his nickname then scampers up the stairs.

Danae is quick to start apologizing to Sam. "I'm so sorry we were late. I got caught up in the discussion and completely lost track of time."

Sam rolls her eyes. "Oh, please. It was not a big deal at all. I'm glad you were having so much fun! We had a great time here."

"How was he? Everything go okay?" Danae asks.

"He was great. Responded fine when I asked him to help with the dishes before we started playing. He'll probably crash hard tonight," Sam says with a wink.

Danae smiles appreciatively. "Thank you so much. It was nice to get to have adult conversation with my friends. Could you text me your Venmo info?"

"No way, you don't need to pay me for tonight," Sam starts to object.

Danae cuts her off, placing a hand on her arm. "Please. Let me pay you."

For a second, it looks like Sam might continue fighting the issue, but in the end, she agrees. "Fine, *this* time I'll let you pay me. But now you owe me an I-babysit-for-free night."

Danae fully laughs, and it's beautiful. A lilting melody. I wish there was a ten-second rewind button for real life so I could push it to hear that exact sound again.

As Sam grabs her coat and bag, Danae thanks me for driving. "I'm sorry again for not paying attention to the time and creating a hassle for you." I see Sam give me a quizzical look over Danae's shoulder.

"Stop apologizing. It's not a big deal at all," I reassure her. "I'm glad you got to have a wild night out."

She laughs again, and I'm becoming addicted to the sound. "Good night, Danae," I say, tipping my hat. In my peripheral vision, I see Sam fighting a laugh. *What are you now, some cowboy? Why did you just tip your hat like an idiot?*

Thankfully, Danae smiles. "Thanks for the ride, Griffin. And thanks again, Samantha!"

Sam and I dart quickly to my Jeep before we can be spotted by a family further down the sidewalk. Once safely inside the car, Sam shifts to face me. "Hassle?"

I give her a brief rundown of my failed attempt to nonchalantly signal the time to Danae in the bookstore. Sam howls with laughter.

"Griffin West, making dreams come true for all the book club ladies," she says, wiping tears from her eyes. "I bet they'll choose a baseball romance for next month's book."

"A what?" I ask, confused.

"A baseball romance. You know, a romance book featuring a baseball player as the main character," Sam explains.

"That exists?" I glance over to see her nod. "Books are weird."

Sam *tsks*. "Don't let Danae hear you say things like that. You might ruin your chance with her book-loving heart."

"I think tonight already ruined my chance with her," I say, voice melancholy. "You should have seen the look on her face when her friends realized who I was and started asking for photos. Like a baby deer in ultra-bright headlights. I don't think that level of attention is the kind of life she's looking for."

"So, you're saying you *are* hoping for a chance with her?" Sam's voice sounds gleeful.

I reach over to shove her shoulder. "That's your takeaway from my statement? You're going to completely ignore the negative reaction Danae had to the attention?"

Sam waves a hand. "Her first impression of the fame is an obstacle that can be overcome. What matters is do *you* want to overcome that obstacle or not?"

I ponder her observation.

"I'm interpreting your pensive silence as a solid 'yes,'" Sam answers for me. She rubs her hands together. "So, let's game plan to win her over."

"Slow down," I say. My thoughts are interrupted by a driver cutting in front of me on the highway. I hit the brakes and lay on the horn.

"I thought you were speaking metaphorically, but literally slowing down works too," Sam quips.

"I mean, *you* need to slow down with the romance game plan. Even though I might be interested in dating Danae, I need to consider if that's even what she would want in her life right now," I say. "She became a mom to a nine-year-old a little over a month ago, and that's a lot to work through with him. Might not be the best timing to start a new relationship, even without the added obstacle of the public attention. I don't want her to take on more than she can handle."

"Danae's a grown woman, Griff. Why don't you let *her* decide what she can handle in her own life?" Sam replies.

I drum the steering wheel. Sam's right—I should let Danae decide for herself what she can and can't handle. But the attraction I feel to her is different from the surface-level physical attraction I've felt for other women in the past. It's even different from the interest I had in the few women I've actually dated. Interest that typically fizzled as soon as I realized they were chasing association with "Griffin West, Wizard of Defense."

Danae is different. She's empathetic and caring but not just in words. She's living it out in huge, significant ways. Not to mention the spark of passion inside her that flares when she talks about books or her role as a librarian.

Plus, she has zero passion for baseball, which means she doesn't care about my athletic prowess or success. That's not what she sees when she looks at me.

Except for the public attention that comes along with it. That, she might see. And she may not want that. Which means, I'm not sure if she'll want *me*. Public attention is part of the package that would come with dating me. It's who I am.

My grip on the steering wheel tightens.

Sam flicks my ear.

"Ow!" I yell, shooting her a chastising glare.

"Get out of your head, big bro. It's unlike you to think so much," Sam says.

I roll my eyes, although I doubt she can see the gesture in the dark car. "Very funny."

"I'm serious," Sam replies. "It's obvious you're drawn to Danae. And I happen to think she's pretty amazing as well, plus Jason's a great kid.

You don't have a lot of time before you leave for spring training camp. So hurry up and shoot your shot."

"Basketball lingo, huh?" I sigh. "What if it's a swing and a miss?"

Sam shrugs. "Then at least you swung."

Chapter Eleven

Danae

Glancing at the clock, I see that I have twenty-five minutes until the first class will come to library. My library aide is still helping clean up breakfast in the cafeteria, so I have a few moments alone.

Moments I should be using to update my substitute lesson plan binder or to make copies for next week or to write a to-do list for all of the spring library activities. This is my busiest season, between the special reading week activities I plan each year, as well as conducting the Battle of the Books competition for the fourth and fifth graders. Throughout the school year, teams of students read twenty books selected by librarians across our district, taking notes about them. In the spring, I conduct a tournament of battles between teams to see who can correctly answer the most questions about the books.

That is what I should be spending this free time doing—getting ahead on battle preparation.

Instead, I walk back to the storage space attached to the library and lean against a counter, staring into space. Thinking about Griffin West.

Last night threw me for possibly the biggest loop I've ever experienced. And that's saying something, considering I recently became a single mother with very little advance notice. Somehow, Griffin's presence in my life is more disconcerting than Jason's presence.

After an hour of lying wide awake in bed, I'd finally succumbed to my taunting curiosity and looked him up online. I didn't fully fall down the rabbit hole, but I read enough (and clicked through enough photos) to outline the basic gist of his life.

He grew up all over during his elementary years before his family settled in Oklahoma. He played baseball for a college in Texas for three years before he was drafted by the Crowns. He eventually became a darling of Kansas City sports fans due to his athletic success and all-around "great guy" reputation. His good looks don't hurt him on the popularity front, either. Apparently, kids all over the city ask their barbers for "The Wizard" cut with the faded sides and longer hair in the middle that makes Griffin's hairstyle stand out so much.

Call me an ostrich because my head was deep in the oblivion sand when it came to Griffin West's existence.

Now, my head has been forcefully wrenched out of that sand.

But Griffin is the exact opposite of everything I want. I like stability and security. I like solid plans with little disruption. I like to assess every possibility and plan for everything.

I *do not like* baseball.

So why can't I stop thinking about him?

"Earth to Danae!" Kara's voice jerks me out of my reverie. She walks over and leans a hand against the counter next to me. "What's got you off in la-la land? Something with Jason?"

I shake my head. "No, Jason's fine."

"But there *is* something on your mind," Kara observes. She glances at her watch. "We have sixteen minutes until the first classes rotate to our rooms. Spill."

My thumb is working overtime picking off the clear polish on my fingernails as I debate whether to clue Kara in to my new friendship with Griffin. *Should I even call it a friendship? Acquaintanceship?*

Kara grabs my thumb and yanks my hand up like evidence. "Spill," she reiterates.

Sighing, I cover my face with my hands. "Swear you won't breathe a word about this to anyone else," I say, peeking out between my fingers.

She holds a hand up. "Of course, I swear."

"Not even Ron. *Especially* not Ron," I clarify. Her husband is a huge sports fanatic.

Kara pouts momentarily but agrees. I blow out a breath. "So, you remember the baseball camp that Jason got to participate in—the one organized by Griffin West?"

"Of course, I remember," Kara says. "Your new son getting to meet members of the Crowns baseball team isn't exactly a forgettable detail. Or Griffin West's sister becoming your new babysitter."

My thumb resumes fidgeting with my nails. "Well, Jason and I have really connected with Samantha, Griffin's younger sister. Turns out she joined Griffin's family through adoption because his parents fostered kids for several years."

Kara nods. "Ohhhh, that makes a lot of sense why he would host a camp for kids in foster care."

"Exactly. And Samantha understands firsthand some of what the kids might be experiencing. As you know, she offered to start babysitting Jason whenever I needed some time to myself. She came over last night to stay with him while I went to book club," I explain.

"That's great! Why would you be acting broody about that?" Kara asks.

"Well . . . when I say we connected with Samantha, I guess it might be more accurate to say we connected with Samantha . . . and Griffin."

Kara's eyes widen dramatically. "Danae, you *know* Griffin West?!" Her voice started out hushed but grew in strength and pitch. I shush her.

"Be quiet, or I won't tell you the rest!" I admonish. She mimes zipping her lips, so I fill her in on last night's events.

After dramatically unzipping her lips, Kara loudly whispers, "You rode in a car with Griffin West and weren't going to tell me?! I thought you were my best friend!"

I roll my eyes. "You are my best friend, but I'm still trying to process all this new information. After I was already processing a lot of new information with Jason moving in."

"What's he like? Is he as charming in person as he seems to be?" Kara asks.

"I mean, I didn't even know who he was the first time I met him"—Kara closes her eyes and shakes her head at this—"so I can't say I'm the authority on whether he matches his public image. But charming might not be exactly the right term. It's not charm just for show. He's . . . well, he's . . ." I feel my cheeks heat as I trail off, searching for the right word.

A grin spreads across Kara's face. "You have a crush on Griffin West!" she squeaks.

"Kara! Stop it! Crushes are for teenagers—I do *not* have a crush," I say. Kara side eyes me. "I just . . . I keep thinking about him. And I'd like it to stop."

"Danae Collins, only you could be friends with Griffin West and wish you could stop thinking about him," Kara says with an exasperated expression.

"We're not friends—more like acquaintances," I try to justify. Kara shoots me a look. "Okay, fine, I guess we're a level up from acquaintances."

"Why are you so averse to thinking about him? If I wasn't happily married, I would *happily* spend time thinking about Griffin West," Kara says. "Especially if I had even the slimmest of chances with him."

"Because he's the opposite of everything I want out of life! You know I hate baseball. You know I hate instability. You know I hate the fanfare that comes with wealth and status," I say. Kara's expression softens slightly. "Griffin West's existence is pretty much summed up by everything I hate. It makes no sense for me to like him. So, thinking about him is pointless. I need my brain to compute that logic."

Kara looks at me with assessing eyes. "Logic has its place. An important place." She pokes me in my chest. "But our hearts also have a place. Maybe your heart is fighting for its place. Not to kick logic out the door, but to at least have a seat at the table."

I mull over her words, not particularly wanting to give credence to them. "This is a silly conversation anyway. It's not like Griffin West is going to think twice about me. I'm a school librarian with a newly-adopted son. Not exactly the caliber of the models or socialites he's probably used to dating. He was doing a favor for his sister last night. My mind has run wild worrying about contingencies that aren't even going to happen."

Kara *tsks*. "Or maybe you're precisely the type of woman who would capture his attention. He'd be a smart man to notice you."

Sighing, I fight a smile. "You're just saying that because you're my best friend."

"Or maybe I chose you as my best friend because it's true," Kara says, smiling fully. "Give yourself some credit, Danae."

We're interrupted by the sound of voices entering the library. "Oops, better get back to the music room!" Kara says. "But don't think this conversation is over. You will keep me up to date on any and all new developments."

"Remember, you're sworn to secrecy," I whisper as we walk out of the storage room.

"As much as it pains me to keep quiet, I promise," she says.

I turn to the room filled with third graders and switch into librarian mode. "Good morning, class!"

Chapter Twelve

Griffin

"Oye, West!" Adrian's sharp voice cuts through the fog in my mind. I shake my head and look down to where he's lying on the bench in front of me. The barbell he'd been bench-pressing is resting safely in the rack.

"You were supposed to be spotting me, man. Good thing I've been working out extra in the offseason and can hold my own," Adrian says, sitting up and swiveling to face me. "Where's your head at?"

"Sorry, man. Got distracted," I say, not offering up further explanation. Adrian quirks an eyebrow at me, and the amused twitch of his mouth indicates that he knows precisely where my head was just now. Or rather, where it's been all day, resulting in multiple extra takes filming the commercial this morning. I already received an earful of opinions from Sam about my distracted mind today.

Adrian grins. "Still thinking about that Danae woman, huh?"

I smack him on the shoulder and signal him to move so I can take my turn lifting. "None of your business." Lying down on the bench, I reach up to grab hold of the bar. Unfortunately, I can't avoid the view of Adrian's gleeful grin from this position. Huffing a breath, I lift the bar from the rack and slowly lower it to my chest.

"It is my business if you're going to let me drop a rack full of weights on my face instead of paying attention," Adrian says. I simply grunt as I push the barbell up. I can hear the other infielders talking around the weight room, but Adrian and I are separated enough that we could have a private conversation. If I wanted to.

I lower and raise the bar again in silence.

"Come on, bro, I'm your best friend. And greatest teammate ever. Not to mention, pretty smooth with the ladies. Tell me what's going on up there," Adrian urges, motioning toward my head.

The head that should be concentrating its brain power on training for the upcoming season. Not working overtime weighing the pros and cons of asking Danae out.

I don't think the ease I felt with her on the drive to the bookstore was entirely one-sided. She seemed to come out of her shell and enjoy the conversation. *Seemed* to enjoy my company, at least a little bit.

The drive home? Not so much.

In her mind, could our connection on the first drive overpower the bitter taste of the attention? Would she consider going out with me? Or has she given me zero thought since last night?

Adrian must read the inner turmoil playing out on my face because his softens from mischievous to uncharacteristically sympathetic. "Why are you overthinking it so much? If you're interested, just ask her out. This isn't like you," he states, his hands hovering below the bar as I reach my final rep.

I strain to push the barbell up, then replace it on the rack. Sighing, I let my arms drop to the sides of the bench, gently stretching the muscles of my chest. Adrian *is* my best friend, and I don't envision him letting this go. So I may as well be honest.

"Yeah, well, Danae's not like other women," I say, voice low.

The sympathy drops from Adrian's face, replaced by a devilish grin. "*Ooo*, you are so obsessed with her."

"You know, for a twenty-eight-year-old man, you act a lot like a fourteen-year-old girl sometimes," I say with an exasperated sigh. I don't really want to admit that he might be right.

"Do I need Sam's help pressuring you to ask her out already?" Adrian asks, voice growing louder.

Shushing him as I sit up, I say under my breath, "No need. She's already been pestering me about it nonstop. But I'm trying to be a mature adult and think through a potentially significant decision. Not rush into something."

I rise to my feet, and we move to the dip stand for triceps dips. The team trainers are circulating the room to make sure we're following our plans, and I avoid drawing any additional attention to the conversation that Adrian and I are having.

He grabs the parallel grips, but before hoisting himself up, he cocks his head, looking at me curiously. "You're really next-level serious about this, aren't you? Not just a casual date or short-lived interest."

I nod and shrug, both affirming and playing off the observation. I speak quietly as Adrian starts his first set of dips. "Danae's not the type of woman to casually date. She's not in a position to have some fleeting fun. If I ask her out, it's because there's potential for something real."

Adrian grimaces as he completes the first set then drops to the floor. "And you see that potential?" he asks.

I move to take his place at the stand, glancing around to make sure no other teammates or trainers are nearby.

"Yeah," I admit. "I mean, I want there to be potential there. She intrigues me. We haven't spent a ton of time together, but the impression I get from her is that she's the type of woman I'd want a relationship with for the long haul. I want to find out if that's true, but I don't know if Danae could see any kind of future with me."

"You won't know unless you ask. It's clearly eating at you. I understand that you're thinking it through, but don't think too long," Adrian says. "We leave for Arizona in a little over a month. And we both know how hectic life will be once the season starts. If you're serious about Danae, you've gotta give her enough time to come around to the idea before we leave town."

Huffing my way through a set of triceps dips is the perfect excuse to delay responding. But as soon as my feet drop to the floor, Adrian gives me a pointed look when I glance over.

"I know."

I zoom in to enlarge the words, triple checking that the voice-to-text got everything right. I hit send and practically throw my phone across the table. After training wrapped up, I arrived home just in time to get another lecture from Sam before she left to meet a friend for dinner.

Her pressuring logic sounded eerily similar to Adrian's. So much so, I'd almost think they're actively coordinating their efforts. Regardless, their individual or collective methods worked, and I decided to take their advice.

I'll shoot my shot, and at least I'll know one way or the other if I have any chance with Danae.

My brain needs to free up some focus for training. I need to either take Danae out or move on if she's not interested. Although, I have a niggling feeling that the holding pattern of my thoughts might continue to hover around her regardless of which way this goes.

No notifications ping through on my phone. I click it open and see that my message is read. But no reply. I get antsy standing around waiting for her response, so I move to my home gym. Lifting weights beats pacing a three-foot area while staring at my phone.

The more minutes that tick by with no text back, the more frenetic my energy grows. I channel it into squats since we focused on upper body at training today. When my phone finally *pings* fifteen minutes later, I almost drop the barbell. After carefully securing the bar in the rack, I pick up my phone.

I'm sorry. I know that's pushy. My thoughts tend to spiral to worst-case scenarios whenever someone sends me a "Can we talk?" text. I won't be able to focus at school tomorrow, and I have kindergarteners, so focus is a must.

I fight a smile at her response. I picture her pacing her small living room, staring at the phone trying to work up the courage to send those texts. The thought makes me smile even bigger.

ME

Sure thing. I didn't mean to worry you. Just wanted to talk in person. I could swing over there now if you're free?

Three dots bounce and disappear, bounce and disappear. Finally, her response comes through.

DANAE

Um, sure, ok. I'm getting ready to read to Jason in bed, but if you get here in like thirty minutes, he should be asleep by then. The kid's a cliff sleeper.

ME

That works. I'll text you when I arrive so you can let me know if you're ready or not. And you'll be explaining what in the world a cliff sleeper is.

DANAE

Deal.

I rush to take a quick shower and style my hair. I decide on jeans and a plain long-sleeved t-shirt rather than anything branded with the Crowns logo. If I'm going to convince her to go on a date, I think I need to come across as much like a normal guy as possible. Not a baseball player.

Fifteen minutes later, I park in the same visitor spot as last night. I send a text letting Danae know I'm here, and then I wait.

And wait.

I drum the steering wheel on beat to the music, trying not to wonder what's taking so long. It's only been thirty-five minutes since Danae texted me to come over. Jason may be taking longer to go to sleep than usual. Or they got caught up reading. That wouldn't surprise me at all.

Five minutes later, Danae texts to come in. I check my reflection in the mirror and nod to myself. "Let's go, West," I say out loud.

I don't even have to knock before Danae opens the door. She's wearing jeans and a pink sweater, and her hair looks freshly teased. At least, I think that's the term Sam uses when she talks about fluffing up the roots of her hair. My eyes are drawn to Danae's lips next, not only because they're a perfectly enticing heart shape, but also because there looks to be a sheen of fresh lip gloss on them.

My heart inflates with hope. *Did she take an extra minute to freshen up before letting me in? Could she possibly have been thinking about me as much as I've thought about her?*

I step into the entryway, and Danae takes my coat to hang on a hook. "Um, come on in," she says, gesturing toward the living room. "Can I get you some water or anything?"

"Nah, I'm good," I say. Although, after staring at her lips, my mouth is a little dry. Danae motions for me to sit in one of the matching high back navy chairs, taking the other for herself.

"So?" she asks, crossing her legs. Her toe starts furiously tapping the air, and I notice her picking at her thumbnail. "What did you want to talk about?"

I give her a teasing smile. "First, you owe me an explanation." Her eyes widen. "Cliff sleepers?"

Her laugh comes out in a short burst. "Oh, I didn't realize that wasn't a common term. Ummm, a cliff sleeper is someone who is awake one second and asleep the next. You know, like you're walking along and suddenly fall off a cliff? Like that." She snaps her fingers to punctuate the point. "Instantly asleep."

"And are you a cliff sleeper?" I tilt my head, assessing her.

"I wish!" she exclaims. "I'm quite jealous of cliff sleepers. My mind fights tooth and nail against falling asleep most nights. Too much to think about."

Her statement reminds me of the anxiety she expressed about the unknown intentions of our conversation. I don't want to be a cause for anxiety in Danae's life, so I decide to cut right to the chase.

"It's a good term—I like it," I say then clear my throat. "Listen, Danae, I'm really sorry that my text earlier worried you, but I wanted to talk in person and not over text. I wanted to ask if you'd be willing to go out on a date with me."

Danae's bouncing foot stills. Her fidgeting fingers freeze, and her perfect lips part in shock.

"I'm sorry? You . . . you want to go on a date with me?" she asks, voice small. Disbelieving.

I maintain eye contact as I nod at her. I'm distracted by the sparkles of gold in her hazel eyes in the process, but I speak up to clarify. "Yes, I'd like to go on a date with you. I realize that we've only seen each other a few times, but I've enjoyed every conversation I've had with you. I really admire the character I've seen in you, and I'd like to get to know you better. In an ideal world, we might have more opportunities to hang out casually as friends first, but my world is less than ideal on that front. Especially considering I'm about to leave town for six weeks for spring training. So I'd like to take you on a date so that we can continue getting to know each other."

Danae takes an audible breath, and I'm amazed that anyone could be so lovely while simply breathing. Her eyes remain wide and round as she stares back at me.

"Are you sure I'm the type of woman you want to take on a date?" she asks. "I mean, you're a famous athlete. I'm a teacher. A new single mom. We're not exactly a headline-worthy match."

I'm not sure if the question reveals her true hesitation about the invitation. Is it merely insecurity and doubt that I would genuinely be interested in her? Or is the question just a front to cover up hesitation about dating *me*? Although I don't know the answer, I want to make *my* interest crystal clear.

"I'm very sure that I want to take you on a date," I affirm. "But I know that you've had a lot of upheaval in your life recently. I'll totally understand if you don't think this is the right time to start dating since you're figuring out life with Jason. And I'll understand if the complicated nature of my life as an athlete isn't appealing to you," I say before pausing to draw a deep breath. My gaze on Danae is intense when I add, "But I'm absolutely positive that I'd like to take you out, to be intentional about getting to know you. If that's something you'd like as well."

I give her a warm, close-lipped smile, trying to communicate both eagerness and patience in my facial expression. Danae purses her lips, and she clenches her fists as though short-circuiting the urge to pick at her fingernails again.

"Can I . . . have some time to think about this?" Danae finally asks. "And talk with Jason about how he might feel?"

"Yes! Of course," I quickly answer. *If she's thinking about needing to ask Jason how he feels, that has to mean it's not an immediate no.* My heart beats a little faster at the thought. "Take as much time as you need."

"When do you leave for your training?" Danae asks.

"Not until mid-February," I say. "Plenty of time. Don't feel rushed to make a decision."

Danae still looks stunned as she slowly nods. Her eyes drop.

"But Danae?" I say, and she looks back up at me. "Me telling you not to rush doesn't mean I consider a date with you just some insignificant possibility. I'd take you to dinner tomorrow if you said yes. I'm serious about this."

A flush shades her cheeks, and she wedges her hands under her legs. "I'm sorry I'm being so awkward," she says. "This has all caught me completely off guard. Being asked out by a professional athlete wasn't on my bingo card for the new year."

I throw my head back in a laugh, and I'm pleased to see a genuine smile crinkling the corners of Danae's eyes when I look back to her. "I didn't exactly see this coming either. I thought it would be another run-of-the-mill Camp Wizard with kids getting dropped off by case workers or foster parents. I never expected someone like you to walk through the door."

Her cheeks blush again, and it's a deliciously addictive sight. I stand up to leave, not wanting to linger past her comfort level. "You have my number, so call me when you're ready to say yes, or shoot me a text to let me down gently," I tease.

Danae laughs in response. I think she surprises herself when she reaches over to playfully shove my arm. "I'll just send you a mysterious 'We need to talk' text either way. Make you sweat a little bit."

My smile widens. I hope her teasing is a positive sign. "I look forward to it. Hope to talk to you soon."

She follows me to the front door but beats me to open it as I put on my coat. "I'll check to make sure no one is outside for you," she says, poking her head out the door. "Coast is clear."

"Thanks," I tell her, and my chest tightens. She took that extra step to ensure our privacy so intuitively, but I hope that extra necessary step doesn't tip the scales away from the possibility of an "us."

Because I really want to explore that possibility.

CHAPTER THIRTEEN

Danae

Kara nearly screams but manages to rein herself in. We're sitting in her music room eating lunch, and I filled her in on Griffin's date request last night. I feel guilty taking up our forty-five minutes of lunch to talk instead of letting her work on lesson plans, but my conversation with Griffin is eating me alive.

"Ron is going to lose his mind when he finds out you're going on a date with Griffin West," Kara states.

"You're not telling Ron anything yet because I haven't even decided if I'm going to say yes or no," I say, narrowing my eyes at her. "You're still sworn to secrecy."

"Look, Danae, I know you don't like baseball—" Kara begins.

I cut in, "*Loathe* baseball."

She rolls her eyes. "Okay, you *loathe* baseball, but you shouldn't let your prejudice stop you from saying yes to a date with a per-fectly agreeable guy."

Now I roll my eyes. "This is not a *Pride and Prejudice* situation, Kara. Prejudice has nothing to do with my hesitation about dating Griffin."

"Oh, so you mean it's not prejudice to automatically write him off because he's an athlete? Or because he probably has some level of wealth? That sounds like prejudice to me, Miss Judgy-Pants," Kara says.

I reluctantly admit, "Fine. Maybe I have a couple of negative gut reactions to his . . . station in life. But it's not only that. He flat-out told me that the reason he was asking me on a date is because his life is too hectic to spend time as friends first. Because he'll be leaving soon for like two months! And we both know how chaotic baseball schedules are. Plus, I saw firsthand how much attention he gets out in public—and that was just a tiny bookstore! I'm not sure I can handle that kind of circus. Especially not after welcoming Jason into my life so recently."

Kara stares at me.

"What?" I ask.

"I'm not saying those are invalid rationalizations. But it sounds like you're working really hard to list out every possible negative thing about Griffin. Which makes me think there are some positives that you're attracted to but aren't admitting," she says.

All the clear polish is gone from my index finger, so I move my thumb to my ring finger. I shrug, not making eye contact.

"What are the positives, Danae? I know you made a list last night. Tell me what they are," Kara demands before taking a bite of her sandwich. When I don't answer right away, she adds, "I don't mean to rush you, but we are down to fifteen minutes. So, I am rushing you."

I sigh. "He has this very magnetic quality to him. Not like he's *trying* to be charming in a false way. More like . . . he makes you feel as though he genuinely enjoys talking with you. Like he really, truly wants to hear the answers to the questions he asks because you're so interesting. And, of course, the fact that he does this camp for kids in foster care every year shows a certain level of understanding he has for my situation. I can sense it in the way he talks to me about Jason. I'm sure that his understanding comes from Samantha and her younger brother joining his family through adoption. He has personal experience with the foster system, even if it's not exactly the same as my experience."

When I pause, Kara motions for me to continue. "Go on. I can tell there's more."

"I like the way he interacts with other people, at least what I've seen so far. He is precious with Jason. And he handled the ladies at my book club so kindly when they mobbed him. It's obvious that he and

Samantha have a close connection, and even watching him interact with that other teammate was endearing."

"Wait, what other teammate? Who else did you meet?" Kara asks.

"Um, I don't remember who he was. He said something in Spanish while we were talking to Samantha. Maybe Andrés or something?" I say.

Kara holds her hands up in disbelief. "You got to meet Adrian Ortiz too? The Crowns' star third baseman? Ortiz and West are the baseball world's favorite duo! Even non-Kansas City fans love them! I can't believe you didn't tell me this!"

I huff. "Kara. I do not pay attention to baseball. I didn't even know who Griffin was, remember?"

Kara rubs her temples. "I know, I know. I just cannot believe you. I'm sorry, back to what you were saying. What else was in the 'pro' column of the list?"

Blowing out a breath, I add, "He drives a Jeep."

"Huh?" Kara questions.

"A Jeep. I followed him out the night he drove me to book club, expecting a flashy car. But he drives a totally mid-range black Jeep. Said he dreamed of owning a Jeep as a teenager, and now that's what he drives," I say. Kara tilts her head in confusion, so I clarify. "It's not what I expected. I'm used to ostentatious displays of wealth and status from people with means. He pleasantly surprised me."

"Elizabeth sees past the outward wealth to the inner Darcy," Kara says, eyes twinkling. I smack her arm, though there's no real malice in the gesture.

"So, what are you going to do?" she asks.

"I don't know," I reply. "This might be the worst timing ever. I'm still figuring out how to be a single mom with a precious boy who's been through a lot. Would it be crazy and selfish of me to consider dating *anyone* right now? It seems a little crazy and selfish."

"Or, maybe this is the perfect timing for you to have someone in your life who understands your experience and can be there supporting you. Maybe even loving you," Kara says, voice serious. "You don't have to say yes, Danae. But don't say no just because you're afraid, okay?"

I've spent four solid days thinking about Griffin West.

Sure, Jason and I had a fun weekend together. Kansas gave us a random sixty-degree day on Saturday, so we went to the park and played for hours. We made chicken chili together the next day when the temperature dropped back down to twenty. We popped popcorn and watched a movie before reading another chapter of *Harry Potter* before bed.

But Griffin's face was never far from my mind's eye.

I've examined every facet of this choice ten times over. I could recite three sub-points beneath each pro and con on my mental (and physical) list. Pretty sure I could win first place with either side of the argument if "Should Danae go on a date with Griffin?" was the question posed at a debate tournament.

Yet, overanalyzing has brought me no closer to an actual decision. The question boils down to two opposing facts. I feel safe with Griffin as a person and *want* to date him. But his career feels risky for my emotional wellbeing—which makes me think I should stay far away. How do I choose? Heart or logic?

It's Tuesday evening, and I'm browning some ground beef for tacos. I hear Jason playing with his Lego set in the living room, which reminds me of his duel battle with Samantha. Which makes me think of Griffin, yet again.

Calling Jason over to the kitchen, I help him assemble tacos before making my own. Once seated at the table, I decide it's time to broach the topic with the other person whose life this decision would impact most.

"Hey, Jason, I have something I need to ask you about," I say.

Jason freezes, taco halfway to his mouth.

"Sorry, I made that sound too serious," I quickly clarify. "There's something I'd like to get your opinion on." He visibly relaxes and takes a bite of his taco, waiting for me to continue. "You know how we've talked with Samantha and Mr. Griffin a few times now?"

Jason's eyes light up as he vigorously nods. "Is Sammi coming back to babysit again soon?" he asks.

"Maybe," I say. "Here's the thing—Mr. Griffin asked me last week if I would maybe want to go out to dinner with him sometime, just the two of us."

"Mr. Griffin wants to go on a date with you?" Jason clarifies. When I nod, he says, "Cool! Can Sammi come over to babysit while you go on your date?"

I laugh. "I'm sure she could if I decide to say yes. Would it bother you if I go out on a date with Mr. Griffin?"

Jason's face screws up in confusion, and I fight to not laugh at his adorable expression. "Why would it bother me? Mr. Griffin is the coolest! I mean, he's the best shortstop in all of baseball—well, okay, maybe not the number-one best, but don't tell him I said that. There are a lot of good shortstops right now. He's still one of the best. But he's definitely the nicest one—you can tell him I said that."

His stream-of-consciousness speech brings a smile to my face. "He is really nice. I just want to make sure that you would be okay with me going on a date with someone. It wouldn't mean that I care about you any less, or that I'm not going to spend special time with you still," I say, carefully observing Jason's face for his reaction.

"Oh, I know that. You care about me the most," Jason declares with confidence. "But can Sammi babysit? Will you ask her? Tell Mr. Griffin you'll only go on a date if Sammi comes over." He takes another giant bite of his taco, clearly finished sharing any opinions about my dating life.

Well, Jason certainly seems okay with the idea. Which takes his reaction out of the "con" column. Is this a sign I should say yes? Or am I putting too much stock in a nine-year-old's opinion?

As Jason begins chattering about everything that transpired in the Gaga Ball pit at recess today, I force my thoughts to tune out Griffin and truly listen. I've learned a different side of the school dynamic over the past month listening to Jason recap his days.

When I tuck Jason into bed a couple of hours later, he gives me an extra-long hug. "Miss Danae? I really like Mr. Griffin. I think it would be cool if you like him too," he says, voice so sweet and sincere. I take a moment to study the freckles splattered across his nose and cheeks, his green eyes made even more vibrant by the contrast of his orange-red hair.

"I do kinda like him," I say with a small smile. "I guess I need to figure out if I *really* like him or not." Jason grins at me before I give him one more hug. "Good night, Jason. And no matter what happens with Mr. Griffin, I'm with *you* one hundred percent, forever."

"G'night!"

Closing his door, I pause in the hallway. *I do kinda like him.*

I head downstairs and find my phone. Pulling up Griffin's name in my contacts, my thumb hovers over the call button. Smiling to myself, I hit the message icon instead.

ME

We need to talk.

I have no idea what Griffin's schedule is like. Does he do baseball training stuff in the evenings or only during the daytime hours? Or could he be out with his teammates or friends? Is the offseason their time to live it up? It's possible he may not even text me back until tomorrow.

My phone starts ringing in my hand, causing me to jump. I fight a smile when I see Griffin's name lighting up the screen.

"I expected you to just text back," I say, unable to keep the smile out of my voice.

"Nope. I need to hear your voice when you either give me wings or crush my dreams," Griffin says with a lighthearted tone.

I laugh. "That seems a little dramatic, don't you think?"

"Maybe so," he says, and I can hear the smile in his voice. "Or maybe it's exactly accurate. So, what's it gonna be? Am I getting celebratory or self-pity ice cream tonight?"

His playfulness serves to bolster my confidence in my decision.

"Yes. I'll go on a date with you."

CHAPTER FOURTEEN

Griffin

"Y ou've got a little extra oomph in your twist today," Adrian says. "Did you finally get some good news?" he asks, waggling his eyebrows.

I glare at him and throw the medicine ball across my body at the wall again before acknowledging his question. "Possibly," I evade, although I'm sure the smile I'm fighting is confirmation enough.

The smile that hasn't left my face since I talked to Danae last night. Five days of sweating over her silence made her affirmative answer that much sweeter when it finally came. Honestly, I haven't really had to wonder whether the women I've asked out in the past would say yes or not. Sure, I questioned whether they were genuinely interested in *me* but never whether they would say yes to a date. For a couple of days there, I was convinced that Danae was going to turn me down.

So, yes, I've got a little extra oomph in my twist today.

Before I can pass the medicine ball to him, Adrian annoyingly pats my cheek. "She really agreed to go out with your ugly face?"

I shove him away. "Yes, she did. We're going out Saturday night."

Adrian hollers in celebration, drawing the attention of the rest of the guys in the weight room. Our infield players make up a pretty tight-knit group of friends, so everyone came to work out today. Drew Sheffield, our first baseman, Luke Powers at second, and our catcher, Carlos Diaz, all make their way over to Adrian and me.

"What's the cheering about? Did West finally manage more than three medicine ball throws in a row?" Luke teases.

I shoot him a look. "Very funny. You know I kept up with you the second the training staff cleared my shoulder."

"Just kidding, man," he says, fake jabbing my ribs. "We're all glad you're back for the start of the season. For real, though—what's the cheering about?"

Adrian grins impishly at me, and pretty soon Drew catches on and points one finger at Adrian's smile and one finger at me. "*Ooo*, this has to be about a woman! West, you sly dog, what aren't you telling us? Is Lily gonna have a new WAG to assimilate?"

Drew's wife, Lily, is the self-appointed welcome committee for any wives and girlfriends of Crowns players. And the ongoing social chair for the group. She's grounded, easy-going, and friendly, so Lily's exactly who I'd want to welcome Danae to the WAG club. But I'm getting way ahead of myself, probably due to the overreactive enthusiasm happening all around me.

Their pestering increases in volume and exuberance until I finally yell at them. "Shut your loud mouths if you want me to tell you." They decrease the volume but continue their laughing and teasing. "I have a date this Saturday that I'm excited about. That's all."

"You're not usually so evasive about going on dates. What makes this one special?" Carlos asks. He rests his chin against his fists and exaggeratedly bats his eyelashes. "Tell us about her."

I smack the back of his head slightly harder than necessary. "Stop it, dummy." They continue snickering and *not* returning to their workouts, so I decide to get this over with. "Her name is Danae. I met her through Camp Wizard a couple of weeks ago."

Quickly filling them in with sparse details, I give enough information to get them off my back without sharing too much about Danae. She seems like more of a private person, and protecting Jason's story is definitely something that would be important to her. So I'm quick to shut down further questions and shove everyone back to their weight machines.

"You're fired as my friend," I mutter to Adrian, who merely cackles.

"Whatever, man," he says. "You could never live without me. Let's hit those throws. You've gotta keep that bod in shape for your lady."

"She's not *my* lady," I correct with a roll of my eyes.

Adrian's eyes twinkle. "Not *yet.*"

Pacing in the living room, I check my watch. "Hurry up, Sam!" I yell.

"Coming!" Her faint voice calls back from her room upstairs.

"You're not even the one getting dressed for a date! What's taking you so long?" I holler again.

Sam appears at the top of the stairs and jogs her way down. "I was getting a couple of things ready for Jason tonight." She holds up a deck of cards.

"Please don't teach the kid Texas Hold'em. Danae will never see me again if she comes home from our date to find Jason dealing poker hands," I say.

Sam walks over to me and pinches my cheeks. "Don't worry, I'd never do anything to ruin your shot with Danae."

"Knock it off." Smacking her hands away, I smooth down my beard.

She smiles at me, a genuine smile instead of her sassy smirk. "The beard trim looks good. As does the suit. Knocking her dead is your strategy, huh?"

"My only strategic move for tonight is taking her somewhere we won't get the overblown attention she witnessed at the bookstore. I want time to talk and really get to know her better without all the distraction. To try and figure out what it is about her that I'm so drawn to," I say.

Sam smirks. "You really don't know why you're so enthralled by her?"

I quirk an eyebrow. "What, like you do?"

She huffs a laugh. "Of course, I do. But I've always known you better than you know yourself. I'm gonna give you a little time to try and figure it out on your own."

"I thought you said you wouldn't do anything to ruin my shot? Why not clue me in?" I grumble. Sam shakes her head. Her antagonism is making me antsy. And I was already infinitely more nervous for this date than any past date, ever. My nerves are on par with my first game back after rehabbing my injury. I subconsciously reach up to massage my left shoulder, even though it feels fine.

Sam's hand squeezes mine on my shoulder, calling my attention to her eyes, which are warm, not teasing. "Stop worrying. I think this is a good match for you. Danae's a real one."

"I know. I think that's what's making it more nerve-wracking," I admit. She gives me a sympathetic look. "Let's go."

CHAPTER FIFTEEN

Danae

"This is ridiculous. Why did I agree to do this? There's no chance of this relationship lasting or going anywhere, so why in the world did I think a date would be an okay idea? The risks far outweigh the positives. What was I thinking? I need to call and cancel." I'm ranting to Kara on the phone, not pausing for even a millisecond to allow her to respond.

"Stop it, Danae," she says. "Give your poor carpet a break and stop pacing."

I halt mid-step, offended by her accurate knowledge of my actions.

"You are *not* canceling this date. You will go out to dinner and have a good time getting to know a nice guy who is interested in you," Kara states.

I scoff. "A nice guy *who's a professional baseball player*," I emphasize.

"So what?"

"I hate baseball. If I'm going to be in a relationship, I need a steady, reliable man. Now more than ever. A pro athlete constantly flitting across the country doesn't exactly fit that bill," I say.

I hear Kara's eye roll. "Stop regurgitating all the cons that you already considered and countered with pros. You said yes to this date after thorough self-examination. This is your classic round of second-guessing yourself. You're spiraling, and you need to get a grip!"

Kara says. "Besides, it's not like he's flitting around the country all carefree for no good reason. It's his job. With a set schedule and reliable income. That's stable."

Huffing a breath through my nose, I process before quietly responding. "This doesn't make sense. Dating a professional baseball player doesn't fit into any of the possible life plans I've mapped out for Jason and me. I'm blaming Samantha for muddling my good sense with her friendship and connection with Jason. I never should have said yes to this. It's too risky."

Kara's quiet for a beat before responding. "Maybe that's *why* you said yes, Danae. Maybe your subconscious knew you needed to take a little risk, to step outside the box of what's safe. I mean, heck, adopting a child out of foster care as a single woman isn't exactly a 'stable and secure' move. Maybe this date with Griffin is precisely what your inner self knows you really need."

I catch myself picking at the clear nail polish on my thumb. *Drat. I was trying to leave that intact for one night.*

"Besides—it's one date. You're not saying yes to a lifetime by going out to dinner, you know," Kara adds. It's the trump card to my objections, and I know she's won.

"Okay. You're right. I can be fun and breezy for one night. Easy, breezy, carefreezy," I say, waving a hand in the air.

"Um, no. Stop that right now. Be your normal self—just scale back the worrying about twenty steps down the line, okay?"

"Fine."

"Now go paint on a new coat of nail polish before Samantha and Griffin arrive," Kara says.

Rolling my eyes but smiling, I tell her goodbye.

After quickly touching up my thumbnail, I walk out to the living room, where Jason is playing the Bluey app on the tablet.

"Hey, bud," I say, taking a seat next to him on the couch. "You still feeling okay about me going out to dinner tonight?"

He nods without looking up then pauses the game. When his eyes meet mine, they grow wide. "Wow, Miss Danae. You look so pretty!"

"Well, thank you!" I respond with a smile. Standing, I do a short spin move to show off my dress to him. "You think I look fancy enough for a date with Mr. Griffin?"

He grins. "You look *real* fancy. Why don't you ever dress up that nice for school?"

I laugh, glancing down at my mid-length cocktail dress. I bought it three years ago to wear to a semi-formal wedding, and it's been collecting dust at the back of my closet since then. I've been wishing for another occasion to wear it, so as soon as Griffin told me "cocktail attire" as the dress code for our date, I knew this would be my wardrobe choice.

The first time I tried it on, I felt confident. I loved the clean lines of the halter dress that was fitted but not too tight, with a slit that made walking comfortable without being too revealing. The deep emerald color complemented my auburn hair while bringing out the green in my eyes.

Hopefully, it can bring me some confidence tonight.

Sitting back down next to Jason, I hold up the three-inch black heels in my hand. "See these shoes? These are the kind of shoes that look nice with a dress like this. I'm not about to wear uncomfortable shoes at school all day!"

Jason solemnly nods his head like he completely understands my logic, watching me strap on the heels.

Ding-dong.

At the sound of the doorbell, Jason jumps to his feet and races for the front door. I hardly have a second to take a deep breath before the door flings open.

"Sammi!" Jason yells.

"Hey, my guy!" Samantha's voice calls back. I hear a loud high five take place before I walk into the entryway to greet Samantha and Griffin.

Griffin is smiling down at Jason, receiving his own high five. But the moment I step into view, his eyes lock on me and freeze. His wide smile slips as he stares.

I clench my fist to stop from chipping at the brand-new coat of clear polish.

"Um, hi," I say, voice tight.

Samantha looks up at me and grins. "Ow, girl, you look amazing!" She pivots her gaze to Griffin, and her grin quickly changes to a smirk when she sees his expression. A sharp elbow jab to his ribs accompanies the exaggerated clearing of her throat.

"Yes, wow, Danae, you look gorgeous," Griffin stutters.

His perfectly tailored navy suit is doing all sorts of good things for his broad shoulders and athletic legs. The top button of his cream shirt is unbuttoned, toning down the formal look of the suit. The longer hair at his forehead looks carefully styled and freshly trimmed. The fade of his faux hawk is so subtly blended, no novice barber could achieve such perfection—a perfection that makes him all the more attractive.

A flush heats my cheeks as his gray-blue eyes remain locked on mine, a twinkle sparking in them as he slowly smiles. I'm suddenly incapable of standing a single inch closer to him without spontaneously combusting.

Swiveling on my heel, I motion toward Samantha. "You can follow me to the kitchen, Samantha, and I'll show you some options for dinner!"

Mercifully, Griffin remains in the living room talking with Jason while Samantha walks with me. I have no reason to open the refrigerator, but I open the door and let the cool air wash over me anyway. "Um, there's a pitcher of filtered water in here if you want that instead of the tap water," I say, as though Samantha didn't already know that from the first time she babysat.

Her dancing eyes let me know she sees right through my water display ruse.

Opening a cabinet door, I show her the boxes of mac and cheese and canned ravioli.

"I've been introducing Jason to more home-cooked, healthy meals, but since me leaving tonight is potentially significant, he can have some of his old comfort foods from . . . you know, before," I say.

Samantha's eyes soften. "Got it. That's cool of you to do. I know that probably means a lot to him, even if he doesn't know how to express that."

I smile at her, grateful for the ways she understands Jason's situation. The less I have to explain, the easier it is for me to think about leaving him for the evening.

"I guess you probably know where we're going, but call me if you need anything. I promised Jason I'd be back before he goes to bed tonight, but don't feel bad if you need me to come back early for any reason at all. Text or ca—"

Samantha holds up a hand, silencing me. "*Shhh*," she says. "You go have a baller night with my big bro. I got this. Stop worrying about Jason or about being alone with Griffin. Whatever it is that's bothering you more."

Cheeks freshly flaming, I wish I could think up an excuse to open the refrigerator again. Instead, I exhale and follow Samantha's retreating figure. "You ready for the best night of your life, kiddo? Because after I win our wizard duel, I'm going to teach you how to play Trash," Samantha says to Jason.

"Wait, you're teaching him what?" I ask.

Griffin steals my breath by taking me by the elbow. That winsome smile is back, and he winks as he says, "Don't worry. It's a harmless card game. Sam's *mostly* harmless, anyway."

"Say '*adios*' to the grown-ups, Jason," Samantha says, saluting us.

"*Adios*! Have fun on your daaate," Jason adds with high-pitched emphasis. Samantha rewards him with another high five while Griffin laughs. He's holding out the peacoat that was hanging on the hallway coat rack, ready for me to slip my arms in. My breath catches as I take in the sight of this very handsome, very *famous* man holding out my coat for me.

Last chance to back out. Can I really do this?

Slipping my arms into the sleeves, I call out final reminders to Samantha. "Don't forget, the fire blanket is under the sink! And be sure to turn on the exhaust fan if you use the stove or the smoke detector will be set off! And—"

Griffin tugs my elbow just hard enough to pivot me in his direction, once again locking those gray eyes on me. "Trust Sam. She's got it. And I got you. Let's go."

After clicking my seatbelt, I immediately sit on my hands to stop myself from picking at the fresh nail polish. Bouncing my knee will have to do as an outlet for my fidgety nerves.

Griffin pulls out of the parking lot and asks how the week at school went. I fill him in on the major happenings of an elementary library (fights over who gets to sit in the giant tub during silent reading time being the most noteworthy). The sides of his eyes crinkle when I tell him how happy Jason is about his exclusive access to the tent after school each day.

"Maybe I would have been more interested in reading during elementary school if there was a tub or a tent at stake," Griffin says with a laugh.

His comment makes me giggle, which makes him smile at me again, which makes my heart beat in funny rhythms. *Maybe this won't be so bad*, I think. Then I look out the window at our surroundings and recognize the familiar path to the Country Club Plaza. My heartbeat stutters nearly to a stop.

"Where are we going for dinner?" I ask, holding my breath.

"I would say it's a surprise, but you strike me as the type who doesn't love surprises," Griffin says, a slight tease in his tone. I shrug my confirmation of his assumption. "I have a reservation at Capital Grille."

I turn away so Griffin doesn't see my brow furrow. *Great. I shouldn't have let the Jeep throw off my instincts so much. Of course, he's going to show off his status by taking me to a ritzy restaurant. Typical.*

My phone rings, and I answer immediately when I see that it's Samantha. "Is Jason okay? What's wrong?" I ask.

"Nothing's wrong," Samantha replies, and my heart rate slows down. "I just wanted to catch you before you get to dinner. Jason wants to bake some cookies together, so I wanted to double check if you're okay if we use up the rest of the flour."

Closing my eyes, I blow out the breath I was holding. "Yes, that's fine. I'm going to the store tomorrow, so not a problem at all. Thanks for checking."

"Now go have fun! We're all good here," Samantha chirps before hanging up.

"Everything okay?" Griffin asks when I put my phone away.

I nod. "Yes, they're fine. She needed the go-ahead to use up the flour to make cookies."

Griffin grimaces. "Uhhh, I don't know how to tell you this, but expect to find flour in every nook and cranny for the next few weeks. Sam takes the saying 'messy cooks are the best cooks' very literally."

A sound that's half laugh and half groan escapes my throat, turning Griffin's grimace back into a smile. The lighthearted moment is ruined, though, as we pull up in front of Capital Grille. The valet quickly opens my door, and I slip out of the Jeep as gracefully as possible in my dress and heels.

"What's up, Jimmy?" Griffin says as he tosses his keys to the valet. "How's your mom doing?"

"Much better," the valet—Jimmy, apparently—replies. "She'll have to be careful about what she eats without her gallbladder, but she's already doing so much better."

"Good to hear, man. We'll catch you on the way out," Griffin says to Jimmy. Then he places a hand lightly on the small of my back while gesturing toward the restaurant with the other. "Ready?"

I'm not ready at all, but I can't exactly tell Griffin that. Logically, I knew we were dressed up. I knew we had to be headed somewhere semi-fancy, but I had not mentally prepared myself for *this* restaurant. I haven't been inside this restaurant in years, but the second I step through the door, I'm hit with a wave of nostalgia. No, *not* nostalgia. That emotion implies a positive wistfulness. And nothing about my memories of this place is positive anymore. My lungs won't fully inflate for deep breaths, and a cold sweat makes me fight the urge to shiver. *Please, don't let me see anyone I know here tonight.*

One of the hostesses smiles at me and says, "Welcome to Capital Grille." I attempt to return her smile. She turns to greet Griffin by name. "We have the table you requested ready for you. By the way, my cousin got that autographed hat from the St. Louis Bluebirds player. Thanks so much for pulling strings to make that happen!"

He says something about it not being a big deal, and we begin following the hostess into the restaurant. Griffin pulls my elbow to a gentle stop as we walk past the bar. He reaches over the bar to give a complicated hand slap to the bartender. "Jeff, my man! How's it goin'?"

"I heard you were coming in tonight," Jeff says, grinning widely. "Should I start up your usual?"

"You can wait till we sit down and look at the menu. But I won't be surprising you," Griffin replies. "This is Danae," he tells the bartender as he places his hand on my back again. The repeated touch feels so natural, somehow both gentlemanly and possessive. It sends a thrill of warmth through my body, counteracting the cold sweat.

Jeff reaches across the bar to shake my hand. "Nice to meet you, Danae. You're a brave soul, going out with this guy."

Laughing, I return Jeff's greeting.

"She is, indeed. Hey, is Krystal here tonight?" Griffin asks.

"Nope, she's staying the night with my parents," Jeff responds.

Griffin turns to me. "He has the cutest little girl who hangs out in the back sometimes. She's what—six years old now?"

"Six going on sixteen," Jeff says with an eye roll as he shakes a drink. I can't help but laugh again. Jeff slides the drink to a customer sitting at the bar a few seats away from us then tells Griffin, "I'll tell her you said 'hi,' though."

"I'm sure we'll see you on the way out," Griffin says before turning back to the hostess. She's been patiently waiting, as though this inter-action was an expected delay. We follow her to an intimate table in the back corner, dimly lit by candles. The restaurant is full tonight, but no one gives Griffin more than a second glance. Well, other than the wait staff he greets by name as we walk past.

Interesting.

Griffin pulls my chair out for me at the table, and I accept the menu from the hostess. "Marco will be right with you. Enjoy your evening," she says.

Seconds after Griffin sits across from me, he stands up again when our waiter arrives. They give each other a bro back-slap hug as Griffin exclaims, "Marco, congrats, man! How was the honeymoon?" He stays standing for a moment as Marco briefly tells him about the beach in Mexico.

Griffin introduces me before sitting back down. Marco tells us the specials for the evening and then leaves to give us a moment to look at the drink menu.

"So, what's your usual?" I ask Griffin as I peruse the wine list.

"Club soda with lime and a splash of cranberry juice," he replies. I raise my eyebrows. "Not what you expected?" he asks, grinning.

"There's been a lot about you that I haven't expected," I respond without thinking. His lips twitch at the corners.

"I don't like drinking alcohol when I'm training or playing, which is pretty much all year. My body feels more sluggish during workouts, even after one drink. But Jeff makes the best cranberry lime soda ever concocted," Griffin declares.

"High praise," I say, relaxing slightly. "I might have to experience this for myself."

When Marco returns, I tell him to double Griffin's usual drink order. While he's away getting our drinks, I look over the menu.

"Have you been here before?" Griffin asks.

I hesitate—which I know Griffin notices. I see the spark of curiosity light up his eyes when I don't answer right away. "Yes, I have. It's been a long time, though."

Griffin somehow reads my reluctance and asks a new, lighthearted question. "If you could only eat one type of food for the rest of your life, what would you choose?"

"Breakfast," I answer without hesitation. He raises his eyebrows, and I giggle. "Not what you were expecting?"

"Absolutely not. I had you pinned as an Italian pasta girl," Griffin says. "Why breakfast?"

"It's like the ultimate comfort food. And so much variety with sweet and savory options. I think breakfast food might be my primary love language," I say, smiling.

Griffin's eyes dance. "Duly noted. Alas, Capital Grille's menu sorely lacks breakfast items. Maybe we should give some constructive feedback."

I burst out laughing, which causes Griffin's eyes to light up even more. "I think I'll be able to find something."

"If not, I'm sure we can locate a Waffle House somewhere nearby," he says. "I'd go wherever you want." The smile on his face is so genuine that I don't doubt that he'd really drive me to a Waffle House right this second if I asked him to.

Suddenly, I'm entirely at ease sitting here in *this* restaurant, with *this* man.

Talk about unexpected.

CHAPTER SIXTEEN

Griffin

Marco returns with our drinks, and Danae orders the salmon while I order a steak. When Marco leaves, I raise my cocktail glass to her. She clinks her glass to mine and takes a sip. I wait with bated breath for her reaction.

"Not gonna lie . . . that's pretty darn good," Danae says. She takes a second drink and adds, "The cranberry splash adds a tart counterpart to the sour fizz of the club soda and lime. It's like a refreshing punch to the mouth."

"I told you," I reply with a grin and take a sip. "Jeff's the true wizard. I've tried ordering the same drink other places, and they never get the cranberry ratio right." I set my glass down on the table. "So, how's it been balancing work along with your new responsibilities as a mom?"

"Okay, I think? It makes it easier that Jason comes with me to work every day. I'm sure it would be a lot more complicated to be working in an office and coordinating getting him to school and staying longer at after-school care," she says. I study her as she takes another sip of her drink. "Of course, there are also challenges to him being at school with me. I knew him as a student first, and I know all of the behind-the-scenes discussions that have happened with administration about him prior to him coming to live with me. And I know about all of the social challenges he can have with his classmates."

I nod. "That would be tough to have a teacher lens over one eye and a protective mom lens over the other eye."

"Exactly!" she exclaims. "I wouldn't have even thought to phrase it that way. Yes—as his mom now, especially being privy to more information about his background, my hackles rise any time something negative comes up at school. But I also know how tiring it is as a teacher to deal with those behaviors. I'm not sure which side of my brain to defer to."

"You don't have to answer this if the question is too personal," I say, "but how did you go from being his teacher to being his kinship placement for adoption? Again, I know that Jason's background is his private story, so don't share anything you don't want to."

"I appreciate your understanding," Danae replies, and I can see the truth of it in her eyes. "I can't tell you the number of well-meaning people who found out I was adopting Jason and immediately wanted to know every sensational detail about why he was in foster care."

I hum. "I get it. I generally don't even tell people that Sam's not my biological sister—I leave that to her to choose to bring up if and when she wants to talk about it. So, while getting to know you better includes learning more about Jason, I never want to overstep. Feel free to shut down any question I ask that seems too intrusive. For real," I say.

Danae nods appreciatively. She leans forward, her voice lowering. "Jason was in and out of foster care a few times. His mom died of a drug overdose when he was a baby. His dad was on the roller coaster of using drugs and then getting clean for a while, back and forth. Jason was removed from his dad's care a couple of times but returned when his dad took the right steps. His paternal grandmother, Cathy, helped take care of him at times, but she also has some health challenges related to decades of smoking."

My heart fills with even more compassion for Jason and Danae as she continues. "A few months ago, Jason's father was arrested for armed robbery and possession with the intent to sell. This wasn't his first offense, so he'll be in prison for quite a while. He decided to terminate his parental rights, believing it was the best thing for Jason to have a chance at being adopted into a stable home.

"There were no maternal biological family members interested in adopting Jason. Cathy had the first rights to adopt Jason as his biological family, but she didn't think that she could handle it, given her own challenges. Apparently, Jason had talked to her about me multiple times. She sought me out and asked if I would consider adopting Jason since I was already a safe, familiar figure in his life. I thought about it for a couple of weeks, but I think I knew the instant she asked me that I would say yes," Danae explains.

My heart hurts in so many ways. Clearing my throat, all I can manage to say is, "Wow. There aren't really the right kind of words to respond to something like that, are there?"

"Yeah, I know," Danae agrees. "Samantha told me that your parents adopted her and her biological brother from foster care. Were they the only kids your parents fostered?"

"Nope—they were the only two who joined our family permanently. But there were over a dozen kids who lived with us for some duration of time. My mom undoubtedly knows the exact number," I say. "I'm sure she'd have some wisdom to pass on if you need a pep talk at any point. Although, maybe you're already getting unsolicited wisdom from your own mom."

I made the statement in a joking tone of voice, but the shadow of pain that crosses Danae's face makes me wish I could take back the words. Marco arrives with our food before I can apologize for my off-hand comment. He takes a moment for me to cut into the steak to check if it was cooked correctly. When we both decline needing anything else, he leaves us to our meal and conversation.

Danae's face is pensive as she takes a small bite of salmon. Before I start eating, I want to recalibrate the mood of our conversation.

"I'm sorry I made that comment about your mom when I don't know anything about your family. That was insensitive of me," I admit. "You're welcome to tell me whatever you want to about your family, or we can move on to talking about the winter storm heading our way next week and the likelihood of you getting extra days off school."

Danae laughs a genuine laugh, her eyes sparkling. But just as quickly, the sparkle dims. She pokes her fork around her plate before responding. "Let's just say, I don't currently have a close relationship with my parents."

She looks up to meet my eyes, and there's so much sadness in her expression. I wish I could reach over to touch her face and absorb all the sorrow residing inside her. I settle for telling her, "That's really tough, Danae. Now that I know you don't have your family to lean on as you adjust to motherhood, I'm even more glad that Sam connected with you to babysit. I mean, completely aside from my own gain in getting to know you as well."

Danae gives me a small smile, and I take a bite of my steak to give her space to talk more about her family or move on.

"The tension with my parents and my . . . initial discomfort with this restaurant are actually related," Danae says quietly, not quite meeting my eyes.

I swallow hard. "I'm sorry I brought you somewhere uncomfortable for you. Geez, I pretty royally screwed up this first date. You'll receive zero criticism if you decide to run away screaming."

She laughs again. "No, it's okay. I'm enjoying it now. I'll admit, when you first told me this was our destination, I might have preemptively judged you based on my past experiences. But I see why you wanted to come here—this must be a comfortable place for you, given the fact that you seem to know the personal life details of every employee here."

I make an exaggerated grimace when she raises her eyebrows. "You caught me," I say. "This is my default dinner spot. The arrival of a professional athlete here isn't unusual enough to draw a lot of attention from the other guests. They're used to people with higher profiles than me eating here. So it's sort of a safe place to come."

"And you're friends with the whole staff," Danae adds, her smile teasing.

"And I'm friends with the whole staff," I agree with a laugh. "It's nice to come here and feel like I'm catching up with a bunch of old friends each time. Not navigating a social circus."

Danae nods in understanding then purses her lips. "I came here countless times with my family—well, here and other comparable restaurants. But my parents weren't coming here to fly under the radar or to get to know the employees. It was all about being seen for them."

She looks so conflicted that I can no longer resist the urge to touch her. I place a hand lightly over hers just long enough to say, "You don't have to tell me more. But if you want to, know that anything you say is safe with me."

Her eyes are locked on the physical contact of our hands, but as soon as I move my hand away, she meets my gaze. "My dad is a financial planner for high-net-worth individuals," Danae says. "He didn't grow up particularly wealthy but had a knack for good investment strategies, so he climbed the ranks at every financial planning firm he worked for. Which was exactly his goal—climbing the social ladder.

"He was never content with what we had, even when it was a lot. He wanted more. More money, more social connections, more status symbols. We bought a home in Mission Hills when I was in high school, and that only made things worse. Because we were the new money in the old money section of town, so Dad had even more to prove. Everything about our lives was orchestrated to move our family up the social food chain—including my dating life," Danae says, voice tightening.

I'm staring at her, hanging on her every word. I'm grateful that she's not making eye contact right now to see the way my mouth is hanging open. *What kind of father does that to his daughter? To his family?*

"My parents expected me to be the trophy wife for Tyler, the son of one of my dad's big clients, to solidify our place in high society. They 'indulged' my desire to get a degree in education, not thinking I would put it to use," she says, emphasizing the statement with air quotes and an eye roll. "At first, I felt like I had no choice but to play along with the game. But the more education classes I took, the more I knew I wanted to teach for real. When I graduated college, applied for my teaching license, and broke up with Tyler all within the span of a week, well . . . let's just say our communication dropped to almost nothing."

I'm speechless. Usually, it's not hard for me to immediately come up with the right words to say in any given conversation. It's like a superpower.

But my superpower is short-circuiting. Because I'm still silently staring when Danae finally makes eye contact again. She shrugs. "You'll receive zero criticism if you decide to run away screaming," she says. Her parroting of my words cuts through my brain fog.

I reach across the table to take her hand in mine, gently rubbing my thumb against her palm. "I'm not screaming. And not running away. Quite the opposite."

"So you're a glutton for trauma?" she says. Her tone is joking, but there's a kernel of serious inquiry behind it.

I shake my head slowly. "Not a fan of trauma in the slightest. I've seen too much of its negative effects to be attracted to it. But I suppose I've been adjacent to it for enough of my life to have the deepest respect for the people who fight their way through it, day in and day out. Even though it lasts a lifetime. And I have so much respect for you being willing to walk with Jason through his when you have your own baggage to carry."

Danae's eyes brim with unshed tears as she fights the quiver in her chin.

Squeezing her hand firmly, I say, "Look, Danae, I like you. I like you even more now than I did coming into tonight. But regardless of what happens or doesn't happen between us romantically, I'm here for you to lean on as you navigate all of this. And I know Sam is all in too. We understand firsthand how much support you're going to need as you continue moving forward with Jason. Sam and I are here for you however we can be, even if our relationship winds up being only friendship."

She squeezes my hand back, and I look at her with a wry smile. "But, in case that was confusing, allow me to clarify that I'd very much like to be more than just your friend."

Everything Danae has shared tonight only confirms my instinct about her—that she's exactly the type of woman I could be attracted to for the long term. Not only attracted to . . . possibly fall in love with. She's genuine and down to earth. She's passionate and tender-hearted. It's not hard to picture the future with her, and it's certainly not hard to get lost in the forest of her green eyes and the soothing timbre of her voice.

I'm suddenly picturing myself coming home from a day of training and finding Danae and Jason playing a game on the back porch. I'd walk over and wrap my arms around her, maybe gently kiss her neck while inhaling the scent of her hair. She'd look up at me with those gorgeous eyes, and I wouldn't resist dropping my lips to hers. I'd sit down and pull Danae onto my lap, snuggling her closer to me. She'd lean her head against my shoulder, and I'd massage my fingers against her scalp while I listened to Jason share what he did at school that day.

The vision is so real, I can almost reach out and touch the image in my mind.

Danae's laugh breaks through her tears and snaps me out of my runaway daydream. She smiles at me when she says, "I'm starting to think I might want to be more than just your friend too."

CHAPTER SEVENTEEN

Danae

I can't even believe how much more relaxed I feel on the drive home versus the drive to dinner. After Griffin's demeanor dissipated my initial anxiety about the date, his thoughtful conversation completely put to rest the lingering hesitations I had about him.

Without question, I like the man.

Which is a revelation I'm positive I will pick to pieces with apprehensive, imagined future scenarios all night. Good thing tomorrow is still the weekend since I don't foresee much sleep happening tonight.

But for these few moments on the drive home, I'm going to embrace the giddy, kick-my-feet hormones flooding my system.

Griffin somehow managed to strike the perfect balance of personal questions and lighthearted banter over dinner. I haven't felt that comfortable talking about myself since . . . well, maybe ever.

How did he do that? Come to think of it, I barely learned anything about him. He kept me so at ease talking about my life—my hopes, my likes and dislikes—that I hardly asked him anything.

I look over at him in the driver's seat. His profile is striking in the near-darkness, and my pulse picks up steam remembering how this *very* attractive man declared he wants to be my "more than friend."

"Okay, you got to know all about me at dinner, but now I get the final ten minutes of our evening to pepper you with questions," I say.

Griffin's eyes find mine briefly, and the calm intensity in them sends a shiver through me.

"Fair logic," he says, eyes returning to the road. "What do you want to know?"

"What does your day-to-day life look like during the season?" I ask.

Griffin sputters a breath through his lips. "Couldn't start off with a soft pitch question first? Had to pull out the curveball right away?"

I bite my lip. "Can we go ahead and acknowledge that I'm going to understand exactly zero baseball lingo or references? You're going to have to spell out that meaning."

He cuts another glance at me, laced with playfulness this time. "Can we also acknowledge that I'm eventually going to pry the story out of you as to why you dislike America's favorite sport so much?"

I wave my hand and make a dismissive sound.

"Soft pitch would be easy to hit, so an easy-to-answer question. Curveballs are trickier, which means the question doesn't have a straightforward answer. Or maybe I don't want to give a straightforward answer. Mostly because I don't want to scare you off with the reality of my schedule," Griffin says.

My face falls slightly, not that he's looking at me to notice. He licks his lips before continuing. "We're away at spring training in Arizona for about six weeks before the official season begins. We get back home but alternate being in town for seven to ten days and then traveling for the same duration of time. Usually, we play six to seven games per week, so it's not exactly a laid-back schedule."

I suck in a sharp breath before I can stop myself. *That schedule is . . . worse than I imagined.* Staring out the window for a moment, I say, "Wow. That's a lot."

"But, you know, I do have free time when we're in town. Not every game is in the evening—some are in the early afternoons. And we do have some shorter days of practice and training when we don't have games," Griffin says, and I detect a note of desperation in his voice. "A good chunk of the season falls over the summer, and players' families are allowed to travel as much as they want to. So it's not like I wouldn't see my wife and kids for weeks at a time or anything outrageous like that."

Realizing what he said, he slaps a hand to his forehead. "I mean, not saying that we're for sure getting married. I didn't mean to imply that. But also not saying that I'm *not* thinking about marriage, because I am, I'm not just looking for something casual with you. Or, what I mean is—"

As I've watched him scramble to explain his thoughts, a smile has slowly grown so large on my face that I can't hold back a giggle any longer. His gaze cuts over to me, and relief softens his features when he sees my smile.

"I know what you meant," I say, putting him out of his misery. Although the verbal scrambling coming from this self-assured man was kind of adorable. "I appreciate the clarity that you're serious. And to reciprocate the clarity, I will say that while a hectic schedule like that isn't my ideal, it's not an immediate deal-breaker for me. I'm open to continue exploring where life might lead us."

"Okay, good," he says. "I was seriously sweating it there for a minute."

We turn onto my street, which means I'm running out of time to glean more information from him. "As we've established, I'm not a baseball fan," I begin.

"Firmly established," Griffin cuts in with a grin.

"An indisputable fact," I add. "But Jason has been talking my ear off about your baseball stats and career. He mentioned that you were injured last year and were questionable to come back. I assume every-thing is all healed up now?"

The light in Griffin's eyes dims, and his face hardens. I didn't expect such an intense reaction to a well-known fact. *Maybe reliving the injury is traumatic for him?* I try to retreat. "You don't have to talk about that," I say in a rush. "Sorry if I shouldn't have asked about it. I shouldn't have brought it up."

Griffin sighs as he pulls into the parking lot of my townhouse com-plex. "No, you don't need to apologize. I don't want you to feel bad asking me anything," he says. He puts the Jeep in park and stretches his neck to either side before looking at me. "Yeah, it was one of our first games to start the season last year. I injured my left shoulder—my catching arm—pretty badly. It was . . ." He trails off, looking out the window.

"Bad?" I supply for him.

"Yeah, it was bad," he says. "The surgeon and rehab team were fantastic, though, getting me back into shape."

"I'm sure you did a lot of the hard work to get yourself back into shape," I add. "That's admirable."

"Sure, yeah. It was a lot of hard work. I'm glad to be back with the Crowns to start the season," he says, still not meeting my eyes.

Apparently, I unintentionally poked a pain point. "We'd better get inside so I can get Jason in bed," I say, pivoting to open my door.

I'm halted by the sensation of Griffin's hand around mine. His calloused palm is rough against my skin, but his fingertips are soft as they wrap around and trace my palm. I turn to look over my shoulder at him.

"Danae, I'm sorry. You didn't do anything wrong asking me about the injury—that's a logical topic of conversation," he says. I turn to fully face him, careful not to move my left arm too much. I don't want to risk losing any of the points of contact between our hands.

"I wasn't mentally prepared for your question. I kinda have to psyche myself up to talk about being injured. Can I take a rain check for that topic? I promise I'll tell you more sometime," Griffin says. One side of his lips hitches up as he adds, "Please don't let that be the lingering memory of our first date."

"Deal," I reply. "I really should get Jason to bed, though."

Griffin lightly squeezes my hand before reluctantly letting go (at least, he seemed reluctant, but maybe I'm projecting my own feelings). We make our way inside and find Samantha and Jason sitting across from each other at the dining table. There's a half-empty plate of cookies and a set of playing cards between them.

"Miss Danae! We made cookies!" Jason exclaims when we walk into view. "And I can play cards now!"

I cross the room to hug his neck, glancing at the kitchen in the process. Griffin was not joking about finding flour everywhere. But knowing that Jason had a good time while *I* had a good time puts a messy kitchen in proper perspective.

"You'll have to teach me how to play this game tomorrow after we go to the store," I tell Jason. "Thanks so much for staying with him, Samantha."

Samantha leans in toward Jason. "Hey, you were gonna show Griffin where you have all the posters from camp hung up, remember?"

His eyes light up. "Oh yeah! Come on, Mr. Griffin! Let me show you in my room." Jason grabs Griffin's hand and leads him upstairs, chattering away about dropping an egg on the floor while making cookies.

Samantha stands and turns to me. "That was my clever ploy to get Griff out of the room so you can tell me how the night went."

I burst out laughing but quickly quiet myself. "We had a great time."

Samantha widens her eyes and makes a "go on" motion with her hands. "You have to give me more intel than that."

I roll my eyes but can't hide my smile. "We had great conversation. He's so easy to talk to. In fact, I think I shared more about myself on our first date than I share with friends who have known me for years," I say with a shrug.

She nods knowingly. "Yep, that tracks. My brother, the human can opener."

"The what?"

"I've always called Griff the 'human can opener' because he can get anyone to open up and start talking about themselves. But not in a manipulative way—just because he's genuinely interested in what people have to say," Samantha explains.

"Huh. That makes perfect sense. He seemed to know something personal about every employee we ran into at Capital Grille," I say.

"Oh, he definitely knows everything about everyone there. He wasn't putting on a front for you. Griff truly considers all of them friends. That's part of the reason he always wants to eat there, and why I always beg and plead to go literally anywhere else," Samantha says with a cheeky grin.

The pitter patter of Jason's feet on the wooden stairs mingles with the solid clomp of Griffin's descending footsteps. Something about the sound stabs a pleasant pain through my heart. Samantha gathers her stuff to leave, and we collectively walk toward the front door.

As we stand in the entryway together, the oddness hits me of ending a first date while standing in front of my soon-to-be son and my date's younger sister. But my life has taken a far-from-typical turn these past couple of months, so I suppose this is a fitting piece of the puzzle. Jason holds my hand as Samantha zips up her boots and Griffin smiles down at me.

"Thanks for tonight," he says quietly. He gives me a small wink that seems to communicate he's similarly aware of the uniqueness of our present situation.

I smile warmly in response. "It was a good *first* date," I say, casually emphasizing the word "first" to see how he'll react.

Fireworks spark in his gray-blue eyes, setting off a series of sparklers in my chest.

"I'll text you," he mouths while his back is still to Samantha and the door. As he turns to face her, he brushes one finger down the back of my free hand with a feather-light touch.

I focus on the weight of Jason's hand in mine to stop myself from melting to the floor.

After getting Jason in bed and the kitchen clean(ish), I indulge in my longest wind-down routine. However, I'm still anything but wound down, lying wide awake in bed. My eyelids won't even stay shut longer than a few seconds at a time.

My mind is fighting a fierce battle with itself.

You barely know this guy. You can't trust him yet.

Even though it's only been a couple of weeks, Griffin has come across as understanding and trustworthy every time we've interacted. He was fun to talk with tonight.

Sure, you had fun, but fun isn't the chief goal. You need stability, especially for Jason. Griffin is chaos.

At least he was honest about how chaotic his life is during baseball season. He's aware and seemed concerned with how to alleviate that chaos for the people he cares about.

It doesn't matter how good-looking or smooth-talking he is. Continuing a relationship with Griffin is not a safe choice.

Maybe it's not safe, but what if it's still the right choice?

You're letting the butterflies from that lingering eye contact and sensual hand graze at the end of the night cloud your judgment.

What if I want the butterflies?

The mental back and forth continues for several rounds until I finally surrender. Propping up on one elbow, I grab my phone from the nightstand. The distrusting antagonist in my brain keeps snagging on the end of my conversation with Griffin in the car. When he tightened up so much in response to my question about his injury.

I know he promised he'd tell me more about it sometime. But curiosity is killing the proverbial cat. The cat can't stand the mystery any longer.

A quick Google search of "Griffin West injury" provides thousands of hits. There must be hundreds of videos providing commentary on the injury itself, the rehab process, and the likelihood of his return to baseball. One of the research techniques I teach the fifth graders is the importance of using original source documents as often as possible. So, I decide to watch the original footage of the injury in real time. I'll wait to hear further commentary directly from the source himself.

The video opens with rapid clips of two strikes being thrown to the opposing team's batter. The announcer sets the stage for the importance of another strike to end the game with the final out before any runners from the loaded bases can score. The pitcher throws, and the loud *crack* of the ball against the bat dissolves hope of a strike. I lean in to listen to the announcer's intense voice.

"It's a popup to short left field, and West is racing to catch it. Left fielder Ethan Farmer calling for the ball as he sprints in. Seems to be a lack of communication as West isn't ceding ground to Farmer, and both players are closing in on the ball. West dives back for the catch, but Farmer's still running full tilt with his eye on the ball and—ohhh, that didn't look good, folks. West's left arm was fully outstretched in his reach for the ball when he collided with Farmer running full steam ahead."

There's a pause in the announcing as the camera zooms in on the left fielder picking up the dropped ball as Griffin rolls around, banging his right fist on the ground. Two runners make it home before the ball gets to the catcher.

"This is not what we wanted to see to end this game," the announcer's voice picks up again. There's a gravity to his tone that's a stark contrast to the excitement leading up to the collision. "Griffin West looks to be in absolute agony as the training staff makes their way out to him. The Crowns will lose the game with the two runs scored, adding insult to West's injury." Another drawn-out pause as the camera stays glued to Griffin's position. One of the training staff moves enough to briefly reveal Griffin's face, etched in unspeakable pain. "It's possible that he could be out for a while, based solely on the amount of pain he looks to be in. It would be a huge blow to the team and their chance at a World Series run if West misses the rest of the season," the announcer says, voice somehow *more* solemn. "We'll keep our eye out for news from the Crowns training staff but . . . this is looking pretty severe."

I just spent the evening with a smiling Griffin. I know that he healed, he rehabbed, he's starting the season back with the Crowns. Considering the way my heart is pounding, I understand why Griffin is averse to talking about that moment. I only watched the video, and adrenaline is sending shivers through my veins. What must it be like to relive that moment? I managed to pick off every last bit of clear polish from my fingernails, and I know how the story ended.

Clicking my phone off, I lean back against the headboard. *No wonder he didn't want to talk about it.* Everything in me wants to call Griffin to come back over here so I can apologize for even bringing that up tonight. And maybe hug him.

Yes, definitely hug him.

CHAPTER EIGHTEEN

Danae

Look, I knew you would be overloaded last night and unable to fill me in on the date. But your time is up. I need information. CALL ME!

I can't call. Little listening ears. But I can text you.

Get those thumbs tapping, ma'am.

I'll explain more in person over lunch tomorrow, but we had a really nice evening. I was super nervous at first, especially when he took me to Capital Grille.

Oh no.

That was my first thought too.

But he knew everyone there. Not the guests, but all of the employees. The restaurant is like his personal friends' club hangout, and none of the guests bothered us. So I understood why we were there. Also, I didn't see my parents or any of their social circle there, so that helped.

KARA

Thank goodness. But tell me more about the dialogue with the main man. Not just the setting.

ME

For being famous, he was shockingly easy to talk to. I felt like I was on a date with a totally normal guy. Well, that's not true. He was way more conversational and attentive than normal guys. Kara, I told him about my parents.

KARA

???? You did? On a first date?

When's the wedding?

ME

Stop it. That does not help.

I had a fantastic night with him. But my inner skeptic is going haywire with all the complications of dating someone like him. I don't know if I can do it.

KARA

You stop it. If you were as comfortable with him as it sounds, he deserves a real shot. YOU deserve a real shot with someone like that. We can figure out the complications.

Also, he's absurdly hot. You also deserve that.

ME

I'm rolling my eyes at you.

KARA

Please please please can I tell Ron about this? You're killing my marriage making me keep this a secret from him.

ME

Fine. But only Ron. And he cannot tell anyone else.

KARA

I will swear him to secrecy upon penalty of a year of bedtime duty with Millie.

ME

Speaking of swearing to secrecy, I probably need to have a conversation with Jason. I need him to not be blabbing about me dating Griffin to the entire school like he did with the baseball camp.

KARA

Don't think I didn't notice you said datING Griffin. I'd say your heart has finally won a seat at the table.

ME

Maybe. Or maybe after another day of overanalyzing I'll end things before they get out of hand.

KARA

Don't you dare. Give your heart a little more time to feel things out. Promise me.

ME

I'll try.

KARA

I'll take it. Now I'm off to have a very entertaining conversation with my baseball-loving husband.

GRIFFIN

Hey there. How's your day going?

I apologize if I'm supposed to be playing it cool and not contacting you 15 hours after our first date ended.

But I'm not really interested in playing it cool in case that wasn't obvious.

Please note that I use voice to text a lot so if my message ever reads weird blame it on the technology.

I'll stop blitz texting you and give you a chance to respond.

ME

Hey there. <smiley face emoji>

The day is good so far. Jason was a little sassier than usual this morning after being so out of routine last night, but nothing terrible. We're getting ready to go to the store to stock up on some groceries before the snow storm Tuesday. And then he's planning to teach me that card game this afternoon. What about you? What do you typically do on Sundays during the offseason?

GRIFFIN

Well typically I work out at home, do something to have fun or relax, and then walk through my schedule for the week with Sam.

But today I've mostly just been thinking about you. Wondering what your impression of our date was. Thinking about the things I still want to know about you that I didn't have time to ask about last night.

ME

More questions, huh?

GRIFFIN

Endless questions.

ME

Like what?

GRIFFIN

Like what's your favorite book? Do you ever watch movies or only read? What do your days in the library look like? What's your favorite season and why? What's been the hardest and the best parts of life with Jason so far? Do you have a favorite flower? Why do you hate baseball so much…

ME

Ha! All of those questions were providing cover for the final one.

GRIFFIN

Not true. I want to know the answers to all of them. And a hundred more. I would go on listing them out, but you haven't actually answered any of them yet.

ME

I'll answer one each day. But only if you also answer one of my questions too.

GRIFFIN

Deal.

ME

My favorite season is winter because I like having a built-in excuse to stay home and be cozy. No one questions why you won't go out and do things during the winter. Curling up with a book, a fluffy blanket, and a warm drink on the weekends is socially acceptable.

GRIFFIN

Insightful. Sorry for disrupting your cozy reading schedule last night.

ME

I'll let it slide. Going out occasionally isn't so bad with good company.

GRIFFIN

So you're saying I'm good company?

ME

Like you need to be told that.

GRIFFIN

<winking emoji> Your turn for a question. But it has to be on par with the depth of question you answered.

ME

So no asking about your deepest childhood fear after telling you my favorite season?

GRIFFIN

Exactly.

Heights. I gave you a freebie.

ME

What type of music and podcasts do you listen to?

GRIFFIN

Podcasts: mostly sports related. Shocker, I know.

Music: I have pretty eclectic taste. Everything from rap to pop to EDM. Anything with a good beat. I like to shuffle the Discover playlist on Spotify that suggests music I might like.

ME

I'll have to scroll through your playlists next time I see you. I'm a creature of habit and tend to listen to the same albums over and over.

GRIFFIN

That's shocking.

ME

Ha ha. <eye roll emoji>

GRIFFIN

I'll let you get to your shopping with Jason. Tell Fireball hi for me.

ME

Will do.

GRIFFIN

And Danae?

ME

Yes? You're freaking me out with the ominous text of only my name and a question mark.

GRIFFIN

Sorry, not ominous. Just wanted to say thanks for talking. Today and last night. Every time we've talked. Can't wait to talk in person again. Hopefully soon?

ME

Soon works for me.

CHAPTER NINETEEN

Griffin

"Tell us every juicy detail about Saturday night," Luke says the moment he sits down with his burrito bowl.

Drew invited all of the infield team to his house for an early dinner after our workout today. Supposedly, it was a chance for us to hang together before the incoming winter storm likely cancels our group training sessions for the next couple of days. However, I suddenly see this for what it truly is.

A setup. To grill me about my date with Danae.

"Lily, I can't believe you were party to this," I yell. She waltzes over and snuggles next to Drew on the loveseat, her own bowl heaping with the rice and taco fixings she cooked for us.

She doesn't even try to play innocent. "What? I needed to hear the details about any potential addition to the WAGs just as much as they all wanted to watch you squirm." She points her fork at Carlos. "Amy is going to be upset that you didn't invite her for this."

He wipes a hand down his face. "Ugh, she totally is. Can we put this on hold for an hour until she can get over here?"

Adrian swats Carlos with a throw pillow. "Heck, no! You're not punishing all of us because you didn't think ahead. You can deal with your fiancée's wrath later."

"Leave my throw pillows out of this!" Lily scolds. "And all of you better shut up so Griff can actually talk."

I take a giant bite of chicken, black beans, and rice as a way to punish them with a delay. The strategy backfires, though, as I'm subjected to five mischievous stares for the extended amount of time it takes to chew.

I already rehashed the highlights of the date with my nosy little sister yesterday. It's not that I don't want to rave about how incredible the night was or how much I enjoyed Danae's company. It's not that I want to hide how close I came to a heart attack at the sight of her in that green dress or how my respect for her skyrocketed over the course of the evening.

But I don't want to spook Danae by drawing too much attention to our relationship. Our future felt tenuous for a moment when I described my schedule during the season. I managed to avoid an onslaught of attention by taking her to Capital Grille, but it's only a matter of time before she's exposed to the full-blown havoc she only glimpsed at the bookstore.

I'm brainstorming how to establish more trust with her before that happens. And I don't think sharing intimate details about her or our date with a bunch of people she would consider strangers qualifies as trust-building.

When I finally swallow, all eyes are still locked on me. Unrelenting.

Sighing, I say, "Guys, all I can tell you is how I feel about it. It was the best date of my life. I get antsy even thinking about the possibility of never seeing Danae again. I would have asked to see her again today if Drew hadn't invited us over here. A decision I now regret knowing the true intentions for this dinner."

"Awww," Lily says, eyes and mouth curling into that expression you give adorable babies and dogs.

"But that's all I'm going to tell you," I state, which is met with exasperated groans. "With her adoption situation, Danae has more of a need for privacy right now than most people. And we all know that privacy isn't a luxury afforded to our significant others," I add, looking pointedly at Lily. She and Drew were college sweethearts, but gossip sites were ruthless toward her when Drew got signed to the majors. They nearly broke off their engagement as a result of the negative press. Thankfully, when he got traded to the Crowns, the fans here have been much more receptive and respectful. Still . . . I don't want to push my luck with Danae yet.

Drew reaches over to squeeze Lily's knee. "We understand, man. Don't we?" he says, glaring around the circle at the other players. There's a chorus of mumbled affirmations.

"Fine, fine, but answer this one question," Luke says. "I'm not saying you're in love or getting married tomorrow, but on a scale of one to ten, how much do you like her today?"

I don't even hesitate. "Ten."

A mug of steaming coffee warms my hands as I take in the fresh white landscape through my living room's oversized windows. The natural light in this room is one of the reasons I chose this house. Of course, the privacy of the gated community was the biggest selling point, but I loved the way the windows illuminated the entire vaulted room. I savor my single cup of coffee for the day as I watch the snow.

Thick flakes lazily drift from the sky, adding to the six inches already coating the ground. I'm keeping an eye on the clock, waiting for an appropriate hour to call Danae. When the area school districts posted messages last night about canceling school today, I hatched a perfect plan on the drive home from Drew's house. I bribed Sam to make a run to the store for me.

Unable to wait any longer, I send a text to Danae asking her to call me when she wakes up. Ten seconds later, my phone rings.

"Good morning," I greet.

"Is something wrong?" Danae immediately asks.

"Oh, no, nothing's wrong," I say. "Sorry, apparently I need to get better at my text message phrasing so I stop unintentionally freaking you out."

"No, I'm sorry," she says. "I need to rewire my brain to stop assuming the worst about every text message."

"You don't need to change anything about that beautiful brain. I'm perfectly capable of changing my text patterns. You tell me—what's the best way to phrase a text if absolutely nothing is wrong and I'm just looking for any excuse to hear your voice?" I ask.

I hear the smile in her tone when she responds. "Well, you could say, 'Nothing's wrong, just have a quick question.' Or maybe, 'Nothing's wrong, but call when you have a free minute.' Or even a blatant, 'Nothing's wrong, just want to hear your voice.'"

"I'm sensing an overt 'nothing's wrong' theme here," I deadpan.

Danae laughs as she replies, "You asked!"

"You're right. Thank you for telling me. I'm going to save 'Nothing's wrong' as an automated message prompt," I say. "Now, I *have* been looking for any excuse to hear your voice again, but I also have a specific ask. Do you have any plans for the snow day today?"

"Uhhh, not really," she responds. "I hate driving in snowy conditions. So I was planning to take Jason over to the little bit of green space by the pool in our complex to see if we could build a snowman before other people beat us to it. Why?"

Perfect. This is panning out exactly how I envisioned.

"Well, I happen to have all-wheel drive and exemplary winter driving skills, so I was going to ask if I could come pick up you and Jason to bring you over here. I have a huge yard, so we can build a whole army of snowmen together," I say.

There's a pause before Danae asks, "You really want to do that? You'd do that for us?"

"I already bought sleds and snow gear for everyone last night. Maybe that was presumptuous, or maybe I'm showing my hand a little too much, but I know the clock is ticking on my shot to convince you to continue dating me before I leave town." Danae huffs a short laugh, making me smile. "I'd really like to spend the day with you and Jason. Sam will be here too, but otherwise we'll have a quiet day to be together without other prying eyes. What do you think?"

Danae *hmmms*, and the sound is teasing, maybe even flirtatious. "I think I love that idea," she says. "Let me run it by Jason when he wakes up, but I can't imagine him turning down that offer. If he tries, I'll convince him otherwise. Because I'd love to see you again."

Her words shoot confidence through my veins, and I abandon my cup of coffee in order to have plenty of time to shower and make sure I look presentable.

An hour later, we've transferred Jason's booster seat to the back of my Jeep, and we're on our way back to my house. Despite my winter driving prowess, I purposely drive extra slowly to keep Danae's nerves at bay.

"Wow! This place is so cool!" Jason exclaims with awe as we pull up to my house. On the scale of professional athletes' homes, it's modest in size. But the gated neighborhood provides security and privacy, plus large lot sizes. Which will serve us well today.

When we walk through the garage door, we're met with the smell of cinnamon. There's a pan of cinnamon rolls on the kitchen counter, but zero mess anywhere in sight. I quirk an eyebrow at Sam.

"Frozen section," she explains.

"That makes a lot more sense," I say.

She smacks my arm before replying, "They'll still taste as gooey and delicious as homemade. You want some sugar before we go out in the snow, my guy?" she asks Jason, who enthusiastically high-fives her.

The four of us sit around the table enjoying cinnamon rolls and coffee. As I pour a cup of coffee for Danae, I decide to break my one-cup rule and pour one for myself. I want to indulge in the ritual of having a morning cup of coffee along with Danae—something about those shared mundane moments feels the most intimate.

After we're all thoroughly caffeinated (or sugared-up, in Jason's case), we sort through the snow gear Sam purchased last night. She impressively guessed everyone's sizes correctly, so we're soon bundled up and ready to head out into the snow. My backyard has just enough slope for some low-key sledding, so she also purchased four sleds.

"What should we do first? What's your favorite snow activity—sledding or building snowmen?" I ask Jason.

His brow furrows seriously. "I've never been sledding before. And my hands and feet always got too cold before I could finish building a snowman." My heart catches at his unaware admission. His eyes meet mine with a look of total trust. "Do you think sledding or building a snowman is more fun?"

I catch Danae's gaze above Jason's head. She gives me a sad smile. "We should definitely start with sledding," I tell Jason. "Do you want to ride with me your first time down the hill?"

"Yes!" he yells with a jump in the air.

Taking one of the longer sleds to the top of the slope, I sit down and help Jason plop down in front of me. I hand him the string and say, "You hold on here, and I'll make sure we don't tip over."

Danae and Sam position sleds on either side of us, and after counting to three, we simultaneously push forward. The gleeful giggles erupting from Jason as we sail down the hill implant in my mind's catalog of "favorite sounds."

We trudge up and fly down the hill countless times over the next thirty minutes. Jason alternates between sledding solo and tandem with each of us until we decide it's time to build a snowman. Jason and Sam form an opinionated alliance on what the snowman should look like, giving me all the grunt work to do.

I don't mind it one bit. Mostly because Danae volunteers to help me push the giant snowballs around until they've reached the right size to match Jason's vision. Which gives me a perfect excuse to bump her shoulder, tease her until she throws snow in my face, and shamelessly flirt with her in general.

Danae's a beautiful woman. It's a fact that my mind acknowledged the moment I laid eyes on her that first day at Camp Wizard. But seeing her in this setting—auburn locks peeking out beneath her hat, cheeks reddened with cold and exertion, eyes sparkling as she laughs and plays with Jason—she's breathtaking.

"I think my boogers are frozen," Jason announces shortly after he declares our snowman complete. "Can I have more hot chocolate?"

We all stifle laughs as Danae responds, "Of course, you can. It would be a good idea for us to warm up for a while."

After leaving all of our wet gear in the mudroom, Sam makes another cup of hot chocolate for Jason while I pull out a couple decks of cards. "Has Jason filled you in on the rules of Trash yet?" I ask Danae.

"Oh, did he ever. We played multiple games yesterday, and he won every single time. Kid's the luckiest card-drawer ever," she responds loudly, winking over at Jason. He covers his mouth with a hand as he giggles.

Sure enough, Jason wipes the floor with the rest of us when we play. I reach over and tickle him. "Are you hiding extra kings and jokers in your sleeves there, Fireball?"

"I'm just good at drawing cards," he says between gasping laughs. "I don't want to play Trash anymore, though. Do you have any lunch?"

"I bet we can find a little food somewhere," I say. "You up for trying some real baseball-player food?"

Jason's eyes light up, and he nods seriously. "I sure am."

"Okay, good, because you've gotta eat the right kinds of food to give you energy if you're gonna play ball," I tell him. I look at Danae and jerk my head toward the kitchen, hoping she'll follow me.

"I'll help!" she says, jumping up from her seat.

Once in the kitchen, I lower my voice. "I confess I forgot to stock up on any kid food. My chef left chicken and quinoa soup for today—what are the odds of Jason eating that?"

"Better after that inspiring speech you gave," she teases as she pokes me in the side.

My shortstop reflexes come in handy as I snag her hand before she can pull it away. I tug lightly to pull her a step closer. I love the way her eyes widen in response as she looks up at me. "I'm glad you agreed to come over today," I murmur, slowly interlacing my fingers with hers.

Danae's exhale is shaky before she replies, "Me too. Thanks for inviting us over. It's been so nice being able to just . . . be with you." She returns my smile and adds, "Plus, this was way more fun for Jason than fighting for space at the townhouse to build his first snowman."

Her statement sobers us, and I gently squeeze her hand. "He's a special kid. I'm grateful for the chance to get to know *both* of you better."

After lunch (which Jason heartily eats after some initial skepticism), Sam announces that she and Jason are going to play Mario Kart in the TV room downstairs and that Danae and I are not invited to join.

"Looks like we're on our own," I tell Danae. Her cheeks flush, and she bites the bottom left corner of her perfect heart lips. My mind floods with questions about what those lips would feel like against mine.

"Guess you're stuck with me," she says.

I take a step closer to her, drawn by the spell her lips are casting. "I won't waste time pretending to be mad about that," I reply, voice low. Glancing down at her hand, I see her finger furiously picking at her thumbnail. I gently take hold of her hand, stilling her fingers.

Leading her over to the large, U-shaped couch, I pause to turn on the gas fireplace. We sit down a respectable distance apart but with bodies angled toward each other.

As Danae pulls her feet up to pretzel her legs, I hand her a throw blanket. After running a hand through my hair, I lean my arm across the back of the couch and look into her eyes. "Can I be honest?"

"Yes, please," she immediately responds, voice breathy.

Taking a deep breath, I launch into the speech I mulled over last night. "I feel a little caught between a rock and a hard place, and I'm not sure how to proceed. On the one hand, I don't want to come on too strong and scare you away. I know your life is . . . a lot right now. And I don't want you to be pressured by me moving too fast. I want to give you whatever time and space you need to figure things out."

Her fingers are back to working overtime on that nail polish, and I can't help but smile. I reach over to wrap my fingers around hers as I continue. "On the other hand, I am very, very interested in continuing a relationship with you. There's a certain sense of urgency to spend the maximum amount of time with you before the craziness of baseball season begins. Because I want to build as much of a foundation to our relationship before that time comes, to give us the best chance of making it."

Danae chews on her lip as she watches me, and it takes all of my willpower not to get distracted. Now is not the time to get lost in a daydream of kissing her senseless. I give her hand a small squeeze, more to focus my own attention than anything. "So, how would you like me to proceed?"

CHAPTER TWENTY

Danae

Griffin looks at me with patient anticipation, but I'm distracted by the thrill of his strong hand so tenderly holding mine. The soft smile on his face isn't helping me concentrate on answering his question, either. I notice a lock of hair sticking up from when he ran his hand through it, and now my thoughts fixate on what it would feel like to run *my* hand through his hair. On what it would be like to have permission to touch him in that kind of familiar way.

His honest question isn't one I know how to answer immediately. *Take it slow, or take every opportunity we have?* My mind is scrambling to dig through all the information, all the possible negative outcomes from either choice. I need a couple of days just to filter through the positives, negatives, and potential side effects—much less make a decision.

As though he can see the spiral of thoughts behind my eyes, Griffin's smile grows wider as he watches me. He reaches his free hand over to gently tap a finger against my temple as he says, "One of these days, I hope to understand what the thought factory in there is like without you having to spell it out for me. But for today, can you spell it out for me?"

The side of my face is now tingling from his momentary touch, which adds to the long list of "things that aren't helping me focus."

I break eye contact in the hope of being able to gather a coherent sentence.

"I'm feeling a little paralyzed by your question. In all honesty, I'd like to sit down with a notepad and pen and make a detailed pro/con list. Possibly even draw a flow chart of potential issues. That's what the thought factory is churning over," I confess. "But that doesn't exactly equal a timely response in conversation."

Griffin tilts his head to one side before he says, "Hang on." He stands and leaves the room.

His abrupt exit starts a new thought spiral. *There's one way to have the decision made for you—show him how high-maintenance you'll be in a relationship. That will end things before they start.*

Without Griffin's hand to still my fingers, my subconscious sets my thumb to work on the nail polish. I mentally fortify myself for him to come back and let me down easily.

I consider beating him to the punch. *Tell him you think this isn't going to work. That the thought factory suddenly popped out a solution: this is over. Don't make him feel awkward being the one to end things when you're the weird one in this situation.*

The words shrivel in my throat when Griffin comes back into view holding a legal pad and a pen. He holds them out to me and says, "Here, you work on your list while I pop some popcorn for Sam and Jason. And maybe show him who's the real boss in Mario Kart for a round or two."

Peering up at him with wide eyes, I slowly reach out to accept the paper and pen. "Really?"

One side of his lips hitches in a lopsided smile, and now I'm distracted by thoughts of kissing him. *Would the beard tickle or feel scratchy? What would it feel like to run my fingers along his jawline? Tyler never could grow a beard. And his kisses were always haphazard at best. What would kissing Griffin be like? He strikes me as the much more intentional type.*

"Really. I'll come back up in a little while," he says, breaking me out of my reverie. A reverie that left me extra warm. I kick off the throw blanket.

Griffin walks away to the kitchen, and soon the sound of the microwave interrupts the silence. I'm not sure how he's going to explain to Samantha why he's joining them in the basement and leaving me alone, but that's the least of my worries at the moment. I stare at the blank yellow paper in my lap then write "Take Things Slow" at the top of the first page. Drawing a line down the middle, I label the two columns "Pros" and "Cons."

I begin neatly writing bullet points on the pro side, soothed by the familiarity of the action. My concentration is interrupted by Griffin's voice. "Holler if you need anything," he says before winking at me and opening the door to the basement.

His voice can be heard through the closed door, yelling at Jason to prepare to meet his match. The sound spreads warmth through my chest, and I move my hand to the top of the "Con" column.

Taking things slow means waiting longer for Griffin to kiss me.

I lose track of time as I complete the lists. Griffin still hasn't emerged from the basement—I've heard loud heckling and Jason's groans of defeat through the door, though. I flip to a third page to start a flow chart of the possible outcomes of either choice. The page is nearly filled by the time I hear the basement door open. Griffin's head pokes around the edge of the door frame.

"Am I up to bat or still on deck?" he asks.

I narrow my eyes in a pointed look.

"Come on, even you have to know what that means. Surely that's a common-enough saying in books you read," he teases.

"Fine, fine," I say. "Batter up."

Griffin's face lights up. "She *does* know some baseball lingo!" he exclaims as he closes the door behind him. He quickly crosses the room and makes a big show of trying to peek at the legal pad, which I swiftly clutch against my chest. "Come on, you have to let me read your notes," he whines.

"Absolutely not," I say, kicking my feet toward him when he tries to lean closer. "My lists are sacred material."

"Okay, okay," he relents, holding his hands up in surrender. "At least show me a glimpse of the level of organization we're dealing with here."

I huff, but then I quickly flash the first page to him. He lets out a low whistle. "Wait, is there really a flow chart?" he asks. Spearing him with a look, I reluctantly turn the pages and give him a quick glimpse at the chart.

He drops his head back in a laugh. "I didn't think you could possibly be any more captivating, but I was dead wrong."

I blush at what I interpreted as a compliment, but then worry that maybe he didn't intend it as a positive. "You're not making fun of me, are you?" I ask before thinking it through, voice unsure.

His face sobers. "I would never." He tucks a strand of hair behind my ear, maintaining piercing eye contact with those gray-blues. A smirk plays at his lips. "Tease you, hoping to make your cheeks flush with that beautiful blush? Yes. Count on it. But never, ever would I make fun of you."

The mixture of gentleness and intensity in his tone gives me a perfect clarity that even my three pages of notes didn't bring. I want the maximum amount of time with this man.

"Maximum," I whisper. His eyes spark. "I choose maximize the time."

Sam and Jason eventually join us upstairs, and Griffin orders pizza (although he cooks chicken and broccoli in the air fryer for himself). Between bites of cheese pizza, Jason bounces back and forth between explaining *Harry Potter* to Griffin and baseball to me, clearly loving the opportunity to spout off facts about his two favorite subjects.

"There are seven books total? Where are you in the series?" Griffin asks Jason.

"We're on the third book. It's taking a while to read out loud, longer than reading it by myself. But I don't want to read it without Miss Danae," Jason says. Griffin catches my eye and gives me an encouraging smile as Jason continues, "Hey, why don't we have the books with the pictures in them? Jackie at school told me there are *Harry Potter* books with pictures."

"Oh, there are, but . . ." I hesitate to answer, not wanting to admit the truth out loud in front of Griffin.

Although my parents paid for my undergrad, once they realized I wasn't going along with their life plans, they cut me off. I'm still paying off the student loans for my master's degree, which eats a chunk of my teacher's salary paycheck each month. I've been far more concerned with building an emergency fund in the bank than purchasing multiple copies of books, though I've coveted the illustrated versions of the *Harry Potter* series. However, I do want to model responsible spending to Jason, to set him up well for adulthood someday.

"Well, the illustrated books are pretty expensive, so I've never bought them just for myself. Maybe we can look into that as a gift later this year," I say. "Although probably only the first couple of books for now—the later ones have some illustrations that are a little bit scary. I wouldn't want you to have nightmares."

"I wouldn't be scared! I'm super brave!" Jason says, looking miffed.

"Of course, you are!" I scramble. "I know you're a super brave kid."

Sam jumps in to help. "Yeah, look at how you marched right into Camp Wizard the first day, not knowing anyone, and you did amazing at everything!"

Jason puffs up his chest. "I was pretty good, huh?"

We all laugh, and Griffin asks, "Where did you learn so much about baseball?"

"I watched a lot of baseball," Jason says around a mouth full of pizza. He swallows, and a contemplative look passes over his face. He looks down as he continues, "I mean, on TV. Never in real life. Sometimes my dad would let me watch with him whenever he was home and not . . . out. And on the days he left me home alone, I would sit and watch the games by myself. You were my favorite player to watch on TV, Mr. Griffin! Well, you and Adrian Ortiz. He's funny." Jason giggles at the end of his statement, and I know that all three of us adults have emotional whiplash from all of those revelations.

"We'll have to get you out to watch some games in person this season," Griffin finally says after clearing the emotion from his throat. "The games are even more fun in real life."

Jason's entire face lights up. "Really? That would be the coolest! Can we, Miss Danae?"

"I'm sure we can figure something out," I reply, feeling conflicted. My desire to go to a baseball game falls into negative territory on the number line. But not only am I dating a baseball player, my new son is clearly obsessed. Mentally, I groan at the prospect of watching baseball, but outwardly I smile and change the subject.

An hour later, Griffin drives us home. The streets are mostly cleared now, meaning school should be back in session tomorrow.

"So, Fireball, when's your first baseball practice? Are you playing on a team this spring?" Griffin asks, looking in the rearview mirror at Jason.

He perks up in his seat and leans forward. "Am I gonna be on a real baseball team, Miss Danae?"

My gut clenches, and I can't stop myself from briefly glaring at Griffin before turning to Jason. "We'll have to talk more about that, bud. I'm not sure that's something we can add to the schedule right now." I give Griffin one more side-eye as Jason's face falls. He sits back in his seat.

Griffin looks at me quizzically and mouths "sorry" before he changes the subject. "What was your favorite part of playing in the snow?" he asks.

Jason perks back up. "Definitely sledding! Or maybe when you hit Miss Danae with the giant snowball," he says, giggling.

"Hey! You should be defending me, not encouraging him!" I say with mock outrage. Griffin reaches a hand back for a high five, which Jason heartily supplies.

"I'll be keeping my eye on you two," I say, using my fingers to motion from my eyes to the two of them.

"I hope so," Griffin says under his breath. I suppose we haven't reached the "hold hands in front of Jason" stage yet, but Griffin reaches over to run a finger across the back of my hand. It's a delicate touch that sends my heart (and hormones) into a frenzy. A touch I'm becoming addicted to after experiencing it just twice. A touch that nearly makes me forget that Griffin put me in a tough position with Jason and his baseball dreams.

There's absolutely no chance I'm signing Jason up for baseball this spring. I can't handle one more thing right now.

We pull into a parking space in front of our townhouse. The lot hasn't been cleared of snow very well yet, which makes the clearance of Griffin's Jeep an advantage. He helps Jason out of the car and grabs the booster seat to transfer to mine. I unlock our front door, but Jason suddenly turns and wraps his little arms around Griffin's waist in a tight hug.

"Thank you for letting us come play, Mr. Griffin. I had so much fun today," he says.

Griffin makes brief eye contact with me before leaning down to return Jason's hug. "Any time, Fireball. You're gonna need a lot of practice if you're ever going to beat me at Mario Kart."

"And you're gonna need better luck if you're ever going to beat me at Trash," Jason says, voice and eyes full of mischief.

Griffin and I burst out laughing, and he ruffles Jason's hair. "You two better get inside out of the cold," Griffin says, and Jason scampers off.

In one smooth movement, Griffin takes my hand and pulls me closer as he leans in toward me. He places a soft kiss on the sensitive skin just below my ear, evoking an involuntarily gasp.

"Thanks for coming over today," he murmurs. "I'll talk to you tomorrow?"

It's a question he already knows the answer to. Still, I nod a yes.

Inside, I lean against the door for a moment to let my heart calm down before facing Jason. When I walk to the living room, he's there playing with his Lego set.

"Did you have fun today?" I ask him. A question I already know the answer to.

"This was the best snow day ever!" he yells, flinging himself at me. I catch him in a hug, rubbing his back.

"Hey, we probably need to talk about how we're going to handle sharing about our snow day at school tomorrow," I say.

Jason leans back to meet my eyes. "What do you mean?"

Wow, this is a hard concept to explain to a nine-year-old. "Well, Mr. Griffin is really famous, right?" I say. Jason nods. "And sometimes famous people kinda like to keep some privacy so people don't know everything about their lives. Since Mr. Griffin and I have only gone on one date, we maybe shouldn't tell other people yet that we've been spending time with him. Does that make sense?"

Jason's face furrows. "You mean, like a secret?"

"Not exactly like a secret," I say, contemplating how to explain. "Here's the thing—you remember the first week back to school when you were telling everyone about how you got to meet Mr. Griffin and the other players at camp, and one of the other kids said some not-nice things to you?"

Now Jason's face falls. "Yeah, I remember."

"Well, that boy might have felt like you were bragging about it, and he was probably a little bit jealous that you got to meet someone famous. So he said some mean things to try to make himself feel better about it. We don't want to brag about being friends with Mr. Griffin right now. At least, not until he and I are a little more serious about our relationship," I say.

Jason cocks his head at me. "You mean, you're not serious about liking each other?"

I blow out a breath. *Wow, I am really screwing this up.* "No, it's not that we aren't serious. I do *really* like him."

"He really likes you too. I can tell," Jason replies with a grin.

I smile back at him. "Yeah, we do seriously like each other. But I'd still like to keep our relationship private for a little longer. Do you know what I mean?"

Jason nods solemnly. "I do. I won't say anything at school, I promise."

"Thanks, bud," I say, pulling him to me for one more hug. "I really love you, you know? With you one hundred percent, forever kind of love."

He squeezes me harder. "I love you too."

And now I'm crying.

CHAPTER TWENTY-ONE

Griffin

Which question are you answering today? Favorite book or favorite flower?

Asking a reader to name their favorite book is considered cruel and unusual punishment. We could never choose.

Come on, there has to be one book that rises to the top.

Nope. I could maybe choose a few top favorites from each genre or for a specific mood. But I can't possibly pick only one book.

Fine then. Favorite flower?

I don't really care for flowers. I'd rather have books. <smiley face emoji> Flowers die. Books are forever.

What hobbies do you have other than baseball?

You didn't really answer either of my questions. So I guess I won't be telling you that I don't really have any hobbies outside of baseball.

Really? Nothing?

I like people. Meeting and getting to know new people. Establishing connections. Not sure where that classifies on the hobby scale though.

I guess we'll just label it "talking." Now you have an answer when someone asks what your hobbies are.

Gun to your head, you have to choose a favorite book. What's your instinctual answer?

Fine. The abridged version of The Count of Monte Cristo. I read it for Honors English my sophomore year of high school, and even though I had always been an avid reader, it was the first book I ever paced myself reading. I didn't want it to end. You might like it!

Is there a movie version?

Why don't you like to read?

That's too deep of an explanation for a text message.

Why do you hate baseball?

It's been three days since our snow day, and although Danae and I have texted a lot, I'm obnoxiously excited to see her again tonight. Our daily texts have helped me slowly learn more about what makes her tick—that her favorite part of being a librarian is helping kids find "the" book that unlocks their love for reading. That the hardest adjustment to being a mom has been constantly second-guessing if she's responding the right way to his emotions. That her favorite color is purple, specifically the shade in the sky at sunset. That she really makes pro/con lists for just about every decision, and books are her means of mental escape.

I've told her a little more about my family dynamic too. How we moved all over when I was young, so I learned to adapt to new social situations everywhere we went. She wasn't surprised at all by my admission that I was quick to win over every coach and teammate I ever played with, regardless of how long we were in one spot. She also didn't seem surprised by my relief that we stayed put once I hit middle school. Most people assume that since I adapt to new situations so well, I must enjoy constant change. But I was elated when my dad stopped working for a big company overseeing construction of luxury hotels and opened his own general contracting business. We could finally settle in one place, and I even grew to love that it was Oklahoma.

We're slowly laying cards on the table, revealing our lives and histories to each other little by little. But I've been stuffing certain cards up my sleeve, reluctant to play the jokers. I get the sense that Danae's doing the same . . . and it's not a long-term strategy if I'm going to win this game. Win Danae for the long haul.

I need to tip my cards if she's going to tip hers. The fact that her trust in me rides on my trust in her is an easy tell to read, so I've been preparing myself for a more serious conversation at dinner tonight. Luckily, I've arranged for my chef to cook dinner for us here at my house, and Sam is going to take Jason to a movie.

"Be expecting a large charge to your credit card tonight because I'm going to buy Jason all the popcorn and candy he can stomach," Sam says as she walks into the bathroom where I'm styling my hair.

"Hey, knock first! What if I was in here showering?" I exclaim.

"Puh-lease, you wouldn't leave the door open if you weren't fully clothed," she responds with an eye roll. "You sent Danae the security code to get into the neighborhood, right?"

"Of course, I did," I say, washing the residual hair product off of my hands.

"I'll text you when Jason and I are on our way back to give you a heads up to stop making out with Danae," Sam says with an impish smile.

"You're such a child," I reply. I flick her arm as I walk past and dodge her returning kick. "We're going to be talking. We need to be intentional about getting to know each other better if we're going to be able to withstand the time apart while I'm in Arizona."

"A little bit of making out might not hurt," Sam says. "You know you want to."

Boy, do I know it. Throughout the week, my thoughts have wandered to Danae's lips on more occasions than could be cataloged. *Maybe a* little *kissing wouldn't hurt.*

"P.S., Joe called earlier, and I actually answered. You're welcome," Sam says, then pauses as though actually expecting me to thank her for doing her job. I narrow my eyes, forcing her to continue talking. "He really wants you to do that cologne campaign."

"The one where they want a bunch of moody, broody shots of me shirtless with a crowd of women?" I ask. She nods. "No, thank you."

"He asked me to remind you of the generous payout they're offering," she says with irritation. "Pretty sure he's concerned about *his* portion of that payout."

"Yeah, no. Never would I want to do that kind of marketing campaign. But especially not now that I'm trying to start a serious relationship with Danae. Parading around shirtless with other women isn't exactly a trust-building move. Hard pass."

"Perfect! I'll tell him to shove the offer up his—"

I cut her off with another glare.

She holds her hands up in a placating gesture. "I'll tell him it's a firm no. Have you told Joe that you're dating someone?"

"Nope," I say, popping the "p" sound. "He'd want to spin it into some sort of PR story. Definitely not doing that to Danae and Jason. I'm going to go check with Robert about the food," I say, heading to the kitchen. The house smells like an all-day brunch café.

Robert pulled some chef strings and borrowed several chafing dishes, which are lined up on the giant kitchen island. It smells like they're already filled with the smörgåsbord of breakfast foods I requested.

"All good?" I ask.

Robert nods. "Just finished washing the dishes. It's not going to taste as good being premade as it would if you'd let me stay and cook to order," he explains with a severe look.

"I promise I won't let Danae judge your chef skills based on the Bunsen burner food," I say, and Robert starts muttering under his breath about his crumbling reputation.

"For real, thanks for doing this, man," I tell him, heartily clapping him on the back.

"Anything for you," he sighs. "Promise me that sometime I can cook a *real* meal for you and your new lady."

"Done."

I spend the ten minutes between Robert's departure and Danae's arrival pacing the living room and trying not to think about kissing her.

Unsuccessful.

The doorbell rings, and I rush to answer it. Jason is all smiles as I swing the door open, and I pause to crouch down into his hug before greeting Danae.

She's dressed more casually for this date in jeans and a long-sleeved top, but she's just as heart attack-inducing as she was in the green cocktail dress. Her lips have a slight pink hue to them, the kind that comes from a tinted lip balm as opposed to flashy lipstick. They're as magnetic as I remember.

A little kissing definitely wouldn't hurt, right?

It's a matter of moments before Sam is on her way out the door with Jason to drive Danae's car to the movie theater. As the door clicks shut behind them, I can't resist the urge to pull Danae into a lingering hug.

"Hi," I murmur into her hair.

"Hi," she murmurs back, her voice vibrating into my chest.

Reluctantly, I draw myself out of the embrace. "Hungry?" I ask.

"Famished, actually," Danae answers with a smile.

"Good thing, because I have a whole dinner buffet waiting for you," I say as I place a hand on the small of her back, gently leading her to the kitchen. I open the chafing dishes with a flourish.

Danae gasps. "Breakfast for dinner?" She returns my wide grin.

"I should clarify that I did not cook this. My chef, Robert, did. And he would like you to reserve your judgment on his cooking skills until he can prepare a fresh meal for you sometime," I say. Danae scans the waiting omelets, pancakes, waffles, bacon, sausage, and biscuits with gravy, her eyes dancing.

"I can assure you—there is nothing else he could possibly cook that will be more impressive than this spread," she says.

We load our plates with food and sit at the smaller table in the kitchen, forgoing the formal dining room. Conversation is light, recapping our weeks as we savor the meal. But as the piles of food are reduced to crumbs, I know it's time to dive deeper.

I have to play the jokers. Even if I don't want to.

Needing some movement, I stand to take our plates to the sink. Danae follows me, carrying the syrup and hot sauce from the table. After rinsing the plates, I dry my hands and then lean them on the counter, facing the sink. Clearing my throat, I say, "So, on our first date, you asked me about my injury last year, and I kinda shut down. But I want to talk with you about it now."

"I watched a video!" Danae blurts. She's standing right next to me, and when I turn to face her, I see the panicked look on her face, eyes wide and cheeks flushing. Her words come out in a rush. "I couldn't stop thinking about it, so I googled it and watched the video of what happened, and I'm so sorry!"

I'm stunned by her admission, not because I'm upset, but because I'm surprised that she cared that much. Danae must misinterpret my silence, though, because she doubles down on her apology. "I'm so sorry. I'm sorry if searching about it behind your back breaks your trust. I'm sure you're tired of people knowing all of your business from the internet, and I'm sorry that I was one of those people."

"I'm not upset," I say, shaking my head. Taking one of her hands in mine, I reassure her. "Not upset at all. Don't worry—I was surprised you gave it a second thought."

Danae sputters a laugh. "Um, second thoughts are all I give. Second, third, tenth. Too many thoughts about everything all the time." She looks down at our hands, at my thumb tracing hers. "It looked really painful. Really awful," she whispers.

I blow out a breath and lean my hip against the counter. "It was. Physically, it was more than painful. Total agony." Her eyes are soft with compassion, and now I draw in a deep breath. "It was the mental toll that was harder to handle, though."

"How so?" she quietly asks.

I stretch my neck, uncomfortable talking about the emotions. "Obviously, there was so much anxiety about my future in baseball. Was it over? Could I come back from a torn labrum? It's a difficult rehab journey after surgery. It wasn't my throwing arm, but the flexibility and reflexes of my catching hand are just as crucial in a defensive position like shortstop. I was plagued by the uncertainty."

Pausing, I look down to see that now her thumb is the one tracing gentle patterns on my hand. "And if it had all been over, it would have been my own fault," I confess.

Danae's brow furrows. "What do you mean?"

I shake my head, weighed down by the memory of that moment. "I should have yielded to Farmer, our left fielder. We'd both called for the ball, but the placement fell within his territory more than mine. If he was able to get there—which he yelled that he was—I should have let up and given him the catch. But coming off the previous season, I'd been getting a lot more attention. The 'Wizard of Defense' nickname had been around for several years, but I was gaining more attention as a five-tool player."

Danae's quizzical expression reminds me that the baseball lingo is going over her head. I explain, counting items off on the fingers of my free hand. "Five-tool players are strong in all areas—fielding, running, arm strength, and hitting for both average and power. I'd always been able to put the bat to the ball and had a decent batting average, but the season before my injury, I'd started hitting with a lot more power in addition to playing well defensively."

I close my eyes, too ashamed to meet Danae's honest gaze. *This beautiful, authentic woman—will she still be interested when she realizes how selfish and prideful I was?*

"I let all the attention over my success go to my head. Felt like I was a bigger deal than I was. So, in that split second running for the ball, I was determined to be the one to make that game-winning catch. Who was I if not the 'Wizard of Defense,' able to make a diving save like that?"

Swallowing hard, I open my eyes to look Danae in the eye. "I wanted to *be* the Wizard of Defense. Wanted to get the catch that would have been on highlight reels for years to come. That would have garnered even more attention, put a greater spotlight on my abilities. So, I assumed that Farmer would yield to me, and I dove for the ball. And I almost ruined my entire life in the process."

Chapter Twenty-Two

Danae

Searching Griffin's face, I see the pain etched there. Pain that's usually buried below the surface of his easy smile and charisma. But there's a vulnerability there now, a piece of him that he seems reluctant to admit exists.

Based on the reluctance and shame in his voice, I know he doesn't see it this way, but that vulnerability is incredibly attractive. Irresistibly attractive.

My heart goes rogue and overpowers my brain's processing speed. Consequently, my mind can't think through my actions before I lean up on my toes and press my lips to his.

Griffin's surprise is evident in the slight flinch of his lips upon initial contact, but he overcomes the shock in record time. His hands are instantly in my hair, holding my lips to his as though he's pictured this moment as obsessively as I have.

Rational thought tries to remind my brain that we still have more to talk about. This is a serious moment that requires more discussion. But the feather-like movement of his lips against mine halts logic before it can yank me away from him. My entire body floods with heat as I relish the sweetness of Griffin's kiss, the soothing melody his lips sing to mine.

We slowly and barely draw back from each other. His mouth is still a breath away from mine when I whisper, "I'm not sure why I did that."

"Do you regret doing that?" Griffin asks, voice laced with restraint.

I ever so slightly shake my head. "No."

It's all the permission he needs to claim my lips again, one arm wrapping around my waist to pull me closer to him, his other hand firmly clasped behind my head. He pivots us so my back is against the counter, and my hands slide up his chest and around his neck. As his tongue traces my lips, I sigh into his mouth, which only serves to turn up the temperature of his kiss. After a light groan, Griffin abruptly pulls away and rubs a hand down his face.

"Hold on, there's still more we need to talk about," he says. He takes a step back to lean against the opposite counter, putting a couple feet of space between us. "Even if the idea of kissing you has infiltrated my every waking thought this week, I came into tonight prepared to be honest with you. And to ask you some honest questions in return." He looks at me with a glimmer of darkness in his eyes. My cheeks flush in response. "But the reality of kissing you is going to take over everything if I don't hit pause."

The realization of what I just did floods over me. *I kissed Griffin West. He was trying to have an honest conversation, and I totally ambushed his lips without asking. Oh my gosh—does he think I'm some floozy throwing myself at him? Does he realize how out of character that was for me, or does he assume I'm showing my true nature—throwing my lips at men?*

My brain halts as Griffin steps forward and grips my face between his hands. "I need you to translate the thought factory for me. I see it swirling."

I bite my lip, terrified about what he must think of me. His thumb brushes over my lip, tugging it free from my teeth. "Without doing that, please," he murmurs, voice laden with heat.

"I'm worried about what you might think of me when I just kissed you when you were in the middle of opening up about your injury," I hesitantly respond.

Griffin tilts his head to one side. "What I think of you? I think you're the most intriguing, empathetic, compelling woman I've ever met. Add sexiest to that list as well." Heat floods my cheeks again, and he brushes a thumb across one of them. "And I'm mystified that you would want to kiss me after I confessed to being an arrogant idiot. I was sure you'd be turned off by the admission of my ego."

I slowly shake my head. "You were being honest and vulnerable about how you felt. That's not a turn off."

His hands slowly drop from my face, finding my hands instead. "I'm not usually very good at being vulnerable. This is a concerted effort. Because I know we need to talk about the hard things if this is going to be real."

I want this to be real, I think as I stare into his gray eyes.

"Baseball ruined my last chance at a happy childhood," I suddenly state. Griffin's eyes spark with confusion. I sigh. "That sounded dramatic."

"That did sound a touch dramatic," Griffin replies with a smirk. His smile softens. "But it must have felt dramatic for you to say it."

I'm so tempted to pick every last fleck of polish off of my nails, but Griffin's firm yet gentle hands hold mine still. "I've told you a little bit about my upbringing," I begin, and he nods in understanding. "When I was in elementary school, I always felt uneasy at home. At school. Everywhere. My dad was constantly scheming ways to elevate our finances, our status as a family. Turning family dinners into board room strategy meetings. It was so disorienting, like we were constantly in danger of losing everything, when now I understand that we weren't."

I focus on the comfort of Griffin's hands around mine, forcing myself to continue speaking. "I had a hard time making friends at the private school I attended. Even there, social status was the undercurrent of relationships. And my dad's voice was always in the back of my mind reminding me who to talk to, who to befriend for the sake of our family's gain. It felt like a chess game that I didn't want to play, but I still tried. It was such a messed-up way to approach childhood friendships. What kind of kid thinks that way?"

Griffin's eyes are full of compassion. "It wasn't your fault. You shouldn't have had to think that way."

I sigh. "I had a cousin on my mom's side, Nina, who was my age. We had the best times together at my grandparents' house over holidays, and it felt like she was my one true friend. Someone I could be myself around without pretense. When I was in fifth grade, her family moved here to the Kansas City area. I was elated—I thought I'd finally get to see her regularly and have a *real* best friend."

Pausing to collect my thoughts, I stare at the floor. It was so long ago, but the disappointment of young Danae is still so fresh in my mind. "Nina's older brother played baseball, and their dad was overbearing about it. Expected him to be the best of the best, all the time. So he was on the most competitive teams year-round, constantly traveling to tournaments, especially over the summer. Baseball took over their lives. Nina's life, by association." I shrug my shoulders. "I tried going with her to a couple of games that first summer, but it was so hot and boring. And her dad would yell at us if we were goofing off with each other instead of paying attention to the game to cheer for her brother. So I stopped asking my parents if I could go, which worked out better for them anyway. Pretty much, I never saw Nina. My chance at having a best friend I could be myself with was ruined by baseball. I've hated the sport ever since."

I finally look up, expecting to see skepticism or judgment on Griffin's face. I'm not prepared to see him looking at me with tenderness. *May as well tell him everything.* "Also," I continue, "I think baseball is unbearably boring."

Griffin's head falls back as he roars with laughter. He pulls me to his chest, which still vibrates with his resounding laughs. I loop my arms around his waist and bury my face in his chest, taking a deep inhale of his spicy, manly scent. "You're not mad at me?"

My senses of smell and touch protest when he pulls back enough to look me in the eyes. "Not mad. I'll admit—a little bewildered that you could think the greatest sport of all time is boring, but we'll work on that."

I shoot him a sassy look, which makes him grin. "You cannot approach this relationship expecting to change my mind about baseball," I say, suddenly serious. "Us working out can't be contingent upon me developing a love for baseball."

Griffin's face turns solemn as well. "Understood. I won't have that as an expectation." He leans down, lips a temptingly-close half inch from mine. My breath hitches in anticipation of his kiss, but instead of erasing the distance, he grazes his lips up my jawline. He whispers in my ear, "That doesn't mean I'm not gonna try."

The hair on the back of my neck stands up, and the shiver that begins in my neck makes its way down the length of my body. My hands involuntarily clench the back of Griffin's shirt, and his eyes are molten when he draws back to meet my gaze.

"Am I allowed to kiss you again, or is there more you'd like to say?" he asks, voice low. He brushes a strand of hair away from my forehead, tracing the lines of my face and neck. Even if I had more to say, there's zero chance that I could form coherent sentences while he's doing that.

"No more words," I breathe. And then his lips are devouring mine again. A kiss I return with reckless abandon.

My heart has officially claimed its seat at the table.

CHAPTER TWENTY-THREE

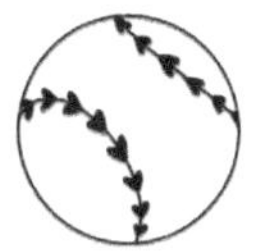

Griffin

I've dated a fair amount. I've kissed a reasonable number of women. But Danae's lips against mine make me think that I have never truly *kissed* a woman before. Because this is a completely different feeling, possessing every part of my mind, body, and heart.

Maybe it's the way that Danae is melting into me when I know she's naturally reserved. Maybe it's the way her kiss is unhesitating when I know she wrestles with anxiety. The thought that *I* could make her feel that way, make her kiss that way—it's intoxicating.

She is intoxicating.

The sweetness of the syrup she slathered over her waffles at dinner lingers on her lips, her tongue. Paired with the natural sweetness of who she is, I'll be on a sugar high for days.

Danae slowly slides her fingers along my beard, and I've never been more thankful to have facial hair. I'm lost in every sensation of her when the tiny voice of reason in my brain tries to speak up.

You still have another joker.

I try to ignore the little jerk, but his insistence grows louder, unrelenting until I finally break away from Danae's lips. The waves of her hair are disheveled by my hands. It takes every ounce of willpower I possess to resist weaving my fingers back through her hair and resuming our kiss.

"There's something else I need to tell you, Danae," I say. "Something else I don't like telling other people." Her eyes were foggy with the intoxication of our kiss, but they suddenly clear as she pulls further away from me.

"What?" she asks, voice hardly more than a whisper.

"You explained why you don't like baseball—which is my favorite thing in the world. It's only fair that I explain why I don't like reading—your favorite thing in the world," I say, and the fear evaporates from her demeanor.

"Okay," she says, then quiets.

I gently tap my fist on the counter next to her. "I'm dyslexic."

Her eyes immediately flicker with understanding, then bounce back and forth between mine like she's putting pieces into place. "Oh," she says. "That's why you said you use voice-to-text a lot. And it's why you chose eleven as your number for the Crowns, isn't it?"

I nod. "Looks the same no matter which way you look at it. Specifically, I deal with vertical dyslexia, and I don't struggle nearly as much as some people do. But it was much harder to get a dyslexia diagnosis back when we were kids. I wasn't officially diagnosed until I was an adult, and I still get embarrassed when people find out," I say. Danae nods in understanding again. "Growing up, I thought I was just dumb. I hated books because I felt like a failure when I tried to read, and I'm not fond of feeling like a failure."

Danae's lips quirk to one side in response to my statement, which tempts me to stop talking and go back to exploring those lips. But my wandering thoughts are reined in by her next question. "They've made a lot of progress in recent years at making books available in dyslexia-friendly fonts. Have you seen those?"

I shake my head. "I use a dyslexia app on my phone to help with text messages and what-not when I can't use voice text. But I haven't really tried reading books with the updated fonts."

She considers my answer before asking her next question. "Have you tried listening to audiobooks?"

I shrug. "Once. But they've really only become widely popular in the past few years, and I was already hooked on podcasts by that point. I guess I'd rather listen to someone share about their own experience than some narrator reading a made-up story."

Danae's face scrunches, and I can see the thoughts running rampant in her mind. "You might enjoy memoirs then. Especially ones narrated by the author. There are a few—"

Placing a finger on her lips to cut her off, I say, "Us working out cannot be contingent upon you changing my mind about books."

Her eyes spark as she smiles smugly at me. "Touché." The smirk disappears as she asks, "How are we going to coexist when we despise each other's greatest passions?"

"In case I haven't made this clear, I'm not interested in merely coexisting with you, Danae," I say, tucking the hair behind her ear. "And I think I'm interested in having a greatest passion other than baseball." I lean in close before adding, "So we're going to figure this out. No matter what it takes."

The magnetism between us takes over, drawing our lips wordlessly back to each other.

After walking Danae and Jason out to her car, I come back inside to an interrogation. "Sooo, how was it?" Sam asks, eyes sparkling. "Obviously I need to know everything."

"It was good," I say, walking past Sam.

"By the looks of your hair, I'd say it was more than good," Sam replies.

I freeze and resist the urge to smooth down my hair. I'd already smoothed it down in preparation for Sam and Jason's return. *Is she just messing with me?*

Sam sashays by and taps the back of my head, where the longer hair of my faux hawk ends. "You missed a spot," she says with a smirk.

I can't help it. I reach a hand up to rub the back of my head. Sure enough, I find the piece that was sticking up out of place. The memory of Danae's fingers there starts to heat my blood again, so I turn toward the kitchen. "You're so juvenile," I call over my shoulder.

"It's not my fault my maturity was stunted by childhood trauma," Sam quips, halting my steps. I turn to face her. She looks like she's joking, but I know that the jokes are sometimes real and sometimes covering a struggle underneath.

"Is being around Jason bringing up memories?" I ask quietly.

Sam shrugs. "A little. But not in a terrible way."

I move toward Sam. "I can find another babysitting solution for when I want to take Danae on a date. You don't have to keep doing it."

"No way! You're not taking my guy from me! I love that kid," Sam says. "And I like that I can be there for him. Not that he's opening up about deep things a lot—he's too young and it's all still too fresh for him to actively process his experiences. But I understand the small comments he makes and feel like I'm somewhat equipped to know how to respond. Like Danae has another person in her corner supporting Jason's journey. That makes me feel good, like I'm doing something good with my life."

I place my hands on Sam's shoulders and bend my knees to meet her eyes. "You're doing a lot of good with your life, sis. That kid is so lucky to have you as someone to look up to. I'm lucky to have you supporting me in my career and every aspect of my life. Danae is lucky to have your support. But I want you to be honest if you ever reach your limit, okay?"

"Deal," Sam says, and I pull her into a hug. "But only if you tell me about kissing Danae."

"You're fired," I joke as I playfully push her away from me. She raises one eyebrow.

"I am *not* giving you details. I'll just say, I hope it was the last first kiss of my life. And it would be a last first kiss of epic proportions."

CHAPTER TWENTY-FOUR

Danae

Nothing's wrong. Just can't stop thinking about you. Or your perfect lips.

<monkey covering eyes emoji>

You're blushing, aren't you?

<eye roll emoji>

I only wish I was there to see it.

I'm not going to answer a question today if you keep distracting me like this. I have things I need to accomplish.

Distracting you like what, exactly?

ME

You know what I mean.

GRIFFIN

Maybe I want you to spell it out. You know, to make sure I'm correctly understanding the thought factory.

ME

You're ridiculous.

GRIFFIN

I'm also patient. And persistent.

ME

Fine. Distracting me with thinking about kissing you. Stop it.

GRIFFIN

I have zero desire to stop thinking about kissing you. Or to stop you from thinking about kissing me. I'm afraid you've made an impossible request.

ME

What was your favorite subject in school?

GRIFFIN

Changing the subject, are we?

ME

Answer the question, or I'm not answering any. And this conversation will be over.

GRIFFIN

Recess.

ME

Does not count. Although absolutely the answer I would have guessed for you.

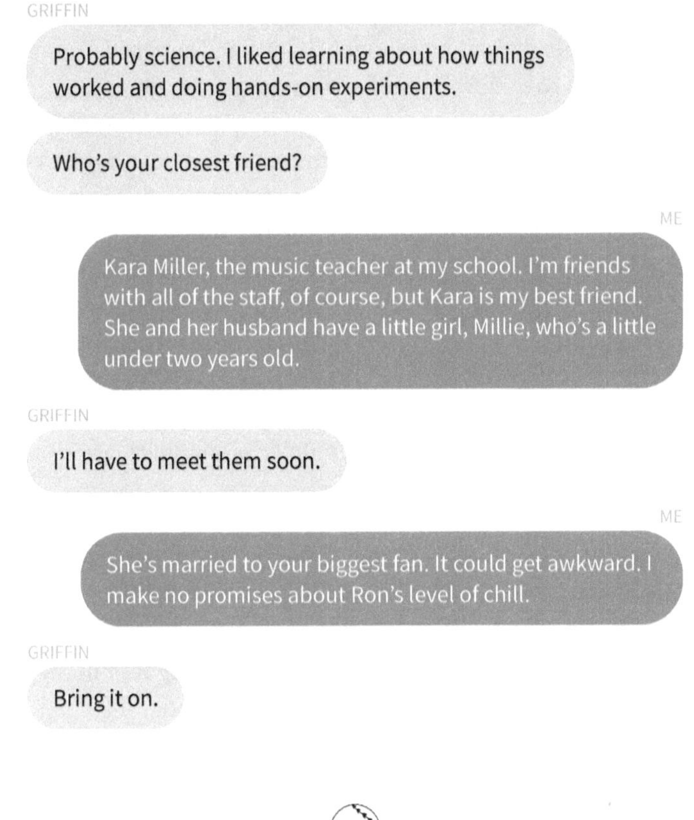

Kara makes a show of fanning herself. "That is so hot. Everything about it—Griffin West making your favorite meal, being vulnerable, and then making out in the kitchen. Holy cow, how is this your life?"

"I've been asking myself the same question, if I'm honest," I say after swallowing a bite of my sandwich. I give Kara a serious look. "Do you think I'm making a mistake?"

"Why would you think that?" she asks.

I drop eye contact. "I don't know. He's just so . . . different than what I pictured for myself in a partner. His schedule is utter madness, and maybe that's the worst kind of position to put myself in when I'm trying to figure out life for Jason. Am I being selfish by pursuing a relationship with Griffin when Jason needs so much love and support?"

"We've been over this, Danae," Kara says with a sigh.

"Go over it again. You know how much I mull things over," I say.

Kara rolls her eyes. "You're like a cow regurgitating its food to chew on again." I scrunch up my nose at her gross analogy. "Swallow this down, once and for all, Danae Collins: you deserve happiness. You deserve love. You having more happiness and more love in your life is only going to make it possible for you to give even more to Jason. Plus, it sounds like Griffin is amazing with Jason. And the sister. I don't see anything about this being negative for Jason. So stop worrying."

"When has 'stop worrying' ever worked with me?" I ask wryly.

"Let this be the first time," Kara admonishes, pinning me with a look. "I'm serious."

I sigh again. "Also, Griffin suggested that we should do something together with you and Ron sometime. He wants to meet my best friend."

Kara nearly drops her fork, laden with leftover pasta. "Do you understand what you'd be getting yourself into, putting Ron in the same room with the Wizard of Defense? Are you sure about this?"

I laugh. "I told Griff the same thing, but he seems to think he can handle it."

Kara smiles and points her fork at me. "Don't think I missed that shortened nickname. You've officially hit the next level of intimacy: pet names."

"Calling him Griff instead of Griffin is hardly a pet name. Can you please eradicate the term 'pet name' from your vocabulary altogether? Along with 'levels of intimacy?' You're so weird," I say.

"Says the one who chooses this weirdo as her bestie."

Susan pokes her head into the library and asks, "Danae, could I talk to you in the hallway for a moment?" Susan is Jason's classroom teacher this year, and my stomach sinks at her request. It's been a long week, and I've been looking forward to a quiet Friday evening to decompress. Griffin has some dinner he has to attend, so I was planning on a date with a book tonight after Jason's bedtime. I get the sinking feeling that my quiet evening is about to be derailed.

Jason is tucked away in the reading tent while I'm finishing up a few tasks, so I follow her out to the hallway. She lowers her voice. "I wanted to get your help with something. There have been several kids in my class over the past couple of weeks who have had things go missing. Nothing major, just little trinkets like pencil toppers, or the erasers and smelly pens I give out as behavior incentives. One of the boys claims he saw Jason take something from another student's desk today. I asked Jason about it, but he was pretty evasive. Could you maybe have a follow-up conversation with him tonight?"

I let out a long breath. "Of course, I can."

Susan looks at me with compassion. "I'm so sorry. I know this is all really hard. I'm on your team, on Jason's team. Let me know if I can do anything to help."

Nodding, I assure Susan I'll keep her posted. The knot of dread twists in my stomach for the remainder of the afternoon as we head home and make dinner.

"Hey bud, I need to ask you about something," I say after we've eaten. I at least wanted his blood sugar to be regulated before having this conversation.

Jason looks at me, waiting. Something about the moment feels like a ticking time bomb.

"Ms. Willard told me today that some of the kids in your class have been missing some items, and someone thought they saw you take something out of another student's desk. Could you tell me about that?" I ask.

His eyes look panicked, but he promptly shuts down the jittery energy as his face reddens. "I didn't take nothing. That student was lying. Or maybe he saw wrong. I swear I didn't take anything."

I'm so out of my depth. It seems obvious that he's not telling the truth, but he swears he *is* telling the truth. How do I get him to be honest without damaging his trust in me because I don't believe him? I'm paralyzed by indecision.

"Can I go play Legos now?" Jason asks. The jittery energy is back.

"Take your plate to the sink first, please," I respond.

You're failing, Danae. He's obviously lying. You can't let him get away with lying. But calling him out on the lie might crush him. He isn't even calling you "Mom" yet. Will he ever think of you as his mom if he thinks you don't trust him?

What do I do?

After doing the dishes, I walk upstairs to go think in my room. I'm itching to write out a pro/con list, but that seems a little much for the situation. As I walk past Jason's room, I decide to take a quick peek around. Maybe if I have concrete proof, he'll respond more honestly.

I look under his bed and even under the pillow. Nothing seems out of place in the closet, but when I open his dresser drawers, I quickly find a secret stash buried under his socks. Like Susan said, there are little erasers, a couple of coins, a tiny container of dried-up slime. Cheap, silly stuff that I would have bought for him if he'd asked.

Gathering the contraband items, I walk back downstairs, steeling myself for this confrontation.

"Jason? I need to talk to you again," I say, taking a seat on the couch. He puts down the Lego pieces he was holding and notices what I have in my hands.

"Where did you find that? Did you look through my room?" he asks, voice rising.

"Jason, we need to talk about why you took the other kids' stuff. You can ask me if you want to have some little things to fidget with. But stealing other people's things is wrong," I say, taking care to keep my voice calm.

"You shouldn't have looked in my drawer!" Jason yells.

My heart pounds, and my hands tremble with adrenaline. "You shouldn't have lied to me about taking this stuff, Jason. I only looked through your room because I knew you weren't being honest with me."

"You're not allowed to do that! You stay out of my room!" he screams, hands clenched in fists.

"I'm your mom now, Jason, so I do get to look through your stuff if I think you're doing something that's not safe or that's hurting other people," I say, my own voice trembling with frustration.

"You're not my mom! I don't have a mom! You can't tell me what to do!" Pure rage engulfs Jason's entire body as he growls with anger. His narrowed eyes might as well be shooting real daggers.

It's unnerving. Almost scary.

He screams with rage and then runs up the steps, slamming the door to his room behind him.

Trying to calm down my nervous system, I take several deep breaths. My thumb makes quick work of the clear polish on my fingernails as I contemplate what to do. Sometimes, being alone in his room helps him calm down. Maybe he'll listen to some music and come down from the anger. Maybe I should give him a few minutes of space.

But when I hear the sound of ripping and more angry growls, I realize that giving him space right now isn't going to be the right choice. I rush upstairs and turn the doorknob, only to be met with resistance trying to open the door. Thankfully, it's only a pile of blankets and pillows blockaded against the door, so I push it open with little effort. I'm not at all prepared for the sight before me.

Jason is standing on his bed, ripping the signed poster of Griffin into shreds. The other players' posters are already on the floor, ripped and crumpled in pieces.

As he continues tearing, Jason mutters, "These posters are stupid. I never wanted these. What a dumb way to decorate a room. I hate these posters. I hate everything in this room."

Tears spring to my eyes as I'm frozen in place. *What is happening? What do I do?*

My body instinctively takes over before my mind can think coherently, and I move toward Jason and try to take his hands. "Jason, stop."

He hurls the remaining strips of poster to the floor before yelling, "No!"

Gently taking his hand, I say, "Bud, I don't want you to hurt yourself. Can we sit down on the bed?" He yanks his hand away, so I lightly place an arm around his shoulders instead, easing him toward me. He resists at first but suddenly wraps his arms around my neck and bursts into tears.

"I'm sorry! I'm sorry, Miss Danae! I'm sorry I made a mess! I'm such a bad kid!" he gasps between sobs.

I ease us to a sitting position and scratch his back. "You're not a bad kid. You're an amazing kid. And I love you so much."

"You can't love me. I did bad stuff," Jason says, still sobbing into my shoulder.

I nudge his chin so that he'll look at me. "I do love you. Do you remember what I told you about what it means that I love you? That I choose you, that I'm with you one hundred percent, forever. You're mine no matter what. No matter what you do, I'm not going to stop loving you, okay? I'm not leaving you, ever. You're not leaving me, ever. You're still stuck with me."

Jason sniffles as he watches my face, as though looking for any signs that I'm lying. "Promise?"

I hug him as tight as I can without hurting him. "Promise."

He sniffs again. "I'm sorry I took the stuff. I don't know why I did that. My brain just told me that I should take it, so I did. I'm sorry."

"I forgive you," I say. "How 'bout we go together to take the stuff back to Ms. Willard tomorrow morning?"

Jason looks resigned but nods his head. His eyes fill with tears again as he looks at the floor. "I'm sorry I tore the posters. I don't think they're stupid. I shouldn't have done that. I really loved those posters."

Wrapping my arm around his shoulders, I nestle him into my side. "It will be okay. We can find some different decorations. Or maybe Sammi and Mr. Griffin could get us a new poster. I'll ask him, okay?"

"Okay," Jason's voice is small. "And Miss Danae? I really am glad you're my mom now. I lied when I said you're not my mom. I want you to be my mom."

I squeeze him one more time. "Well, good. Because I want to be your mom."

Chapter Twenty-Five

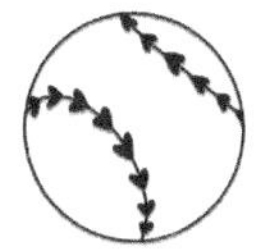

Griffin

"Bro . . . I need you . . . to sign a poster . . . after we're done," I huff between breaths as Adrian and I run on curve treadmills next to each other. We've completed our strength training for the day and are finishing off the session with cardio conditioning.

"No prob, old man," Adrian replies before increasing his speed with an impish grin. "All that time with your lady getting in the way of your conditioning?" He sounds hardly winded as he asks, but I know he's making an intentional effort to hide his own breathlessness.

The closer we get to spring training, the harder our trainers push us.

"Remind me to . . . slap you when time is called," I huff again.

"When do we . . . get to meet her?" Drew asks from my other side. "Lily keeps pestering . . . me about it."

"Time! Next rotation!" one of the trainers yells, and I take deep breaths as the treadmill slows to a stop. The three of us move to rowing machines, which should make conversation slightly easier. Despite Adrian's show-off nature, he's breathing just as heavily as I am as we sit down on machines and wait for the start signal.

"We're having dinner tonight with Danae's best friend and her husband," I tell Drew. "So I think Danae will be open to meeting some of my friends if tonight goes well. Even the friends I'm stuck with," I add, giving Adrian a hearty shove right before the trainer yells to begin.

"I've already met Danae," Adrian gloats as we begin rowing. "We should do a group thing—my familiar presence would definitely put her at ease."

He's half-joking but likely not wrong. Maybe getting all my teammates together to meet Danae at one time would be less overwhelming in the long run than multiple instances spread out.

"We could do a team dinner at our house sometime," Drew offers. "You know Lily would love to plan that."

"I'll talk with Danae about it tonight," I respond through the back-and-forth motion of the rowing machine. "It might overwhelm her to meet everyone at once—"

"Because we can be a lot?" Adrian playfully interjects.

"Pretty much," I say. "But that's probably the easiest way to introduce her to everyone before we leave for camp."

Drew exhales sharply as he pulls the rower cables back. "Sounds good. I'll tell Lily to start planning."

"Hey, I need you to sign a poster before we leave today too," I say, glancing over at Drew. "There was a mishap with Jason's posters from camp, and I want to replace them."

"Sure thing," Drew says. "Mishap?"

I'm silent for a couple of rowing cycles. "The kid's been through a lot. Sometimes the trauma responses are too much for him to hold in," I say.

"I know I don't understand trauma all that well," Drew replies, "but you know we've got your back as you've got Danae's, okay, man? Anything you need from us, you let us know."

"You know I love giving you a hard time, but, yes, what Sheffield said," Adrian pipes in. "Fireball is such a cute kid. Let me know anything I can do to help."

"Thanks, guys," I say, masking the swell of emotion in my chest with an extra-deep inhale and exhale.

"That's time! Next rotation!"

When I arrive at Danae's townhouse, I glance around the parking lot before jogging up to knock on the door. Danae opens it with a wide smile, and Jason quickly comes sprinting into view.

"Mr. Griffin! Are you excited to go to dinner tonight? You'll get to meet Ms. Miller, my music teacher. Music is only my third favorite specials class because I like P.E. and library better. Don't tell her I said that because we don't want to hurt her feelings," Jason rambles. "But at least music is better than art."

"Your secret's safe with me," I say, holding my hand out for a fist bump. "Hey, Fireball, I've got something for you."

Squatting down to his eye level, I pull three posters out of the bag of Crowns merchandise I'm carrying. I unroll them to reveal one of my posters, one of Adrian, and one collage of multiple starters, all signed.

Jason's eyes grow wide but then flicker with worry. He darts a glance at Danae. "Miss Danae told you about the posters?" His voice trembles, and his eyes drop to the floor.

I tell him, "She told me that you were having a hard time calming down your big emotions and that the posters got damaged in the process. She asked if I would mind bringing you some new ones—of course, I didn't mind!"

"Are you mad at me for ripping up the first one?" he asks, voice still small.

I reach a hand up to rest on his shoulder, encouraging him to look in my eyes. "I'm not mad. We all have to learn good strategies to calm us down when we're angry or hurt or frustrated. It's kinda like how most ball-players have the same at-bat routine—going through the exact same motions each time helps us calm down our nerves. You've just gotta find some strategies that work for you when you need help calming down, ya know?"

Jason nods slowly, and although I can't be sure that he fully understands, I know he's trying. I ask, "Should we go hang up the posters now?"

"Actually, we should probably go so we aren't late," Danae says, and I look up to see her eyes shimmering with moisture. She raises an eyebrow as she adds, "But maybe Mr. Griffin could help you hang them up when we get back from dinner?"

"Sure thing," I say, my heart pounding double-time from her hint at spending time alone together later tonight. I hand the posters to Jason. "Why don't you run these upstairs to set on your bed?"

Jason takes them and runs with enthusiasm for the stairs, and I match his enthusiastic energy, swiftly pulling Danae into my arms. She whispers, "Thank you," and I plant a firm kiss on her lips, followed by her jaw and her neck. She sighs and runs a hand along the faded buzz on my scalp, and I force myself to remember that we probably have two seconds until Jason is back at our feet.

"Anything for you. Anything for him," I whisper back. I manage to squeeze in one more quick kiss to her lips before our time is up.

I extricate myself from the passenger side of Danae's car and stretch out my limbs. She didn't want to call attention to our presence at Kara's house by parking my Jeep in the driveway, so we rode in her car.

It's been a while since I folded myself into a sedan.

Grabbing the bag of autographed merch for Kara's husband, I follow Danae and Jason up to the front door. Jason rings the bell, and a few seconds later, the door swings open to reveal a woman with sandy-blonde hair and a beaming grin. Her hair is swept back in a low bun, and the smile lines around her eyes are visible even behind thick-rimmed glasses.

"Welcome! Come on in, Jason! There are drinks on the counter that you can pick from," she says before giving Danae a quick hug as we step into the entryway. Jason scampers out of sight, I assume headed to the kitchen, and the woman immediately turns to me. "I'm Kara—and you're obviously Griffin, who I've heard *so much* about," she adds with a smirk in Danae's direction.

I like her already.

Danae's cheeks flush, and I place a hand on her waist, giving her a teasing grin. "Glad to know you're talking about me *so much*," I say with a wink. Danae starts to take a step further inside the house, but Kara holds up a hand to halt us.

She lowers her voice. "Listen. I've given Ron several pep talks about playing it cool tonight. But you deserve to know that Ron has no chill. He's a huge sports fan—a huge Kansas City sports fan—and the Crowns team is the epitome of all sports fandoms for him. So . . . please set your expectations to zero chill."

I chuckle because I can tell that she's dead serious. "I have appropriate expectations. It probably won't help that I have signed merch from the team for him," I say, holding up the bag in the hand that isn't rubbing circles on Danae's back.

Kara abruptly takes the bag from me, hiding it beside the shoe rack. "Let's just save that for later. *After* you guys have left. I don't need him completely embarrassing himself."

At that moment, a tiny girl with strawberry-blonde hair comes toddling up behind Kara, and Danae immediately crouches down to scoop her into her arms.

"There's my little Millie girl!" Danae exclaims. She tickles the girl's neck with kisses, making her laugh that adorable toddler giggle that universally turns people into mush.

"Aunt Nay-Nay," Millie says, grabbing a fistful of Danae's hair. "Come over eat!"

"Yes, we're going to eat with you tonight," Danae says, voice like honey. "Millie girl, this is my friend, Mr. Griffin." She angles toward me with Millie on her hip, smile wide. Anything inside me that wasn't already mush from Millie's giggle is now a pile of goo seeing Danae with her.

I reach a hand over to gently pat Millie's back. "Nice to meet you, Millie," I say quietly. She smiles but then decides to be shy, burying her face in Danae's neck. I understand the appeal.

"Why don't we head into the kitchen and rip off the proverbial Band-Aid? Ron's pulling the meat off the smoker, but I imagine he'll be coming inside any second now," Kara says, turning to lead us to the kitchen. Jason is already there, downing a lemonade juice box.

The back patio door opens and a red-headed man walks in holding a large aluminum pan covered with foil. He pushes the door closed with his elbow, then turns to face us, mouth dropping open. I'm grateful that he collects himself enough to not drop the pan he's holding because the smell has my mouth watering.

"Hey, Ron," Danae says, still holding Millie. "It's good to see you. That meat smells amazing."

Danae's comment about the meat returns Ron's attention to the giant pan in his hands, which he quickly sets down on the kitchen counter. Removing the hot pads from his hands, he walks the few steps over to where we're standing. He starts to hold a hand out but quickly retracts it, mouth opening and closing.

Smiling, I extend my hand toward him. "Ron, nice to meet you. I'm Griffin. Thanks so much for having us over and cooking dinner tonight."

Ron shakes my hand a moment longer than your standard handshake, then abruptly lets go when he catches sight of Kara's meaningful glare.

"Griffin West, it's amazing to meet you. I'm a huge fan. Enormous. The entire Crowns team—enormous fan," Ron gushes. "I can't wait to see how the season pans out. I think we're in for a good run this year, especially now that you're back."

"Ron, why don't you slice the meat so we can continue talking over dinner?" Kara suggests. "Jason, would you like to help me crush the Oreos to sprinkle on top of the pie for dessert?"

Jason hops down from the barstool he's been sitting on with an excited, "Yes!"

As he moves to assist Kara, Millie continues sneaking glances at me in between snuggling Danae's neck. I run one knuckle along Danae's hand that's rubbing Millie's back, softly smiling at her.

"So, Ron, tell me how you cooked the meat tonight," I say, moving to stand next to Ron. "I love Kansas City barbecue but haven't attempted to smoke anything on my own yet. What's your process?"

Ron's eyes light up as he begins explaining the process he's honed over the years. I ask follow-up questions and eventually steer the conversation to find out what he does.

"*Oof*, so you're gearing up for your busiest time of year as a tax accountant, huh?" I observe. "I'm even more honored that you made time to cook for us tonight when you're heading into tax season. That meat looks perfect."

"Oh, it's nothing," Ron says, puffing up but brushing aside the compliment. "I'm the one who's honored to cook for you. Having the Wizard of Defense in my house—that's certainly something I never expected! I can't bel—"

"Let's get food, everyone!" Kara jumps in to cut off whatever Ron's next statement was going to be. "I, for one, am starving!"

Danae holds Millie while Kara prepares a plate of tiny pieces of food for her, and I help Jason load up his plate with meat and sides. When Kara takes Millie to strap her into the highchair, I place a hand on the small of Danae's back to move her to the food line.

She smiles up at me with such a pool of happy contentment in her eyes—it kills me to not lean down and kiss her. I love spending time alone with her, but seeing her here with her best friend is bringing out a totally new side of her that I haven't seen yet. A soft, beautiful side.

As we sit down to start eating, I turn my attention to Kara. "Danae told me that you teach music. What got you interested in music education?"

Kara explains her choral background and the impact of her choir teacher in middle school. "In the same way Danae's safe place was books, music was mine. Elementary level isn't quite the same as specializing in choral music at the secondary level, but I do enjoy giving kids an introduction to the various forms of music."

I screw up my face. "I still remember learning the recorder in elementary school. In retrospect, that must have been torture for the teacher."

Kara laughs. "Of the worst degree. A couple of years ago, I switched to teaching the ukelele to fourth grade instead of recorders. It's a much more pleasant experience."

"I love the ukelele!" Jason exclaims, mouth full of cheesy potatoes.

"Would you like to move up to a secondary position someday?" I ask Kara before taking a bite of a rib. It's a perfect fall-off-the-bone texture, requiring zero false praise for Ron's cooking abilities.

Danae spears Kara with a look. "You'd never leave me, would you?"

Kara rolls her eyes. "You know I love you, but, yes, I would like to teach choir in middle or high school eventually." Danae fakes a pout, and I can tell this is a conversation they've had repeatedly. "Danae landed her dream position way earlier than most librarians do. I've had to wait my turn for a secondary choral position to come open."

"Serving your time on the farm team before getting called up to the majors?" I joke, and everyone laughs—even Danae. I elbow her in the side. "Look at you, catching all the baseball lingo now."

My comment opens the door for Ron and Jason to start talking baseball. It naturally leads to me fielding question after question from Ron about my experience, the coaching staff, the other guys on the team, and strategy for the upcoming season.

"I know you're not a baseball fan, Danae," Ron says, "but you should know that this guy earned that Wizard of Defense nickname for a reason. The Crowns are lucky to have him. A true wizard at the shortstop position."

"I'm sure he is," Danae says, reaching over to squeeze my hand under the table. "You should know that he's amazing at a lot more than baseball. Like connecting with anyone and everyone, making kids feel special, taking care of the people he loves, remembering minute details about people's lives—there's a lot more to him than just the baseball Wizard."

Her sweet smile curves as she looks at me with shining eyes. My heart is choked up by her affirmation and praise. I lean over to kiss her on the cheek, barely containing myself from landing the kiss squarely on her lips instead.

Conversation continues, but a piece of my mind keeps circling around Danae's observation. The qualities she sees in me. I'm used to variations of the exact conversation I'm having with Ron and Kara tonight—conversations revolving around my identity as a professional baseball player. I'm not accustomed to hearing praise about anything else I do.

It only makes me fall for Danae a little further, a little harder than I already was.

CHAPTER TWENTY-SIX

Griffin

When's the last time you talked with your parents?

Going straight for the kill today, huh?

Opening myself up to an equally devastating question. But you can divert to something more lighthearted if you wish.

Thanksgiving. Our interactions have been mostly limited to tense holidays for several years now. I let them know that I was going to be adopting Jason. Needless to say, they did not approve.

Why wouldn't they approve of you providing love and support to a little boy who needed it? Who you already knew and loved?

A single mother of a "troubled" child isn't exactly marriage material to wealthy, eligible bachelors.

In their minds, I was further ruining my prospects. Or their prospects for me, I guess I should say.

ME

So they haven't met Jason, I assume?

DANAE

No. I've danced around explaining why to him.

ME

Their loss.

Ok, hit me with your best shot.

DANAE

How much flexibility do you have in your training and game schedule? If something comes up and I need you, how likely are you to be available?

ME

The ugly truth or the glossy truth?

DANAE

The TRUTH truth. I need to know what I'm setting myself up for.

After a minute of the text bubbles of Danae's response starting and stopping, they ultimately stop. I run a hand over my beard, worried that I was *too* honest. I send a follow-up text when I can't take the silence any longer.

Normally, I'm chomping at the bit to leave for spring training and dive into the excitement of the upcoming season. Excited to see friends from other teams I haven't seen in a few months. Ready for the hype of interactions with fans who fly in for games, hoping for autographs. Happy to spend quality time with my teammates and skip out on the end of winter in Kansas.

This year, I'm counting down the days with a degree of dread mixed into the excitement. And not only because of the constant anxiety of proving that I'm "back" from my injury. It's also because of who I'm leaving behind.

When Danae asked me last Saturday about the flexibility of my schedule, I could sense something deeper behind the question. Once I made it to her house, she filled me in on another minor explosion that Jason had the night before. He didn't physically destroy anything this time, but I know it's destroying Danae's heart to see him hurting so much and not being able to fix it. A feeling I identify with. I wish the embrace of my arms could be enough to fix everything for *her*, to reassure her that she's doing an amazing job, that things are going to be okay. But her defeated demeanor for the remainder of the day let me know that my arms weren't enough.

We had a few tense moments that day discussing the reality of the months ahead of us. I had to run a lot of interference for Danae's poor fingernails. Although I was able to drop everything and go to her house that morning, in just a few days, I'll be in Arizona for six weeks, followed by six months of games almost daily.

I don't know how to prove to her that I'm there for her and Jason when I honestly don't know how *there* I can be. I haven't navigated a serious relationship during baseball season.

Let's be honest—I haven't navigated a *serious* relationship, period.

Which makes me even more anxious about being so far away from her for so long.

Unfortunately, this week has been packed with final agenda items and endorsement appointments that have to happen before I leave town. I've had to make do with daily text message conversations instead of seeing Danae in person, which is not an adequate replacement. I'm more eager than ever to see her tonight. Hold her hand. Run my fingers through her hair. Kiss her. All the things I'll be missing out on for six weeks.

Drew and Lily are hosting a team dinner at their house tonight so everyone can finally meet Danae. At least she's confident enough in our relationship to spend a night socializing with my teammates and their wives and girlfriends.

Then again, it's possible I haven't accurately prepared her for exactly what that will entail.

Normally, Sam would tag along to a gathering like this, but she was more than willing to stay with Jason so that Danae could accompany me. Sam's been doing everything in her power to keep Danae around, and I'm not arguing with her meddling in this case. I'll take any assist I can get to keep Danae in my life.

When we arrive at Danae's townhouse, Sam immediately surprises Jason with the new *Harry Potter* Lego set we brought for him. He whoops and goes running to the dining table to start building. Danae smiles at him and then turns a nervous smile to me.

"Am I dressed okay?" she asks, looking down at the cream sweater, black skirt, and black tights she's wearing. "I wasn't sure how to dress for tonight, so I googled 'baseball wives and girlfriends,' and I should not have done that. My entire wardrobe is spread out across my bed, and I'm still afraid I chose the wrong outfit."

I loop a hand around her waist, pressing the small of her back to move her closer to me. "You look beautiful. You could have worn sweats and a hoodie tonight, and I still would have proudly shown you off to everyone. Because *you* are amazing. And gorgeous."

Leaning in, I press a gentle kiss to her lips, resisting the overwhelming urge to deepen it into something more. Drawing back, there are still lines of worry around her eyes.

"But is this outfit okay?"

I can't help but chuckle. "It's perfect. You'll fit right in. The other gals are going to love you, and the guys are all dying to meet you," I say, which only serves to deepen her worry lines. I snatch her hands in mine before she can pick at the glossy nail polish. "Everyone there tonight already knows about your situation with Jason, and they know not to ask you tons of questions about it. These guys are like my brothers—they know I'll beat them up if they mess with my girl," I say before pressing a kiss to her knuckles.

She finally cracks a smile, and I inwardly pump my fist in victory. "I am excited to put faces and personalities with the names you talk about," she says. She puffs a determined exhale. "Let's go."

When we arrive, Lily is there to immediately wrap Danae in a welcoming hug. "It's so great to meet you! Griffin has been pretty tight-lipped about your relationship, but you've brought out this whole new smitten side of him we've never seen before. I'm excited to get to know you—oh, and I'm Lily. I'm married to Drew, the first baseman. Let me introduce you to the other ladies here."

Lily starts to usher Danae toward the kitchen, but I follow closely so the security blanket of my presence isn't ripped away too abruptly. I brush one finger down the side of Danae's hand, reminding her that I'm here as she faces the waiting crowd. She grabs at my hand, clutching it as Lily announces her arrival to the eager group.

I should have been a little more specific with everyone beforehand about *not* scaring Danae away.

Amy, Carlos' fiancée, steps forward to introduce herself, followed by the other three ladies here. Adrian swoops in with an enthusiastic hug, and Danae looks genuinely relieved to see another semi-familiar face. All of the starting position players are here, plus one of our pitchers, bringing the total to fourteen people, aside from Danae and me. Maybe throwing her into the deep end like this wasn't the best idea—then again, this *is* my world, my circle of people. If we're going to last, she needs to know my world.

By the end of the night, Danae's smile is coming easily. The other WAGs have freely shared experiences and tips for staying connected with their men during baseball season, a ploy I did not even put them up to. I hope it's helped ease Danae's mind somewhat about our impending separation.

The guys, for their part, do all they can to embarrass me in front of Danae. Little do they know, I'd cough up endless embarrassing stories so long as she keeps laughing and looking at me with that twinkle in her eye each time.

As the night winds down, we say our goodbyes. Danae looks entirely comfortable as she gives hugs to the ladies (and Adrian). "Thanks so much for hosting tonight," she says to Lily as we linger in the foyer. "It was really nice to meet everyone."

"Will I see you at spring training at all?" Lily asks, and Danae looks over to me.

"People are allowed at spring training?" Danae asks. I'm not sure how I fell for a woman who knows nothing about baseball.

I've absolutely fallen for this woman. The realization hits me like a line drive straight to the glove. I cover up my thoughts with a smile and tell her, "Yes, we actually play around thirty games during spring training that fans can come and watch. The starters usually don't play much at the beginning since the team is feeling out which backup guys they're going to keep on the roster. I was hoping I could maybe fly you and Jason out over part of your spring break, if you'd be open to it."

"If you do come, I'll show you all the ropes," Lily adds. "I'll get your number from Griffin and text you so you have mine."

On the drive back to Danae's place, she asks, "You'd really want us to come out to spring training?"

I glance over at her and respond, "Of course, I would. I mean, I'd beg you to fly out there for the entire six weeks if you didn't have that pesky job." Danae snickers, and I reach a hand over to hold hers. "I'll pay for the tickets for both of you, a hotel room, everything. I'm going to be dying to see you by then."

"Could you find a place to pull over for a minute?" Danae asks.

Concerned that she might be car sick, I pull off on the next exit, even though there are no gas stations or restaurants to park at. I pull to the side of the road and put on my hazard lights. "Are you okay? Are you feeling sick?" I ask, pivoting to face her. She looks fine.

"No, I'm not sick," Danae says. She tilts her head to one side, studying me. "It's just that this is the last time we'll be alone before you leave, since we're doing dinner together with Jason tomorrow."

Danae leans closer to me, raising the temperature of the blood in my veins. The temperature reaches a boiling point when she runs her fingers along my beard. "If this is the last time I get to be alone with you, I wanted to do this."

She places a gentle, tantalizing kiss to my lips before drawing back enough to search my eyes. When her lips meet mine again, it's desperate and pleading, matching the hungry passion in my kiss, in my grip on her waist, her neck, her face.

When I feel moisture on her cheek, I lean back to search for the source. Tears pour from her eyes. "*Shhh*, it's okay. What's wrong?"

Her voice cracks as she says, "I really don't want you to leave."

I pull her head to rest in the crook of my neck, clutching her to me like she'll disappear if I lose contact. "I know. I don't want to leave you either."

"I'm scared, Griff. Scared that I let myself get close to you only for you to be gone," she whispers, clutching a fistful of my shirt.

"But I'm coming back. I'm not gone forever," I try to reassure her. I reach a hand up into her hair to scratch her scalp.

Her voice is thick as she says, "I know it's not that long, but what if I can't handle it? The time apart? Things with Jason are so overwhelming sometimes, and I don't know if I can bear the emotional burden of being away from you on top of it. We've only known each other for six weeks, but I . . . I get so anxious every time I think about not seeing you. Which is ridiculous. I should be able to handle it. I shouldn't be breaking out in cold sweats when I think about a guy I've known less than two months not being around for a few weeks. I'm being—"

"Danae," I cut in, hoping to break the thought spiral she's having. "I get a pit in my stomach every time I think about leaving you. I get this buildup of anxious energy when I think about not seeing you for six weeks too. When I think about not being able to hop in my car and drive to your house to help if Jason has another bad day. I don't want to handle the time apart either. It's not only you feeling this way."

She sighs, and her breath warms my neck. I'm scanning my memory for everything I've learned about Danae, trying to think of how to help her feel better in this moment. "Hey, why don't we make a list of all the ways we're going to cope with the time apart?"

Danae sniffs, still clinging to me. The sensation of her so tightly holding me—not wanting to let go—is spellbinding. As much as I don't want to break the spell (or the physical contact), I do want her to end the night feeling more confident. I continue, "I don't have any legal pads handy, but we can use the notes app on your phone. Let's write down all the things the other WAGs told you tonight about how they handle the time apart, and we can come up with some of our own ideas."

She nods against my chest before sitting up. Cold air rushes in to fill the void of her warmth nuzzled into my neck, a stark reminder of what lies ahead of us. My chest seizes as I get choked up at the thought, but I will it away while Danae is distracted retrieving her phone from her purse. *You're supposed to be the strong support right now. Not the one falling apart.*

As Danae pulls up a blank note on her phone, we start listing out the suggestions that Lily and the other women gave her tonight. Some of the advice included daily text messages, video calls, and a trip in person if possible.

"Amy mentioned she focuses on a hobby she doesn't usually have time for to keep herself distracted and busy. I'm not sure how applicable that is for me. I'll still have teaching and Jason and everything about regular daily life," Danae says, sounding defeated.

"Sam will still be here in KC for the majority of the time," I say. "I guarantee you she still wants to babysit so you can go to book club. Maybe even join a second book club."

A smile cracks through on Danae's face. "Two book clubs, huh?"

"All the book clubs you want, babe," I say, and her eyes flicker at the term of endearment that slipped out. Her smile grows wider.

"The other day, I was talking to Kara and called you Griff. She totally freaked out that I shortened your name—she would lose it completely if I called you 'babe.'"

I reach over to run a strand of Danae's hair between my fingers. "I did internally freak out a little when you just called me 'Griff' a minute ago. And I also might lose it completely if you called me 'babe.'"

Danae lowers her gaze with a bashful smile. A smile that begs me to cover her lips with mine, but I'm trying to stay focused on our list.

"Video and phone calls would be great, but what about when our schedules don't align? What if that happens a lot, and we're left to rely on only text messages? You know my tendency to overanalyze text messages. And I don't want our main communication to be a point of frustration for you with your dyslexia," Danae says.

"No form of communication with you is going to frustrate me. I know you have listening ears around and can't always listen to voice memos. I've spent years learning to manage my dyslexia and text messages—you don't need to worry about me," I say.

Danae nods. "Okay, if you're sure. And . . . I would like to come out over spring break, if you're serious about that."

"Deadly serious," I say. "Tell me the dates you can come, and I'll arrange everything."

She gives me a coy look when she responds, "You mean Samantha will arrange everything?"

I reward her flirtation with another sound kiss, but I'm careful not to get totally lost in it. Breaking away, I ask, "You feel a little better now that we have a list and a plan?"

Danae sighs. "I guess so. I still just . . . wish you weren't leaving. Not when things are so hard with Jason. Not when things are really clicking between us. Right when I'm fal—" she cuts herself off and takes a deep breath. "I wish we didn't have to say goodbye."

I can't make any promises about how hard or easy the next six weeks are going to be. She doesn't need any platitudes about how well she'll handle things with Jason on her own. So I give her the only promise I can.

"I'm coming back to you, Danae."

CHAPTER TWENTY-SEVEN

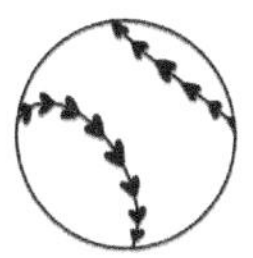

Danae

Where's your ideal place to sit and read?

You mean everyday location or dream locale?

Both.

Everyday would be at one of the nearby parks when the temperature is perfect. Dream would be sitting by the fireplace of a ski lodge in the mountains.

You mean after a full day of skiing? <winking emoji>

Do you even know me at all?

So we're going to a ski lodge but not going skiing?

ME

You're welcome to go skiing. You could even take Jason. I will sit by the fireplace with my book.

GRIFFIN

Yeah my coaches would kill me if I went skiing. They don't appreciate us doing any injury-prone activities.

ME

Looks like you'll sit by the fireplace and read with me then.

GRIFFIN

I'll just watch you while you read.

ME

You can't watch me if I'm snuggled up in the crook of your arm while I'm reading.

GRIFFIN

I can get on board with this dream.

ME

What's your favorite city to travel to during the season?

GRIFFIN

Ooo that's a tough one. Probably Baltimore, but that's mostly because one of my buddies from college plays there. We always try to catch up somehow when we're in each other's cities.

ME

I haven't traveled to the northeast before. My mom always preferred beaches, so we never went north for vacations growing up.

GRIFFIN

So we'll hit up Baltimore on our way to the ski lodge in Vermont this winter. Sounds good to me.

Closing myself in the staff restroom, I take a deep breath, willing myself not to cry. Griffin has been gone for two weeks now, and although that means I'm two weeks closer to seeing him again, it's been two of the hardest weeks of my life.

Jason has been struggling more than ever, which means I'm doubting myself more than ever. I know he's having an equally hard time with Griffin's sudden absence, considering how quickly he'd become a regular fixture in our life.

Last week, we got together for lunch with Cathy, his grandma, for her birthday. On the one hand, it was really good to see her, to continue that connection for Jason, and for her to see us doing well. I know she loves and cares about Jason, even if she didn't feel equipped to raise him. But his angry reactions were off the charts at school and at home for the three days following our visit, complete with another destructive outburst smashing all of his Lego sets. At least those can be rebuilt . . . I'm not sure how much of my confidence in myself as a mother can be repaired.

To top it all off, Jason's huge blow-up happened on a day that Griffin was completely unavailable. I talked things through with Kara, who encouraged me to also talk to Samantha. I didn't want to burden her when I know her own troubled childhood is probably difficult to relive. But when she came to babysit while I went to book club, she could immediately tell things were off. She stuck around after Jason went to bed, and I unloaded the whole story on her. Samantha listened intently and encouraged me to find a therapist who specializes in working with adoptees and children who have experienced trauma. She even helped me find some options, and after calling around, I found a therapist who was able to get us in this week.

I already did a telehealth meeting with her yesterday to give her information about Jason's background and current behavior challenges. We're leaving school a half hour early today to meet with her in person for the first time, and I'll have a debrief with her alone tomorrow.

I'm overwhelmed. I've wondered more than once what it would be like to have loving parents lending their support in this journey. I'm beyond grateful for Samantha's understanding, for Kara's encouragement, and for the support of all my coworkers and friends. Simultaneously, my heart aches with the deep void of Griffin's absence in the midst of such an emotionally and mentally challenging time.

And I'm ticked off at myself that I would be thrown for this much of a loop missing a man I've known less than two whole months.

Now here I am, crying in the staff bathroom right before the library is about to fill up with twenty third graders. And all I want is to burrow myself against Griffin's strong chest. To feel his arms fold around me. To drown in the spicy scent of his cologne. To have his hands wrapped around mine, stopping me from picking off my nail polish. He was the only one who seemed able to subdue that anxious habit.

I blow my nose, wash my hands, and pat a wet paper towel under my eyes. *Pull yourself together, Danae,* I lecture my reflection. *You're a grown-up, not a lovesick teenager. Start acting like it.*

"Jason, it's been so nice getting to know you a little bit this afternoon," Miss Jessica says. We spent the first thirty minutes of the therapy session getting acquainted while Jason played with water beads. "Before you go home today, could we do a little puppet show?" she asks.

Jason responds with enthusiasm, so she pulls out a basket filled with puppet animals. Miss Jessica says, "These puppets help me explain some of the things that go on inside our brains, some of the things that I'm going to help you with while you're here. Can you put this puppy on your hand?"

He slips his hand into the puppet and immediately starts barking. Miss Jessica continues speaking in her soothing tone of voice. "You are *very* good at making dog sounds! Do you know that we all have lots of different animals inside our brains?"

Jason's eyes grow wide. "I have animals in my brain?"

Miss Jessica smiles, "Okay, we don't *really* have animals in our brains. But different parts of our brain act in different ways, a lot like how different types of animals act." She holds up her hand, which is now covered by an owl puppet. "We all have something called the prefrontal cortex toward the front part of our brain," she says, tapping Jason's forehead.

"A what?" he asks, face screwed up in confusion.

"I know, it's a fancy word, huh? That's why I like to use the animals," Miss Jessica says. "That part of our brain is like this wise old owl. When the wise old owl is here in our brains, we can make good decisions, we can pay attention and solve problems, and we can regulate the emotions we're feeling." I'm watching her puppet show with rapt attention, positive that I'm learning more than Jason is.

"But we also all have part of our brain that's like your watchdog there," Miss Jessica continues. "When the watchdog thinks we might be in danger, he barks to sound the alarm." She points at Jason, who barks and growls aggressively. "Exactly! The watchdog is trying to keep you safe, so he lets you know if he thinks you're going to get hurt, whether that's physically or emotionally. And if the watchdog doesn't calm down and stop barking, he scares away the wise old owl." Miss Jessica flaps the owl puppet's wings and flies it away behind her.

"Now, when the wise old owl leaves, there are different animals that might take its place. Some people have the same animal all the time, and other people might have a different animal depending on how they're feeling that day. One of the options is the porcupine," she says, pulling out a porcupine puppet. "The porcupine raises its spikes, ready to fight the danger. It wants to keep you safe, so it's ready to get into a fight in order to do that. Have you felt that way sometimes? I know I have."

"Yeah, I do think I have a porcupine in my brain sometimes," Jason answers.

"But sometimes it's not a porcupine that answers the watchdog's alert. Sometimes the bird pops up, and it flies away to try to run from the danger. Other times, we have a turtle that takes over. It freezes and draws inside its shell to try to hide from the danger because it doesn't know what to do. Do those animals make sense?" Miss Jessica asks, as she lays each puppet out in front of Jason.

"Uh-huh," he says. "Which animal is the best one?"

"Well, there's not a good or bad animal," Miss Jessica responds. Even though *I'd* like to point out that the fighting porcupine seems less than ideal. She continues, "All of the animals are there trying to protect you. But sometimes, those animals can make us act in ways that might be harmful to ourselves and others, so we have to learn how to calm down the animals when that happens. Once we can get wise old owl to come back, then we can make better choices with our words and actions. So we're going to work on some strategies to help you be able to tell when your watchdog is barking, how to tell if you're *really* in danger, and how to get wise old owl to come back faster. Does that sound like a good plan?"

"Yeah!" Jason says. "Can we play with water beads again too?"

Miss Jessica leans forward like she's whispering a secret. "We have *lots* of fun things to play with. We have water beads, shaving cream, and a whole room full of sensory toys like a swing and a trampoline. We'll play with different things each time until we figure out your favorites."

"Awesome!" Jason yells.

"Our time is up for today, but I can't wait to see you again, Jason," Miss Jessica says.

I clutch the bottle of water in my hand, trying to ground myself. I took the whole afternoon off today so that I could meet with Jessica privately to discuss her perspective on Jason's needs. She's spent the first twenty minutes explaining the science behind how trauma wires a child's brain, even beginning in utero with heightened cortisol if the mother has a stressful pregnancy. She's explaining all the scientific reasons that Jason's brain is so quick to react to perceived threats and slow to regulate his emotions.

The amount of information feels paralyzing.

I'm incredibly grateful to understand the physical realities of Jason's brain chemistry contributing to the behaviors and outbursts. But understanding certainly doesn't "fix" it. And it only makes me grieve all the more for what that sweet boy has been through. That he'll forever deal with the effects of neural connections that weren't his fault. I want to take it all away—love it all away—but I'm overwhelmed by how *not that simple* this all is.

"There are a variety of strategies that we can use to help Jason learn to regulate what he's feeling. Remember—we all learn to self-regulate through co-regulation," Jessica explains. "That's typically provided by birth parents responding to a baby's cries and soothing them. But if Jason missed out on that period of co-regulation—which it sounds like he did—then he's never been taught to regulate. That's going to come from you, now. When Jason has these angry outbursts, you need to switch your brain from looking at it as 'my child is destroying things in anger' to 'my baby is crying.'"

I sigh as I process what she's saying. "That sounds easier said than done."

"It's one hundred percent easier said than done," she replies with a supportive laugh. "It's really hard to regulate your own emotional response when you have a kid violently tearing things apart in front of you."

"That's something else I don't understand," I say. "It's not like he's destroying things he doesn't like. Or even things that are mine. The posters, especially, but also the Lego sets—those are his prized possessions. Why would he destroy the things he cares most about? There's no logic to that at all."

Jessica hums. "Well, first of all, it's important to remember that when Jason is having these outbursts, his wise old owl brain has flown away. So his actions and words are not going to make logical sense. But I could see a handful of underlying feelings that could be causing him to destroy things he cares about. Children who have been through trauma and abandonment almost always have a lifelong struggle with shame from feeling like they weren't good enough for their parents to care for them. They feel unworthy of love. They're often convinced that there's something deeply wrong with *them*, rather than the adult figure, even if they don't consciously realize it."

My heart clenches thinking about Jason feeling that way.

"One explanation could be that deep down, Jason thinks he doesn't deserve to have those special things because he's a bad kid. He *must* be a bad kid if his parents and grandmother left him. So he has an urge to destroy those good things when his 'bad behavior' is discovered," she says, miming air quotes. "It's also possible that he could be subconsciously testing you, seeing how you will respond to him destroying something special. Whether you will continue to care for him or if you will also leave. Or, he may have seen destructive behavior modeled by his father when he was upset. It will likely take a while before Jason is able to recognize what the thoughts and emotions are underneath his actions."

Teary-eyed, I blow out a long breath. "And in the meantime? How do I support him and help him get to that point of understanding?"

"Like I said, there are a variety of tools available that we can add to Jason's toolbox," Jessica says. "Of course, we will continue talking and doing some hands-on sensory play. But we can also explore neurofeedback therapy that helps him learn to soothe his brain activity. EMDR therapy is also a very effective tool to help process the stress of traumatic memories. Medications could be an option. We'll take it slow—as I get to know him better, I'll give you my thoughts on what might be most effective, so this isn't something you need to decide right now."

Well, I know what all of my Google searches tonight will be.

"There is one tool that I think could be very critical for him to start immediately, though, and that's working with the occupational therapist here at our practice. In order for Jason to be able to regulate his feelings, he first needs to be able to identify *what* his body is feeling. Our OT specializes in helping kids connect with what's happening in their bodies when they experience certain emotions. I think he could really benefit from working with her in addition to seeing me," Jessica explains.

"Okay," I say, mind reeling to process all this information. "I hate to even ask this, but on a practical note, I need to know what I'm looking at financially to get him the help he needs. So I can make a plan."

Jessica gives a gentle grimace. "I can tell you it won't be cheap. While Jason is still in foster care, some sessions will be covered by his insurance. But once the adoption is finalized, your medical insurance doesn't provide coverage for the talk therapy or this particular type of occupational therapy. It will be out of pocket, but we can work with you on payment plans and possibly staggering weeks with me and OT. I'll email you some concrete numbers after I talk with our OT."

My heart sinks. Of course, I want to roll out the red carpet for anything that would help Jason to work through the trauma he carries with him. But, as a single mom on a teacher's salary, still paying off student loans and living in an area where rent is *not* cheap . . . I'm afraid to find out what dollar amounts I'm looking at.

Jessica must see my inner turmoil. She reaches a hand over to pat mine. "I know this is a lot to take in. Not just financially, but emotionally and mentally. The fact that you're here exploring these options is proof of how much you love Jason. And remember that even though your love for him isn't enough to fix what's happened in his brain wiring, it's not nothing. Your day-in and day-out expressions of love for him are going to be a huge piece of the healing puzzle. Even if we don't see the immediate results we wish could be possible, you *can* help to rewire those neurological connections for him. Over time, you can help his brain learn that he is safe, that he is wanted. Your love is a powerful thing."

"Thank you," I murmur, vision still blurry from tears.

"Make sure you have a good network of people you can lean on for support through this," Jessica says. "You're going to need others holding you up as we work through this with Jason. We have a long road ahead of us."

When I leave Jessica's office, I sit silently in my car, processing. Although, processing is probably too productive of a word to describe what's happening in my brain. The thought factory, as Griffin loves to call it, is not churning out functional thoughts. It's a muddled mess—an overloaded machine on the verge of breakdown.

I press my palms over my eyes, trying to suppress the tears. I'm overcome by the longing to feel Griffin's arms around me, to press my ear to his chest and listen to his heartbeat. When did his embrace become *my* preferred form of regulation?

Focus, Danae. You can't help Jason if your thoughts are constantly pining after Griffin.

Sighing, I close my eyes and lean back against the headrest. A few moments later, my lap is covered with tiny flecks of clear nail polish.

I call Griffin.

Chapter Twenty-Eight

Griffin

"Yes! That's the way to do it!" I yell as Adrian hollers next to me. One of our new outfielders from the farm team managed to hit a home run, bringing in a runner on first for a two-run hit. He'll be a great backup player on the bench, assuming the coaching staff chooses to keep him for the season. After his performance today, I don't know why they wouldn't.

As the guys run into the dugout, Adrian and I are there giving celebratory back slaps and jumping shoulder bumps. We always make a big show of celebrating the runs and good plays during spring training games. It's partially to boost the morale of the players who are here working hard for their shot at the big leagues. And also partially to distract us from the boredom of not getting to be the ones out there playing.

Adrian's always pushing the boundaries of rambunctious behavior, hamming it up for the cameras he knows are watching. As his best friend, I play right along with him. He makes it easy to get swept up in the fun, and Joe never complains about the extra PR attention that comes from all of the YouTube views.

"You're gonna need to work on your dance moves for some new celebrations this season," Adrian tells me.

"I don't know what you're talking about—I have plenty of moves. You'd better focus on your baseball moves so you have something to celebrate over," I rib him back.

Our team goes on a run in the seventh inning, stretching our lead to 9–2, which we hold through the end of the game. Spirits are high in the locker room as we recount the highlights.

"How's the shoulder?" Adrian asks after we've showered and changed. It was bothering me this morning during practice after I pushed it a little too hard in the training room yesterday.

"It's fine now," I answer. He raises an eyebrow. "I'm serious—it really feels fine now. The trainers worked their magic, and it's good as new."

He gives me a hearty slap on the back, near my shoulder, as if watching to see if I'd flinch. I fake sucker punch him in the gut in response. "Watch it, Ortiz. I'll report you to the trainers for screwing up my shoulder if it hurts again tomorrow."

Pulling my bag out of my locker, I check my phone. My heart plummets to my stomach when I see I have four missed calls from Danae, spread out across the past two hours. Today was an afternoon game, which means she was calling while school was in session. There are no texts from her explaining her reason for calling.

I break out in a cold sweat.

"Hey, I've gotta go call Danae," I tell Adrian.

"Uh-oh, what's wrong?" he asks.

"I don't know yet. But she called me four times during school hours. Something must be wrong," I reply, already walking toward the doors. "I'll catch you at the condo."

Once outside, I try to give a semi-sincere smile to the fans who have lingered hoping to catch sight of players as we leave. Normally, I'd pause to sign a few autographs and take photos with kids. Right now, talking to Danae is all I can think about. She's an hour ahead, so school is officially over for the day.

Quickly making it to the privacy of my rental car, I dial Danae's number, hoping she'll answer. My heart sinks even further when she doesn't. We'd exchanged our usual morning texts today, but I was a little shorter with the conversation since I had to have the training staff look at my shoulder before practice. Still, she'd given no indication that anything was wrong.

I dial her again, wondering if she didn't hear it ring the first time. No answer.

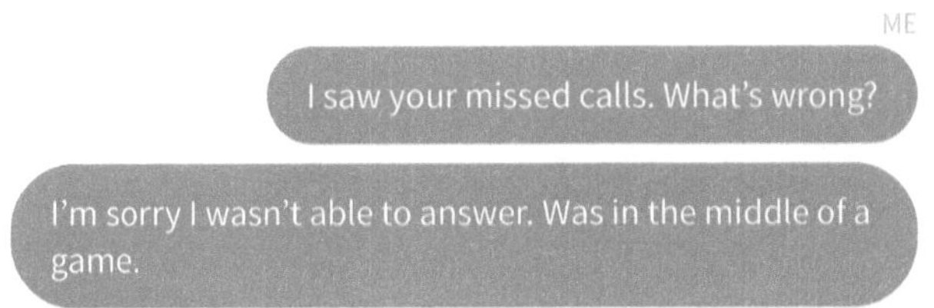

After excruciating silence that stretches for what seems like an eternity (although it was likely only a minute), I decide to text Sam. She leaves tomorrow morning to come to Arizona for a few days, but she's still in KC for the night.

I'll let you know if I hear anything. And let me know once you hear something.

I debate whether to drive to the condo Adrian and I are sharing or wait here longer to see if she'll call back. Finally, I get a text from her.

I'll have to call you later after Jason is in bed.

Is everything ok?

I'll call you later.

I have no secondary cues to go off of—no facial expressions, no body language, no tone of voice—only the written words of her text. But I don't need any secondary information to sense the disappointment, the hurt behind Danae's message.

Clearly, something is *wrong*. And I wasn't available when she needed me.

This scenario is my worst nightmare, precisely because it's *her* worst nightmare. The number one fear she vocalized about our relationship is playing out in real time, and there's nothing I can do to change it. I can't have my cell phone in the dugout. And even if I could, I can't up and leave in the middle of a game. I certainly can't hop on an airplane back to Kansas before spring training ends.

Is this going to be the straw that breaks everything apart for Danae? Is she going to realize she can't be with a professional athlete? Can't be with me? This is who I am—what if that's not enough for her? Too much for her?

I text Sam to let her know that Danae's going to call me tonight. Then I head to the condo to pace my room for the next three hours.

I stare at Danae's tear-streaked cheeks on my phone screen, wishing I could be there in person to take her into my arms. To kiss the tears away.

She filled me in on everything she talked about with Jason's new therapist, and it's no wonder she tried to call four times. It's a lot of information to process—a heavy load to carry. I hate that I wasn't available to help her carry it right away.

In all of our conversations over the past few days, Danae never mentioned that they were going to meet with this therapist for the first time. Apparently, she wanted to fill me in afterward, thinking that she could handle it on her own without burdening me. I wish I had known that she was walking into this, so I could have tried to think of a way to support her. I know that therapy sessions with Sam and Ian weren't easy experiences for my parents.

Her screen tips to the ceiling briefly while I hear the sound of her blowing her nose. Danae didn't want to video call, probably for this reason, but I insisted I wanted to be able to see her face. When she picks it back up, she leans her head against the pillows on her bed, looking exhausted.

More than exhausted. Utterly defeated.

I want to crawl through the phone screen and lay down next to her, wrap my body around hers. Protect her from the heaviness. Hold her so she knows she's not alone in this.

But I can't. I won't see her for almost three more weeks.

I can see in her eyes the shadow of what she hasn't openly addressed yet. The disappointment of me not answering the phone when she'd tried to call after meeting with the therapist. I decide I should be the one to face it head-on.

"I know it had to feel extremely frustrating that I couldn't answer when you called today. I'm sorry that you felt alone coming out of such a hard meeting," I say.

I know I hit the mark when fresh tears well up in her eyes. Even through the video, I can see the quiver of her chin as she fights against the emotions. She presses her thumb and a finger to her eyes, then wipes her cheeks.

"You had a game. I looked it up. I know that's why you didn't answer," she says, voice small. "You're doing your job."

I can see her fighting to maintain her composure. Fighting to rationalize away the frustration and even anger. It's written all over her face, her demeanor.

"I really hate this, babe," I say. I'd hoped the term of endearment might reel her in to me a little bit, but her eyes bounce away from the screen to the ceiling.

"I wish I could be there to hold you right now. To help you navigate this with Jason," I say. "You have to know I would be there in a millisecond if I could."

Danae purses her lips. "Yeah, well, you can't." Her chin quivers again. "And it's his birthday in a couple of days, and I already know that's going to be a whole minefield of potential explosions for him. Especially with—" she breaks off, wiping her eyes again before exhaling deeply. "Especially with you not being here. He got too used to having you around. It's been hard for him to not see you."

I didn't think it was possible, but my heart manages to sink even deeper. Below ground level. "Danae, I'm sorry. I don't know how to fix this."

She shrugs and sits forward on the bed, as though trying to brush this off and pull herself together.

"There's no fixing it. It's not your fault—this is your job. There's nothing you can do about it. This is what it is," she says, tone resigned.

"Danae," I say with an edge of pleading. Her eyes aren't meeting mine through the screen. "Please look at me." She sighs but moves her phone to make eye contact. "Please stay with me. We need to figure out some ways to cope with situations like this. We *will* figure it out. Please don't give up on us."

Her quivering chin stops as she fully gives in to the sobs, covering her eyes with one hand. It's then I notice that her fingernails are much shorter than usual, picked off below her fingertips. What I wouldn't give to take that hand in mine, to do anything to take her pain and transfer it to my heart instead of hers.

"What's the thought factory churning out?" I ask, and Danae gives a choked laugh.

"That I hate how much I want you here with me. That I hate how it hurts so badly not having you here, but ending things wouldn't fix it because it hurts even more to think about never seeing you again." She pauses briefly to throw a hand up in the air. "That I hate baseball even more now. That I hate feeling overwhelmed by helping Jason because I'm the adult and should be able to handle this better. That I hate that Jason has to learn to rewire his brain because the people who were supposed to take care of him and love him didn't, and that just *sucks.* That I hate how I can relate to him by feeling like I wasn't enough to be loved by my parents. That I hate everything about everything in this situation," she says, voice strained from sobs.

"I just miss you," she adds, blowing out a breath. "It's ridiculous that I lived thirty-one years of my life without you, but then knowing you for eight weeks suddenly has me falling apart when you're not around. It physically hurts to be so far away from you. I hate it."

"Well, I don't hate it," I murmur, and she spears me with a look. I smile as warmly as I can through the screen. "I *do* hate that I'm not there physically with you. And of course I hate everything Jason's been through, everything you've been through. I hate how overwhelming all of this is—and it *is* overwhelming. You shouldn't feel guilty for being overwhelmed," I say, and she inhales slowly. "But I don't hate that you want me around. I kinda love that."

I've managed to coax a smile out of her with those words, and I'm taking every small victory at this point. "I can change your flights to get you here the first day of spring break so we can see each other two days sooner."

Danae sighs. "Tempting. But I promised Jason he could go to a birthday party for a friend from school that weekend and that we'd go to the zoo."

"I bet there's a zoo here. I could find some kid's birthday party for him," I joke. Now the smile spreads fully across her cheeks, erasing the sorrow lines.

"It will be okay. We'll be okay," she says.

"Will you really? Are we really okay?" I ask.

"Yes," she replies. "We're okay. I'm sorry I got so upset earlier. There was nothing to disrupt the overdrive cycle of the thought factory, and I completely overreacted. That was unfair to you."

"Nope, no apologizing for that," I cut in. "You're allowed to feel the feelings. This isn't an ideal situation, especially for a new relationship, and you don't need to pretend like it is. It sucks. End of story."

"Speaking of stories, how's the audiobook coming along?" Danae asks.

I groan. "Sly change of subject there, babe. I'm gonna give it to you, though, since you had a rough day." She fights a smile, and what I wouldn't give to kiss those lips right now. "I'm trying. I swear I am. But I'm only on, like, chapter three or something. I can't multitask while I'm listening, so I haven't had a lot of time to listen."

When she quirks a knowing eyebrow, I add, "And I still don't really enjoy it. But I'm trying it. For you."

"And for Jason," she adds, eyes twinkling. "He'll be so excited when you finally know who Ron, Hermione, and Draco are."

Covering my eyes with one hand, I pretend to grimace but then grin and run my hand back through my hair. "I'll give it my best effort. No promises." Staring into her eyes, I cup the phone in my hand as though I was cupping her face. "I really wish I could kiss you right now. Just so you know."

Danae kisses her fingertip and then places it over the camera briefly. I mimic the gesture and sigh. "Nothing like the real deal, but that'll do for now. I'll talk to you tomorrow, okay?"

After we hang up, I quickly video call Sam.

"So what's the situation?" Sam asks, forgoing a greeting altogether.

After I fill her in on the basics of what Danae shared with me, I say, "Hey, I need you to stay there in KC. I'll cancel your flight."

"You mean I'll cancel my flight," she says with an eye roll. "Why?"

"Jason's birthday is in a couple of days, and I'm not gonna be there," I say.

Sam clucks her tongue. "Yeah, that sucks."

"Exactly," I say. "Danae said she's having a small party for him with a few friends from school, but I need you to take a present over there and say hi in my place."

"You know Joe is gonna throw a hissy-fit when I'm not at the meeting tomorrow to sync schedules for the season? Not that I'm complaining about getting to annoy Joe," Sam says.

"I'll take care of Joe. You take care of Danae and Jason," I respond.

"What present am I getting?" she asks.

I smile. "I'll tell you exactly where to go and what to get."

CHAPTER TWENTY-NINE

Danae

GRIFFIN

Happy birthday to Jason! Give him the biggest birthday high five from me.

ME

Thanks! Will do.

GRIFFIN

What are the big plans for the day?

ME

Just what I told you about already. Having a few of his friends from school over from 6:00-7:30 p.m. for pizza and games. He's so excited for his first party.

GRIFFIN

Wish I could be there with you guys.

ME

Me too.

GRIFFIN

What's your favorite flavor of ice cream?

ME

Ooo, there's this local ice cream place that has a flavor called Maddy's Mud. It's coffee ice cream with brownies, Oreos, and fudge swirl mixed in.

GRIFFIN

That sounds rich.

ME

The coffee ice cream balances out the sweetness. It's perfection.

Ok, same question to you today.

GRIFFIN

Strawberry.

ME

Plain strawberry?

GRIFFIN

Yep.

ME

Boring.

GRIFFIN

It's a classic. I'm a classy guy.

ME

Then what does my favorite flavor say about me?

GRIFFIN

That you're perfect, obviously.

"Thanks so much for coming!" I say to the final parent picking up their kid. Even though we kept the invite list to Jason's party small (since my townhouse is small), I was not prepared for the fact that parents drop kids off without staying.

It was chaos. But happy chaos.

Although, I suspect I'll be finding pizza stains in questionable locations for the next few weeks. Maybe by next year, I'll have saved up enough money to rent out a fun birthday party location. On second thought, every spare penny I have is going to be paying for therapy bills. I doubt we'll be having a giant birthday bash next year.

The smile on Jason's face is well worth the effort and chaos, however. It's been a roller coaster of a day—he was initially thrilled when he woke up to balloons and donuts, but his mood had dampened by the time we left for school. Cathy mailed Jason a birthday card, but there's an inescapable reality that this is his first birthday away from his father. The first of all of them.

It's a heavy reality for a child to not fully understand.

Thankfully, by the time the party rolled around, Jason was in high spirits. The thought of having a party and receiving presents from friends for the first time was enough of an enticement to bolster his mood. We'll see how the night ends.

A few minutes after the guests have left, Jason is looking through his gifts again while I start cleaning up trash. A knock on the door surprises us both.

Jason rushes to the door, but I yell for him to wait for me. Looking through the door viewer, I recognize our guest and pull the door open.

"Surprise! Happy birthday, my guy!" Samantha yells, grinning widely.

"Sammi!" Jason screams, lunging at her.

"Careful, careful, you're going to make me drop your present!" Samantha exclaims as she comes into the entryway.

Jason jumps up and down, nearly bouncing off the walls in a literal sense. "I can't believe you're here!"

"Of course, I'm here! I couldn't miss your big day. Griffin wishes he could be here too," Samantha says.

Jason's countenance falls ever so slightly, but he perks back up. "It's okay—he has to get in shape for the season," he says seriously.

Samantha nods. "Yeah, it's gonna take a lot of work to get that guy in shape for opening day," she replies with equal seriousness before cracking a smile. Jason giggles.

"Can I open my present?" he asks.

"Yes! But let's go to the living room, and I'm supposed to video call Griffin so he can watch you open it too," Samantha says. Jason's eyes light up, as I'm sure mine do as well. Samantha pauses to hug me as Jason bounds over to the living room. "You holding up okay?" she whispers.

"Surviving," I reply honestly. "I thought you were supposed to be in Arizona for some meetings?"

"Griffin canceled my trip so I could be here tonight," Samantha says quietly. "It was the closest he could get to being here himself."

Tears spring to my eyes, and Samantha squeezes my arm. "Just give me a second," I say, fanning air into my eyes. Samantha makes her way over to Jason while I compose myself. By the time I join them, she's propped her phone up on the coffee table, ready to call Griffin. I nod when she makes eye contact with me, so she hits dial.

Griffin answers almost immediately, as though he's been sitting around waiting for this call. *Probably because he has. He's trying to make the best of this.* The thought brings a small smile to my face.

"Happy birthday, Fireball!" Griffin says, his grinning face filling the screen. *Good gracious, he's so handsome even through a video.*

Jason's enthusiastic response brings an even bigger smile to my face. "Can I open my present now?" he practically yells.

"You'd better open it! I'm dying to see what you think," Griffin responds.

Samantha jumps in. "I'm just the bearer of the gift—Griffin was the one who picked it out and told me where to go get it."

Jason lifts the wrapped box and says, "*Oof,* it's heavy!" He sets it back down on the table and rips the wrapping paper off. Samantha helps him undo the small pieces of tape holding the lid of the box together, and Jason gasps when he opens it.

"The picture *Harry Potter* books! Look, Mom!" Jason exclaims, pivoting to show me the book in his hands.

He called me "Mom."

I barely control myself to avoid bawling. Samantha must read in my reaction that this is the first time because an emotional smile springs to her face.

"That's amazing, Jason!" I manage to say, voice thick. I sit down next to him and put an arm around his shoulder. I can't help but squeeze him in a little hug after that moment.

Now that I'm sitting next to Jason, Griffin can see me in the screen also. His eyes flit to mine, full of tenderness. He clears his throat and says, "It's only the first two books for now, but when you're a little bit older we can get the next books."

For the second time in the past minute, I'm choked up and barely holding it together. Not only because of the thoughtfulness of this gift, but also because Griffin used the future tense. He really is committed to making this work. Committed to us.

Jason talks nonstop, filling Griffin in first on his birthday party, then on the whole day, and then on the entire past week. As he chatters, I thumb through the pages of the first illustrated book, marveling at the intricate details.

I've always wanted these for myself. But I've always been too financially practical to purchase them. Even though these are Jason's birthday present, I know they're just as much Griffin's gift to me as well.

"Christin says hi, by the way," Samantha says as Jason walks the phone around the room showing Griffin his other presents. "Her bookstore is the cutest—no wonder you love it. I told her I know you but didn't mention my relation to Griff," she adds with a wink.

"Thanks for this," I tell her. "For getting the books and for coming over. This really means a lot."

"Consider it a sign of how much *both* of us care about you two," Samantha says. "Griff told me it's been a tough week. It really is killing him to be far from you while this is all happening—I can hear it in how he talks. It's probably a good thing he doesn't have to play much at spring training yet because I don't think he would be doing so hot."

"I feel guilty that I made him feel bad," I say with a sigh. "I know there's nothing he can do about his schedule."

"There's no need for guilt. It's important for you to express your emotions. And especially important to have people to lean on for support," Samantha says. "But you might need to widen the net of support for when Griffin's away. You're not close with your family?"

I shake my head. "They're the polar opposite of supportive. I do have friends from book club who I know would be eager and willing to help if I told them I needed it. And my coworkers at school are all incredibly supportive, but I've felt guilty thinking about burdening them with this struggle when they also have to see Jason in the context of school."

"Do any other staff members have kids at the school also?" Samantha asks.

"Well, yeah, of course. One of the benefits of being a teacher is having your kids there with you," I reply.

"Then they're all used to compartmentalizing the kids as both students and the children of their friends. I bet they'd be glad to help ease the load for you," Samantha says, giving me a pointed look.

"You're probably right," I admit.

"And you've got me. I may not be as muscular as Griffin, but I do think I'm funnier than he is. So I've got that going for me," she says. "Seriously—if there's ever a time you need to get away, or if you need to call and vent to someone who understands, I got you."

"Thanks, Samantha," I say.

"P.S., you really can call me Sam, if you want," she adds.

"Is that your preference?" I ask.

She shrugs. "I honestly don't care. Like I said the first day, I'll respond to just about any variation of my name. I know Samantha is a mouthful. I don't want my long name to inconvenience people."

"I like it, though," I say, smiling. "So as long as you genuinely like it, I'll stick with Samantha."

"Mr. Griffin wants to talk to you now, Mom," Jason says, holding the phone out to me. Samantha catches my eye and motions me upstairs.

"You showed Griff, but I want to see all the other presents you got today," Samantha says to Jason, pulling his attention away. I quickly sneak upstairs to my room.

"Hi," I say as I fall back against the pillows on my bed.

"Hey, gorgeous," Griffin replies. "How long has he been calling you 'Mom?'"

"First time," I reply, getting misty-eyed again.

"Wow. I feel privileged that I got to hear it," he says. "I only wish I would have been sitting right next to you when it happened."

"Me too," I say. "But thanks for sending Samantha over. For changing her schedule when you can't change yours. For picking such a meaningful gift and even having Samantha go to a meaningful store to buy the books. I really appreciate your thoughtfulness."

Griffin gives me a soft smile. "You're welcome. I wish I could do more, but I'm always going to do the most that I can. I promise."

Rolling to my side, I stare into Griffin's gray eyes on the screen. "I really wish I could kiss you right now."

"That makes two of us."

CHAPTER THIRTY

Griffin

Morning. Have I mentioned lately how much I'd like to start the day seeing your beautiful face instead of Adrian's?

Only every day for the past week.

Well. The point still stands.

Three more days until we get to see you. Although you still won't see my face immediately upon waking.

Counting down the hours. Thanks to a handy countdown widget doing the math for me.

How was book club?

It was wonderful. I mean, the book itself was mediocre. I probably would have DNF'd if it wasn't the book club pick. But being with my friends was wonderful.

ME

DNF?

DANAE

Did Not Finish.

ME

<shocked face emoji> You mean sometimes you don't finish a book you start? This surprises me about you.

DANAE

I don't do it very often. Usually only in dire circumstances. With my plate being more full with Jason and having less personal time to read, I'm finding it more tempting to quit when a book isn't exciting me. But I persevered for this one. And I had a great time with friends while Jason had a good time with the neighbor who came to stay with him. Angie was so sweet and good with him. Very grandma-ish.

ME

I'm glad you have another babysitting option for when Sam's not around. You know she'll be upset if you replace her as your number one option though.

DANAE

She'll always be number one. What's the question today? Fluffy or deep?

ME

If your parents knocked on your door tomorrow and said they wanted to be a part of your life again, would you let them in?

DANAE

I'm not sure I'm emotionally prepared for that level of a question today. Or ever.

The typing dots start and stop multiple times until they ultimately disappear. After waiting a couple of minutes for a reply, I pivot.

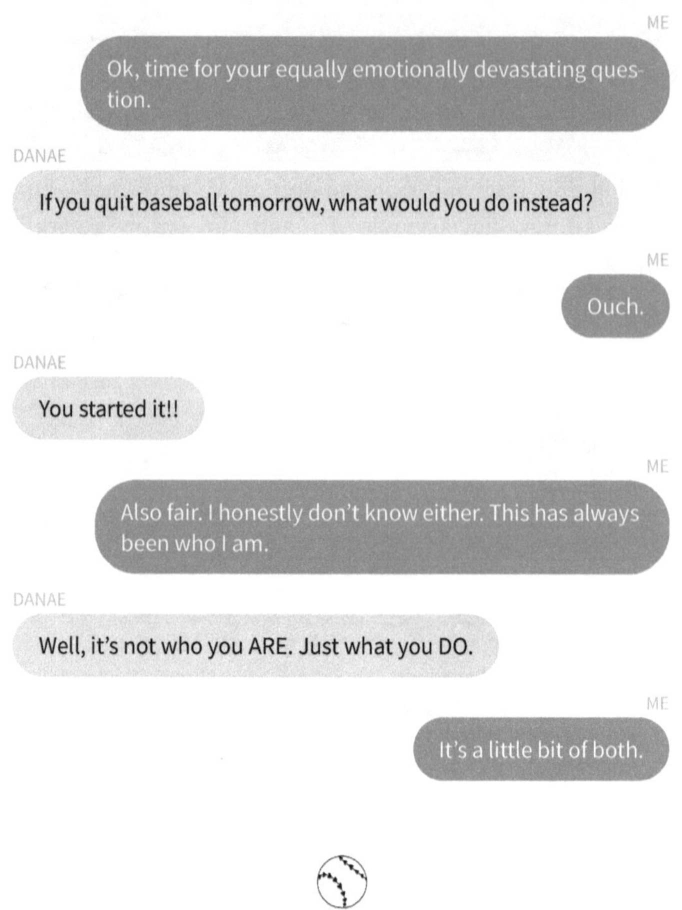

Crack!

I know it the second the bat makes contact with the ball. I hear it in the sound. Feel it in the reverberation.

Home run.

Starters have been playing full games for over a week now, cut days are all behind us, and the roster is finalized. I came into the season knowing my spot with the Crowns was essentially secure, but there's always that tiny kernel of doubt that needles you until the day final rosters are posted. I had ultimate peace today knowing I'd officially made the squad—knowing I *deserve* this spot—but this walk-off home run feels like the exclamation point declaring that I'm back.

The roar of the crowd buzzes through my veins as I pump my fist in the air and jog the bases. Hopping onto home plate with a flourish, Adrian is right there to ambush me with a celebratory half-tackle. Drew and Luke follow his lead, then the rest of the guys quickly form a mosh pit around me. You'd think we won the World Series, not a spring training game.

I love this game. The thrill of a good hit, the screams of the crowd, the camaraderie of my teammates—I love it all.

"Too bad your lady wasn't here to see that," Carlos teases, slapping me on the back.

"Guess I'll have to do it again tomorrow," I reply, grinning widely.

"Will she be here in time for tomorrow's game?" Adrian asks.

I nod as we jog to the dugout to gather our stuff before going to greet fans and sign autographs. "That's the plan. Pending no flight delays, she and Jason will be here to watch."

"Are they sitting in the suite with the other WAGs?" Drew asks. "Lily didn't mention it."

"Nah, Danae isn't ready for public attention yet. She and Jason are going to sit in regular seats and meet me after the game," I say, stuffing gear into my bag.

"Well, if she changes her mind for any of the games this week, let me know. I'm sure Lily would be thrilled to show her the ropes," Drew offers.

"Thanks, man. I'll play it by ear and let you know." As we make our way to the stands, I stay to sign more autographs and pose for more photos than ever, anticipating that I'll be cutting time with fans short over the remainder of the week. Because starting tomorrow, I'm going to be racing away to spend every available second with Danae and Jason.

It killed me that I couldn't be the one to pick Danae and Jason up from the airport instead of Sam. But we still had morning batting practice and workouts, so I couldn't be there to greet them when they arrived. Not that Danae would *want* me picking her up and publicly outing our relationship like that. I'm desperate to touch her, to remind myself that she's *real*. That she cares about me.

These weeks apart have been torture in more ways than one. I know the months ahead will still be chaotic, but at least we won't have to go more than a week to ten days without seeing each other during the season. Whoever said "absence makes the heart grow fonder" must have gained that wisdom from painful personal experience. Because being away from Danae this long has made me crave her. It's like nothing I've ever experienced in my life—this inescapable melancholy that a piece of my happiness is missing.

I begged Sam to bring them down pre-game and meet up outside the locker room, but in typical Sam fashion, she made a big show about reluctantly complying. I'm confident she'll make it happen, though. Well, mostly confident.

Sure enough, about ten minutes before we have to take the field for warm-ups, Sam texts me that they're here. I walk out of the locker room to the hallway, where I'm immediately bowled over by an enthusiastic hug from Jason.

Laughing, I pull him into my arms to lift his feet off the ground. "It's good to see you, Fireball!" Setting him back down, I make a show of measuring his head against my waist. "Hold on a second—did you grow a couple inches while I was gone?"

He grins up at me, standing on his tiptoes. "I think so! I've been eating real good food like you said I should. I bet that made me taller! I can't wait to watch you play today," he says, swinging an imaginary bat. "I watched the highlights from yesterday—that home run was a-MAZ-ing!"

Nudging down the brim of his baseball cap, I tell him, "I'll try to hit another one for you today. But first I need to hug your mom."

I turn my attention to Danae, who's looking more gorgeous than I even remembered, dressed in jeans and the Crowns t-shirt Jason picked out for her at Camp Wizard. Every one of my dreams and daydreams have been filled with her face, but I still somehow forgot the delicate lines of her beauty. The sparkle of the gold flecks in her hazel green eyes. The copper-streaked brown waves of her hair brushing against the tops of her shoulders. The blush-pink shade of her lips.

Wrapping her in my arms, I pull her against me as tightly as I can manage, just shy of squeezing too hard. Burying my face in her neck, I murmur, "It's so good to see you. To really *see* you."

The tight grip of her arms around my waist and the way she nuzzles her face into my neck would be confirmation enough that she feels the same. But she also sighs, "Finally." When she tilts her head to meet my eyes again, there's relief in her gaze. A rightness to being together that I also sense in the depths of my being.

I've felt that rightness in Danae's presence ever since the first time we met, before it made any logical sense. Like she was meant to be there all along—almost as though a phantom piece of her *had* been with me all along, waiting for us to find each other for real.

I don't care that Sam and Jason are standing right beside us. I don't care if any other Crowns players or staff walk in and out of the locker room. I will not resist the weeks-long yearning to kiss those perfect heart lips.

One arm still firmly around her waist, I cup the other hand behind Danae's head and gently press my lips to hers. The kiss is chaste in every sense of the word, given our audience. Nonetheless, passion and desire flood through me at record levels.

I think I love this woman.

At the sound of Jason's dramatic, "Ewww!" Danae smiles against my lips. I dip her backward, never breaking lip contact. Jason's moans turn into laughter, and I stand Danae upright again.

Time is ticking, and I know I need to get back into the locker room. I know I'll see them after the game. Still, my heart is a stubborn mule when told to leave her for even a second. Placing both hands on her cheeks, I drink in the real-life, physical reality of Danae.

"I'm so happy you're here," I say. She leans forward to kiss me again, and I muster all my willpower to step away after a moment. "I'll see you after the game, okay?" I say to Jason, who gives me a high five for good luck.

Trailing my fingers down her arms to her hands, I slowly back away toward the locker room. She holds on as long as possible.

CHAPTER THIRTY-ONE

Danae

Peals of laughter compete with the shouts of concession workers walking the stands. Self-confident armchair commentary surrounds me, drowning out the announcements from the speakers. Peanut shells crack and beer cans pop open as I try to retrain the negative associations in my brain. *Try* to hate this atmosphere a little less.

In the bottom of the first inning, Griffin's turn at-bat comes. I perk up in my seat for the first time, watching him approach home plate. As his name and position come over the speakers, the announcer says, "And we've got a new walk-up song for Griffin West today."

I listen closely as the song starts off quietly, but a smile spreads across my face as I realize what it is. Griffin twirls the bat in one hand and looks toward our seats with a huge grin. *Be still, my heart.*

"It's the *Harry Potter* theme, Mom!" Jason yells, standing to jump up and down. "I bet he picked that because of—" I quickly but playfully clap my hand over Jason's mouth, giving him a look to remind him we're not calling attention to the fact that we know Griffin while we're here.

"Looks like the Wizard of Defense decided to play up the nickname with the music this year!" the announcer says in a vibrant voice.

Wrapping an arm around Jason's shoulders, I squeeze him in a hug. "That's definitely for you, bud," I say, voice low.

Jason grins at me. "For us."

After one ball and one strike, Griffin makes contact and sends the ball past the opponent's shortstop, successfully running to first base. Unfortunately, the next two batters strike out, and Griffin is left stranded on first as the inning closes out.

Play continues, and I'd say the energy of the crowd is contagious, but I'd be lying. Aside from the moments that Griffin is at-bat, I'm mostly bored to tears.

Jason, on the other hand, is living his best life. No, not just *his* best life. *THE* best life there ever was, if his smiles and enthusiasm are any indication. His running commentary of every swing, every catch, every out keeps me amused, at least. It also informs me of all the appropriate lingo for what's taking place in the game.

Eight innings in, the score is still 0–0. Very few batters have even made it on base for either team. Thus far, none of the opposing team's hits have gone in Griffin's direction, so we haven't really been able to see him in action. He did get a double on his second at-bat, but he was left stranded once again. I'm really and truly baffled by the level of passion fans have for such a snoozefest.

As the game transitions to the ninth inning, I stifle a yawn. *I wish I had my Kindle with me.* Trying to dismiss the thought, I remind myself: I love my son, who loves baseball. I really, *really* like (love?) Griffin, who loves baseball.

But I do not love baseball. Facts are facts.

I hope that Griffin can see that I care about him, even if I don't share this particular passion of his.

The first batter for the opponents strikes out, but the second hits a double. The next batter makes a base hit, giving the runner at second the opportunity to make it to third base with only one out.

As the next batter comes up to the plate, I see Griffin crouch and ready himself. When the batter makes contact with the ball, it bounces on the field right in Griffin's direction. Almost before I can track where the ball is going, Griffin fields it and throws to second base at lightning speed. The second baseman, Luke, stomps the bag and immediately throws to first, where Drew catches it with his foot on base just in time to make the out.

The Crowns fans go wild cheering, and I stand up to jump and scream along with Jason. Adrian makes a flourishing curtsy toward Griffin, who tips his hat and bows in return. He looks over his shoulder at us as he jogs off the field, and I hope he could see us cheering for him. "That was the fastest double play I've ever seen in real life!" Jason exclaims as we take our seats. "I mean, it was the only double play I've seen in real life, but I bet it would still be the fastest even if I'd seen lots."

Drew is the first at-bat in the bottom of the ninth inning, and he hits a triple. Griffin comes up to bat next, doing the same series of warm-up moves he's done the past two times. The first pitch is a ball, and Griffin settles back into his stance. With the next pitch, his swing is followed by that satisfying *crack* of the bat, and he takes off running to first. It's only a single but hit in the perfect direction to give Drew time to make it home and end the game with a run.

When the cheering over the win dies down, Jason looks up at me. "Well, it wasn't another home run, but it was still the game-winning hit. So I think it still counts for me."

Laughing, I give him a playful shove. "I'd say so! Don't get too greedy!"

Jason's eyes widen with shock. "You got me the game-winning ball?!"

Griffin grins at Jason from where he's kneeling at eye-level. "Sure did! I tracked the ball down, and then Drew and I both signed it for you."

Holding the ball with reverence, Jason whispers, "Thank you." In the next breath, he's diving forward, wrapping his arms around Griffin's neck. "I'm gonna display this on top of my dresser forever," he says.

Griffin looks up at me as he hugs Jason, a tender expression in his eyes. He winks in response to the smile I give him, and heat floods my core. As if he can sense the effect of his wink on me, his own smile twists into a self-satisfied smirk. He gives Jason one more squeeze before standing up to immediately plant a kiss on my lips. A move I'm not protesting at all, especially since we finally have the privacy of his condo.

"Adrian and Sam should be here with the tacos any minute. Can I get you something to drink?" Griffin asks.

"Water is great. Unless you have a cranberry club soda from Jeff hiding out in your fridge," I reply.

"I wish," Griffin says, opening a cabinet door to get two glasses. "As soon as I get back to KC, I'm taking you to Capital Grille again. We'll have two rounds of the Jeff special." He turns to Jason. "You want water or a Gatorade?"

"Gatorade!" Jason chirps with a little bounce.

A few minutes later, Samantha and Adrian come through the front door of the condo, laden with bags from a local taco shop. We stuff ourselves with delicious food as Jason gives his full breakdown of the game today, causing all of us to stifle our amused laughter. Adrian and Griffin regale us with stories from training camp and the games so far, causing multiple rounds of unstifled belly laughs.

When the tacos are gone and the chips are down to crumbs, Adrian leans over the table toward Jason. "I think it's about time you tried the best ice cream in Arizona. What do you think?"

"Yes!" Jason yells, pivoting to look to me. "Can we, Mom?"

"I'm too full for ice cream, but you should definitely let Ortiz take you, Fireball," Griffin says, eyeing me meaningfully.

"I'm in!" Samantha says, giving me a similarly pointed look.

"Oh, yeah, I'm pretty full, too, after all those tacos. I'll pass on ice cream this time," I say. Standing up, I start gathering the trash to throw away, trying to look occupied and not like I'm obsessing over finally being alone with Griffin again.

Adrian fist bumps Jason and ushers him toward the front door, closely followed by Samantha. She gives us a sly look over her shoulder as they exit the condo, their laughter echoing behind them.

It's a matter of milliseconds before Griffin spins me toward him and captures my lips with his. I loop my arms around his neck, melting against him. When he pulls back from our kiss, he trails the tip of his nose from my chin up the line of my jaw. The resulting shiver that skitters through my body must delight him because he smiles against the skin below my ear.

"Have I mentioned I missed you?" he murmurs, voice warm and tantalizing. "That I thought about you constantly the past five weeks? That every day I've been daydreaming about drinking in your kiss again?"

Before I can respond, his lips are back on mine, his hands moving from my waist to my hair. I sigh, so blissfully happy to be back in his embrace.

"Everything about you is so soft," he whispers. "Your skin," he says, placing a gentle kiss to my cheek. "Your hair," he adds, running a lock of my hair through his fingertips, his eyes tracking the movement. The gray has almost completely clouded out the blue in his irises as he stares at me. "Your lips," he breathes as his fingers trace the outline of them.

I move my hands from behind his neck to his shoulders, slowly sliding them down to his chest. When I feel his heart thundering beneath my hands, I mimic his self-satisfied smirk. "I'm really glad to see you again," I say. "That was way too long apart."

"Agreed," he says. "Let's not do that again." He leans in to press a kiss to my neck, then takes one of my hands and leads me to the couch.

"Listen, I could stand here kissing you for the entirety of however long Adrian and Sam manage to distract Jason. But I want to talk with you too," Griffin says as he sits on the couch. He pulls me down next to him, and I drape my legs over his as he tucks me under his arm.

"Would this be an appropriate seating position for reading at the ski lodge?" he asks, voice teasing.

"*Hmmm*," I say. "Realistically, if I was going to be able to hold my book, I'd have to face the opposite direction and lean my back against your chest."

"I can get on board with that too," Griffin says, "but for now, I'm happy just like this." He kisses the top of my head, pausing to noticeably smell my hair. "What kind of shampoo do you use?"

I laugh. "Some cheap stuff from the grocery store. My days of regular highlights and high-end hair products got left behind when I cut ties with my parents. But I like the mango citrus scent of this shampoo, so I don't even care."

"Well, that makes two of us," Griffin replies. "Don't ever change it. I can't believe you used to highlight your hair. It's already the perfect shade of auburn. Why would you mess with perfection?"

I shrug, his arm wrapped around me rising and falling with the movement. "It was part of the lifestyle my parents wanted for us. Regular beauty treatments to look as chic and posh as possible were as much a part of my upbringing as learning to ride a bike."

"I'm almost surprised you know how to ride a bike," Griffin remarks.

Slapping him on the chest, I lean back to give him a fake scowl. "We weren't *that* out of touch with reality," I say. He raises his eyebrows. "I'm not saying I could tell you the last time I actually rode a bike, but I did learn."

Griffin laughs, and I lean my head against his chest to fully appreciate the thundering sound. I trace lazy patterns on his forearm as I ask, "How has training been?"

"Different this year. Mentally harder than usual," he says. "Mostly because of the separation from you. But also because the seed of doubt about whether I'd be good enough to make the squad was bigger than ever after coming back from the injury."

"I can imagine that weighed on you," I reply. "You were amazing today, though."

"Did you think so?" he asks, pulling back from me enough to look at my face. The tentative smile on his face looks as though he's genuinely searching for my approval. To know if I'm proud of him.

"Of course," I say, reaching a hand up to trail my fingers along his beard. "Even from someone who doesn't care for the sport, I can appreciate the talent you had in fielding that double play. Not to mention three hits." He smiles more fully, looking pleased. "But the walk-up song was by far my favorite part."

His smile breaks into a grin. "I thought you might appreciate that. Good thing my nickname lends itself to a little *Harry Potter* magic. What did Jason think?"

"Oh, he was beside himself. Thought it was the coolest moment ever. Well, until your double play. Then that was the coolest moment ever. Although *now* he probably thinks getting the game-winning ball is the coolest moment ever," I say. My voice drops to a murmur as I add, "You're giving him a lot of coolest moments ever."

"And you're giving him all the everyday forever moments," Griffin says tenderly. "How have things been going since the most recent therapy appointment?"

"Up and down," I say, sitting back a little. "We had our first appointment with the occupational therapist, and she's going to teach me some of the exercises to do at home with him as well."

"Will you see both of them every week?" he asks.

I frown slightly. "Maybe? I need to figure things out as far as how much we can do."

Griffin's brow furrows. "What's the hangup?"

Shrugging, I say, "Nothing's covered once he's on my insurance after the adoption is finalized. So I need to plan everything out and set up a reasonable schedule with Jessica and the OT when we get back home. Speaking of home, when will you actually fly back to KC?"

"Unfortunately, not soon enough," he says. "We still have one game left here the day you leave, and then we fly to Texas for two exhibition games. We'll only have a couple of days back in KC before the home opener. Thank goodness our first series is at home this year. I don't think I could handle seeing you and then immediately having another two-plus weeks apart."

"Thank your season scheduler for me," I tease. "They might be saving my sanity. Which will already be stretched to the limit watching so many baseball games this week."

Griffin gives me a mischievous look. "No closer on converting you to a fan, huh?"

Slowly shaking my head, I smirk back at him, causing his eyes to narrow.

"Good thing I'm finding another passion, then," he says, voice nearing growl territory as he leans toward me. "Another very enticing passion."

Our lips find each other like two oppositely charged elements that can't stay apart. That won't stay apart. That don't *want* to stay apart.

CHAPTER THIRTY-TWO

Griffin

Taking another step off the base, I analyze the pitcher's cues. We're currently tied 3–3 at the top of the ninth with two outs against us, and I've been sitting at second ever since I hit a double. I'm contemplating stealing my way to third to give us a better chance at a run scored to possibly give us the win.

I haven't even attempted stealing any bases throughout all of spring training. It's as though my mind is averse to the physical sensation of my shoulder stretching out in a dive. But having Danae and Jason here these past few days watching us play—watching *me* play—has bolstered my confidence. Hearing them praise my good performance each evening together has brought back some of the swagger that drained out in the aftermath of last season's injury.

I'm pretty sure I have a good read on this pitcher's habits, and I'm fairly confident that I could successfully steal the base. The third base coach has signaled the same, giving me that extra assurance. Making up my mind, I watch for the right moment and take off sprinting.

I focus on pumping my arms, on the grip of the dirt beneath my cleats, on the oxygen in my lungs, so that when the time comes to slide, my body dives without thinking about my shoulder. The crowd roars as the umpire signals "safe," and I leap to my feet in celebration. As subtly as I can, I look up to the seats I know Danae and Jason are occupying, grinning when I see Danae holding Jason in her arms, jumping up and down.

The team celebration is exuberant when Adrian bats me in for a score, giving us the lead. Our next batter strikes out, which means it's time for some good defense to close out the game. My eyes can't help but find Danae's in the stands as I jog to position, heart seizing when I see her on her feet clapping.

I need to get that woman a West jersey. The thought of looking up in the stands to see Danae wearing number eleven gives me an extra push of motivation to finish this inning with a win.

Our closer strikes out the first batter, getting us one step closer to victory. When the second batter makes contact with a curveball, I know it's coming to me. Shuffling two steps toward second base, I catch the ball before it can hit the ground, gaining the second out. Adrenaline floods through my body, setting all of my reflexes on high alert.

The next batter has a count of three balls and two strikes, meaning this next pitch could be the decider. That familiar *crack* of the bat resounds through the stadium, and the ball is a pop fly a little above my territory. I start running that way but hear Ethan calling for the ball, triggering an alarming sense of déjà vu in my body. Exhaling a breath, I pull up and back down, allowing him to make the final catch and out of the game.

I slap Ethan on the back and say, "Great catch, Farmer!" He claps me back, recognizing the moment, and I'm bordering on emotional. Thankfully, Adrian snaps me out of it by using my shoulders as a springboard to launch himself up, jumping piggyback on me with his fist in the air.

This will be the latest addition to the Ortiz/West compilation videos, I think as I laugh and run to the dugout with him on my back. *Hopefully Jason's getting a kick out of this.*

For as much as I've loved getting to know Danae (and probably falling *in* love with her), connecting with Jason has been a close second on the enjoyability scale. I've yet to witness one of his big blow-ups firsthand, although it's easy to imagine, knowing how sensitive and emotional he is. I'd witnessed the full gamut of behaviors in our home as I grew up with a revolving door of kids in foster care coming in and moving on.

I know that being in his life long term wouldn't be smooth sailing. I've watched Sam and Ian work through the hard stuff, watched my parents support them, even been a closer support specifically for Sam. Listening to her process the trauma she endured, watching her fight to change her brain's natural reactions to triggers—I understand, at least in some sense, what it will be like to be one of the main players supporting Jason's lifelong journey.

And I want it.

Spending time just the three of us this week, after so long apart, has illuminated how right it feels to be together. I want to help that effervescent, enthusiastic little guy grow up and forge his own path. I want to be there to listen when he's had a hard day, to assist his mind in calming down when something triggers a memory. To let Jason know he's loved no matter what he does.

It's as though my past experiences—our family doing foster care, welcoming Sam and Ian into our family, even interacting with the kids at Camp Wizard—have been the breadcrumbs guiding the way and opening my heart to a life with Danae and Jason. I want to walk into the hard alongside Danae, to be a team.

I only hope she wants that as much as I do.

"Another baseball game?" Danae asks, a slight groan in her tone. "We literally *just* finished your game."

Jason, on the other hand, starts doing some ridiculous dance move that I can only imagine started as a dance trend he's trying to imitate. We're standing in the hallway outside the locker room, and one of the assistant coaches passes by, chuckling at Jason.

"Come on, we can leave early if you want to," I tell Danae, looping an arm around her waist to tug her toward me. "And this time I'll be sitting there with you. I've been wanting to watch one of Rogers' games, the friend who plays for Baltimore that I told you about. We can go and enjoy the experience of watching together."

She gives me a sassy look. "Enjoy, huh?"

Pulling her even closer to me, I tickle her neck with my beard. "I can bribe Sam to take Jason out for ice cream afterward," I murmur in her ear. I feel the goosebumps break out on her skin, and I steal a quick kiss before standing back to beg. "Please, pretty please?" I say, nudging Jason with my elbow. We both give her our saddest puppy eyes.

"Fine, fine," Danae says, rolling her eyes. But she can't hide her smile.

I'm elated at the prospect of getting to watch a game *with* Danae and Jason. She has good reason to be hesitant to bring our relationship into the open, so I called Rogers for a favor. He came through with three standing-only spots in a suite, so we can stay hidden from the public eye while having a good time together.

Just to be safe, we stop by their hotel so they can change out of Crowns gear. I'm already wearing a nondescript t-shirt and plain hat. I throw on sunglasses before we walk into the complex to keep a low profile. It's familiar territory, so I'm able to navigate us through the back channels to the suite. It's mostly family members and WAGs of Baltimore players. I greet Rogers' wife, Tammi, with a one-armed hug (considering my other hand is currently occupied as Danae's lifeline).

"Griffin West, it's good to see you!" she says. "Lawrence told me you were the surprise guest joining us today! He's going to be so excited to see you after the game."

"Thanks for letting us squeeze in," I respond. "This is my girlfriend, Danae Collins, and her son, Jason." I keep the explanation simple, leaving it up to Danae or Jason to offer any additional information as the night goes on. Danae lets go of my hand long enough to shake Tammi's.

"Help yourself to any of the food and drinks back there," Tammi says, waving her hand behind us. "I'm sure people will be in and out of the seats, so feel free to sit outside at any point if seats are open. We're all pretty chill in here."

"We'll probably hang back inside the whole time. We're trying to lie low," I explain, and Tammi nods.

"Totally understand that. Don't rush the jump to media attention," she says to Danae with a sympathetic smile. "There's something special about the secrecy of having the relationship just between you two. And your inner circles, of course."

"Yeah, Mr. Griffin gets tired of too much attention," Jason inserts matter-of-factly. "That's why we don't talk about him dating my mom yet."

I can't help but chuckle. "Oh, do I now?" I ask, shooting a teasing grin at Danae. Her cheeks flush.

"It was the simplest explanation I could come up with for why we shouldn't tell everyone at school about it," she says quietly, even though Jason has moved on to scout out the snacks. "It might need a little workshopping."

Fully laughing, I loop my arm around her shoulders and kiss her temple. "It's okay, I can pretend to hate attention." She pinches my side and offers a brief explanation to Tammi about her situation with Jason.

Tammi's eyes soften. "That totally makes sense. I'll be sure to let everyone in the suite know to be careful about posting photos, to check to make sure you aren't in the background or anything."

"Thank you. I really appreciate that," Danae says.

Glancing over my shoulder, I notice Jason balancing a plate with one hand while trying to overload a ridiculous amount of chicken tenders onto it with the other. "Whoa there, Fireball. Let me give you a hand with that," I say, quickly making my way over to him.

We naturally rotate between paying attention to the game, conversing with other guests in the suite, and talking to only each other. Jason has downed his body weight in chicken and cookies, and he's entertaining everyone with his running commentary about the game play.

During the seventh-inning stretch, I rest an arm around Danae's shoulders as everyone sings along to "Take Me Out to the Ball Game." Jason is belting out the lyrics, and Danae smiles, watching him.

"You really hate all this?" I ask, disbelieving.

Danae shrugs. "I mean . . . yeah."

I lean in to whisper in her ear. "Come on, even me in the uniform? You hate that?" She slaps my stomach, but I see it coming and manage to flex my abs just in time. Her cheeks flush an adorable shade of pink. "You're telling me the uniform doesn't do it for you *at all?*"

Danae tosses her head. "Nope. It's the man inside the uniform that does it for me."

Who is the man inside the uniform? The question crashes through my mind like a 95mph fastball, and I usher it out the back door just as quickly.

I quickly put my teasing grin back in place. "You're seriously not having fun?" I ask Danae, bumping her hip with mine.

She sighs. "I like being with *you*, but I'd rather be at home playing a game with you and Jason, or reading a book on the couch. Baseball is still super boring to me," she says unapologetically. "It's such a slow-paced game."

"Well, that's part of the charm of baseball, though. It was intentionally designed to be a slower-moving game, to make attending games about more than just the action. It's about sitting and shooting the breeze with your friends between pitches. Although the pitch timer has sped things up a little, which surely you appreciate. But it's also about enjoying the food, the spectacle, the hot dog races—not having to have your eyes glued to the field as the only source of excitement," I say. "The whole event is an experience for fans, not just watching the guys on the field."

Danae cocks her head, looking intently in my eyes. "And melting in the summer heat, watching men spit sunflower shells into the stands, and sitting for hours with no set end time?" Although I'm positive these are real grievances for her, a smile plays at the corner of her lips. I remind myself that we're lying low to halt my instinct to lean in and kiss her.

She sighs. "I guess I see what you're saying. I can appreciate how other people enjoy the whole experience."

"Just not you," I clarify with a chuckle.

She shakes her head, eyes dancing. "But I enjoy *you*. That's enough, right?"

Present circumstances are seriously hindering my vibe, because it's excruciating to not be able to kiss her senseless in answer to her question.

"More than enough," I reply, voice husky with the desire I can't physically express. Danae must read it in my eyes, though, because she winks at me. Which adds gasoline to the desire fire.

Whose idea was it to spend time together in a public location tonight?! I need to have a stern word with that idiot.

Danae

"**T**hank you for flying with us today. Welcome home to all the Kansas City locals, and, to everyone visiting this vibrant city, enjoy your stay."

The captain's announcement gives the signal to unbuckle seatbelts and fight for inches in the aisle. Jason is still dead asleep, his head resting against the window. The past four days of nonstop fun and baseball wore him out, which means he slept the whole flight home. He'll be so upset he missed the drink cart, but I wasn't about to risk startling him awake and gambling on his mood. Thankfully, the sounds of overhead bins opening and voices calling to let loved ones know they've landed gently awakens Jason.

We're not in a huge rush, so I let the aisle clear before I stand to pull out our carry-on suitcases. Jason follows me, and by the time we reach the interior of the airport, he's back to non-stop chatter about all the fun we had this week. As we make our way to the car, I find myself thankful that Griffin paid for the close parking garage, saving us a shuttle ride. Money can't buy everything, but it can buy a bypass around herding an energetic ten-year-old through endless rows of parking spaces.

On the drive home, Jason fills every sliver of silence recalling plays from the many games we watched this week. I try to play along with his enthusiasm, asking questions about which games were most exciting or which players were his favorites (aside from Griffin, naturally). I'm genuinely enjoying his lively observations, distracting me as we pull into the parking lot.

The second we get out of the car and close the doors, everything changes.

Cameras, voices, phones, people ambush us all at once. I drop my purse in the chaos, quickly bending to retrieve it and pulling Jason to me. He clings to my waist as I push my way through the mob, leaving our suitcases in the trunk of the car.

"Danae Collins, can you confirm that you're dating Griffin West?"

"Can you tell us what Griffin is like in a relationship?"

"When did your relationship begin?"

"Are Griffin and Jason close? When is the adoption final?"

The sound of Jason's name on the lips of a strange reporter sparks an explosion in my mind. Whirling around, I glower at the offender. "Leave us alone," I bark, trying to keep the tremor of fear out of my voice. Increasing our pace, I lead Jason to the front door, breathing out slowly to still my trembling hand enough to unlock the door.

I double lock the door and pull Jason into a hug.

"What happened?" he asks. "Why are all those people here? How did they know where we live?"

How, indeed.

I can't tell if Jason's body is shaking as well, or if he's caught in the ripple effect of my own panic. "Why don't you go grab a snack and hang out in your room while I get some things figured out. You can play on the tablet. Would that be okay?" I ask. Thankfully, Jason doesn't argue, and I quickly check the locks on the back door while he shuffles to the kitchen.

The second his feet hit the stairs, I dial Griffin. Of course, it goes to voicemail. I practically growl with frustration. Dialing Samantha, I cross every finger and toe hoping she'll answer.

"Danae, what's up? You guys make it back to KC?"

"There was a crowd of reporters waiting at my townhouse when we pulled in," I answer in a rush. "They somehow knew that Griffin and I are dating, and they know about Jason's adoption. HOW DO THEY KNOW ABOUT JASON?" I don't even attempt to stifle my yell.

Why do they know about Jason? How did they know where we live? What else do they know? Could this hurt my adoption case? My thoughts are yelling louder than I could ever yell at Samantha.

"Oh no. This must have been why Joe was blowing up my phone this morning," Samantha replies.

"Who's Joe?" I ask.

"Griff's agent. He's an annoyance, so I try to ignore him as much as possible," she says, and I hear the change in her voice as she switches to speaker. "That's not good."

"What's not good?" I clarify.

"Have you not googled yourself?" Samantha asks. "That wasn't your first thought when there were a bunch of reporters around?"

"No! I've never had a reason to google myself!" I exclaim, frustration rising again. I switch the phone to speaker and type my name into the browser search bar. My screen is immediately filled with news articles with headlines like "Who's the Single Mom Who Stole the Wizard of Defense's Heart?" I'm reluctant to give them engagement clicks, but I have to see what's being spread.

There's a zoomed-in photo of Griffin and me in the suite at the Baltimore game. It looks like we were in the background of a photo a fan was taking of other people seated in the outdoor section of the suite space, but we were visible behind the glass. Griffin's arm is around my shoulders, and we're smiling at each other in a way that implies a more-than-acquaintances relationship.

The original photo was posted to social media last night, and apparently reporters can manage to dig up an entire dossier of information about a person in less than twenty-four hours. Including my pending adoption case with Jason and "rumored" (but accurate) details about his biological parents, despite the fact that his case files should be sealed.

"I think I might throw up," I say, falling to my knees, my forehead dropping to the floor. I barely hear Samantha's voice from the phone next to me as my blood makes the *swooshing* sound like a seashell when you hold it over your ear.

"Does Griffin know?" I ask, eyes closed against my fists on the floor. I still don't know anything that Samantha said over the past indeterminate number of seconds.

"He can't possibly know or he would have called me. And you. The game starts in thirty minutes, but I'll catch him before. I can get an emergency message in to him," Samantha replies. "Danae, I'm so sorry."

"What if they take Jason away from me?" I whimper. My body falls to one side, curled in the fetal position. "What if the invasion of privacy is considered a strike against me? What if they think I'm not taking motherhood seriously if I jumped into a relationship with a professional athlete a month after Jason moved in with me? What if the media won't leave us alone and Jason spirals more than ever? What if the judge thinks I'm unfit to be a mother if I couldn't stop this from happening?" Each question tumbles over the previous one, a torrent of panic bubbling out.

"Danae, stop it," Samantha says firmly. "Jason is home with you now, yes?"

"Yes," I say.

"Then you need to pull it together right now so you don't scare him. You hear me?"

Rolling onto my back, I confirm, "I hear you."

"We're going to figure this out. I'm going to hang up so I can get ahold of Griffin before he goes out on the field. But you are going to be okay. Jason is going to be okay. We will never let anyone take him away from you, okay?" Her voice is the calm, commanding wind to scatter the fog of anxiety suffocating me.

"Okay. Yes, okay," I say, sitting up. "We're going to be okay."

For the first time in my life, I voluntarily turn the channel to a baseball game.

I tell Jason he can have unlimited tablet time as long as he stays in his room with the door closed, a bribe I may pay for later. I jump when my phone rings in my hand. My stomach becomes an acrobat when I see that it's Sandra, Jason's social worker, returning my call. Swallowing hard, I answer.

"Hey, Danae, I got your voicemail and looked up the articles you mentioned," she says. My heart is pounding and frozen at once, disabling my vocal cords. Luckily, she continues speaking without pausing for me to say anything. "I'll admit, this is a situation I've never dealt with before, which is really saying something." There's a level of amusement in her voice that slows my panicked thoughts.

"Is this going to hurt my adoption case in any way? That's all I need to know." I squeeze my eyes shut as I wait for her answer.

"I really don't think so," Sandra says. "Although it's unfortunate that Jason's privacy was invaded—and you know I'll help fight on that front to get these taken down—it's not like you're being abusive or neglectful. I mean, this is a genuine relationship you have with Griffin West, correct?"

"Yes! Absolutely, yes," I exclaim. "We initially met through the baseball camp, but it's a real relationship with real feelings."

"Good, yeah. It's not like you've used Jason to get to Griffin or to gain media attention," Sandra says. My stomach flips again at the thought that someone might misconstrue the situation that way. "I'll do everything I can to make sure that there are no hiccups here. But I honestly don't see this being an issue. In fact, I still think we'll be able to expedite the waiting period and move up the official adoption date, if you want that."

"Yes! I do! Please let me know anything I can do on that front. And thanks for getting back to me so quickly," I say with a grateful sigh of relief.

"Will do," Sandra replies. Her tone changes as she asks, "The Wizard of Defense, huh? I thought you didn't like baseball?"

"Yeah, I don't," I say.

Sandra is quiet for a beat before she prods, "Buuut?"

"But I do like Griffin. Never saw that coming," I say.

"Good for you," Sandra replies, and I hear the grin in her voice. "Don't worry yourself about this—I'll let you know if there are any updates, okay? No news is good news on this front."

Hanging up, I drop my hands to my knees and breathe deeply. One kernel of anxiety about this situation has been put to rest, at least halfway. My phone immediately rings again, and Kara's picture displays on the screen.

"Kara! Talk me off the ledge. Or over the ledge. Should I be talked off the ledge or over the ledge in this scenario?" I ask, frantic.

"Off the ledge for sure," Kara says. "This is not end-your-relationship level bad, okay?"

I cover my eyes with one hand but don't answer.

"Acknowledge, Danae," Kara says, louder. "You are not ending things with Griffin because of a little media attention."

"A *little* media attention?!" I whisper yell. "There was an entire crowd of reporters *outside of my house*. Asking questions about Jason. I'm not prepared to deal with that kind of thing! You're my best friend—you know me!"

"Yes, I am your best friend, and that's how I know that you are panic-spiraling about this right now. But if you abruptly make the decision to end things with Griffin in response to this situation, I also know that you will regret it forever. Because you love that man."

I still at her words. *You love that man.*

"Am I right, or am I right?" Kara asks. "I already know I'm right, but you can still give me the satisfaction of saying that I'm right."

"You might be right," I quietly admit.

Kara sighs. "Close enough. What was it that Jason's therapist told you about the animals? Calm down your dog brain and get your owl brain back, Danae. This is not real danger. I've got your back. All of us at school will have your and Jason's backs. Reporters won't get within five miles of the school building. I'm sure Griffin will figure out how to deal with this. Don't do anything dumb because you're afraid, okay?"

"Okay," I say with a sigh. "Thanks for talking me off the ledge."

"You promise you're off? I don't need to call back in a few minutes for a second round of pep talks?" Kara asks.

Smiling at how well she knows me, I pause to thank my lucky stars that Kara and I wound up teaching at the same school. "I promise I'm off. I will calm down."

Despite the assurances to Kara, my heart is in my throat, in my stomach, and pounding out of my chest all at once for the duration of the nine innings. Griffin is very obviously off his game—evidence that Samantha was able to get in touch with him. On the one hand, guilt over him playing badly due to my phone call gnaws at my stomach. On the other hand, panic and the utter loss of knowing what to do eat away at my mind, and it only seems fair that he would be plunged into the same turmoil.

By some unknown mercy, no mention of the photo or news about our relationship is made by the announcers of the game. The Crowns end spring training with 4–2 loss, due in part to an error made by Griffin. As the game ends and smiling players from the winning team are interviewed, the gnawing guilt starts to win out over the panic.

I should have waited until after the game to tell him. I shouldn't have ruined his game. What kind of girlfriend am I? Will Griffin even want to be with me after today? Is this the wake-up call for him that being in a relationship with me is only going to hinder his career? Surely, he'll realize that it was a mistake to think that a guy like him could be with a girl like me. With all my baggage, I am not an easy person to be with. What was I thinking, believing that we could do this? How could I think I could handle this kind of attention? This was a ridiculous mistake. I never should have let myself get close to him when I knew that something like this could happen.

I'm seconds away from a trip to the bathroom to revisit the Biscoff cookies I ate on the plane when Griffin's face suddenly fills the TV screen, standing next to the sideline reporter.

"Griffin, can you tell us anything about why today's game was such a struggle?" the reporter asks.

"Not every game is going to go our way, and it's normal for players to have off days. But I'd like to address some media attention that broke this morning regarding my personal life," he says. He shifts his eyes from talking to the reporter to speaking directly to the screen. My lungs freeze in place.

"News outlets have been spreading a photo of me and my girlfriend watching the Baltimore game yesterday, where I was supporting my college buddy, Lawrence Rogers," Griff says. "While I will confirm that

I am in a serious relationship, I'd like to ask for privacy at this time. This is especially an appeal to all the Crowns fans in Kansas City—the greatest fan base in the country—to please respect our privacy until we choose to share more openly about our relationship. While I've chosen this public life as a professional athlete, Danae is a private citizen with a need for confidentiality regarding her personal life right now. She means a lot to me, and I won't stand for her getting dragged into a media circus. Please show her respect by not invading her privacy or disrupting her daily life."

The reporter asks a couple of follow-up questions, but my ears tune everything out as Griffin's statement loops through my thoughts.

My girlfriend.

Serious relationship.

She means a lot to me.

Show her respect.

Standing abruptly, I turn off the TV and pace the room. I clench my phone as though I'll miss the call I'm sure is coming if I lose physical contact with the device. When a video call request pops up, tears immediately fill my eyes as I answer it.

"Babe, please don't end things. Please don't leave me over this," Griffin says, eyes full of anguish. His hair is a mess, and his hand aggressively rubs over his beard as he stares at the screen. "I'm so sorry, Danae. I wouldn't have taken us to that game if I would have known this would happen. It was dumb. I should have thought about the possibility and not pushed you to go. We should have stayed in the privacy of the condo. This is all my fault, but please, *please* don't let this be the end."

Warmth trickles down my cheeks as the tears spill over, coating my lips with salt.

"Please spell out the thought factory for me. I'm dying over here," Griffin says, leaning his forehead against his palm. "I'd pay every cent I have, or ever will have, for someone to give me a teleportation device so I could be there wiping those tears away right now. Please tell me what you're thinking."

Wiping my cheeks with one hand, I lean against the wall and slowly slide down to sit on the floor. Propping the hand holding the phone against one knee, I blow out a long exhale. "We're not over," I say, and Griffin lets out a similar exhale. "I mean, there were definitely some moments when the 'this is over' column had significantly more bullet points in it. But everything you said in your interview tipped the scale back the other way."

Griffin's entire body droops, his torso collapsing against the desk he's been leaning on, as though relief has released all the panic ballooned inside him. "Thank you," he says, wiping a hand down his face as he sits back up. "Thank you for not giving up on me. On this. On us. You would have every right to wash your hands of all this nonsense."

"I can't lie—I feel very unequipped to deal with the nonsense. Twenty kindergarteners screaming and flailing and sometimes vomiting in a room filled with books—that nonsense I can deal with. Media attention and people digging into Jason's past because I'm dating a famous athlete? Not the nonsense I'm prepared for," I say, wiping the remainder of my tears away.

Griffin's face hardens. "As soon as Sam told me what was going on, I was ready to hop on a plane. If I wouldn't have been in breach of contract, I would have skipped the game and been there throwing those vultures off your front lawn."

I huff a small laugh. "Well, it's a townhouse, so I don't exactly have a lawn."

A smile slowly breaks across Griffin's face. "Did you just make a joke? At a time like this? Here I was, suffocating the whole game thinking that you would be showing me the exit door from your life, and now you're joking about the mob of reporters outside?"

"Like I said, the exit door column did have more selling points for a minute there, the mob being a rather large one," I say, smiling to soften the statement. I lean my head against my free hand. "But Jason's social worker called and said nothing about this should inhibit the adoption moving forward. That was my biggest concern."

Griffin's head drops back slightly, and he takes a big inhale of relief. "Thank goodness," he says on the exhale.

My voice falls to practically a whisper. "I'm sorry about the game. I should have waited until afterward to call you or Samantha."

"Absolutely not. A situation like that is not something you carry by yourself, not even for a minute. You did the right thing calling to make sure I knew. I couldn't care less about losing a game, not right now. All I care about is that you feel safe," Griffin says, voice slowly warming with each word, like a pot of water set to boil.

We stare at each other through the screen, wordlessly watching each other's faces. He hums. "Did you know that your eyes turn fully green when you cry?" he asks. Smiling, I shake my head. "It's like every fleck of gold gets chased away by the saltwater. They're like a vibrant meadow green all of a sudden. So beautiful." His final statement is a whisper.

Blushing, I glance down, breaking eye contact. When I look back up, his smile is soft. "I really wish I could kiss you right now," he says. "Hold you. Run my fingers through your hair. Sit next to you for hours."

"Right after I get to watch you throw all the reporters off my imaginary lawn. I'd kinda like to see that," I respond with a smirk.

He sits up, puffing out his chest. "Would that display of alpha male protection impress you?"

I burst out laughing, the reverberation chasing away the lingering worry still hiding in my nerves. "I can't say it *wouldn't* impress me."

Griffin's face turns serious. "Are they still out there?"

Blowing out a breath, I rise to my feet so I can peek through the blinds on the kitchen window. It's quiet, empty. Normal. "They're gone," I say, surprise in my tone. "I guess word traveled fast about Griffin West not standing for media circuses on my doorstep."

"You let me know the second anyone else bothers you," Griffin says. "Sam's already contacted a lawyer about getting any article mentioning Jason's personal information taken down. I'm going to do everything I can to protect him. Both of you. I'm sorry that it's necessary. That I've brought this mess into your life."

"I'm not sorry that you're in my life," I say, hearing his unspoken need for reassurance. "I'm only sorry that I can't be there to kiss you right now."

CHAPTER THIRTY-FOUR

Griffin

I get to see your beautiful face in person today. Can you come to my house straight from school? I should get there by three.

I can't wait to see you, but it will probably be a couple of hours after the end of school before we can make it over. I have to decorate the library for a special event tomorrow.

Then can I come there to help you?

Are you sure you want to do that?

I'm positive I want to see you every second that I possibly can. And also positive that I want to help you in every way I can.

Then come on over. Maybe wait till the pick-up line dwindles down. Maybe around 3:30? I'll let you in the side door.

ME

Sounds good. What's your go-to coffee shop order?

DANAE

Morning or afternoon?

ME

Both.

DANAE

Mornings = hot vanilla latte. Afternoons = decaf caramel cold brew.

ME

Of course that was my general question of the morning, not relevant to any occurrences today.

DANAE

<winky-face emoji> What's yours?

ME

One cup of black coffee in the morning. Never in the afternoon.

DANAE

So I'm drinking alone this afternoon, huh?

ME

You'll be the only one with a coffee, but you absolutely won't be alone.

"Sneaking me in past the principal, huh?" I tease as I step into the building with Danae. "This is giving forbidden vibes, and I can't say I dislike it."

Danae slaps my chest, and I catch her hand to hold it there while I take a step closer to her. We're in the entry between the locked outer doors and the second set of glass doors opening into the hallway of the school, and I intend to take advantage of this illusion of privacy. A quick glance ensures that the hallway is empty, so I wrap an arm around Danae's waist and pull her to me.

I graze a gentle kiss across her lips, smiling when she sighs and relaxes against me. Threading my fingers through her hair, I kiss her a little more firmly but still stay on the low end of the "passionate" spectrum. Breaking away from her lips, I brush the tip of my nose against hers.

"These past four days have been worse than the post-surgery pain," I murmur.

"Worse than a first grader swiping an entire display of book fair knick-knacks off the table," she replies.

I lean back and raise an eyebrow. "Wait, has that actually happened?"

"He didn't have enough money left over for the chocolate bar calculator. It was very distressing," Danae says gravely. "And a huge headache to clean up."

"I have a confession to make," I say. "I just realized I left your iced coffee in the car. But I don't want to let go of you to go get it."

Trailing one finger down her arm, I take her hand in mine, pleased by her shiver that follows my touch. She shakes her head slightly, as if clearing her mind. "I don't care about the coffee."

"Good," I say. "Let's go get that library decorated so we can get to my house."

Following her through the hallway, we step through the double doors of the library. I recognize her friend, Kara, standing there keeping Jason occupied, and I make a mental note to thank her for running interference to give me that first moment alone with Danae. An autographed jersey for her husband should work, after hearing about Ron's ecstatic reaction to the first round of autographed merch I gave him.

When Jason sees us enter, he sprints across the room. I kneel down to catch him in a hug. "Fireball! I missed you!"

"Mr. Griffin! You're here at my school! This is so cool. Too bad all my friends are gone already because they know that my mom is dating you now, and I promised that someday I'd bring you here to meet everyone, and they act like they don't believe me, but I think they're just jealous." His words are one unending, stream-of-consciousness sentence.

Pulling back to see his face, I scan his green eyes, the freckles that have multiplied under the spring sun, that red hair that stands out like a fire signal. *Man, I missed this kid.* My heart is suddenly tight, like a fist clenching to brace for the impact of a punch. "It's good to see you. I'll definitely come visit sometime when your friends are here. I'll work it out with your mom, okay?"

Standing up, I nod my head at Kara. "Good to see you again, Kara. We'll have to get you and Ron out to some games with Danae and Jason sometime this season."

She turns to look at Danae. "This friendship is winning me 'wife of the year' status for the rest of my life." Turning back to me, she adds, "I gladly accept the offer. Not all of us are baseball-haters."

"Hey!" Danae exclaims with mock offense. "No need to make me look bad."

"Nothing could make you look bad, babe." I watch both women melt before my eyes. I wink at Danae and add, "Now put me to work. What are we decorating?"

"I've gotta go pick up Millie from daycare," Kara says. "But I'll talk to you tomorrow, Danae." Her insistent tone adequately communicates the demand behind her statement. I hide a smile.

"Okay, we're transforming this space from regular library into reading café extraordinaire," Danae says, pulling out a tub labeled "Reading Week Supplies."

"And why's that?" I ask, mostly because I want to hear her passion for her job come through in the explanation.

"We've been celebrating reading all week, but tomorrow we have an extra-special experience," she explains. "The fifth graders get to dress up and act like the servers at a fancy reading restaurant, helping the younger kids find books they might like. Then they serve cookies before sitting down at the tables to read a book aloud to a small group of students."

Grinning at the enthusiasm in her voice, I say, "I love it. What a great way for the younger grades to see reading as a special experience."

Danae beams at my praise. "*And* it's an opportunity for the oldest kids to model helpful behavior for the younger students. Plus, work on their reading fluency. It's one of my favorite days of the year, even if it's a lot of extra work."

We spend the next thirty minutes draping twinkle lights from the ceiling and covering the overhead lights with sheer fabric to soften the fluorescent glow. We rearrange tables and cover them with tablecloths and book character-inspired centerpieces. Jason flits around adding finishing touches and filling me in on the many, many things that have transpired in his life over the past four days. As the space comes together, I let out a low whistle.

"Looks pretty amazing. Maybe I would have enjoyed reading slightly more if it had been approached this way when I was a kid," I say.

"Speaking of you enjoying reading, have you made any progress on the audiobook?" Danae asks, layering excessive amounts of casual into her tone.

"I'll have you know I finished it on the flight here," I say, feeling far too proud for a grown man who just admitted to completing a children's fiction book.

When Danae's eyes sparkle with delight, the pride runs deeper. Jason's enthusiastic cheer only serves to pile it on.

"And?" Danae asks.

I clear my throat. "And it was . . . good."

"Just good?" she clarifies.

"You know how you told me that you could see how *other* people enjoy the atmosphere of baseball games?" I ask. Her mouth quirks as she rolls her eyes and crosses her arms. I smile and continue, "I can see how you and Jason love it. But I'd still rather be listening to a sports podcast than a bunch of kid wizards learning how to make objects float in the air. I think this was a one and done experience."

Jason immediately lets out a wail of offense, launching into an explanation about how this is only the beginning, and the books get so much better as you learn more about the characters . . .

His voice fades from my consciousness, though, as Danae saunters toward me, a flirtatious smile on her face. She leans onto her tiptoes and places her hand on one of my cheeks and her lips on the other. "I appreciate you trying it," she says. "Even if you sorely lack literary taste."

I catch her in my arms and tickle her sides, burying my face in her neck under the guise of punishing her for that comment, but really I want to inhale her scent. That smell I've been aching for the past four days that felt more like four decades apart from her.

How did I get here? So completely gone for a woman I've known less than three months?

I'm not sure how it happened, but I'm definitely gone. And I don't want to be found.

After completing the library transformation, I convince Danae to transfer Jason's booster over to my Jeep to ride over to my house together. I don't care that I'll have to drive them back to her car later tonight—I don't want to spend a single second apart. Not even a twenty-minute drive.

I answer all of Jason's questions about the exhibition games in Texas and ask him about his predictions for the upcoming season. The kid has a remarkable grasp on the game, not only from an enjoyment level, but an analytical level.

We're getting out of the car in the garage when the second garage door opens and Sam pulls in. Jason immediately starts jumping up and down next to the driver's door, and I see the enamored grin on Sam's face. I think she's almost as far gone for Danae and Jason as I am, in her own sister and auntie way.

"My guy, you ready for some dinner and Mario Kart?" Sam asks as she hugs Jason. "I picked up the best Chinese food in town. Can you help me carry it?"

"Ma'am, yes ma'am!" Jason yells, throwing in a serious salute. Sam hands him the lighter bag of food, then pauses to hug Danae before grabbing the other bag.

I heat up the meal that my chef left in the fridge because the start of the season means sticking to my assigned food regimen as much as possible. I enjoy watching Jason's attempts to use chopsticks, though, before he gives up and reaches for a fork.

Danae and I start clearing the table after dinner, and Sam convinces Jason to go with her to get warmed up on Mario Kart. "I promise I'll come join you here in a little bit," I say. "After I get everything cleaned up and talk with your mom."

"And after you smoochy-kiss," Jason adds, making ridiculously cheesy kissing faces.

Rising to the teasing challenge of this ten-year-old kid, I take Danae's hand, twirl her around, and pull her to me for a quick "smoochy-kiss."

"Ahhh, my eyes are melting," Jason says, palms covering his eyes. His toothy smile gives away his true feelings, though.

"You better get some practice rounds in before I totally school you at Mario Kart," I say, shooing him toward the basement door. As soon as the door closes, I pull Danae back into a true smoochy-kiss. "You can leave the dishes. I'll clean up later."

It's one of those spring days when the sun is warming the earth to a just-right temperature, so I lead Danae to the back porch. The saucer magnolia trees in my backyard are in full pink bloom, turning the covered porch into an oasis with a view. I have several seating options available, but I guide her to the large, cushioned porch swing. She pulls her feet up, and I wrap an arm around her knees, locking her in close to me.

"So, tell me how the past few days have been. And be honest," I say. She seemed okay by the end of our video call that first day the news story broke. Still, I've worried that the cons column of the "Being with Griffin" list may have multiplied in my absence. From what I could tell, news stations seemed to mostly kill the story, and she hasn't told me about any other media ambushes at home or at school. But there was always the niggling doubt that she could be secretly reevaluating our relationship without telling me.

Danae pauses a moment to take in the view, as though gathering her thoughts from the corners of the yard. "Weird," she finally answers.

"Weird doesn't sound great. Weird makes me nervous," I say.

She looks at me with a half-smile. "Oh, good. Finally, I'm not the only one who's anxious all the time. I finally found something for you to be nervous about."

"You underestimate the amount of anxiety I consistently have that at any given moment you're going to see right through me and walk away," I say. I've pushed levity into my tone to cover up the very raw truth at the surface of my statement.

Danae's eyes soften, and she reaches up to trace my jaw with her fingers. "I see you, Griff. *You*. And I'm not tempted to walk away from you. It's the rest of the circus that makes things confusing." Her eyes drop, and my heart follows.

"I'm sorry about the circus. I'm sorry that who I am isn't always the soft, quiet place you need," I say, studying her fingernails. They're growing back after clear evidence of an attack, freshly painted with glossy clear polish. I take a deep breath, willing myself to press forward. "What's been the hardest part?"

"My parents keep calling me," Danae says, and my eyes shoot up to hers in surprise. "I haven't answered any of their calls. I'm pretty sure I know the gist of what they might have to say, and I'm not sure I'm strong enough to withstand their manipulation."

"What do you mean?" I ask, taking her hand in mine to halt her thumb's assault on that fresh coat of polish.

She sighs, long and slow. "I'm sure they saw the news about us dating. And I'm sure that they're suddenly very interested in being back in my life now that I'm in a relationship with someone famous. Someone famous and wealthy."

Sadness and rage wrestle in my chest as I watch tears prick her eyes as she continues. "I'd be worthwhile to them again now that I'm not throwing my life away as a teacher and single mom to a 'broken kid.'"

The phrase is emphasized by her sarcasm and air quotes, and the rage wins out over the sadness that her parents actually spoke those words to her. About Jason.

"Why don't you call them right now? While I'm here with you," I say before even thinking it through. Her eyes are the ones to shoot to mine with surprise now. "I'm serious. You can't avoid them forever, and that's not a confrontation you should have alone."

"Are you sure?" she asks. Her tone is hesitant, but her eyes shimmer with hope.

I lean in to gently kiss her lips, sealing my assurance. "I'll go get your phone. You're not doing this alone, Danae. We're a team. I'm with you."

CHAPTER THIRTY-FIVE

Danae

I tems *not* on my bingo card for this year?

    1. Calling my parents.

2. Calling my parents while in the presence of Griffin West.

I knew, in theory, our relationship would eventually progress to a point where I would have to communicate *something* to my parents about us. But that anxiety can of worms was one I was nowhere near opening. Or touching. Or even acknowledging its existence.

But now, here I am, pacing Griffin West's back porch while I listen to the *ring, ring, ring* of my outgoing call. To my parents. Griffin went inside to retrieve my phone and a box of tissues, correctly anticipating how this will likely go. Now he's standing guard next to me.

When my mom answers, she quickly announces that she's putting me on speaker so my dad can talk too.

"Danae, it's so great to hear from you, darling," my dad says. Like nails on a chalkboard, the sound of his voice grates against my ears. His words—subtly scolding, as though I'm the one who cut off communication—add insult to auditory injury. I'm tempted to hang up without a word, until I meet Griffin's eyes and see the encouragement there. Encouragement that he's here to support *me*. Not encouragement to blindly patch things up with my parents.

"Mom, Dad, hi. I'm just returning your missed calls," I state.

"Well, it's been such a long time since we heard from you, we wanted to check in and see how things are going for you and that dear little boy who's living with you," Mom's saccharine voice cuts in. It's the overly-soothing kind of tone that you think is only used by actors in soap operas, but, nope—Judy Collins has it down to a real-life art.

"Need I remind you, I'm not the person who exited our familial relationship," I say. I hear the wobble in my voice, but Griffin rubs my back, infusing me with strength. "Why are you calling now?"

"It certainly seems like you're rewriting history a little bit," my dad says, his voice gaining an edge of frustration.

"What your father means"—Mom cuts in with that falsely soothing tone—"is that you might have overreacted and taken things the wrong way in the past. But we want to know how you're doing. Especially with the news story that broke last week. Of course, we want to make sure our daughter is okay after such a dramatic turn of events."

Pinching the bridge of my nose, I squeeze my eyes shut. "I'm fine. Thanks for checking. Is that all?"

"Well, if you really are in a new relationship, don't you think we should meet whoever it is that you're dating?" my dad asks.

Pursing my lips, I choose my words carefully. "You didn't seem at all interested in meeting the guy I dated right after I started teaching. So, no, I don't see your point."

There's a jealous glint in Griffin's eyes, and the sight is enough to bring a small smile to my face. I reach up and stroke my fingers through his beard, and his fingers dig more possessively into my back. *I'd really like to end this phone call so I can pay more attention to the man in front of me.*

"That relationship was over before it started," my dad says, prompting an eye roll on my end.

"Besides, it's a different story now that you have Jason with you. We should probably meet any man who's going to spend time around our grandson," my mom adds, and my circulatory system floods with fire.

"Don't you dare try to make this about *your* grandson. You didn't want anything to do with Jason or me before now. Be honest about why you suddenly care," I demand.

There's an awkward moment of silence, and I can envision the back and forth pointing going on between my parents. Dad must have drawn the short straw because he's the one who finally speaks. "Danae, darling, if you're dating someone like Griffin West, it certainly seems appropriate that we be included in your future plans for your relationship. I can't believe you haven't introduced us already."

"And there it is," I say, wobble returning to my voice. "I'm dating someone useful to your ambitions, and suddenly you care that I exist again."

"That's quite the accusation to make," Mom says, soothing tone evaporating. "We're your parents, and we've always loved you and wanted what's best for you. Do you think your private education and college paid for themselves? You think all the head starts we gave you in life aren't evidence of our love for you? Just because you made some ill-advised choices doesn't mean that we—"

"Ill-advised choices?" I cut her off. "You mean my choice to become a teacher instead of a trophy wife? Or my choice to adopt Jason instead of trying to bag an eligible bachelor with a trust fund? I'm very sorry that your view of the world would categorize my choices as ill-advised."

My entire body is shaking from anger, adrenaline, anxiety, fear, disappointment, all of the above. Just as the phone—the conversation—starts to feel too heavy to hold anymore, I'm pulled tightly against Griffin's chest. His arm wraps firmly around me, supporting my weakness with his strength, as he takes the phone out of my hand.

"Danae is finished with this conversation. Please don't contact her unless she contacts you first," he states. His voice is calm, but I sense the raging undercurrent of protective anger. He ends the call and stuffs my phone into his pocket before securely fastening his other arm around me.

I bury my head into his chest as my tear ducts detonate. I'm sobbing against him, not even attempting to stem the flow of sadness. Anger. Hurt.

This is not a pretty, staring-sadly-out-the-window movie-scene cry. This is an ugly, eyes-on-fire, snot-dripping-like-water-from-my-nose cry.

I cry for Jason not having loving grandparents on top of everything else he's missed out on.

I cry for my childhood, for all the unnecessary anxiety little Danae carried around.

I cry for my future, unable to imagine a cordial relationship with my family, much less a loving one.

I cry for the shame, the embarrassment of Griffin witnessing the fact that I wasn't worthy of my parents' attention until I was associated with him.

I cry for the possibility that someday Griffin could wake up and realize I'm not worth keeping around. Even as he holds me close to him, holds me like he'd never dream of letting go.

The adrenaline crash takes my shaking body to the next level on the Richter scale. Griffin swivels his torso and threads an arm under my knees, scooping me into his arms in one flawless movement. I wrap an arm around his neck, although let's be honest—I'm completely useless. In no universe could a case be made that I am supporting any of my own weight. The sobs that won't stop are sucking up every ounce of energy.

Griffin carefully eases us onto the cushioned couch and hands me the tissue box. He holds me on his lap and gently scratches my back, occasionally pressing kisses to my temple or forehead or cheek. He lets me cry until my body has evicted every spare ounce of water, which is not a short amount of time.

As the tears wind down, my body goes rigid as the thoughts wind up. The thought factory is spiraling off the rails. My muscles tense in preparation to stand, to back away, but Griffin's arms tighten around me right before I can move.

"Nope," he says. "You're not going anywhere. Because I'm not going anywhere. Let me go ahead and directly address some of what I think is going on up here," he says, motioning toward my head.

"Yes, I overheard most of what your parents said. Yes, it's taking a tremendous amount of self-restraint not to track them down and show them exactly what I think of them. No, I am not your parents. I don't love you because you add value to my life—even though you do. I love you because of who you are, because of your heart, your tenderness, your concern for others, your passion for books and Jason and teaching. I love you for all the amazing ways you bring light to the world. I am here, and I am not leaving," he says.

I love you. His words register in my mind, and my eyes double in size.

"You love me?" I whisper.

Griffin slowly tucks a strand of (wet) hair behind my ear and gently wipes my (wet) cheeks with his thumb before he answers. "I love you, Danae. And before you say anything, I should tell you one other thing. Now that I better understand the context of your suspicion toward people with financial wealth, I want to be up-front and tell you that this past week I paid in advance for six months of Jason's weekly therapy and occupational therapist appointments."

Jerking back, my brain struggles to choose an emotional direction. "You what? Griffin, you can't just—"

"I am not throwing my wealth around to show off. I'm not trying to buy anyone's affection or good graces. I have resources, and I'm investing them in something I care about. Someone. Well, two some-ones. Because I care about you and Jason. So paying to make sure he gets the professional help he needs to process his trauma—to support *you* in that way—is an absolute no-brainer. And it's already done, so there's no point in trying to talk me out of it. And I'll continue paying as long as he needs to keep going," Griffin states, no-nonsense tone engaged.

I flop against his chest, dead weight once again.

"I know that being with me is complicated. And . . . unideal, in a lot of ways, but I'm doing anything I can to show you that you and Jason are safe with me," Griffin murmurs against my ear. His fingertips graze paths up and down my forearm, and my eyes track the movement, slowly calming my body.

"Griff?" I whisper, still watching his fingers.

"*Mmhmm?*" he hums.

Lifting my head to face him, I say, "I love you too."

His hand finds my cheek, thumb tracing the line of my lips, then making its way up to brush the final tear from under my eye. He whispers, "I hate to see you cry, but the green of your eyes is even more emerald in person. You're so beautiful when you cry—even though I wish I never had to see it happen ever again."

I lean in to his lips, my heart calming at the contact.

Safe. We're safe.

Aren't we?

CHAPTER THIRTY-SIX

Griffin

The energy of the locker room is one part nerves to three parts excitement.

It's opening day.

We're lucky to have our first series at home, which means it's also our home opener for the season. Kansas City fans show up ready to tailgate the minute the parking lot opens, and a lot of people take the day off of work and pull their kids out of school in order to attend the afternoon game.

Unfortunately, Danae and Jason are *not* taking off of work and school in order to be here today, which means my own energy is in reverse proportion to the rest of the team's. I'm so ready to get back out on the field in our own stadium, to hear the roar of the Crowns fans—I only wish the two individuals who have skyrocketed to the top of my "most important people" list could be here.

When Danae was weighing the decision of whether or not to skip school today for the opening game, I convinced her not to. They'll be here for the games on Saturday and Sunday, where they'll get to meet my parents, which is way more important. Expecting Danae to play hooky for me would be unreasonable, especially after the media fiasco last week and the ensuing catastrophe with her parents.

Did I find out where they live and casually drive by to scope things out?

I plead the fifth.

It's the right call to not make her come today. But that doesn't mean I'm happy about it.

My vision suddenly goes dark as the visor of my baseball cap tips down to cover my face. I know without seeing that it was Adrian's doing, so I flail a fist to make contact with his body as I pull my hat up. He feigns serious injury for a split second before breaking into a grin and plopping down next to me.

"Ready for the day, West?" he asks.

I nod.

"Head? Shoulder? Heart? All ready?" he asks, uncharacteristically serious.

No, I'm absolutely terrified. Scared that my shoulder could give out. Scared that I'm not going to play up to snuff, despite a great training camp. Sad that the woman I love isn't here to watch me play. Nervous that my mind is too distracted by her to play my best.

Forcing a grin, I smack his visor down. "Readier than you," I say. "Let's get out there."

As I rise to follow Adrian out of the locker room, I hear the *ping* of a message notification from my phone. When I check the screen, there's a new voice memo from Danae. My fake grin becomes genuine as I hit play.

"Hey, Griff. I assume you'll be heading onto the field soon for warm-ups, so I hope I catch you in time. Please ignore the squeals in the background. I'm hiding in the library storage room while the first-grade class plays at centers. I just wanted to tell you good luck and that I wish I could be there to hug you before the game. You're going to be amazing, and I can't wait to talk to you tonight. I love you."

Although the rest of the team has filed out of the locker room, I take an extra minute to listen to the memo one more time. When I make my way to the field, I have a lot more pep in my step.

The starting position players do our typical dynamic stretches and warm-up throwing routines. Smiles are big as we watch the stands fill in and fans hold up homemade signs with our names. Drew points out a giant cutout of me giving Adrian a piggyback ride off the field last week, and we laugh until we get yelled at to focus.

As we head to the dugout after warm-ups, Adrian jogs next to me. "Sam's here, but not Danae and Jason?" he asks.

"Yep," I say. "Con of having opening day be an afternoon game on a Thursday. But Danae sent me a good-luck voice memo, so I know she's thinking about me."

"Yeah, it sucks that they can't be here," he agrees. "You know she'll be watching at home, though, once they get out of school."

Huffing a laugh, I say, "Actually, I don't know that she'll be watching at home. She still hates baseball."

"She seems to love you, though. That's gotta count for something," Adrian says, face serious. In the next second, his goofy grin is back. "Besides, you know that Jason is going to demand she turn it on as soon as they get home from school. The nickname Fireball suits him for more reasons than one."

Chuckling, I clap Adrian's back. "You are not wrong, my friend."

"Let's go out there and have some fun," he says, eyes twinkling.

I take a second to look around the stadium. The grass, the red dirt, the white lines. The mass of individual bodies dressed in blue and white. The laughter, the chatter, the music playing over the speakers. I inhale the earthy scent of the field, the buttery aroma of popcorn, the salty smell of sweat. I feel the leather of the baseball mitt on my hand, the comforting squeeze of how the material has molded around my fingers over time.

Exhaling, I smile over at Adrian. "Let's go have some fun."

"It was the best catch ever!" Jason practically screams into the phone, and I can't hold in my laughter any longer.

"I'm glad it's that easy to impress you," I say. The kid has broken down practically every play of the game, but he's taken extra time to gush about one particularly tricky catch I made in the eighth inning.

I'd be lying if I said it hasn't made my heart double in size.

"No way, it was just that good. A total Wizard of Defense move!" Jason says. "I can't wait to watch in real life on Saturday!"

"Yeah, I'm excited for you to be there, too, Fireball. Make sure you save a few chicken tenders for your mom, okay?" I say. "Can I tell her hi real quick?"

"Oh, okay. I'll give her the phone. See you Saturday!" he chirps before yelling, "Mom! Mr. Griffin wants to talk to you!"

I'm not sure how Danae doesn't break down crying every time he calls her "Mom," because that's certainly the response I'm fighting every time I hear it.

"Hey, babe," Danae says softly a few seconds later.

"We've officially moved to 'babe' territory, huh? Have you alerted Kara?" I tease.

"Ha ha," she says. I imagine Danae rolling those beautiful hazel eyes and kick myself for not starting this as a video call. There's a smile in her voice when she continues. "I will gladly call you 'babe,' Griff, and whatever other terms of endearment come with the 'I love you' territory. But never will I ever call you 'Wizard of Defense,' so strike that from your expectations."

"I think I can handle that," I say. "Remind me again why I didn't drive straight to your house right after the game tonight?"

"Because Jason is getting into bed right now," she reminds me.

"Seems like all the more reason for me to be there," I say, dropping the octave of my voice.

"*And* it's a school night," she adds, but her tone sounds flustered now.

"Whatever you say. I'm looking forward to dinner tomorrow, though," I say. "You okay if we sit at the bar instead of at a table? I want to catch up with Jeff a little bit."

"You just want easy access to bottomless cranberry lime sodas, don't you?" Danae says, and the teasing tone in her voice makes me want to drive straight over there and kiss her. For a long time.

I smile at the ceiling instead. "You caught me. I'll see you tomorrow. I love you."

"Love you too, Griff."

CHAPTER THIRTY-SEVEN

Danae

"You really don't need to be nervous. Our parents are awesome. They're friends with everyone. Heck—they love Griffin, so of course they'll love you," Samantha says. Jason and I are following her through the inner labyrinth of the Crowns stadium, toward the locker room. We'll head up to Griffin's suite soon, but we're meeting him to say hello before the game starts. Maybe eventually I'll feel comfortable enough to greet him from the front of the stands like some of the other wives and girlfriends do during warm-ups.

But today is not that day.

For now, we're flying under the radar. I'm not prepared for another onslaught of media attention. We'll tell Griffin good luck, and then I will focus on deep breathing while we make our way to the suite, where I will be meeting Griffin's parents for the first time. There are way too many games for them to travel up from Oklahoma for every one, but they're here for the games today and tomorrow.

I spent most of last night writing out flow charts of every possible way this first meeting could go. I am well-prepared for whatever turn our conversation might take, and yet, in an equally real sense, not at all prepared.

My eyes glaze over as my mind chases itself down the rabbit hole of "What if his parents ask about such and such" questions, and I'm startled when Jason yanks his hand out of mine. Pulling my vision back into focus, I see him sprinting to Griffin down the hallway. My heart squeezes at the sight, and I pick up my own pace.

When Griffin's eyes find me, his grin turns just this side of wicked as I approach. It only takes two giant steps from him to close the distance between us. He immediately grabs my hand, guiding me into a slow-motion twirl before securing me in place with a hand on either hip.

"Number eleven, huh?" he says, huskiness permeating his tone. His gaze languidly travels down my body and back up to meet my eyes again.

I trace the numbers on his jersey, mirrored on the one I purchased earlier today.

"Only ever number eleven," I murmur, feeling a blush creep to my cheeks.

Griffin skims a kiss over the hottest part of my cheek, only adding to the flush.

"Good luck!" I blurt. "Break a leg? Is saying 'good luck' bad luck in baseball? I wish you well. You got this. Go get 'em, cowboy? Please help me out here."

A deep laugh echoes in the hallway as Griffin loses the battle to stifle his response to my verbal tripping. Samantha and Jason join in with their own giggles. "'Good luck' is fine," Griffin says. He leans in and adds in a lower tone, "Although we could further explore this cowboy talk."

I smack him on the arm before he pulls me into a hug. "It's good to have you here today," he says in my ear. "My parents have talked about nothing other than meeting you and Jason the last three times I've called them."

Abruptly pulling back, I grill him one final time. "Anything else I need to know? Have you thought of any last-minute pieces of information that I should be equipped with heading into this meeting? What additional intel do I need?"

His lips quirk in a half-smile. "Not a thing. They're going to love you both. And I really think that you're going to love them too," he says, voice warm. "And the camera crew knows not to take any video footage of our suite for the jumbotron, so don't be worried about that. I've gotta get back into the locker room, but I'll see you after, okay?"

Griffin receives a final high five from Jason as he says, "I had an extra dish of chicken tenders sent to the suite just for you, Fireball."

"Let's gooo!" Jason says, eyes lighting up. "See you after the game, Mr. Griffin! I'll be cheering as loud as I can!"

"You must be Danae!" a sweet, feminine voice exclaims.

So much for beating Griffin's parents to the suite and having time to shut myself in the bathroom to mentally rehearse my preparation lists.

"I'm Cinda, Griffin and Sammi's mom!" the woman says as she pulls me into a generous hug. "I've been aching to meet you ever since Griff mentioned you back in January." She leans back but keeps her hands on my arms as she looks me over. "This is a real treat," Cinda adds, voice like honey and blue eyes dancing.

"Are you gonna give me a chance to introduce myself, too, or are you hogging her all to yourself today?" The deep voice has an uncanny similarity to Griffin's cadence, and when I look over to the source of the voice, I'm struck by the physical similarities as well. He's a couple of inches taller than Griffin, but with the same jawline and winsome smile.

Allowing myself to breathe and smile widely, I say, "You *have* to be Griffin's dad."

His laughter booms just like Griffin's belly laughs, and he holds out a hand to shake mine. "I'm David. It's a pleasure to meet you. Now where's the little guy I've heard so much about?"

At his question, I realize that Jason has been hiding behind me, but he peeks his head around my side. David crouches down and holds out his hand in an open invitation for a handshake or high five.

"You must be Jason. I'm David, Griffin's dad. He's told me a lot about how cool you are. I've been dying to hear some of those baseball stats you know so much about."

Jason takes a step to the side, revealing his full self from behind me. "You like baseball too?"

"Of course! You have me to thank for getting Griffin to start playing. Of course, he flew well beyond my coaching abilities after a season or two, but watching baseball is my favorite hobby," David says, tone warm and inviting. "It sounds like I might finally have a baseball buddy who likes to break down the plays as much as I do. Mrs. West here is all about the atmosphere, not so much the technical part of the game."

The whole time David's been talking, he's stayed eye-level with Jason with his palm outstretched. I watch the guards slowly retract from Jason's eyes, and he finally slaps David's hand with a hearty high five.

"I'm most worried about the Crowns' batting lineup. They might need to change the order from what they did in spring training," Jason says.

"You think so?" David asks. "Tell me more about that. Well, tell me more about that after we get some snacks." He stands to his full height and motions toward the food trays, and Jason happily scurries to check out the offerings.

Samantha has been quietly observing the exchange but suddenly shrieks, "What are you doing here?!" Her body is a blur as she launches herself at someone who just came out of the bathroom.

"Heya, sis," a muffled voice says from underneath Samantha's smothering.

"I can't believe you didn't tell me you were coming!" she says as she releases him. She looks over her shoulder at me and gestures toward the young man in front of her. "This is my baby brother, Ian."

Ian rolls his eyes. "I am not a baby. I'm in college, Sam. A legal adult."

Samantha playfully pinches his cheeks. "But you'll always be my baby."

"You're worse than Mom," Ian says with a sigh. From the looks of his expression, he's used to this kind of behavior from Samantha. Despite his more stoic demeanor, he doesn't seem upset by it at all.

"I'm Danae Collins," I say, holding my hand out to Ian. "It's great to meet you! What are you studying at college?"

"Right now I'm majoring in biology, but I'm debating if I should double major in environmental science as well," Ian states matter-of-factly. "I was originally considering medical school, but now I'm intrigued by pursuing a career in research."

My eyes grow as I say, "Wow, sounds ambitious!"

Ian shrugs as Cinda beams at him and Samantha's smile turns forced. She twirls a finger through one of the pink lengths of her hair. Sparking brightness back into her expression, Samantha tells Ian, "I want to hear all about your semester. Tell me everything."

There are other people milling around in the suite, but with Samantha occupied with Ian and Jason fully absorbed in baseball talk with David, that leaves Cinda and me to chat. Which feels much more approachable than a full-family inquisition.

After filling plates with food, we sit at one of the high-top tables in the suite, leaving the good seats for the avid baseball fans.

"So," Cinda begins, "I want to hear about you and Griffin getting to know each other from your perspective. I've heard all about you from him, but I'm curious to hear about the relationship from your point of view."

I take a long sip of water to buy time and hydrate my brain. "That's quite the open-ended question!" I say, making her smile. "It's been a roller coaster to say the least. A roller coaster I never expected to get on."

Cinda smiles even bigger. "Yes, Griffin told me that you're not exactly a baseball fan."

"I assume he told you I didn't know who he was the first time we met?" I ask sheepishly.

"Oh, Sammi told us that. It's her favorite story to tell now!" Cinda says with a chuckle.

I fill Cinda in on the basics of our relationship thus far, toeing the line of guarded and honest. We pause our conversation to watch the opening of the game, cheering loudly when Griffin's name is announced. Jason sits next to David, talking his ear off about the team. David is a much better partner for Jason than I am, though, because he seems to ask appropriate follow-up questions that keep Jason talking even more. I'm suddenly blinking back tears as I watch them.

"That little boy has David eating out of the palm of his hand already," Cinda says, voice echoing my sentimentality. "He always connected so well with the boys who came into our home."

"How many kids did you foster?" I ask quietly.

"Fourteen kids over the course of six years, not including Sammi and Ian," she responds. "We closed our home for foster care after we decided to become their forever family."

I shake my head slowly. "Goodness, I can't even imagine what that would be like. I'm barely hanging on with one kid to focus on."

"Well, that's a totally different situation you have on your hands," Cinda says as we sit back down. "Similarities, of course, but you dove right into forever all on your own. That took a lot of bravery. How much preparation time did you have?"

"It was a couple of months before Jason moved in that his paternal grandmother approached me about the possibility of adopting him. I took an expedited foster care class and had several weeks to read as many books as possible. As valuable as the books are, I'm not sure anything can prepare you for the in-the-moment emotions, though," I say.

Cinda asks several gentle questions about my experience with Jason so far, and I find myself slowly opening up more and more. *This must be where Griffin got those human can opener skills.*

"And have you found a therapist yet?" Cinda asks.

"Yes, we see Jason's therapist once a week right now," I reply. "Plus the OT appointments."

"No, honey, I mean have you found a therapist for *you* yet?" Cinda clarifies.

"Oh, um, no, I haven't," I stutter. "I mean, I talk with Jessica, Jason's therapist, and learn a lot from her about what's going on in his mind and how I can help him regulate."

"But you need a professional to talk to just for you, hon," Cinda says. "Supporting a loved one as they work through their trauma isn't a light load. You'll need help processing your own secondary trauma if you want to continue being there for Jason."

My brows furrow. "So you had your own therapist apart from who Samantha and Ian saw?"

"Absolutely," Cinda says. "David went sometimes, too, although not as often as I did. Griffin and his older siblings even talked with her a handful of times. You make sure you're finding the support *you* need to stay healthy and regulated."

We're interrupted again by the announcement that Griffin is up to bat, so we turn our attention to the field. The remainder of the game is a dance between our conversation and watching Griffin, and by the end, I realize it's the most I've ever enjoyed a baseball game. As a bonus, the Crowns win 4–2, with Griffin scoring two of the runs. Jason gets a huge kick out of watching Adrian douse Griffin with a cooler of Gatorade during the post-game interview. Let's be honest—I get an equally big kick out of the sight, and the grin on Griffin's face has me weak at the knees all the way up in the top of the stadium.

Everyone hangs out in the suite until Griffin is cleaned up and able to join us. Despite the fact that his parents and brother are here, Griffin gives first attention to a very eager, very excited Jason. He places his hands on his knees and bends to look Jason in the eye.

"Did you see my long throw from deep in the shortstop hole in the sixth inning?" Griffin asks Jason, as though there's any doubt that Jason watched every single second.

"Yes!" Jason says with a fist pump and leap into the air. "I was afraid the ump was gonna call him safe when I just *knew* you got the ball to Sheffield in time. Good thing he called it right." Jason swings an imaginary bat so hard he spins himself in a circle. "And then you had that triple in the seventh inning—epic! Did you hear your dad and me cheering for you? Because we were super loud."

At Jason's mention of Griffin's dad, he finally has license to look around and greet everyone else. He's equally surprised by Ian's presence, giving him some sort of intricate handshake that must have taken years to perfect. After a bear hug from his mom and a manly slap on the back from his dad, Griffin turns to me and picks me up in a spinning hug.

"All my people here in one room after a solid win—nothing could make me happier," Griffin says, his face bright.

"I believe you're forgetting that you have two other siblings plus a sister-in-law," Cinda says sternly. "Should I tell Miranda and Sawyer that you've kicked them out of the family?"

Griffin rolls his eyes. "No, Mom, I didn't forget them. But they're too busy with their own grown-up lives to come to my games anymore."

"You can tell them that Ian and I are Griff's *favorite* siblings," Samantha chimes in.

"Now, Sammi—" Cinda begins, but David jumps in with a change of subject. "Jason here might have a future career in sportscasting. Kid's a natural at narrating the game-play."

We all watch with smiles as Jason visibly inflates, standing two inches taller and lifting his chin. Griffin holds his clenched hand out for a fist bump from Jason.

"Oh yeah, Fireball here has an incredible grasp on the game. And wait till you see him throw the ball," Griffin says, matching Jason's grin. "What do you say we all head back to my house to hang out for the evening? Mom and Dad, the guest room is ready for you, but you'll probably have to sleep on the floor somewhere, Ian."

"Whatever, I'm kicking Sam out of her bed," Ian retorts. A round of sibling bickering and teasing ensues that gives me a glimpse into the West family household, bringing a smile to my lips and a splinter to my heart.

And in that intuitive, charismatic way of his, Griffin is immediately right there, sensing my thoughts. He presses a kiss right below my ear and whispers, "I love you."

CHAPTER THIRTY-EIGHT

Griffin

First of all, it's been less than a day since my parents headed home and I flew out, and I've received no less than fourteen texts from my mom gushing about you.

<smiley face emoji> You were right. I loved her. Both of them.

What's second of all?

If you could have a lifetime supply of any one thing, what would it be?

You're not allowed to say new books.

Rude.

Think outside the box. Or should I say the pages.

DANAE

Dad jokes already, huh?

ME

Just proving I have what it takes in the Dad jokes department. I learned from the best.

You still have to answer.

DANAE

Snow days.

ME

???

As in, actual play in the snow days? Or snow days in the school schedule that you don't have to make up?

DANAE

Both. I'd need the unlimited days in the schedule so that I could choose to have an actual day in the snow with you and Jason anytime I want.

ME

I love it.

DANAE

I should clarify that the majority of these snow days would include me reading by the fireplace while you continue to play outside with Jason after my very short stint in the snow. With my lifetime supply of new books.

ME

Deal.

DANAE

If you could have any food be calorie-free so you could eat it any time, even when you're training, what would it be?

ME

Oooo, probably chips and queso. Definitely.

Hey, I wanted to ask you something else. Don't say no right away.

DANAE

What's wrong???

ME

Sorry, forgot to lead with nothing's wrong. I have a request that I know knee-jerk Danae would not say yes to. So please reserve judgment until I've fully pled my case.

DANAE

I'll make a concerted effort. This is not the best start, though.

ME

I want you to take off work on Thursday and pull Jason out of school.

DANAE

You have an uphill battle ahead of you.

ME

I know, I know. But we have one day off with no game on Thursday after we get home from this series before we start our stretch of home games. I'll still have training in the morning, but I want to take Jason to do something fun together. And Sam wants to hang out with you by herself for the day. She has something special planned and specifically asked to take you with her.

DANAE

What is it?

ME

I'm sworn to secrecy.

DANAE

But I'm your girlfriend. You love me.

ME

Ughhhh you can't do that. Not a fair fight. I promised Sam she could surprise you.

DANAE

This is all a part of your ploy to get me to take the day off, isn't it? Intrigue me with a mystery that I won't be able to stop thinking about.

ME

Is it working?

DANAE

It might be.

ME

I'll make your sub plans for you. "Have the kids read books for an hour." Done.

DANAE

You know that's not what I do.

ME

I do know. I just love to picture your cute furrowed brow and gorgeous pouty lips when I tease you.

DANAE

I am not pouting. Besides, I had an entire semester's worth of sub plans ready to go back in January. You never know when you'll wake up sick or have an emergency without time to plan.

ME

I am not even a little surprised by that.

So??

DANAE

Fine. I'll put in the request for the day off. On one condition.

ME

What's that?

DANAE

I get to see you for a little bit of this day off too.

ME

I wouldn't dream otherwise.

CHAPTER THIRTY-NINE

Danae

"Are you going to tell me where we're going?" I ask Samantha from the passenger seat. She and Griffin drove separately to my townhouse, where Griffin loaded Jason into his Jeep and I got into Samantha's car with her.

"Nope," Samantha replies, emphasizing the "p" sound at the end of the word.

"Not even a hint?" I plead.

Samantha shoots me a side eye, then looks back to the road. "I'm afraid you wouldn't agree to go with me if I told you where we're going."

"Samantha West, if you love me as a friend at all, you will tell me where we're going right now," I say. "You know I can't handle the anxiety of you making a statement like that."

Her smile turns smug as she continues staring straight ahead. "Consider this my way of stretching you into your growth zone. It's good for you."

Crossing my arms over my chest, I lean back in my seat with a *harrumph*.

Ten minutes later, we park in front of a tattoo parlor.

"Absolutely not. I am not getting a tattoo," I practically shriek. "What in the world would cause you to peg me as a spontaneous tattoo type of person?!"

Samantha rolls her eyes. "Not you, me! I'm getting a tattoo. I've been thinking about it for a long time, but I'm finally gonna do it. And I wanted you to be with me."

As my heart rate slows, a warm feeling spreads through my chest. "Really? You wanted *me* to come?"

"Yes. It's . . . pretty meaningful to me, and there aren't a ton of people here in KC who know about my full history, so I wanted you here with me," Samantha says, looking almost embarrassed.

I reach to place my hand on her arm. "I'm sorry I freaked out. I'm honored that you would want me here. Why not Griffin?"

Samantha bursts out laughing. "Because he's such a chicken about needles. When he gets shots, he has to lay down on the floor with his legs up so he doesn't pass out. No way he could handle being in a tattoo parlor. The man would faint before they even started."

I'm instantly laughing along with her, picturing Griffin lying on the floor to get a simple shot. "I finally have something good to tease him about," I say.

"You're most welcome," Samantha replies. "Now let's go before we miss my appointment time."

We head inside, where the tattoo artist leads us back to the chair. He pulls up an extra seat for me on the opposite side of Samantha from him, and she shows him the drawing of what she wants tattooed on her left wrist. When the tattoo artist leaves briefly to answer the phone, Samantha looks to me. "Um, Danae? Would you mind if I hold your hand while he does the tattoo?"

"Of course, I don't mind," I say, holding my hand out to her. "Are you sure you want to do this?"

"Yes. I'm sure. I don't have a fear of needles or anything," Samantha says. Her voice gets quieter. "But sometimes physical pain . . . I can sometimes have a hard time controlling my response to sudden pain. Holding your hand will help."

I give her hand a squeeze as the tattoo artist returns and disinfects her skin to prep for the tattoo. She's breathing methodically in through her nose, out through her mouth as he prepares to begin.

"Why don't you tell me about the meaning of the tattoo?" I say, hoping to distract her thoughts. "Why the bird on the branch?"

"Oh, it's because of a painting my mom has in their living room," Samantha begins. She flinches and tightens her grip on my hand at the first touch of the needle. Closing her eyes, she takes more calculated breaths.

"What's in the painting?" I prompt.

"It's a big tree with tons of branches, and it's like you can see below the surface of the soil to the root system as well. There are fourteen birds flying above the tree, and five birds perched in the branches," Samantha says, slowly relaxing as the artist continues his work. "Mom always said she wanted their home—for her and my dad—to be a safe place for kids to land, for however long that might be. The birds flying above the tree represent all the kids who eventually moved on from their home, and the five in the tree represent her forever kids. I'm pretty sure she stops by that painting every morning and thinks about each individual child those birds represent. Prays for all of our wellbeing."

The tattoo artist must have struck a nerve because Samantha flinches again. I trace a soothing pattern on her hand with my thumb.

"I'd love to see the painting someday. What made you decide to get this tattoo now?" I ask.

"Two reasons, really. One, I want a visible reminder that I'm loved and I belong. For any time that I'm tempted to doubt it. I know it's probably hard for you to look at how amazing my parents are—at how amazing Griffin is—and think that I could ever doubt that. But trauma does weird things to your sense of reality sometimes," Samantha says, blowing out another slow breath. "And two, I want it to be a sort of motivation to find my own place to roost now."

"What do you mean?"

Samantha's expression is thoughtful as she searches for the words to explain. "Lately, I've been feeling like I don't really have any clear direction in my life. Coming up here to live with Griffin and help him out was supposed to be a short-term gig, something to do while I figured out what I wanted to *do*. But I still haven't figured out what that is."

"I know that Griffin loves having you here, though, Samantha," I say. "It's not like Griffin's going to kick you out."

She smiles. "I know. The big softie is wrapped around my finger. Both our fingers," she says with a wink. "But seeing him with you and Jason made me realize I need to put some serious thought into what *I* want for my life. Because he's not going to need me forever."

My eyebrows knit together. "Even if Griffin and I are together long term—"

"Get married. You can say it," Samantha says with a mischievous smile.

Rolling my eyes but smiling back, I say, "Okay, even if we *get married*, that still doesn't mean we wouldn't want you around. Or that Griffin couldn't still use your help as his assistant."

"I know," she says. Our conversation is successfully distracting her thoughts, if her loosened grip on my hand is any indication. "But having my parents here and seeing Ian last weekend, it reminded me that I do want to have a real direction for my life. A real career. Ian is so driven and so smart, and I'm so stinkin' proud of him, but . . ."

"But?"

"It's hard not to feel like a lame screw-up in comparison to him. He doesn't have any of the same issues I had at school with focusing or learning. Makes me feel a little dumb sometimes," she admits.

"Just because you don't have ambitions to be a research scientist doesn't mean you're dumb, Samantha," I say. "We all have strengths and passions that lead us to different ways of having an impact. What sort of things do you like to do?"

"Talking to people," Samantha says, grinning. I can't help but laugh. "For real, I do enjoy talking to people. I've learned a lot of social skills from Griffin, to be honest. Watching the human can opener do his thing constantly couldn't help but rub off on me. I like asking questions and drawing people out or giving advice. But I don't think I could handle working as a social worker or therapist or anything like that," she says, hesitating.

"I can confirm that you're good at talking, asking questions, and helping other people," I encourage her. "I'm confident you can find a way to use your talents that doesn't require tons of academic work. We'll brainstorm."

"Really?" she asks, and the expression in her eyes is strikingly vulnerable.

"List-making happens to be my area of greatest expertise," I say, gratified by the smile that spreads across her face.

"All done," the tattoo artist announces, turning off the needle. "Look okay to you?"

Samantha holds her wrist up to inspect the adorable, tiny bird perched on a branch.

"It's perfect."

CHAPTER FORTY

Griffin

I'm back at my house. Samantha dropped me off before she went to meet her friend.

How'd the tattoo turn out?

It's perfectly adorable. And she told me about why she was getting it.

Oh yeah? I still need to hear the full explanation.

It's definitely something you should ask her about. Work your winsome magic on her. I think it will be a bigger conversation.

Will do. Jason and I should be back to your place in about 20 minutes.

"This was the best day ever," Jason says. "Well, *maybe* it was the best day ever. I don't know. Coming to spring training was pretty awesome. But so was sitting in the suite to watch the games with your dad. But also that day that Mom and I played cards and Legos at home was pretty nice too. I'm gonna have to think about which one was best."

I stifle a chuckle at how seriously he's taking this ranking of his favorite days. I also rub a hand over my chest, feeling a tightness there in response to him listing off so many good days he's had since moving in with Danae. I *know* it's not this simple, that his problems aren't all magically fixed just because Danae loves him. But it sure moves the needle.

Danae must have been watching out the window because I see her come out her front door from across the parking lot. As Jason hops down out of the Jeep, I give him a fist bump. "Thanks for going to the park with me and throwing the ball around. This was a super fun day, Jase."

The way his face morphs from utter delight into a mask of simmering rage is something that will haunt my dreams for the foreseeable future.

Jason's eyes are suddenly shuttered with an almost inhuman filter. His lips turn down into an angry frown, and his fists clench into tiny, tight balls.

"That's not my name." His voice is eerie—deep and quiet. But his volume rapidly rises as he screams at me, "You only call me Fireball or Jason. YOU DON'T CALL ME THAT!"

He pivots on a heel and sprints across the parking lot toward the house, not pausing to check for cars. Reflexively, I run after him, leaving the door to my Jeep wide open. Thank goodness, the parking lot is clear, and Jason makes it safely to the sidewalk leading up to the house. He runs right past Danae, and her head whips to me, utterly confused.

"What just happened?" she asks as I run up to her.

"I don't know. I called him 'Jase' and he suddenly got really upset," I say.

The look of terror that transforms Danae's facial features is another sight to haunt my dreams. As quickly as Jason, she turns to the townhouse and starts sprinting inside, so I chase after her.

"What is it?" I ask.

"His father used to call him 'Jase' on their good days. He doesn't want anyone calling him that," she explains as we tear through the front door.

I thought I had seen just about all there was to see from kids experiencing trauma responses. But still, I'm not at all prepared for the sight before me, of this kid I've grown to love absolutely losing his mind in rage.

Jason is standing in the living room, shredding pages out of one of the illustrated *Harry Potter* books I gave him for his birthday. He's yelling exclamation after exclamation of how he hates the books and hates me and hates Danae and hates all people and hates birthdays and hates just about every random thing about life he can think of to hate.

Danae's hands are tented over her mouth, tears rapidly streaming down her cheeks. "Jason, stop!" she says, taking a step toward him.

I grab her elbow and hold her back, giving her a look to let me step in. After all, this was my fault. I triggered this.

Slowly walking toward Jason, I hold my hands out at my sides and speak with an even tone. "Hey, Jason. I'm really sorry that I upset you. How about we put the book down so we can talk?"

When he looks up at me, his eyes are like lava—the kind of lava that's sloshing, sparking, exploding. He finishes ripping out the page in his hand, and then he throws the book at me. My shortstop reflexes kick into gear in time for me to dodge, but he moves to pick up the next book.

Taking quicker strides to reach him, I kneel down on one knee and reach my hand out to him. He jerks his arms away, clutching the book but not destroying it yet.

"Fireball, I'm really sorry I called you that name. I didn't know you wouldn't like it, and I'll never call you that again, okay?" I say quietly. I can hear Danae's heavy breaths behind me, and I watch the temperature of Jason's eyes cool ever so slightly. Holding my hand out a little closer to him, palm up, I say, "Will you forgive me, Jason?"

His tiny chest rises and falls dramatically with his gasping breaths, and his eyes dart from my eyes to my hand to the book in his hands. His chin starts to quiver right before he wails, "I'm sorry! I don't hate these books! I'm sorry! Why am I such a bad kid?! I try to tell my brain not to do bad things, but it tells me to do bad things because I'm a bad kid!"

He drops the book to the floor as he covers his face with his arms, and I gently reach out to touch his shoulder. When he doesn't flinch away, I press against his back to pull him into a hug. He melts against me, sobbing into my shoulder, continuing his string of apologies and remarks of self-loathing.

I hold his head against my shoulder with one hand, firmly rubbing his back with the other. "Hey, I forgive you, man. You're not a bad kid. You got really sad and mad, and that's okay. Those are just books, a bunch of pieces of paper. I don't care about the books. I care about you. I love you, Fireball," I say quietly. I feel Danae's touch on my shoulder as she kneels down to join us in a group embrace.

"Jason, it's okay, we love you no matter what. We want you to be safe," she says, voice still choked with emotion.

Several waves of tears later, Jason has calmed down enough to drink some water and eat a snack. A little blood sugar regulation certainly won't hurt things.

"I'm really sorry, Mr. Griffin. I'm sorry I said mean things, and I'm sorry I ruined the present you gave me," he says. I hear the threat of renewed tears in his guilt-laden voice.

I tap a knuckle under his chin to get him to look at me. "Hey. You don't need to apologize anymore. I said I forgive you. And you forgive me for calling you a name you didn't like being called, right?" He nods.

"So we're both forgiven, and we're not gonna keep thinking about it all the time, okay?" Another nod. "Would you want to play a game of Trash before I have to leave tonight?"

Jason shakes his head. "I'm really tired. I think I might want to go to bed. Is that okay, Mom?"

"Of course, bud," Danae says, stroking his hair. "Should we have Mr. Griffin sit with us while we read a little bit from our book?"

"You're still gonna read to me tonight?" Jason asks, voice and eyes thick with tears again.

Danae wraps him up in her arms, tears springing to her eyes as well. "Of course, I'm still going to read to you. I love you. Just because you got mad doesn't mean I'm not going to read to you. That's our thing!"

Jason nods and looks over to me. "Will you sit with us? Even though you don't really like books very much?"

Smiling, I say, "I wouldn't miss a chance to sit with you and your mom while you read together. I may not love books, but I love you both. So I'm in."

While Jason changes into pajamas, I return to the parking lot to close the back door of my Jeep I'd left open in my rush to follow Jason. When I get there, I discover that a good neighbor already shut the door at some point. I pause to take a deep breath before heading back inside to join Danae and Jason.

If I wasn't already head-over-heels in love with this woman, listening to her read to Jason would have put me over the edge for sure. The three of us squeeze onto Jason's twin bed with him wedged between us. The only way we can possibly fit is for me to drape my arm around Danae's shoulders, and she doesn't seem to object.

Her voice is like spun sugar as she reads, equally drawing you into the story and lulling you into a state of utter relaxation.

I could get used to ending every day this way. I could get on board with books for twenty minutes every night if it means listening to Danae's reading voice.

Jason is half-asleep by the time Danae places a bookmark in the book, so I carefully extricate myself from his bed. She crouches down and leans close to Jason, voice so hushed I almost don't catch her words. "I'm with you one hundred percent, forever."

"Love you too," his voice murmurs back before she kisses his head.

We exit the room and walk down the stairs in silence. Danae heads straight for the living room and lowers herself onto the couch, dropping her head in her hands. I ease myself down next to her and gently massage her neck with one hand.

"Is that what it's always like?" I ask, voice library-low. The muscles of her neck strain beneath my fingers as she nods. I wrack my memories from the times I saw my mom's therapist for any sort of appropriate words that will ease Danae's mind. Words that will show her I'm with her and not come across like an "it will all be okay" platitude.

My memory comes up empty.

I sit still, continuing to rub the tension from Danae's neck as she breathes. Her hands are still holding her forehead, so at least her fingernails aren't presently in danger.

"I hate these moments. The helpless feeling of having zero idea what to do. Sure, I've read books, I've learned strategies from Jessica, but it's so hard to hang on to those threads in the emotion of the moment. I hate that this little boy I love so much is going to continue experiencing these things and dealing with these wild emotions. Knowing it's not his fault, that he can't help it, not really. That choices adults made created these connections in his brain."

She takes a deep inhale, and I continue gently kneading the muscles of her neck.

"But I hate how I know those facts in my mind but still get so frustrated, so angry with him in the height of the moment. Sometimes I think—" Danae abruptly stops speaking.

"You think . . . what?" I ask, waiting for her to fill in the gap of her thoughts.

"Never mind," she says, dropping her hands from her face and staring straight ahead.

I lean forward, attempting to make eye contact that she doesn't allow. I nudge her knee with mine. "You can tell me. Whatever it is."

She shakes her head, eyes still boring a hole into the wall across from us. "No. I don't want to say it out loud. Just . . . never mind."

"Danae, I won't—"

She holds up a hand to cut me off. "Please, stop. I don't want to talk any more right now."

Her posture is giving loud "back off" vibes, so I stop pressing the issue. Instead, I wrap my hand around her shoulder and tug her toward me, murmuring a quiet, "Come here."

Danae leans into the invitation, laying her head on my chest as I sink back against the crook of the couch. Her legs curl beside her, knees resting on my thighs. I move to prop my feet on the coffee table but pause to ask, "Is this allowed?"

She sighs deeply, and I bite back a smile. "Normally, no. But these are extenuating circumstances."

Legs stretched in front of me, I wrap both arms around Danae and hold her tightly against me. She's not crying, not speaking. Just staring and breathing. The lack of tears pricks at me with concern, but I quietly trace my fingers along her spine, up and down her arm, up the curve of her neck to her scalp.

"What was that you whispered to Jason in bed?" I ask.

"I'm with you one hundred percent, forever," she says, voice tiny. "It's something I told him early on to try to explain what it means when I say 'I love you' to him. I think he needs the reminder a lot." Her voice sounds so hollow—drained and empty—despite the significance of the words she's saying.

Closing my eyes, I start mentally brainstorming ways to fix this for her. When problems arise, I lean into my competencies to find solutions. I take action to make things better.

But if my upbringing has taught me anything—if being Sam and Ian's big brother has taught me anything—it's that there is no simple solution to what's happening in Jason's brain, in his body.

And I hate the feeling of powerlessness that brings.

My arms tighten around Danae, hoping that she has a sliver of comfort in not being alone.

Chapter Forty-One

Danae

A familiar tune pierces through the bubble of unconsciousness. I've heard it before, but it doesn't sound quite right. Straining my ears, I finally place the tune as the alarm on my phone. But it sounds muffled, distant.

Moving my head a fraction of an inch, I realize my cheek is resting against something much firmer, much warmer than my pillow. Something moving up and down, slowly and methodically. My eyes squint open to see not my white pillowcase, but the navy blue of Griffin's t-shirt.

My body slowly wakens and consciously recognizes every point of contact with Griffin. My cheek against his chest. My knee draped over his leg. My fingertips clutching the neckline of his shirt. His arm around my back, hand resting on my waist. His fingers wrapped around the back of my knee.

I'm suddenly very, very warm.

The alarm on my phone doesn't sound right because it's not sitting on the nightstand next to me—it's across the room in my purse. We still have school today. Griffin has a flight with his team today. We have to get up.

Even armed with full consciousness and logic, I'm reluctant to move. I could stay right here in this cozy bubble and pretend that all my troubled thoughts from last night don't exist. For just a moment longer.

I carefully raise my head enough to look at Griffin's face to see if he's awake. His head is dropped back, lips parted. I'm positive that he's going to have some serious neck pain today after sleeping in that position all night. A half-snore escapes from his mouth—the kind that isn't quite pronounced enough to be called a snore, but throaty enough to disqualify as heavy breathing.

The sound brings a gentle smile to my lips, followed by stinging behind my eyes.

If people could see the real man behind the Wizard of Defense persona, they'd only be even more impressed. How did I get lucky enough to be the one curled up on the couch with him?

The spiral from last night creeps its way back into the thought factory, increasing the burning sensation in my eyes.

Why does Griffin the man have to be tied up in the Wizard of Defense player?

The sound of the alarm is becoming more impatient, and I know it's time to be a responsible adult. Blinking to dismiss the tears still fighting to squeeze out, I run my hand up Griffin's neck, up the fade of his haircut, massaging my fingers into the length of his hair, attempting to wake him softly.

His mouth claps shut as he jerks slightly. His hands at my waist and my knee tighten, either reflexively or possessively. Maybe both. I need to pry myself away from all these points of physical contact before the tears defeat my determination to hold it together.

"Morning," I whisper, attempting to sit up. Griffin's eyes flutter open, and he promptly traps me with his arms, pulling me back to his chest.

One lone tear finds its way to victory, leaving a temporary blemish on Griffin's shirt.

"Where are you going?" he asks, and his husky morning voice nearly does me in altogether.

"Work. School. Flight for you," I reply quietly. The word "flight" is apparently the right button to push because he jerks fully awake. I untangle my limbs from his as he sits upright and stretches his neck.

"Shoot, what time is it?" he asks, checking his watch.

"I'm hoping it's still close to six o'clock and that my alarm hasn't been going off for an hour," I say, standing to retrieve my phone.

Griffin lightly slaps a hand on his face, waking himself up. "Okay, I'm okay. I can make it home and get ready quickly and still get to the airport on time. Mostly on time," he says, standing. I swipe the alarm off, and Griffin's arms appear around my waist. His beard tickles as he presses his face into the curve of my neck. Before I can stop myself, my hand reaches up to rest behind his neck, fingertips tracing the fade on his scalp.

"As much as I want to kiss you, I should probably confess now that I have the worst morning breath known to mankind. Probably because I'm a mouth breather," he says. I huff a laugh, and he pivots me to face him. He holds one hand in front of his mouth, which only makes me fully laugh. I see the smile lines around his eyes as he says, "I'm going to miss you these next few days. But then we have back-to-back series at home, so I'll be here for a solid week before we travel again."

It's dark, so I know he doesn't see the conflict in my eyes before he wraps me up in a goodbye hug.

"Call me if you have trouble with Jason and need someone to talk to," he murmurs. "I'll . . . I'll try to answer. I'll keep my phone nearby as much as I can."

Nodding against his chest, my arms instinctively clutch tighter around his waist.

"Tell Jason bye for me. I love you, Danae," Griffin says.

A few decibels above inaudible, I whisper, "Love you."

"So, that's why I'm here," I conclude, looking intently at Monica. She's the first therapist recommended to me who had immediate availability. Kara is keeping Jason for an hour after school so that I could be here for our intake meeting.

Monica sits back in her chair, processing everything that I've said.

Dumped. Unloaded. Poured out with wild abandon.

I surprised myself with the instant and thorough word vomit that came out of my mouth, but I suppose that's what happens when the thought factory has been churning overtime with frenzied zeal. When I'm pressed for time and answers.

Monica now knows at least the bare bones about my childhood with my parents, my situation with Jason, my relationship with Griffin, and my terrifying anxiety regarding how all of the above fit together.

"There's a lot to sift through here," Monica begins, and I nod vigorously. I want to make sure she knows that I am in agreement, that she is on the right track, that *this is a lot.*

"We're going to put a pin in the history and current state of your relationship with your parents. Not because it's not important—it absolutely is. And those memories are shading your current relationships with other people," Monica says. More nodding from me. "And I think it's going to be important for us to really dig in to what's behind your general anxiety. But for today, let's talk a little bit more specifically about your anxiety regarding Jason's behavior and your relationship with Griffin. Because those seem to be the most urgent on your mind right now."

I think my head might be in a permanent state of nodding.

Monica gives a small smile. "Here's my first question for you. *Why* do you feel so anxious about not knowing how to help Jason when he gets into those dysregulated states?"

My brow furrows. "Why wouldn't I be anxious about that? Shouldn't every parent be worried in a situation like that?"

"Yes, of course," Monica says in a calm voice. "I'm not suggesting it's an irregular reaction. I'm curious to know what thoughts are below the surface of your particular anxiety in those situations."

Blowing out a breath, I'm instantly engaging in every fidgeting habit I've ever tried to break. Aggressively picking at nail polish with *both* thumbs? Check. Aggressively chewing my lip? Check. Aggressively bouncing my foot? Check.

"You know you can be honest about your thoughts, and I'm not going to judge you," Monica prompts. She preemptively hands me a tissue box.

Clutching the box with both hands, the torrent of thoughts bursts forth again. "Because I'm afraid I made a mistake. I'm not a good decision maker. I agonize over them. And then I second-guess myself within an inch of death. But I was so sure about the decision to adopt Jason. I *knew* it was right. But now I'm worried that I was wrong. Not because I don't love him or because I don't want to deal with these behaviors. Because I'm afraid *I* wasn't the right person for *him*. When he spirals into those rages, I almost feel . . . afraid of him," I admit, and the tears fully unleash. "And my mind sprints ahead to years down the line, fearful of what these outbursts could look like when he's a teenager. It frightens me. What kind of mom is afraid of her child?"

Monica waits patiently as I pause to blow my nose before continuing. "Jason is so incredible. He's such a sweet kid. But even if he wasn't, he would still deserve to have parents who love him and support him through everything. I want to be that for him, but I'm afraid I'm not enough. That he deserves more than me. That I can't provide the stability and security and strength that he needs. I'm worried that I can't love him enough to make up for all the ways I don't know how to help him."

After I blow my nose again, Monica gives my arm a gentle pat. "I'm assuming that Jason's therapist has already explained the brain science behind trauma to you?" When I nod, she continues. "So you know that love, while crucially important, isn't going to be enough to help Jason?"

I sputter a breath through my lips. "I know. I know those words in my head. But I still wish that loving him could be enough."

"I understand," Monica says. "We all wish that love was a magic tonic to cure all injuries. Although that's not the case, I do want to affirm some things for you, Danae." I sit up straighter to meet her eyes as she continues. "You chose to upend your life in order to welcome Jason into it. You are showing him love in small and big ways, meeting his needs in both tangible and intangible ways. You are providing a safe, healthy home for him. You have arranged for him to see therapists who are helping him learn coping strategies as he learns to regulate his emotions and trauma responses. You've expressed that you are open to other therapy and treatment options for him—anything that could help him. And you chose to take all of this on as a single mother. You are a *great* mom, and you are the *right* mom for Jason."

Her face grew blurrier with each statement she made, until I burst fully into tears again. When I finally calm down, I look at my watch. "We're over time," I say. I give her a watery attempt at a smile. "When are you free next?"

Monica smiles. "I don't have any clients after you, so how about we extend our session until we've reached a natural stopping point. Will that work for your babysitter?"

I shoot a quick text to Kara, who immediately responds with a thumbs up.

"For today, there's one other thing I'd like to explore further that you seem to be tangling up with this anxiety over Jason. I'd like to know why you have reservations about your relationship with Griffin. From what you've said, it seems obvious that you care deeply for him, and that he feels the same toward you and Jason. So, why the anxious thoughts?" she asks.

Dropping my eyes, I fidget with the hem of my shirt. "I don't know," I say.

"That response isn't going to work," Monica says, a teasing tone softening the admonishment of the words. "I need you to dig below the surface of your thoughts. *Why* are you so anxious about your relationship with Griffin?'

Chewing my lip, I search the flow chart of my thoughts, looking for patterns.

"It's probably similar to my anxiety about Jason. That I'm second-guessing my decision to date Griffin. That I wonder if that was a mistake too. I love Griffin for who he *is*. I know that I do. He's thoughtful and magnetic and kind. He has the ability to make anyone feel like a friend after one conversation because he asks such good questions—and genuinely wants to know the answers. He disarmed all of my defensive walls in one date. He's funny and charming and protective of the people he loves. He's amazing with Jason. He's . . . he's everything I think I could want from a life partner," I say.

"But?" Monica supplies.

"But I don't love what he *does*. His life is so all over the place. Literally, all over the country. His schedule during baseball season—which is three quarters of every year—is incredibly demanding with very little margin. As much as I know he wants to be there for me when things get tough with Jason, there are very real restrictions beyond his control that limit his ability to *actually* be there," I say. "I know there are couples who deal with so much more time apart than we have. But this level of instability and public scrutiny is hard for *me*. It's why I tried to talk myself out of liking him in the first place. For as safe as he feels as a person, the persona of Griffin West, professional baseball player, feels very risky. So, maybe my decision-making skills are broken. Maybe I never should have agreed to go on a date with him in the first place."

Monica tilts her head, assessing everything I've said. I start to worry I've said something wrong the longer she sits there with her head cocked and eyes narrowed.

"Could I make an observation, Danae?" she asks.

Swallowing a lump in my throat, I return to nodding.

"While the limitation of Griffin's schedule is certainly a valid reason to be anxious, I'm not sure that's *the* reason you have so much anxiety about your relationship. You hadn't met Griffin prior to Jason moving in with you, correct? And Jason exhibited some of these difficult behaviors prior to your relationship with Griffin beginning?" Monica asks.

More nodding.

"You made the decision to adopt Jason as a single mother. You prepared to face those challenges alone, knowing you did not have the support of your family, with only the assistance of the friends you already had in place," Monica says. My nodding slows as I process what she's saying. "So, it doesn't seem like Griffin's inability to be available any time you need him should be *the* issue, at least, not in and of itself. I think it's much deeper, much more nuanced than that. I think you're frightened by the fact that you *want* him to be there for you. He already *is* a safe place for you, after you never felt that way with your family of origin. You're afraid of losing your safe place, so your brain is trying to convince you that it's not actually safe. Because the thought of losing a safe place is more terrifying than never having a safe place to begin with."

I drop back in my chair, like her statement was a physical blow. Monica allows the seconds to tick by in silence as I mull over her observation.

"So," I begin, voice small. "What do I do?"

Monica huffs a laugh. "I think you're misunderstanding the purpose of therapy. I don't prescribe what decisions you should make. I listen and help you see your own thoughts from another angle. I guide you through coping strategies and point you in the direction of applicable resources. But I don't tell you whether or not to break up with the guy," she finishes with a wry smile. "I'm afraid that's all on you."

Covering my eyes with the crook of an elbow, I moan. "Did you not hear the part where I'm terrible at decisions?"

Monica chuckles again. "That's certainly something we can work on together."

Sighing, I uncover my eyes. "And I suppose there's no magic tonic for that either?"

She holds her hands up and shrugs. "Fresh out of magic tonics, I'm afraid."

CHAPTER FORTY-TWO

Griffin

At what age did you stop believing in Santa?

I never believed in Santa.

Seriously?!

My parents never did Santa. They were too serious about everything to engage in something so impractical. And they probably wanted the credit for the gifts they gave me.

That's seriously sad.

<shrugging emoji>

Did you get lost? No question for me today?

When Danae hasn't responded to my flirty text after fifteen minutes, I hit the call button. I need to be on the team bus to the stadium in ten minutes, but I'm going to use all ten of those minutes getting to the bottom of why Danae has been acting so weird the past week.

There was another minor incident with the press, which could be to blame. Someone managed to get a photo of Danae and Jason watching a game in the suite and sold it to a tabloid. The basic facts of Jason's adoption case were dredged back up—which made it easy to get the article taken down in under twenty-four hours. Still, I know it spooked Danae all over again with the adoption hearing approaching, despite reassurance from Jason's social worker that it wouldn't be held against her.

She was evasive most of the week I was in KC for our two series at home and quieter than usual the one time I did see her. She said she didn't want to risk rocking the media boat by coming to any home games again until after the adoption is finalized, which I completely understood. Still, it killed me not to have her and Jason there. Their absence combined with her acting so cagey has me second-guessing everything about myself and our situation.

We're in the middle of a ten-day stretch of away games, in the middle of a seventeen-day stretch of daily games. For the first time in my life, I'm cursing the man who decided that baseball should be a 162-game season. Connecting with Danae has felt next to impossible with her cold shoulder on top of my packed schedule. She doesn't know that I got special permission to miss a game so that Sam and I can fly home after tonight's game in order to be there for the court hearing tomorrow. I still want to maintain the surprise, but it's time to cut to the chase of what's behind her mood. I can't take it anymore.

The call goes to voicemail, so I immediately dial her again.

"Hello?" she answers, sounding annoyed.

"What's wrong?" I ask.

"Nothing," she answers.

"There's an 'everything' behind that 'nothing' if there ever was one," I say. "Babe, you've been acting closed off ever since the morning after we fell asleep on the couch together. Are you upset about that for some reason? Or upset with me for setting Jason off that day by calling him the wrong name?"

"No, it's not that," she says, voice exasperated.

"Ha! So it is *something*," I say. She audibly huffs. "Danae, please open the window to the thought factory. I can't figure out what's going on when I can't see you."

"How long until you retire from baseball?" she asks. Her sudden assertiveness catches me off guard.

"What?"

"How many more years will you be playing baseball?" Danae asks.

"I can't say that for sure. There are too many variables," I say.

"Ballpark guess," she demands.

"I mean, some guys push forty before they retire, but shortstop is a pretty demanding position physically, so thirty-six or thirty-seven is probably more realistic," I say. "But you can't hold me to that—it's not a hard and fast rule."

"So, anywhere from three to five more years, give or take?" Danae clarifies.

"I guess so. Why? What point are you getting at?" I ask.

"I'm trying to mentally prepare myself for how much longer it will be until I get to be with just Griffin," Danae says, voice thick.

"What do you mean?" I ask, my blood pressure barreling higher. "You are with me, with Griffin. What's stressing you out so much?"

"I don't know, Griff! I'm really overwhelmed by . . . e*verything*. My anxiety is on high alert, and I'm really wishing that Griffin the person was free of Griffin West, The Wizard of Defense right now," she says, then abruptly halts at what she said.

We're both silent for a beat, but I start pacing the room.

"This is who I am, Danae. You've known that from the first day we met," I say, the irony suddenly hitting me. "Well, from as soon as you knew who I was."

"I'm sorry," Danae says before she sighs deeply. "I didn't mean it that way. I don't know what I mean. I'm sorry. I shouldn't have even answered your call, should have gotten my mind in a better place before we talked. There's just been a lot of . . . never mind. I need to go. I promised Jason we would go to Lego Land today, which was a huge mistake to promise something exhausting that requires driving downtown and figuring out parking and generally stressing me out when we have court tomorrow. Can we please talk when you get back to KC later this week?"

"Fine," I say, voice hard with frustration. Sighing, I swallow down the desire to tell her we can talk tomorrow, still not wanting to ruin the surprise factor. But I can't leave the conversation hanging this way, not when she thinks I won't talk to her again before her big day. "Hey, good luck tomorrow. Have Kara take tons of pictures. I love you."

Her voice sounds pained when she replies, "I love you too."

There's a loud knock on my hotel room door right as I hang up.

"Griff! You've gotta be on the bus in two minutes! Adrian texted me that you're not down there!" Sam's loud voice is extra annoying in my current state of mind.

I swing the door open, and her brow immediately furrows. "What's wrong with you?" she asks, coming in.

"Bad conversation with Danae," I say.

Sam hums. "You guys have seemed a little off lately. What gives?"

"I don't know the whole of it, but the short of it is that she can't accept me for who I am," I say.

Sam quirks an eyebrow. "Um, okay. That's one very dramatic way to look at things, but it doesn't sound very Danae-like. What makes you say that?"

"She was grilling me on how many years I have left until I retire, complaining that she wishes I could be separate from the Wizard of Defense, when she can't accept that the Wizard of Defense *is* me. Griffin West, the baseball player—that's who I am. I don't know how to sustain our relationship if she won't see that," I say, pacing and throwing my hands up in the air.

"Don't be an idiot," Sam says, and I glare at her. "Don't you dare push Danae away for the very reason you love her."

Narrowing my eyes, I take the bait. "What do you mean?"

"Griff, have you never figured out why you were so drawn to Danae in the first place?" Sam asks.

I shrug. I begin listing off the things I love about Danae, "Of course, I know why I'm drawn to her. She's tenderhearted and empathetic, she's—"

"No, not all the things you *grew* to love about her," Sam says, cutting me off. "I mean the reason your heart altered its orbit around her in the first place. Before you knew all of those things, you were drawn to Danae because she sees *you*. She cares about *you*, Griffin. Not the baseball player. Not the persona. The person."

My eyebrows knit together, and I know I'm scowling when Sam laughs.

She takes a deep breath before diving in. "Listen, for being exceptionally socially aware, you're acutely lacking in the self-awareness category. You got injured last year and came face-to-face with the expiration date on this whole persona that's wrapped up in your baseball career. Even though you clawed your way back to playing, for a minute there, you were confronted with the possibility of who you are without baseball. Deep down, you're scared to face that idea—but that's who you are to Danae. Just Griffin, not the baseball player. The baseball was a *downside* to her. I think the suppressed, scared part of you was finally at peace finding someone who wouldn't move on when your professional baseball era ends. She's going to care about you long past the death of the Wizard of Defense persona. So don't fault her for the very reason you love her."

Sam's words click into place as visions of my first interactions with Danae scroll through my mind. I drag a hand down my face. "You're right," I state simply.

"Yep," Sam gloats.

I shake my head but smile at her. "Where'd you get so smart?"

"Therapy," she quips, smirking at me. "You gonna be able to pull yourself together and play well today, or is this about to be a train wreck I have to watch in slow motion?"

Lightly punching her on the arm, I roll my eyes. "I'm gonna play lights out, and then we're gonna hop on a plane so I can be there for the woman I love."

"That's the spirit!" Sam says. "High spirits are good because Coach is probably about to chew you up one side and down the other for being late to the bus."

CHAPTER FORTY-THREE

Danae

I've felt terrible about what I said to Griffin yesterday. I haven't told him about everything I've been processing through with Monica, even though I know I should have. I've only met with her twice, but the clarity she's given me about the roots of my anxiety regarding Griffin has actually made me *more* confused. They say going to therapy often makes you feel worse before you feel better, and whoever "they" are, they were not wrong.

My brain can only handle one major topic at a time currently, so I'm going to get through this court hearing today and celebrate Jason *officially* being my son. Later tonight, I'll try to call Griffin after his game and see if I can smooth things over. Because I do think I want things to be smooth. I don't want us to be broken, and I'm hoping that Griffin still feels the same way.

Jason looks adorably handsome in his button-down shirt and dress pants. But his face looks like a tumultuous bundle of emotions. Carefully tucking my dress under my knees, I crouch down in front of him.

"Hey, bud. You know how much I love you?" I ask, and he nods solemnly. "Jason, I want you to know something. Today is really exciting and really happy because it means that we get to be family forever, no matter what. We already felt that way in our hearts, but now it gets to be legal and official." He nods again, smiling slightly.

"But it's also kind of a sad day because it means that you'll officially never be with your dad again," I say, and Jason's smile falls, chin starting to quiver. "It's okay to feel happy *and* sad today, or any day. It will never hurt my feelings if you're sad about not getting to be with your dad. It will never hurt my feelings if you're sad about the fact that you never knew your first mom. Because I'm sad that you don't get to be with them, even though I'm so, *so* happy that I get to be your mom forever. We can feel both things."

Jason throws his arms around my neck, hugging me tightly.

As much as the entire staff team would have loved to be here today, finding that many substitute teachers would have been essentially impossible. Kara and Ron will be here, as well as most of my book club friends, and Angie, the sweet neighbor who has become a regular babysitter and friend. Jason's grandmother, Cathy, originally intended to be here but has been battling pneumonia, complicated by her years of smoking. She sent Jason a sweet card and gift yesterday, so we know she's supporting us in spirit.

I hold Jason's hand as we turn down the hallway to the designated courtroom, but my feet stop short when I catch sight of who's standing outside the door waiting for us.

"Mr. Griffin! Sammi!" Jason exclaims before sprinting down the remainder of the hallway. Griffin gives him an enthusiastic but brief hug before handing him off to Samantha when I reach him.

His arms are immediately around me, clinging to me like a lifeline. No—anchoring me like *he* is the lifeline.

Liquefying into his embrace, I *feel* all of my hesitations melt away. *He's safe. I'm safe. We're safe. We can be safe.*

"I'm sorry about yesterday, Danae. I'm sorry for being short with you, for not being understanding. I'm sorry for anything I've said or done to make you feel hesitant about me, about us," Griffin murmurs by my ear. "I have to fly out early tomorrow morning, but, please, can we talk tonight?"

I blink hard and rapidly to force myself not to cry so I don't ruin our photos of today with mascara streaks. Nodding my head against his chest, I pull back and look into his eyes. It takes all of half a second staring into the love in those gray-blues before I'm kissing him, pressing my lips to his like a promise.

"Ahem," a throat clears behind us. I recognize that "ahem," and it is not welcome.

Turning around, I face my parents. My dad's suit looks freshly pressed, and mom's dress is complete with a strand of pearls. The smiles on their faces look equal parts forced and fake. These are the versions of my parents that showed up to important social events—plastering on the pretense of being happy individuals in a happy marriage with a happy child. There's not even the smallest sign of remorse or contrition in their expressions or body language.

"What are you doing here?" I ask through gritted teeth. The slow quivers of adrenaline begin shooting through my body, but I tighten a fist to ground myself. Griffin's hand comes to my waist, giving me a gentle squeeze of support.

Over my parents' shoulders, I see Kara and Ron walking this way, Kara's pace quickening as recognition dawns on her face. Thankfully, Samantha seems to have picked up on the tension and has ushered Jason away.

"We couldn't miss the official declaration of Jason being a part of our family," my mom says, using that falsely soothing tone.

"Jason is being declared a part of *my* family," I say. "You were not invited to be here. How did you even know this was happening today?"

My dad's eyes flicker to Griffin, and he conceals his embarrassment with a smile. "We wanted to come anyway to show you our support. We have our sources who knew this would be an important day for us. Surely you're not going to turn your parents away from such a monumental moment in your life."

"You turned yourselves away a long time ago," I say. My voice is small, even though my determination is not. Griffin gives me another "I'm here" squeeze, and it gives my voice more strength. "I will give some thought to if and when I'd be open to talking about what our relationship could look like in the future, but this is not the time or place for that conversation. I will contact you if that day comes. For now, I'd like you to leave, please."

Both of my parents scoff, as though they can't believe that I would possibly stand up to them. When they make no move to turn around, Griffin takes a half step forward.

"I'm sorry to butt in, but Danae has made her feelings pretty clear. We're going to head inside the courtroom, but you're not going to follow us," he says, voice a deceptive calm. I know there's a raging river underneath, waiting to be provoked.

Apparently, my father is wise (or cowardly) enough to not cause a scene confronting the darling of Kansas City in a public setting. His eyes narrow, but he quickly adjusts his expression. "We'll be in touch, Danae," he says, artificial smile back in place. Placing a hand on my astonished mother's back, he retreats down the hallway.

Griffin takes my hand and asks, "Are you okay?"

"No, and yes," I say. I look up to meet his concerned eyes. "Sometimes we can feel both."

He traces a knuckle down my cheek, then brings my hand up to his lips to kiss my fingers.

I smile at him and call for Jason. "Let's get in there. It's forever time."

After court, we have a celebratory lunch with Griffin, Sam, Kara, and Ron. By the end of lunch, I can tell that Jason is teetering between the happy and sad emotions of the day, so we part ways with the larger group. Jason isn't ready to go home yet, so we decide to go to a park and enjoy the gorgeous spring day. Kara has a key to my townhouse, so she and Ron offer to drop my car off there so that Jason and I can ride with Griffin. He suggests we make an ice cream pit stop on the way to the park, and I heartily agree. We drive to my favorite local ice cream shop so I can get my beloved Maddy's Mud flavor. Griffin stays true to his "classy" self and picks strawberry, and Jason also stays true to character, choosing the Kansas City Crowns-inspired blue ice cream. We find a quiet park nearby, and I cross my fingers that the handful of people out on the walking trails won't give us a second glance.

Jason is quieter than usual and only eats a few bites of his ice cream before scampering off to the swings. Hopefully the sensory back-and-forth movement of the swing will help his body calm down after such an emotional roller coaster of a day.

We spend a couple of hours at the park, going for a slow walk together when Jason tires of the swings. By early evening, Jason's clearly running out of steam but trying his hardest to stay upbeat. When we get back to the parking lot after our walk, Griffin opens the door for Jason to climb into the backseat while I open the passenger door. I notice that Jason's chin is quivering, but before I can ask him what's wrong, Griffin's already leaning through the open door toward him.

"You feeling kinda sad, Fireball?" Griffin gently inquires.

A tear forges a path down Jason's cheek, dripping off his chin. "Maybe a little."

Griffin nods in understanding, giving Jason enough courage to whisper, "I just still kinda miss my dad sometimes, ya know? I miss my good-day dad."

"That totally makes sense for you to miss him and be sad sometimes. You love your dad. Today doesn't change that. Your mom and I are always here if you're sad and need to talk about it. It's safe for you to talk about missing your dad, okay?" Griffin says, and Jason nods. "Would you like a hug, Jason?"

Jason nods again and lunges forward to wrap his arms around Griffin's neck, a tiny sob escaping as he does. Tears freely flow down my own cheeks. "I love you, little man," I hear Griffin whisper. When he meets my eyes, still embracing Jason, I see that all three of us are crying.

It's a happy, hard, sad, heavy, celebratory day, all wrapped into one. A constant conflict of feelings that we'll face together. Safe together.

We grab dinner on the way home to my townhouse, which Jason picks at before practically falling asleep at the table. He gets ready for bed early, and the three of us pile onto his twin bed to read half a chapter of our *Harry Potter* book before we say good night.

Once Jason is asleep, I change out of my dress and into a matching sweatsuit, needing every tangible form of comfort available. Griffin's still dressed up, although he's unbuttoned the top buttons of his dress shirt by the time I join him on the couch—a fact I'm not sad about. I trace the line of his collar bone as I sit snuggled under the crook of his arm, my legs draped over his.

"Thanks for rescuing me today," I say.

"Apparently, you lived a different day than I did, because I did not rescue you. You needed no rescuing," he says, tilting my chin to look at him.

"Okay. But thank you for being here today. Thanks for missing a game so you could come," I respond, eyes already swimming with tears.

"I know I was going for the surprise factor, but did you honestly think that I could miss out on such a huge day for you and Jason?" Griffin asks. He grins wryly as he adds, "Not to mention Sam. She'd never miss this either."

"Fair point," I say with a giggle. Withdrawing myself from Griffin's side, I sit on my knees next to him, taking his hands in mine.

"I'm not sure about this body language," he says, sounding concerned. "This seems like a backward step from your legs draped over mine and your fingertips on my skin."

"I need to look at your face when I tell you this," I say.

"You're not helping," he says.

"Sorry, I should have led with 'nothing's wrong,'" I tease, and that finally cracks a genuine smile out of him. "Or, maybe it would be more accurate to say there were some things wrong, and there probably always will be some things wrong, but I'm choosing to not be afraid to have things be wrong sometimes."

"You've lost me," Griffin says, and I cover my face with my hands. He's quick to grab my wrists and pull my hands down. "Nope, don't do that. Let me see those beautiful eyes, no matter what it is you're going to tell me."

The look on his face is so tender, so real, so open—I can't believe I let myself consider turning away from this love.

"You're safe for me," I say. Griffin's eyes squint slightly as he computes what I'm trying to say. I shake my head and start over. "Your mom encouraged me to start seeing a therapist for myself, separate from Jason, and talking with her has made me realize some things."

He gives my hands a gentle squeeze, and I take a deep breath. "I grew up feeling like I didn't have a safe place. Home was not safe for me. School wasn't safe. When Jason moved in, I was *being* the safe place for this precious little boy. And it was a lot, even though I didn't fully realize how overwhelming it was going to be. Then, suddenly, I had you. And you quickly became very, very safe for me. You proved yourself trustworthy far more quickly than I've ever trusted someone before. You felt like the safe home I never had, even if I couldn't consciously name that feeling. But logically, it didn't make sense for you to be safe because your schedule is so unreliable. On paper, a life with you doesn't appear secure. So, my brain was trying to sabotage me into pushing you away because I was afraid to lose my safe place."

Griffin's expression has slowly softened as I've explained, and I'm sorely tempted to stop explaining and start kissing him. But this isn't the totality of the thought factory. He deserves all the thoughts.

"I love you. For *all* of you. Including Griffin West, Wizard of Defense. I want you to keep playing this game you love for however long you want to play it. I will find a way to manage when you're traveling or playing games twelve days in a row during the school year. And I will travel with you during the summer and come to every home game that I can because it will mean being close to you and supporting *you,* and I'm with you one hundred percent. You're safe for me, and I don't want to lose you," I say, my voice cracking on the final phrase.

Griffin moves to embrace me, pulling me tight against his chest. I tuck my face into the crook of his neck, inhaling deeply. Grounding myself in the safety of his arms, his scent further soothes me with each new breath.

After a few seconds, Griffin's arms loosen as he pulls back to look in my eyes again.

"I love you, Danae. As I've gotten to know you over these past few months, I've grown to love you for so many reasons. But as my sassy but wise younger sister assessed, my heart was drawn to you before I ever knew all there is to love about you. And that's because when we talked, I *wasn't* the Wizard to you. You could see me in a way that most people never do—in a way that I didn't consciously know I needed. You're my safe place too. And that's one of the many reasons I love you so much."

He pauses to press a gentle kiss to my lips but then continues. "I'm not naive to think it's going to be smooth sailing from here. We're still going to face challenges. With my career, with Jason, with your parents, with everyday life and conflict. But I'm committed to working through those challenges *with* you. Committed to protecting our relationship, our safe place together."

Tears have gathered in my eyes again, and I quickly wipe them away. Raising one hand to Griffin's jaw, I skim my thumb along his beard. "Safe together," I murmur.

Griffin swiftly pulls me onto his lap and kisses me with authority, with finality, with determination. He sprinkles verbal affirmations of his love between his kisses to my lips, my neck, my jaw, my forehead, my lips again.

And these kisses feel like forever.

CHAPTER FORTY-FOUR

Griffin

"I've been thinking about something," Danae says. We're sitting in the dark corner of the bar at Capital Grille, chatting with Jeff in between our moments focused solely on each other.

"You realize how much you would be freaking out if I started a sentence that way," I tease. I'm rewarded with an adorable smirk that twists up half of her heart-shaped lips. I don't even bother resisting the pull to lean in and kiss her.

Danae kisses me back but playfully pushes me away before we get too lost in each other. "Okay, okay, I need to say this before I chicken out," she says, and that sobers me up. "Nothing's wrong," she adds in response to my furrowed brow.

I pull her hand to press a kiss to her fingers—nails grown out and polish fully intact—and ask, "What is it?"

She takes a breath and says, "I think we should do a media interview."

I raise an eyebrow. "You think you *want* to interact with the media?"

Danae shakes her head slightly and smiles. "I will never ever *want* to interact with the media. But like I told you that night after court—I'm committed to this. To you. You—Griffin West, the Wizard of Defense, darling of Kansas City," she says. I pretend to wave to my fans, causing Danae to snort with laughter.

Her face turns serious before she continues. "I understand that media attention comes with that territory, but I'd rather try to control the interaction as much as possible. Your post-game interview after the first fiasco kept the press at bay for a while, but if the second hiccup was any indication, there could be an expiration date to that courtesy if we don't feed them any kind of information. So let's schedule our own interview to give them the information that we want to share."

My chest aches with the love I feel for this woman. I reach up to cup Danae's chin. "You sure about this?" When she nods, I brush a kiss to her cheek. "How many pages was the pro/con list?"

Her cheeks pinken, and she drops eye contact. "I mean . . . let's just say it was lengthy."

I skim a kiss along her jaw. "Were flowcharts involved?"

She hums as goosebumps break out along her arms. "There might have been."

I trace her nose with mine. "Do I get to see them?"

"Not on your life," she whispers before leaning her lips into mine.

"She's still sure she wants to do this? Because I can totally call and make up an excuse to cancel," Sam offers.

"We're good to go," I confidently respond as I swipe product through my hair. "I mean, she's nervous, and there's a one hundred percent chance that all of her clear nail polish will be picked off by the end. But we're doing it."

Sam was able to set up an exclusive interview with a local Kansas City lifestyle magazine in exchange for full rights to nix or approve anything in the article before it's published. She agreed that feeding the press a little information on our terms will go a long way in continuing the bubble of privacy they've given us. Joe was elated that I was finally leaning into some media attention—until I told him we were doing the interview for free. I'd rather have control over the narrative than a paycheck any day.

Washing the hair product residue off my hands, I eye Sam in the mirror. She's lingering. In a weird, awkward manner.

"Uhhh, is there something else we need to talk about?" I ask, drying my hands on a towel.

Sam jerks up, pushing her hip away from where it was resting on the counter. "Oh, um, maybe? Or maybe not," she says, avoiding eye contact. She rubs her right thumb over the tattoo on her left wrist.

Tossing the towel on the counter, I repeatedly poke Sam in the arm until she looks at me. My raised eyebrows are enough of a question.

"There's something I need to tell you," Sam says, and the uncertain tone in her voice has my emotions swinging from one extreme to the other.

"Am I going to be leaving this conversation ready to go beat someone up? Because you're going to need to cancel the interview if that's the case," I say.

"No, no, put away the protective older brother zeal," she replies with a very Sam-like roll of her eyes. She tucks her hair behind her ear, finally giving me full eye contact. "I'm quitting."

"Huh?"

"After this baseball season is over, I'm resigning as your personal assistant. I thought I should give you a little bit of a heads up in case you need to make other plans," Sam says, standing up straighter.

"Okaaay," I begin. "You're allowed to quit. But *why* are you quitting? Are you not happy with the job anymore? Is this because of Danae? Because even though things are moving forward with Danae, I still want you around, sis."

"It's not that. I've really appreciated the space you gave me to leave the nest without crashing and burning on my own. And I have truly loved helping you with all the little things you can't do for yourself," she says, her signature smirk returning.

"Hey, now," I retort, giving her a mild shove. "I'm perfectly capable of doing all the stuff you do."

She raises an eyebrow.

I huff. "I didn't say I *want* to do all that stuff, but I *could* do it if I needed to."

"Just admit you'd be lost without me," she says.

"How am I supposed to admit that when you just resigned?" I say, pointing a finger at her.

"Fair point," she concedes. "But the real point is that as much as I've loved helping you for a season of time, I want to find my path, you know? Where I'm supposed to be, what I'm supposed to be doing with my life for the long haul."

"I can understand that. Do you know what you're going to do?" I ask.

Sam gets a bashful look on her face. "I haven't for sure decided anything yet, but I've been researching cosmetology school. I kinda like the idea of being a hair-stylist—getting to have a creative outlet but also an excuse to talk to people and ask questions all day. Do you think that's a bad idea?"

The vulnerability on Sam's face when she asks what I think cuts to my heart. I wrap my arms around her in a full hug. "I think you'd be amazing at that, Sam. It's a great idea."

She hugs me back for a long second before she speaks again. "For the record, I'm interested in styling women's hair. You know, high-lights, layers, et cetera, et cetera. I'm not touching your fade with a ten-foot pole." She lightly smacks the back of my head before she pulls away, grinning.

"But think of all the PR opportunities—the Wizard's sister giving the Wizard haircut to all of Kansas City's youngsters. It's genius," I tease.

Sam smacks me again. "I'm forging my *own* path, thank you very much. But don't worry—I'll get you through the rest of the season first. After that, I'm leaving you to fend for yourself with Joe."

"I can fend just fine, thank you very much," I say, following Samantha out to the living room. "Especially after the interview today. Joe's been practically salivating at all the positive press and wider media attention this is going to bring."

"I'll have the calendar ready to start scheduling all the new sponsor-ship requests," Sam teases. "Kidding, not kidding."

"How'd the interview go, man?" Adrian asks as he laces up his cleats.

"Awesome," I say, tugging my jersey on over my head. "The lady asking questions was really laid-back, which helped Danae not freak out so much. She didn't press when we purposely kept certain answers short."

Drew messes up my hair as he walks by. "And the photo shoot? Was it heaven to have an excuse to act all lovey-dovey with Danae?"

I throw my mitt at him. "I don't need an excuse to act lovey-dovey. You losing your charm after all these years married?"

"My charm game has only increased over time," Drew replies, waggling his eyebrows. "As evidenced by the fact that Lily's pregnant."

"What? You serious?" I ask, and Adrian abruptly jumps to his feet yelling in Spanish.

Drew grins. "Dead serious. She's about nine weeks along and beginning every morning in the bathroom throwing up."

Adrian screws up his face. "I'd throw up every morning, too, if I had to look at your face first thing." He breaks out in a grin and slaps Drew on the back. "*Felicidades*, Sheffield."

I give Drew a full-on hug. "That's amazing, man. So happy for you. Do you think Lily will tell Danae and the other WAGs today?"

"That's the plan," he says. "Your little guy might have someone fighting him for the chicken tenders today. They're one of Lily's current food cravings that she can actually keep down."

Your little guy. The phrase rolled off Drew's tongue with such ease, and it feels like a favorite shirt that fits like a glove.

We need to get out on the field to warm up, but I pull my phone from my locker to shoot Danae a quick text.

ME

Tell Jason I love him. And I love you.

Can't wait to see you after the game.

DANAE

<kiss face emoji> Love you too. Good luck today.

CHAPTER FORTY-FIVE

Danae

"I am wanted. I am loved. I have people who care about me and will never leave me. I am safe. I belong. I am loved."

Jason slowly reads the phrases from the notebook, holding an EMDR tapper in each hand. Soothing spa music plays lightly in the background, and lavender scent fills the air from the diffuser.

After meeting with Jessica for about six weeks, Jason began working through his life story with her. They colored pictures and wrote down the major events of his life—everything from his mom's overdose to his dad's struggles, his time in foster care to his permanent adoption with me. We now end each therapy session with Jason sitting next to me on the couch with a weighted blanket over our laps. He holds the EMDR tappers and reads his own story out loud, ending with the affirmations of how very loved he is.

Jessica says the EMDR therapy will help to connect the two hemispheres of his brain while he revisits his own life story, slowly working to heal some of the trauma woven into his history. We've been meeting with her twice a week over the summer months, sometimes together and sometimes on his own.

At times, I get discouraged when I realize that we're still only a few steps into a lifelong road. But I have moments of hope, too, when I see Jason's brain respond to a trigger and it doesn't end in a dysregulated rage. We still have our fair share of those moments, though. Sometimes

I remember all the de-escalation strategies I've learned from Jessica and Monica, and sometimes I wind up in a dysregulated panic along with Jason.

But no matter how long or twisted the road ahead may be, we're taking baby steps together. And Griffin has stepped up to be present and available as much as he conceivably can be. I've still struggled with moments of frustration here and there when I want to call him about something going on with Jason and he's in the middle of a game, but the summer weeks have been an easier rhythm to manage. Jason and I have traveled along on several of the Crowns' away series, making our times apart from each other less frequent. Those trips have been opportunities not only to stay connected with Griffin, but to get to know the other players' families even better. Lily and Jason typically down an entire pan of chicken tenders together.

The summer has also given me more time to adjust to the public attention that comes with dating Griffin. Capital Grille is still our safe place to hide out in public, but I've gotten used to getting stopped for autographs when we venture to other places. I was shocked the first time someone asked for a picture together with Griffin *and* me. The media frequently circulates photos of me greeting (and often kissing) Griffin from the front row of the stadium at the end of home games. We're okay with the attention, so long as they leave Jason out of the photos.

As the end of July approaches, I'm dreading August and September. The beginning of a new school year is always chaotic, and I'm extra anxious wondering how the school year is going to go for Jason. He's made a lot of headway in therapy, but sometimes it feels like one step forward, two steps back. Which Jessica constantly assures me is the norm for working through trauma. I'm not sure how we're going to juggle starting school along with attending as many baseball games as possible, but I'm determined to be there for Griff as much as he is for us.

I'm committed to teaching again this school year, but I've already started my pro/con lists and flow charts regarding whether to continue after this year if Griffin and I get married. If taking a break from teaching would mean seeing more of Griffin during baseball season, I'm willing to explore it, even though it could be difficult to find an open library position again in the future. It's a struggle to balance thinking through what the future could be versus focusing on the present.

The Crowns have serious potential for a World Series run, and, as overwhelming as it is to think about the season extending through October, I'm crossing my fingers that they'll make it. Griff is always minimizing his hope and optimism in order to not be disappointed if it doesn't happen, but Jason has enough optimism for everyone. He's constantly ready with analysis of how good of a shot they have and exactly how many games they need to win at any given point in order to clinch the chance. It helps that Griffin has risen again to the status of "five-tool player." I'm now the girlfriend using baseball lingo and eagerly bragging about how Griff is playing lights-out defensively and batting with power.

Even though I still can't classify myself as a baseball fan, I'm a Griffin West fan, one hundred percent.

My mind comes back to the present moment as Jason throws off the weighted blanket. Jessica asks him if we have any fun plans today, so he tells her that we'll be attending the Crowns game tonight.

"I hope you have so much fun!" Jessica says. "It's fireworks night—will you stay to watch?"

Jason looks over at me hopefully. "You didn't tell me it was fireworks night! Can we stay? Please?"

"Maybe if you promise to go to bed a little early tomorrow, we can stay late tonight," I reply with a smile.

CHAPTER FORTY-SIX

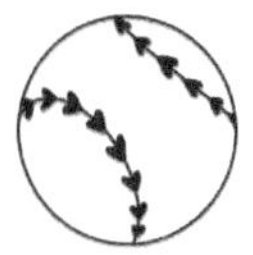

Griffin

Thwack!

I watch as the ball leaves the bat and shoots up in the air toward me. It's a few paces above my head, but I loudly call out "I got it! I got it!" as I run to the location where the ball will drop.

Chasing down the ball's arc, I hold out my glove in the perfect spot, feeling that satisfying *thud* against the palm of my left hand.

"Woo hoo hoo!" Adrian whoops as he runs over to me. He pulls my baseball hat from my head, tossing it up in the air like a graduation cap. "Amazing catch, *hermano*!"

Ethan picks up my hat on his jog in from left field, tossing it to me. "Nice out, man! Way to end the inning."

We celebrate on the way to the dugout, swapping our baseball mitts for batting gloves. We're behind by one run at the bottom of the ninth inning, so the fate of the game is in our hands now.

Our first batter strikes out, but then Drew hits a single before me. As I leave the on-deck circle, *Harry Potter* music plays over the speakers, my constant reminder to Danae and Jason that I'm thinking of them. I look up in their direction, waving my bat like a magic wand casting one of the spells from the first movie we watched together last week.

As I approach home plate, I drink in the atmosphere around me. The roar of the crowd, the hand-painted signs with my name on them—a visual reminder of how much we mean to these fans. I hear the cheers of my teammates from the dugout and make eye contact with Drew on base, who claps his hands before taking his lead off first.

Under the guise of adjusting my batting glove, I breathe it all in for an extra moment. I picture Danae and Jason sitting up in the suite—Danae wearing her West jersey and Jason probably talking her ear off about everything that's happened in the game thus far. The thought brings a smile to my face as I step up to the plate and settle into my stance.

The first pitch is easy to read as a ball, way above the strike zone. I swing and miss a curveball next, so I step back to get my head in the zone. Settling back into my stance, I see the fastball flying toward me and swing at the perfect moment, feeling that reverberating *crack* run through my arms. As I sprint toward first base, I see the coach motioning to continue to second, where I easily make it before stopping. Drew slid safely to third base before the ball touched him, so we're set up to take the lead. We just need someone to hit us home.

Luke hits a pop fly that's an easy catch for the opponent's shortstop, bringing it all down to Adrian. With a count of two balls, one strike, Adrian makes contact with the next pitch, sending it bouncing into right field.

Drew is on his way home as I sprint to third. The third base coach hesitates but then gives me the signal to run home. Kicking my legs into the next gear, I round the base and run toward home. The catcher is ready, awaiting the ball that I'm sure is sailing through the air somewhere close by.

As I near the final few feet, I stretch out my arms and slide toward home as the catcher's mitt closes and his body pivots my direction.

I see it happening in slow motion—the catcher's knee lining up perfectly with the trajectory of my shoulder. The *crunch* of impact fills my ears, drowning out the sound of the umpire yelling, "Safe!"

And I know. I see it in the catcher's reaction, immediately waving wildly at our dugout. I taste it in the howl that must be coming from my own lips.

Drew is kneeling next to me as the catcher hovers above me with his mask off and his hands on either side of his head. I think of Danae—here but not here—so far away at the top of the stadium.

By the time the training staff make it to me, there's only pain.

CHAPTER FORTY-SEVEN

Danae

The world stops.

Time freezes in the stadium as every mouth is covered by a hand, as every voice is stilled in an unfinished gasp. Hearts cease to beat, bodies halt all movement.

"No!" I rasp. "No, no, no!"

The images of the video I watched of Griffin's injury flash through my mind, heightened by the image playing out in front of my eyes. The man I love thrashing on the ground, stomping a foot, wildly clenching Drew's jersey next to him.

"How do I get down there, Samantha?" I ask, frantic. She's still frozen, mouth gaping and eyes like saucers. "Samantha!" I scream. "How do I get down there?"

The tears blurring my vision spill over on my cheeks, and suddenly Jason is crying and shouting and the entire suite is chaos. Lily's hands come to my shoulders, and her firm touch grounds me back into myself.

Turning to Jason, I hug him and say, "Bud, I need to go down and see Griffin. Sammi is going to stay right here with you until I get back." Jason's eyes are pools of terror. Kneeling down, I tell him, "Mr. Griffin is going to be okay. He's not leaving us. But he is hurting, so I'm going to go be with him for a little bit, okay?"

Jason nods slowly, and Samantha takes his hand. Her own eyes are brimming with tears as she places her other hand on my shoulder. "Get down there. He'll need you. He'll need the person who loves just Griffin," she whispers.

Lily leads me out of the suite to the elevators, through a series of hallways I never would have navigated on my own. I tune out the sound of the speakers throughout the stadium broadcasting Griffin's pain. Surely, they've gotten him off the field by the time we finally make it to the hallway outside the locker room.

Pounding on the door, Lily yells, "Someone open up! Let Danae in there with Griffin!"

A few seconds later, the door opens, and an unfamiliar face appears. Likely someone from the training staff I haven't met yet. He grimaces at me. "I don't think you really want to come in and see him like this, ma'am. Wait a little while until we've got his pain better managed."

My chest nearly explodes as I inhale, the oxygen fueling the fire building there. "No! I'm not waiting until his pain is under control—I'm going to stand by him through it. You let me in there right now!"

The man looks taken aback. "Don't say I didn't warn you," he says as he holds the door open. Once inside the locker room, I don't need a guide to find the room where Griffin is. The rest of the locker room is deathly quiet, and I follow the sound of his agony, tears endlessly flowing from my eyes with each step.

As I enter the room, Griffin spots me, and the pain on his face crumples with relief. "Danae," he says, more a sob than a word. I rush over to the training table where he's propped up and grab his right hand. Training staff buzz around the room, assessing and gathering supplies and creating the atmosphere of a bee hive.

"Griff, I'm here, babe," I say, cupping his face with my free hand. "I love you, Griff."

Tears have streaked paths through the dirt on Griffin's face, and he grunts in pain as they shift his position. I try to stay out of the way yet locked by Griffin's side as they discuss the course of action.

"We're going to give you a shot to manage the pain, West," one staff member says, approaching with a tray of disinfecting wipes and a syringe.

"He's afraid of needles," I say, voice quivering. "We need to elevate his legs first."

The shadow of a smile crosses Griffin's face. "Needles are the last thing I'm worried about right now," he says. "Just stay here with me while they give me the shot."

I trade hands so I'm holding his with my left hand, using my right hand to shield his eyes toward me as they clean the area for the shot. "I love you," I say. "I love you, and I'm going to be here with you through every step of this recovery. We're going to get through this together."

He grimaces, and I don't know if it's due to the immediate physical pain or the memories of the arduous rehab process. "What if I can't do it again?" he whispers. I know that there are a dozen other people in the room around us, yet it's only the two of us as we stare into each other's eyes. Griffin swallows hard. "What if this is it for me? If the Wizard doesn't make the comeback this time?" His voice is a shadow of his usual self.

A tear slips past my lips as I smile. "You've never been the Wizard to me. You've always been Griffin—the man who makes people feel special. The man who takes time to value everyone, from the bartender at the restaurant to the book club ladies ambushing him to the kid at camp whose world was turned upside down." A tear skates down Griffin's cheek as his eyes search my face, and I wipe it away with my thumb before it hits his beard. "You're the man who got me to open up about some of the most painful parts of my past on our first date. Because you ask real questions in the most inviting, unassuming way. The man who broke through all of my prejudices against people with financial wealth because you don't use it to manipulate the world. You're the man who opens up his life to people who need him—to Samantha, to Jason, to me. You might be the Wizard of Defense to some people, but not to me. You're my safe place, Griffin. And I'll be yours too, now and long after the Wizard is gone. I'm with *you*."

CHAPTER FORTY-EIGHT

Griffin

"Griff! We're here and brought food!" Danae's voice calls from the entryway. I hear the pattern of Jason's bare feet running on the wood floors next, drawing closer to my spot on the couch in the living room.

It's been almost a month since I reinjured my shoulder and had surgery two days later. I'll never forget the vision of Danae's face peering over me as I came out of the anesthesia—her eyebrows furrowed with worry, then springing back in relief at the sight of my small smile.

Last year, when I woke up from surgery, it was a matter of seconds before my mind dove deep down the dark pit of worry over whether my career was over. Whether I could be my old self again—the self I thought was the totality of who I am. But this time, my first conscious thoughts were about how much I loved the woman looking at me. At *me*. The woman who was worried sick over whether I would be okay—not if I would be able to play baseball again. The woman who spent every possible moment with me throughout the first two weeks of my recovery—time she normally would have spent planning for the start of the school year. Jason was usually with her, and he kept me apprised of all significant baseball-related news. I've taken a break from watching the Crowns games because it all felt too raw. Too fresh.

Instead, we spent time watching a couple more of the *Harry Potter* movies with Jason, until Danae decided the series would be too scary to continue with him. I finally beat Jason at a couple out of a hundred rounds of Trash played together on the back patio. We had lots of long evenings with Danae tucked under my right arm, quietly reading while I binged popular shows I've never had time to watch before. The unfamiliar change of pace was refreshing—simply existing with the people I love instead of immediately working toward the next goal.

Sam and my mom filled in the gaps when Danae couldn't be here, but I'm back to being an almost-fully functional adult again. Which is good, since Danae and Jason have been in school for two weeks now. We're celebrating a successful start to the school year for Jason by going to the Crowns game tomorrow night together. We'll be watching from the suite, which will be an entirely different experience for me. But I'm excited to watch my teammates play again with my safe person by my side.

Jason greets me and instantly starts chattering a mile a minute about his day at school, bringing a smile to my face. He's in the middle of a story about one of the kindergarteners bringing a hamster to school hidden in her backpack when Danae's gorgeous face fills my vision.

"Hey, babe," she says as she leans over me from behind the couch. I tilt my head back to catch her kiss, earning an "ugh, gross!" from Jason.

"I'm going to go get drinks out of the fridge," he says, covering his eyes.

Danae glances up at him with a smile, then looks back down at me, leaning her hands against the back of the couch. She takes in the heating pad on my shoulder. "How did physical therapy go today?" she asks, eyes filling with concern.

I reach behind me to grab her right hand and steer her around the couch to come sit beside me. "Painful, awful, hard—about what I expected."

She tucks one knee under her to sit facing me on the couch and leans in to brush a soft kiss against my lips. As she draws back, I catch her chin between my thumb and forefinger. Glancing down at her perfect lips, I murmur, "You know, my lips aren't broken. You don't have to be so gentle."

Danae gives me a wry smile as I pull her chin closer to me, and she responds with a kiss that is not at all delicate. Remembering that Jason is in the next room, I playfully nip at her bottom lip before releasing her.

"How was school today?" I ask.

Sighing, she responds, "I'm gonna need food for sustenance to rehash the day."

I smirk and remark, "That good, huh?"

"Let's just say the hamster incident is the tip of the iceberg with this new kindergarten class. They're keeping all of us on our toes," she says. "But I had the most precious conversation about books with a new fourth grader today. I'll tell you all about it. Do you want me to bring your food over here so you can keep using the heating pad?"

Clicking the button off, I sit forward. "Nah, I'll come eat at the table with you. I've about hit the time limit for heat anyway."

Jason takes the lid off of my burrito bowl when we get to the table, then starts building his tacos. I'll still wear the sling for another week or two, but this is food I can easily eat with one hand. Danae and Jason take turns sharing more about their days, and Jason asks about what I did in therapy today.

He switches into sports commentator mode, filling me in on the Crowns' latest games so I'll be fully briefed going into tomorrow night. His commentary churns up conflicting emotions in my gut—emotions I need to share with Danae.

"Hey, Fireball, Adrian came by earlier and set up that new rebounder net in the backyard. You could grab your glove and go out to get some fielding practice in—get in shape to start playing next spring." I add that last thought with a wink at Danae, who rolls her eyes.

"I already agreed to try it out in the spring. Adding in practices and games on top of everything this fall was too much," she says. I wink at her again to make sure she knows I'm on her side.

Jason gets up from the table and starts to run off, but Danae reminds him to throw away his trash first. He goes the extra mile and takes all of our trash, which brings a shine of pride to Danae's eyes.

"Why don't we sit out back so we can keep an eye on him?" I suggest. The patio is raised high enough that we can still have a private conversation while keeping Jason within our line of sight.

We take a seat on the porch swing, and I pull Danae close, wrapping my right arm around her. I'm not sure how to go about easing into such an emotional conversation, so I throw us straight into the deep end.

"I've decided to retire from baseball."

Danae launches herself back, the jolt of movement sending a flare of pain through my shoulder. I try to hide my grimace, but her effusive apologies must mean I failed.

"I'm so sorry, I didn't mean to move so quickly! Are you okay?" she asks, face stricken.

"I'm fine," I assure her. "Pain is part of the process. I can handle it. I don't like you sitting so far away from me, though."

She scootches closer to me but remains sitting upright, peering at my face. I point and flex my foot, gently rocking us on the swing, needing the soothing movement.

"Why would you say that, Griff? We've talked about this with the doctors, the coaches, the trainers. You should be back in shape to join spring training—you might not even have to spend any time playing for the farm team if camp goes well. I have your entire rehab schedule organized and color-coded. We're doing this," Danae says, voice firm, eyes blazing.

I reach my hand up to tuck a strand of hair behind her ear, savoring the silky texture between my fingers. "I don't want to do it anymore."

Danae's eyes bounce back and forth between mine. The thought factory is in overdrive, but I know her well enough now to know what's churning in there.

"I'm serious," I say. "I know that you're supportive of me continuing to play. But I don't want to do it again."

Tears sparkle in her eyes, and as much as I don't want her to cry, I'm ready to drink in the emerald green show that's coming.

"Griff, this is your dream. You love this game. I know you do. You love everything about it, and you're amazing at this," Danae says, practically wringing my hand in hers. "I know that some of the guys could get traded, but Adrian and Drew will for sure still be playing next season. They want you back. Everyone wants you back. We want to keep watching you play. I know the rehab is hard, but I also know that you can do it. You're the most determined man I know. Why are you second-guessing yourself?"

"It can't be second-guessing if it was my first thought," I confess. Danae's eyes narrow in confusion. "I know we've talked with everyone about how I could still come back. I know you have a beautiful color-coded rehab schedule all mapped out. But in that moment when you were standing next to me in the training room after my injury, my first thought was, 'I'm ready. This could be over, and I'll be okay.'"

The tears are spilling down Danae's cheeks now, and I reach up to cup her face.

"I remember every detail of how hard it was the first time around. The rehab, the not knowing how strong my shoulder would be, the fears over not being good enough again. There's zero guarantee that my shoulder recovers from a second tear and I get back to how good I used to be. And I have enough pride to not want to be the has-been who didn't know to quit while he was ahead," I say.

Danae sniffs and wipes her nose with the back of her hand. "But you could try. You could do the rehab and see how things go, see how your shoulder is healing. Will you be constantly second-guessing yourself if you give up on your greatest passion without seeing how it might go?"

Sitting up, I lean closer to Danae, wiping the tears from her cheeks. "Baseball isn't my greatest passion anymore. Yes, I love it. For sure, I'm going to miss it. Will I second-guess myself? Yeah, but I constantly second-guess myself anyway. But I am one hundred percent positive that I will never truly regret it. Because I'm ready to shift my focus to the other things in my life that I love—the *people* I love."

Danae's expression cracks with emotion, and I gently pull her face closer so I can kiss away her tears.

"Griffin, are you sure about this? You're not going to lose us. I'm going to support you every step of the way through recovery and getting back into playing shape. You don't have to give this up. Are you *sure* about this?" she presses.

"I'm absolutely positive," I say, echoing the words from the night I first asked her on a date. "I'm ready. The Wizard was an amazing chapter in my life, but it's not the whole book. And I'm ready to turn the page."

Danae's stricken expression breaks into a watery smile at my book lingo. I stroke her cheek with my thumb, feeling a settled sense of peace now that I've spoken these thoughts aloud to her.

"You with me?" I quietly ask.

She mirrors my position, bringing her hand up to my jaw.

"One hundred percent, forever."

Epilogue
Griffin

Seven months later...

"Go! Run! Go, go, go!" Danae jumps to her feet, screaming and clapping. I stand up next to her, yelling similar encouragement as we watch Jason run to first base. The ball flies over the first baseman's head, and the coach yells for Jason to run to second. By the time the kid at first base has recovered the ball, Jason is already rounding third, determined to make it home.

"No, no, go back to third!" Danae screams as I yell, "Pick up the pace! Sprint home!"

Danae clutches my arm as we watch Jason dramatically slide home. Which turned out to be wildly unnecessary, considering the ball sailed past the catcher and never came close to getting Jason out. Which is pretty much expected for a bunch of kids playing rec baseball for the first time.

Jason jumps up and fist pumps the air, looking over to the stands where Danae and I are jumping and celebrating. He gets high fives from his teammates, and I shoot him a double thumbs up.

As we sit down, Danae blows out a breath. "Nothing like a single-turned-home-run thanks to two errors," she says.

Grinning, I wrap my arm around her neck and pull her forehead to my lips. "Look at you and all this baseball lingo," I tease.

She rolls her eyes but presses a quick kiss to my cheek. "Only for that cute little redhead out there."

"Are you forgetting that we are *not* supposed to use the word 'cute' to describe him anymore? Not now that he's eleven years old and nearly finished with elementary school?" I chide.

Danae waves a hand in the air. "I'm his mom. I get to call him cute as long as I want to."

Although it took some convincing to get Danae to sign Jason up to play baseball this spring, she's all in now that she sees how happy it's made him. It's been good for him to develop some new friendships outside of school and have an activity to look forward to. We're working on convincing her to let him try out for a slightly more competitive team next fall, but this has been a good first experience for Jason.

When the game ends, Danae passes out sports drinks and snacks, since it was our turn on the snack sign-up. Jason's team is used to my presence by now, but a few families of the opposing team come up to ask for photos and autographs. I can hear Jason dissecting the game for Danae as they wait at the side of the field, and I can't help but smile at how lucky I am that this is my life.

When I join them, I wrap an arm around Danae's shoulders as we walk to the parking lot. "You'll need to hustle to get changed if we're going to make it before the game starts," I tell Jason.

"More baseball, yayyy," Danae says, voice laced with smiling sarcasm.

Several hours later, we're sitting in the stands of the Crowns stadium, cheering for Adrian as he steps up to bat. "You taking notes to share with the coaching staff or something?" I ask Jason, gesturing to the small notebook in his hands.

"Naw, I thought I'd better start keeping better track of the games for the podcast so you don't get confused about what happened in which game," Jason says. "You forget sometimes."

"You calling me old?" I tease, swatting the brim of Jason's baseball cap.

"Last week you thought Ortiz's home run was in game three when it was in game two!" Jason exclaims, looking indignant.

"All right, all right, I see your point," I say, then stand up to clap as Adrian makes it safely to first. Jason cheers along with me, then marks a note down.

The podcast is an organic thing that may or may not continue for the long term. Although I'm completely at peace with my decision to retire, I haven't figured out exactly what I want to *do* as my second career. So far, past investments along with continued endorsement and speaking opportunities have more than paid the bills.

When spring training started up, Jason and I began recording an audio-only podcast breaking down the Crowns' games just for fun. As it turns out, a lot of people in the country get a kick out of listening to the commentary of a former player and a fiery kid with an uncanny knowledge of the game. We started breaking down major games across the MLB teams each week but maintained our obvious favoritism for talking about the Crowns.

As listens skyrocketed and sponsors came knocking, we set up a foundation that will cover the costs to provide free therapy for kids with experience in the foster care system. Whether they're being reunified with their biological families, joining new adoptive families, or aging out of the system—they all deserve help processing their experiences.

Danae is still working as a librarian and has zero interest in sports podcasting. With Sam happily pursuing her cosmetology career, that means I'm going to have to look into hiring an administrative assistant for the podcast. Turns out, I still don't enjoy doing all those tasks Sam used to do—tasks that are rapidly multiplying as our reach continues to grow.

As the music starts for the seventh-inning stretch, I yank the Kindle out of Danae's hands.

"Hey!" she yells. "Don't swipe the screen and lose my spot!"

"It's time to stand and sing with us," I say, falsely serious. I hook my hand under her elbow and playfully pull her to her feet. "Come on."

She half-heartedly sways along with us and promptly holds out her hand when the song ends, demanding her Kindle back. She gives me a coy smile and a kiss on the cheek when I hand it over. As Danae plops back down into her seat, I look over at Jason and wink.

Little does she know that I'm not taking them straight to their townhouse after the game. She's completely clueless about the surprise waiting for her on my back patio. A surprise including elaborate flowers and candles set up by Sam, a very special sign made by Jason, and a very sparkly diamond chosen by me.

I sit down and wrap my arm around her shoulders. When she looks up at me, I capture her lips in a kiss. Raising a hand to her cheek, I hold her in the kiss a moment longer than "quick." Tracing my thumb down her jaw when I pull away, I watch her lips turn up in a smile.

"What was that for?" she asks.

"Just love you," I say. "What book are you reading? For book club or for fun?"

"Well, reading is *always* fun," she starts, and I exaggeratedly scoff. I've no more become a book lover than she has become a baseball lover, but we love each other plenty. "This particular book happens to be for book club. You still good to hang with Jason while I go this week?"

"Always," I say. Jason is on my other side cheering for something happening in the game, but I continue my appreciative perusal of Danae. She perches her sunglasses on top of her head and reaches over to nudge the rim of my ballcap a little higher.

Then she leans in to kiss me again, several seconds longer than "quick."

"What was that for?" I ask, smiling at her.

"I just love *you*."

BONUS

Want to read about Griffin's proposal?

Check out the bonus epilogue:

Click here

Or scan here:

Author's Note 2.0

No book is ever produced by just one person, but this story in particular was a team effort.

Dear Reader, I need to tell you a little something about me . . . I hate baseball. I obsessively love football; I love soccer; I dislike basketball; and I *hate* baseball. I didn't have to reach far to tap into Danae's feelings about baseball throughout this book.

In the summer of 2024, I publicly swore on Instagram that I would never write a baseball romance because I dislike the sport so much. My good friend Danae messaged me her disapproval of my declaration, and we started joking back and forth about potential plot lines for a romance about a woman who hates baseball when it starts . . . and still dislikes baseball by the end.

There are plenty of sports romances out there where the female protagonist doesn't like the sport for *xyz* reason, but she's won over to it by the end of the book after falling in love with the athlete. I was intrigued by the idea of ending a book with the woman still hating the sport, despite loving the man.

The idea wouldn't leave me alone, and now here we are.

I wanted to take a stab at exploring the question: what do you do if the person you love has a passion you don't care for? Do you *have* to come around to enjoying that interest if you truly love that person? I don't think so. I think we can love someone without sharing all the same interests, even if they are great passions.

The idea snowballed into wanting to explore how two characters who had a lot of differences between them could fight through the consistent conflicts that would arise from their opposing desires, interests, and personality traits. In light of this "opposites attract" goal, a professional athlete who's obsessed with achieving success must be in want of a new single guardian who's obsessed with stability and security. Their perceived needs were sure to provide plenty of conflict to work through together.

And that's exactly what I wanted them to do—repeatedly face conflict, and repeatedly work through it together.

I wanted them to learn to love each other in spite of not sharing one another's passions—and discover that *that is okay.*

Creating these characters and this world took a lot of outside help (have I mentioned I hate baseball yet?). That dear friend, Danae, became my inside source for all things related to baseball—along with her husband, Griffin (yes, the characters' namesakes!!). They answered my endless questions about baseball with painstaking (and patient) detail. They helped me understand the schedule of the MLB baseball season, the training habits, the time spent in the minor vs. major leagues, and the responsibilities of the different positions. Any baseball action lingo in this book pretty much came straight from them. Real-life Griffin also helped spell out fictional Griffin's injury story. In summary, this book would not exist without them.

Additionally, the brain science of trauma shared by Miss Jessica did not originate with my ideas. I learned about it from a licensed therapist, whose information I'm keeping private. The "animals in the brain" explanation came from her, not from my own imagination. The scientific explanations of how trauma shapes the neurological wiring of a brain can be surprising when you first learn about it—I hope that these small glimpses give an introductory understanding and encourage you to learn more (there are many books available on the subject, but I'll suggest *The Body Keeps The Score* by Bessel van der Kolk, M.D., as a possible starting point).

One of the main messages of this book is that two things can be true: love is powerful, and childhood trauma is not "fixed" by love. I hope that viewing Jason's character evokes a sense of compassion and understanding for the real people who are affected by childhood trauma, because it has lifelong effects.

I would also like to point out that I explored one possible manifestation of trauma responses through Jason's character, but trauma responses do not look the same for every person. There are also many possible pieces to the treatment puzzle in the world of mental health. While the treatments mentioned in the book are *some* tools used to address the effects of trauma, effective treatment will not look the same for every person. If you or someone you love has experienced trauma, please seek out a licensed professional for personal, individual assistance.

Although I had help in expressing the different themes of this book, any mistakes are entirely mine.

I chose to use the OpenDyslexic font for the chapter numbers and headings in a nod to Griffin's character.

Also, I feel obligated to report that even after writing this whole book and falling in love with Griffin and Danae . . . I still don't like baseball.

Acknowledgements

If you read the Author's Note 2.0, then you already know that I had a lot of help on this book. I pulled inspiration from so many different places and had support from so many different people . . . I feel very nervous that I'm going to forget to thank someone crucial!

Danae, this book literally would not exist without you. Thanks for not taking my "never" as a true "never." Thank you for all of the work you and Griffin put in to the baseball questions Google doc, for all of the voice memos, for the insight and encouragement and *everything*. You know how much you contributed to this book, and I'm so incredibly grateful to both of you. And thanks for letting me borrow your names!!

Kyle, the OG human can opener, thanks for being my personal muse to shape Griffin's character. Your Enneagram 3 insights were invaluable, and I feel like I understand even more about what goes on inside your mind since I forced you to spell it out for me to create Griffin. You've been my number-one supporter along this author journey—helping me brainstorm, listening to me externally process sticking points, advising me on the "business" side of things, and encouraging me to do whatever I need to do in order to meet my self-imposed deadlines. Thanks for being *my* safe place in every way.

Alpha Hannah, this book may have wound up in a trash can lit on fire if not for you. Thank you for encouraging me and cheering me on *and* helping me figure out where to push and prod to get Danae and Griffin to be their very best. Your voice memos and GIFs and sass are the wind beneath my wings. I'm excited for what's next, winky face.

Lynsey, thanks for being a sensitivity beta reader extraordinaire. I'm thankful that I decided to start writing books simply because it means I got to "meet" you. I'm so grateful for your friendship. Thanks for your encouragement with this one—you understand how much it means.

Krystal, you really helped me find those final pieces of the puzzle that this story needed to get the full picture. Thanks for being the final check to make sure I got all of the baseball right, haha! I'm so grateful for your beta reading skills, your organization skills, and your friendship skills. You're the best friend-turned-PA I could ask for!!

Paris, this cover. Mic drop. Your skills blow me away, and I just *love* how this cover design turned out. Thanks for giving me slow nudges over time to try a different style eventually—this couldn't be more perfect for Danae and Griffin's story.

To the World's Greatest Librarian (name redacted for privacy), thank you for answering my questions about the education requirements and logistics behind being an elementary school librarian. But even more than that, thanks for helping to instill a love for books in my children. All of the above-and-beyond work you do to make reading magical is what inspired Danae's character—the Reading Café, the Battle of the Books, the special reading nooks. You're making such a huge difference in the lives of children and families in our community, and I feel so blessed to know you.

To my line editor, Olivia at Winston Editorial, and my proofreader, Diana at Paper Plane Prose, thank you for helping me smooth out rough edges and catch all the errors that my brain stops seeing after reading these words two hundred times.

The inspiration for the tree and birds painting that Griffin and Sam's mom had came from Jamie Finn at Foster the Family. She has a tattoo with the rooted tree and branches for the reason explained in the book. I thought it was such a beautiful depiction of a foster parent's role and love. If you have any interest in learning more about foster care or being involved, she's the very first person I suggest you follow. Find her on Instagram at @fosterthefamilyblog, and be sure to pick up her book for deeper education.

In a story with a bookish heroine, I had to include a nod to Christin at Monarch Books & Gifts in Overland Park, Kansas. She's been gracious enough to host book launch events for me, and I just love her store. Here in the Kansas City metro, we are blessed to have so many *incredible* local indie bookstores providing our area with books and community. A huge thanks to Erin at Ink & Page and Kate at Monstera's Books for not only having inviting bookstores, but also for being advocates for local authors. You contribute so much to the amazing bookish community in Kansas City.

My people—Amity, Amy, Diana, Haley, Jen, Lani, Leah, Megan—I haven't officially thanked you since the acknowledgments of *Love and Other Goals*, but you all know that I wouldn't continue doing this author thing without you. I wouldn't have written this book aside from all the ways you sit with me and support me in the hard stuff of life. "Thank you" will never be enough for how much you mean to me. Love you all so much.

Also by Tracy Baack

Love and Other . . . Series:

Love and Other Goals
Love and Other Chances
Love and Other Distractions

Christmas in Noel Series:

Saved by Noel
Joy to Noel

Kansas City Crowns Series:

Home Safe

Find them here:

Click here or scan the QR code:

About the Author

Tracy Baack connects with readers through relatable romance. She enjoys writing character-driven contemporary romance novels with so much character depth and development, you just might think they're real people. Her books are always closed-door but full of heart-melting swoon, and they end happily ever after (after a little dose of angst).

Tracy lives with her husband and four children in the suburbs of Kansas City, Kansas, where she loves supporting indie bookstores. Her primary love language is sending the perfect GIF for any moment.

Tracy is the author of *Love and Other Goals, Love and Other Chances, Love and Other Distractions*, *Home Safe, Saved by Noel,* and *Joy to Noel* (with more on the way because she just might be a writing addict).

Connect with Tracy on Instagram at @authortracybaack or through her website www.tracybaack.com.